A Fou,
Treasures Novel

CAROLINE
LOGAN

First published in 2020 by Gob Stopper

Gob Stopper is an imprint of Cranachan Publishing Limited

ISBN: 978-1-911279-52-5

eISBN: 978-1-911279-53-2

Cover Illustrations © Anastezia Luneva

Map Illustration © Caroline Logan

www.cranachanpublishing.co.uk

@cranachanbooks

cranachan

To Vince

"I still can't believe
someone left you
laying around."

Chapter 1

*T*he mapmaker was lost.

Still, he'd made it further than they had said he would. No one could find Ephraim, Queen Nicnevan's faerie court, without a fae guide. It was preposterous that a young army cartographer would even try.

He pulled out his sketchbook again, flipping through the pages of notes and drawings until he reached the end. The mapmaker had all of Eilanmòr sketched out—except the woods around Ephraim. That space only had blank paper. Back at the base, he had books and plans from the rainforests of Avalogne to the deserts of Kemet. He'd braved dangers and befriended locals across the continent, yet still he hadn't mapped out this one piece of his home country.

"How hard could it be?" he had told his comrades. "It's not like we don't know the general direction."

Now he chastised himself. *You've been wandering the Forest of Frith for two weeks. If it was there to find, you'd have found it by now.*

It must be a mere legend then. There could be no other explanation for it. All that talk of faeries, selkies and changelings when he was younger, and they probably didn't even exist. Just like he'd always said.

He cursed his superstitious grandmother. How different things would have turned out if she had only known the truth.

He dropped his rucksack on the ground and found a boulder to perch on. He just had to find his way back home again.

His compass was attached to his belt with a braid of coloured string. He stroked the soft-worn fabric and allowed himself a moment to reminisce about the boy who had made it for him. What would he look like now, he wondered. Three years was an awfully long time.

Gods knew, he had changed so much himself. Gone was the strict military haircut—his commanding officer didn't bother to discipline him anymore.

"You're an artist," he'd said. "I don't care if you tattoo your whole face, as long as you turn your maps in on time."

He didn't need to be told twice. At the first opportunity, he'd shaved the sides of his head and dyed the rest a bright purple. Whenever he thought about his grandmother's face when she'd last seen him, he chuckled. It had been easy to walk away from her forever when she was struck dumb by his hair. The nose piercing had helped too.

The mapmaker stretched and surveyed the forest around him. Something was different, but he couldn't quite work out what. Had the wind changed? He watched the trees ahead shift lazily in the breeze. The smell of pine resin brought a familiar ache to his chest. *I'll take a boat to Edessa after this,* he thought. Eilanmòr was too familiar now.

No, it was something else. Something else was strange about the land around him. It took him a while, but when he finally recognised what it was, his blood ran cold.

The forest was silent.

There were no birds chirping, no insects whirring around. Aside from the whisper of the wind through the trees, there was no sound of life.

The mapmaker leapt up from his perch and grabbed his pack. The only thing that could quiet a forest was a predator. He scanned the spaces between the trees. Was it a bear? A pack of wolves? It didn't matter, it was time to leave.

Scrambling in the leaf litter, the mapmaker threw himself forward. *Go, go, go,* he ordered his feet. He made it ten paces before the forest's silence was pierced by a hair-raising shriek. Turning to look in the direction of the noise, his feet tangled in a branch. Throwing up his hands just in time to catch his fall, he groaned. The scent of blood filled his nose and he did his best to clamp down on his panic. *It's only a few scratches,* he thought, wiping his hands on his shirt.

The smell of blood was suddenly masked by something

altogether less alive. The mapmaker had smelled this before, when he'd come across the corpse of animals. But it was getting stronger, the stench clawing up into his nose. Nausea washed over him in a wave, and he threw up onto the leaves, still red with his bloodstains. Distantly, he heard the pounding of footsteps, coming closer and closer. But the rotting smell was stronger still, so overpowering that the world swayed. He only managed to roll over, away from his vomit, before succumbing to unconsciousness.

Chapter 2

Ailsa stared at the ground, watching as an inky-black beetle picked its way through the maze of roots tunnelling into the earth. Fighting the ache above her left eye, she concentrated, motioning with her fingers, imagining the fattest root pulling out of the mud like a snake. The wind blew a strand of her dark hair across her face and she groaned. "It's still not working."

"You haven't been trying for long," grunted the monster beside her.

"I don't think I have this power," she murmured, half-heartedly trying again to raise the root. She knew better than to quit without the Fear-Laith's permission.

"You are impatient."

Ailsa held in the growl she felt bubbling up her throat. They had been travelling across Eilanmòr for a week now and she had barely been able to move a leaf. Her body itched to run into the heart of the Unseelie Court, to swing her axe and fight with her own hands... but this was a battle that required a greater strength. So they had crept through the Forest of Frith at a snail's pace, while Gris tried to prepare her for what was to come.

It was maddening.

"You are impatient," he repeated. "But maybe we should try something else."

That was all the encouragement she needed to give up. Unfolding herself from her crouch, Ailsa peered up at the face from her worst nightmares. It was still hard to get used to the hulking body of the Fear-Laith, with the grey fur that covered his skin and the red eyes that still haunted her dreams. Even harder was trying to reconcile the monster with the face of her once-mentor.

Gris was the reason she was alive, not only for teaching her to hunt and fight when she needed it most, but also for protecting her - being her shadow throughout her whole life.

My faerie godmother, thought Ailsa, her mouth twisting between a scowl and a smirk.

It was a ridiculous thought. The Fear-Laith had been following her since she had left home, his red eyes always watching between the trees. To think that the whole time she'd been trying to avoid the woods and the presence she felt there stalking her—but it had been him all along, guarding her.

Staring up at his concerned face, she was struck again with the same worry that had dogged her thoughts since they had started their journey: *what will I be afraid of now?* It should have been a comforting thought, but her concern was that something much worse would replace him. *Perhaps a Faerie Queen with golden hair?*

"That's enough for today. You had better get back to your prince," said Gris.

She snorted. "Are you coming?"

He stared off into the trees. "I'm going to train for a bit longer. On you go." He flexed his shoulders and stalked off, leaving her to make the short walk by herself.

It was times like this she could almost remember him as the man who had rescued her. She had been sixteen-years-old when he had found her, beaten almost to death by a farmer. Back then, he had appeared in his human form, as a great Edessan warrior. He had nursed her, then taught her how to fight and hunt, how to use the axe that he had gifted her.

She had promptly developed a crush on him, until he gently turned her down then disappeared into the woods for three years. Not exactly the reaction she had hoped for.

Back at the campsite she found both of its occupiers in varying states of undress. Prince Angus was shirtless, due to the heat from the fire he was working on. Iona was naked, due to the fact she was currently a seal. She poked her nose out of the water, but stayed submerged under the cool of the stream. Ailsa marvelled again at how such a graceful woman could look so... well, cute... as a pinniped.

That's how they get you, she thought ruefully as Iona's

dark, glassy eyes followed her movements. *They lure you in with soft fur and large eyes and then before you know it you've fallen for a selkie.*

It was why she was in this godsforsaken forest after all.

"Ah, you're back." Angus grinned. "I've made us some dinner."

Indeed, the smell of cooking flesh rose to meet Ailsa's nose, making her stomach twist in hunger. She grabbed a place beside him. "What is it?" she asked, regarding the meat suspiciously.

"A weasel," he replied, offering her a skewer. "It's all I could find."

He threw a dirty look at Iona when he said this and gave a huff.

"I suppose this has something to do with why Iona is hiding in the riverbed?" asked Ailsa.

"She seems to think that weasel isn't good enough for her, that there's not enough. I told her to go find her own food then, but there doesn't seem to be any fish around." His voice lowered as he said, "She's really in a huff because she tried to catch a hedgehog and it poked her in the nose."

While he had been talking, a drop of water landed on Ailsa's cheek, right where her wine-red birthmark was. *Changeling mark*, she corrected herself, wiping the liquid away absently. When another landed, she looked up to find a large bubble of water suspended in mid-air above Angus's head.

He followed her gaze. "What the—"

With a pop, the water broke free from the bubble, pouring all over Angus, making him yelp from surprise and the cold.

"Iona!" he shouted, jumping up from the fire, but the seal was nowhere to be found.

"At least you were shirtless," pointed out Ailsa, wiping away the few droplets that had splashed her.

"That's what you get," came Iona's voice from somewhere between the trees.

Angus shook his head, careful not to send any towards the flames. "I guess you're not hungry then," he grumbled back. He flopped down beside the fire, allowing the heat to dry him. "Selkies," he muttered, "are a pain in my butt."

"I agree wholeheartedly," Ailsa mumbled, gnawing on a piece of meat.

"So, how did we get into a selkie rescue mission?" he asked softly.

It's all my fault.

She put the half-eaten skewer down, not hungry anymore.

Angus watched her out of the corner of his eye. "It could make quite a romantic story... faerie princess saves selkie from her evil mother, the Queen of Faeries—"

"I am *not* a faerie princess," Ailsa growled.

"Fine," he smirked. "But '*grumpy changeling*' doesn't have the same ring to it."

She brought her heel down on his foot in reply, eliciting another yelp.

"Okay, sorry," he grumbled, rubbing the tender skin. "You can just be '*mystery woman*' if you like."

Ailsa took a swig of water from her canteen and grimaced. "How about no one tells the story and we all just go back to living our lives?"

"And where would that be?" he asked. "When this is over, are you going to go back to your beach?"

She pictured her home, the smell of seaweed, the crash of waves upon the sand. It felt like years ago when she had found Harris and Iona on that beach and they had asked her to help them find the Stone of Destiny.

What would her garden look like by now? Would it have died or flourished in her absence? Gardening had been one of the only joys in her lonely coastal existence. Though, even growing things was beginning to feel tainted.

Did I enjoy it because of what I am?

Faeries had earthly powers: tending plants, controlling animals. At the beginning of their journey she had asked Gris why he thought she could control the weather if she was a faerie. He reasoned it was to help things grow. Was that why her plants had gotten so big? Is that why she liked to spend hours with her hands in the dirt?

How much of me is just... me?

That would have to wait to be answered.

"No," she replied, to Angus's question. "I think I would return to Dunrigh, if you'll have me." Just for a while...

He nodded. "Of course." Then his mouth twisted. "And Harris?"

"Well, I am assuming he'll come back to Dunrigh too—"

"No, I mean, what will you do when you rescue him?"

She scowled. "What do you mean?" She hadn't spoken to anyone about what had happened in that inn...

"Oh come on, Ailsa." Angus fixed her with a level stare. "I know why he went after you in the first place. He was trying to win you back."

Memories of his lips on hers, on other places, his arms holding her body. instantly filled her mind.

But then she had been captured by raiders and he had been left for dead.

"So," Angus pressed, "are you together?"

Ailsa turned her face towards the fire. Were they together? She had no idea. Back at the inn, he had said that he liked her. That he wanted to *try*. At the time she had thought that he was giving her space, but now she couldn't help but wonder if he was avoiding the commitment. Which was fair enough, of course. But then there was the fact of his lying to her. He'd had so many opportunities to tell Ailsa what he knew about her—that she was something... *other*. But he had never confessed.

"We're friends," she decided. If there *was* anything more, that was for them to decide—after he was rescued.

The prince nodded but didn't reply. He seemed to sense that would be her last word on the subject.

"I think I'll go find Iona," said Ailsa, standing up.

The woods were starting to get darker and the old thrill of fear shot through her as she peered through the trees.

Ridiculous, she thought. *I know my monster.*

But there were other monsters in the dark places of the world. How long would it be until she met another?

Chapter 3

Ailsa traipsed through the trees, trying to keep her mind on the task of finding Iona—wherever she had wandered off to—but it returned to what lay ahead. She'd hardly had time to explore her feelings about her blood since destroying the Avalognian ships and losing Harris, but she had often picked at the subject in her head, like an old wound.

Some things she still didn't know, and others she was sure of. She would start there.

First, she wasn't human, just like everyone had always told her. Changeling, they had called her, and she had cursed their superstitions all her life. Never once thinking they were right.

Second, Gris had found her when she was a baby and brought Ailsa to her human mother to be looked after. Which meant her mother *wasn't* her mother. Cameron, her brother, wasn't her brother at all. Not that it mattered anyway, she hadn't seen him since their mother died and he had been stolen away by frightened relatives. It was probably for the best.

Last, Gris had watched over her and when he thought

it was the right time, he had told her the truth. Or what he *believed* to be true. He only *thought* that she was Nicnevan's daughter and the heir to the faerie court. If he was right, she could not only be the key to saving Harris, but to protecting the kingdom and uniting them all, fae and human alike.

And if he was wrong, she doubted very much that Nicnevan would allow them to live.

All of these half facts left more questions in their wake. Who had stolen her from her birth mother? Had her human mother known what she was? Had Cameron? How was she going to convince Nicnevan to let Harris go?

Her thoughts swirled round and round like crows on a corpse. She was so distracted that she didn't notice the coil of rope around her ankle until it was too late.

Suddenly, gravity was reversed and Ailsa shot into the air. A scream crawled up her throat as her body swung upwards and then bounced on the rope wrapped tightly around her leg.

A trap.

Ailsa dangled from the tree branch, trying and failing to free herself.

"My, my, what have I caught in my web?" came a melodic voice. "Something with more meat than a weasel?"

"Let me down, Iona," Ailsa shouted, allowing herself to relax.

The selkie sighed from somewhere. "Shame, I thought I had caught my dinner. You smell too bad to eat."

Ailsa heard sawing and then she was lowered to the ground, grateful that Iona was doing so carefully. She reached out her hands to the forest floor first, then rolled, landing in a crouch.

"Has anyone ever told you that you are very graceful when you're captured?" Iona rounded the tree, a smirk on her freckled face.

Ailsa smiled back. "I never thought to ask the Avalognians. I don't intend to become a captive again, though."

"I have an idea for a pact. When all of this is over, let no one be held captive again." Iona extended a hand to help Ailsa up with surprising strength. The top of her head came to the selkie's chin, so she had to look up to meet her sharp green gaze. The same shade as her brother's.

Ailsa nodded. "Agreed."

Iona placed a hand on Ailsa's shoulder. "I know you can do it." She winked. "And I'll be right there beside you, fighting that old crone."

"Should I be offended?" asked Ailsa. "That 'old crone' is supposed to be my birth mother."

"Really, I see no family resemblance." Iona looped an arm through Ailsa's, pulling her into a stroll.

"I was wondering about that…" Ailsa's mouth twisted

as she considered. "Will she look like me? I mean, I'm a changeling… surely I've been… changed?"

"Honestly, I'm not really sure how it works." Iona paused as she regarded the foliage. "Changelings are left to replace a dying child. I suppose you'd have to resemble that child in some way for your mother to accept you. Or be made to resemble them…"

There were so many things about Iona's answer which hurt, but Ailsa pushed the feelings down as far as she could.

"You certainly don't look like Nicnevan," Iona continued, squeezing her arm. "I saw her once, when I was young. Blonde hair… sneer…" Iona made a show of leering down at her, "small breasts."

Despite herself, Ailsa shook her head and smiled. "I don't think I wanted to hear that."

"To be honest," Iona grinned, "you look more like Angus than Nicnevan. Apart from the breasts."

"Which I am very glad of," said a deep voice behind them. "They would just get in the way of fighting."

"Depends what type of fighting you mean, Angus," mumbled Iona, and Ailsa couldn't help a burst of laughter from escaping her lips.

The prince shrugged himself between the two women, placing an arm on each of their shoulders. "Have we forgiven each other for our earlier squabble?"

The selkie sniffed. "It depends on whether you've

found me more food."

"That depends on whether you're planning on soaking me again."

The smell of cooking meat wafted through the trees as they approached the campfire again. Ailsa's stomach rumbled. Trying to harness her powers had been using up all her energy and she was struggling to refuel enough.

Iona sniffed the air. "That smells like... pheasant?"

"Grouse," said Gris from where he was cooking the bird.

"See, Angus, there were other things to catch." Iona skipped to the Fear-Laith's side and happily accepted a leg.

Ailsa snaked an arm around Angus's torso and gave a squeeze. He rolled his eyes and pursed his lips. Angus did not enjoy Gris's company. Ailsa was sure Iona was only joking around, but it seemed like she had been playing the two men off each other and it was a testament to Angus's sweet nature that he hadn't been more than a little grumpy.

As for Gris... well, he had more than once questioned Angus's purpose on their mission. At the beginning, he had urged Ailsa to send him home, but she had snapped that she needed him with her. The truth was, she was sure that Gris was jealous. Angus, for all his lack of experience, was still a trained warrior. They argued often about strategies and, on several occasions, Gris had disagreed with a good idea, just because Angus had supplied it. The battle of egos was testing her patience. Gris was her old mentor; he had saved her life. But then he left. She felt she hardly knew him now. Or he hardly knew her. Angus though, was the closest to a best friend she had ever had; he understood in a way she hadn't felt since her brother. The prince and the Fear-Laith were both important to her and she valued both their council. Why couldn't they just get along?

Angus, Iona, and Gris ate in silence, savouring the meat. But Ailsa could hardly taste it. Thoughts swirled in her head all the time. Worry over Harris, worry over Nicnevan, worry over her magic. She felt like she didn't do anything but worry. It seemed a lifetime ago that she was sitting on a beach, her only care whether she'd find something to hunt or if she'd be eating a salad.

"What you need," Gris's hard gaze met hers from across the fire, "is to be in a position where you can't help but show your powers."

"Why do I not like the sound of that…" Angus pressed forward, putting an arm around Ailsa's shoulders. She savoured the warmth his body provided, easing the chill in her heart just a little.

"You need to be thoroughly terrified."

"You've been terrifying me my whole life. Why didn't I show my powers before?"

A moment of pain crossed his features, but he

shuttered the look before she could comment. "I clearly wasn't terrifying enough."

Angus cleared his throat. "Can I just cut in here? I don't like this idea."

"Oh?" said Gris. "And why is that, prince?"

Angus scowled. "The problem with things that are terrifying is that they're often extremely dangerous. And I think Ailsa has been in enough danger lately."

"Playing with plant roots is not going to bring out her magic. She needs some pressure."

"Do you not think saving Harris is enough pressure?" argued Angus, then whipped his head towards Iona. "What do you think about this?"

The selkie was quiet for a brief moment. She looked Ailsa up and down and it felt like a dissection. "It might be what she needs," she replied in a soft tone.

"What the hell?" Angus stood from his spot, shaking his head. "You both want to put her in danger just to save a bit of time? We've already got one person captured by a vindictive Faerie Queen; we don't need another dead."

Ailsa took a deep breath and put a hand on the back of his knee. "It's okay, Angus. I think I need to do this."

He rounded on her. "Do you have a death wish?"

"No, I don't have a death wish," she growled. "I have a wish to save Harris. And I'm willing to try anything."

He passed a hand over his face, taking a seat. "I don't want to lose you," he mumbled.

Now she wrapped an arm around him, hoping she could provide some of her own warmth. She appreciated his concern, but unknowingly he had provided her with just enough courage to face whatever monster Gris had in mind. If Angus was more worried than she was, then maybe she could pretend for him that she was brave.

"You won't lose me, silly. Can't get rid of me that easily."

He gave her a weak smile at that, and she turned her attention back to Gris who was watching their exchange with mild annoyance. "So how do I become thoroughly terrified?"

Chapter 4

eep in the forest, there lives an un-something, a creature that is both there and not.

Of course, Ailsa had heard these stories, but with a distinct *something* following her, she often forgot to be afraid of the *nothing*.

Gris had a name for it: Brollachan. She didn't need to know its name, just how to kill it. But the problem with these stories is that they often like to leave that part out.

"It is not of the earth, but you're a faerie, you can bind its form," he had explained, helping strap new knives to her clothing. "Just let the earth's magic flow through you; it'll know what to do."

"And if I fail?" she gritted out between clenched teeth.

"You won't," he growled, turning to face her fully. His gaze roamed over her, taking in her rigid posture, her defiant expression, and he nodded. A general assessing his soldier. Just like he had done those years ago. As before, his gaze brought mixed emotions. Pride, that he believed her ready. Fear that she wasn't.

However, gone was the lovesick girl she had been back then, starved for companionship, for love. She no longer blushed when she stared back.

He nodded again, seeing something in her face, before handing her her axe from where it had been propped beside her pack. "Just don't let it get too close. The Brollachan would love to possess a being of flesh and blood, if only for a while. It would eat you from the inside then discard your body when it is done."

She clenched her shoulders together to stop the shiver that wanted to run across her body. "And where will you be?"

"With the prince and the selkie. Nearby," he reassured her.

"We have names you know," muttered Angus from behind her.

Gris just huffed and went off to grab his things.

"He's cheerful as usual." Angus watched his back before taking her hand. "Are you sure you don't want me to help?"

"I need to do this myself." She flashed him a half smile. "Still, don't go too far."

"Well, I think you're terribly brave." Iona appeared at her side, leaning down to brush a quick kiss to her temple.

"Ailsa," Gris called.

She distinctly heard Angus grumble under his breath, "So *she* gets a name…"

Shaking her head she followed to where the Fear-

Laith was holding both their packs.

"This way."

Together, Ailsa, Angus, and Iona followed the grey man deeper into the forest, climbing over twisting roots and fallen trees. They walked for more than an hour, in silence, until the trees were so thick that most of the light had been blocked out.

It came on slowly, the feeling that something wasn't quite right. It started off as an itch, that crept under the skin and then into the very marrow of her bones. Ailsa wondered if the others could feel it, but up ahead Iona and Gris continued their stride without a falter. Only Angus beside her seemed uncomfortable, rubbing his chest with one hand as he gripped his sword with the other. As they walked, the chittering of bird song petered out, until all that remained was the crunch of leaves and twigs underfoot and the howling of wind through the trees. It brought with it the bitter stench of decomposition.

"Here," muttered Gris finally, coming to a stop before a gnarled, dead tree.

As Ailsa came up behind him, she wondered at the stupidity of monsters. If she had been trying to catch some prey, she would have done everything in her power to choose a trap that was appealing. She would find a place of sunshine, trickling water, perhaps some food to tempt them.

She couldn't imagine any mortal creature finding the lair of the Brollachan in any way appealing. Beyond the old tree they stood at, the forest dipped into a deep hollow, with steep sides, and waterlogged mud. A bowl, thought Ailsa, designed to catch and keep things inside. All of the plants had died and turned black with rot, the branches of bushes and trees tangling together. A few dead trees littered the ground like fallen soldiers on a battlefield.

And in the dead centre—a boulder, perhaps the only stable ground in the death trap before her. Surely nothing would venture into such a place willingly. The Brollachan must find food very rarely.

Which meant that it was probably hungry.

"Where is it?" asked Angus.

Iona sniffed delicately. "Can't you smell it? Like metal..."

Ailsa pursed her lips. She couldn't smell anything but the rotting mud.

"You'll have to climb down. Keep on top of the logs and the boulder or you'll get stuck," Gris instructed.

"What, exactly, is the point in this? Is she supposed to kill it? Fight it?" asked Angus.

"She's supposed to survive it," said Iona.

"The lair of the Brollachan seems like a death trap, but to a faerie it is anything but," Gris explained. "You are going down into the earth and that should fuel your power. Bind the creature with the plants and dirt and clay, then it can't get what it wants."

"What does it want?" Ailsa asked, feeling the dread pool deep in her stomach.

"To possess you. Brollachan like to creep into bodies, since they don't have one, and devour their prey from the inside. You could be walking around with one inside you for days and no one would know... except that its victims always have a tell…"

"What's that?"

Gris stuck out his tongue, which was surprisingly pink instead of grey. He held it there a moment, giving Angus a suspicious side-glance. "Black tongues. Those possessed by the Brollachan have black tongues."

"Well," said Ailsa, fighting the urge to roll her eyes at the Fear-Laith. "I suppose you'll be able to check me when I'm done."

"Ailsa," said Angus. "You don't have to do this."

She squinted down at the hole. "I do." Because if she could prove she was a faerie, that she could control her powers, she would know who she was. Not some changeling, but fae royalty. And then she might not only be able to save Harris, but maybe the whole of Eilanmòr. If she could stomach killing the woman who had given birth to her…

"I guess I'm ready," she mumbled. "If I die, please tell Harris that he's an eejit for me."

"I promise," said Iona solemnly.

Ailsa lowered herself to the ground and hung her legs over the ledge. Turning round, she gripped the roots of the trees around the lip of the bowl and kicked until she found a foothold. Up ahead Angus, Iona and Gris had lain down on their chests, their heads peeking over the edge in a row. It was slow work, lowering herself down, looking over her shoulder for places to stand, until she deemed herself a safe distance to jump without accidentally falling into the muck. Her boots hit the end of a dead tree trunk and for a second, she thought it might collapse under her weight, but it held strong, toughened by its muddy coating. Ailsa took a breath and let go of the wall of the hole, turning so she could face the centre.

"I don't see anything," she called as she surveyed the basin. "Only mud and rotting trees."

"You're too close to the edge," Gris shouted. "It won't come out if it thinks it can't get you."

Ailsa gulped, even as Angus's muffled curse made the side of her mouth quirk in laughter. Was she going mad? Giving herself a mental shake, she placed one foot in front of the other, travelling along the log, all the while watching her peripherals for signs of movement. Not even a leaf stirred as she walked. She reached the end of her tree and a short leap had her back on solid ground, on the huge boulder.

"Come out, come out," she murmured, scanning again. Had it gotten darker? It was still springtime; they should have had daylight for at least another three hours. Or had she been debating with Angus longer than she thought?

Her hand grazed the handle of her axe. Before all this, when she had just been Ailsa, a human woman, she would have had that axe in her hands as soon as her feet had touched the earth. But now? She still wanted to grab it—her hand was itching for its weight—yet she knew that it would do her no good. No, the Brollachan would have to be killed with her other weapon.

She looked to the sky, to the grey cloud she was so familiar with, barely peeking through the thick branches of the forest. It called to her, a gentle whisper. *Use me. I am yours.* But what use would a storm be? How would that help her trap the Brollachan? If what Gris said was true, then her only power would be in making it rain enough for plants to grow in this godsforsaken mud pit. That would take weeks!

A twig snapped to Ailsa's right and she froze, peering into the gloom. A child, of no more than ten was standing with her feet stuck in the mud. Ailsa hadn't seen her before because she was covered in thick clay, right up to her chin. Even her hair was covered in it.

Not right, a voice whispered in Ailsa's ear.

I know, she thought back.

Legs shaking, she crouched on one knee, becoming smaller. "Are you alright?" she asked the child.

"I got stuck," she said, her voice thick with tears.

"Are you all alone?"

The girl nodded. "I was running away."

"What were you running away from?"

"There were footsteps behind me." The girl shuddered. "I was trying to get away and I fell in."

Ailsa took in her mud-caked clothes, fighting the bile that crept up her throat. "Where are your parents?"

"I don't know my father. My mother is dead," said the girl. "I have a brother though, Cameron... but I don't know where he is."

Ailsa pushed down the anger that threatened to reveal her. She had to make the Brollachan believe she was falling for this deception. But to use her image as a child... that it knew her brother's name... she would enjoy sending this thing to the depths of hell.

The creature was talking again, its face tilting so that Ailsa could see the changeling mark, a perfect replica of her own. "If you help me get out, then we could look for him together. And then we could look for my mother. Not my human one, but the one that's still alive. She's a queen, you know, so that makes me a princess." The girl gave a small smile. "Wouldn't it be nice if we could be princesses together? We could, you know, if you helped me. Then we'd be together always."

Ailsa had heard enough. "How do I help you out?"

"You have to come over here and pull my arms."

"Oh really? But what if I get stuck?"

"Would you really leave a little girl?"

Ailsa tightened her jaw. "I don't really like kids."

The girl looked affronted. "I could die here!"

"You're already dead," Ailsa told the creature, standing to her full height, the sympathy on her face gone. "You were weak." She stared down at the face of her nine-year-old self. "I killed you every time I fought for myself. I am better than the girl I was back then, and I don't miss her, so you can stop all this inner-child-crap and show me what I'm really facing."

The girl opened her mouth as if she would start shouting, but instead Ailsa watched as black smoke poured from it, the Brollachan emerging from the image it had created. It rose out of the figure, unravelling it like string, until it had disappeared and all that was left was a swirling mass, floating above the ground. Formless, just like Gris had said.

The Brollachan seemed to draw in a breath, rearing back, before releasing it again in a bloodcurdling scream. Readying to strike.

But Ailsa had been waiting. Since she had spotted the girl and her stomach had plummeted in fear, she had been pulling at the string of power which connected her to the sky. She had been frightened when she had heard that voice urging her to *take, take, take*—a whisper of what she had heard on the ship—before the storm had destroyed the vessels. But she wasn't in the churning water. There was no one around to be in harm's way—except the monster.

She extended a hand and grabbed a handful of that energy. The Brollachan flew closer, bucking and thrashing like it could feel the charge in the air—the charge Ailsa was wielding.

With a shout, she pulled that power down, her veins crackling with energy as she aimed the lightning right at the creature before her.

It split the swirling mass in half and she allowed herself a tight smile.

A shout from Gris had that smile slipping from her mouth. "You can't use the storm, Ailsa. It doesn't yet have a form! You have to bind it to the earth before you can destroy it."

Sure enough, the scattered parts of the Brollachan were reforming into the black cloud. Ailsa could almost feel the blood draining from her face as she watched the creature dart to her left, coming to rest upon the very tree that she had used to walk on. The black smoke cleared, revealing another figure, taller this time.

"You'll have to try better than that," the not-Harris chuckled, the mischievous tilt of his lips uncanny.

Ailsa ignored him, trying her best to latch on to

power—any power—that might help her. "Gris, how do I bind it?"

"It isn't made of flesh and blood, but you can make it a vessel to reside in if you use faerie magic. Look inside yourself and find it."

Look inside yourself. The words echoed in Ailsa's ears as she watched the Brollachan fly for her. Well, there was one way to bind the Brollachan to an earthly vessel.

Ailsa again raised a hand, becoming a conduit for the electricity crackling high in the sky. The lightning pulsed down her hand. She watched as her skin glowed with it, swallowing all the energy she could, ready to be used on the monster. Finally, she faced the creature, expecting it to be across the forest floor, as another figure from her past perhaps. She hadn't expected to find frost-blue eyes inches from her own.

A mixture of horror and longing stirred within her, even as she fought to keep control of the power within. She hadn't seen that face since she was a girl of twelve, yet here she was smiling down at her. Not like she had been just before she had died, gaunt and weakened. No, now her mother smiled down at her, healthy and glowing.

Ailsa thought she might vomit.

"Ailsa, *mo ghaol*, it's been such a long time." Ailsa's mother brought a quivering hand to her lips, a look of warmth in her gaze as she beheld her daughter.

"You're sick," Ailsa spat.

Her mother's face maintained a dreamy expression. "Not anymore. I know it was hard for you and your brother when I was unwell, but I'm better now." A single tear escaped her eye. "We can be together again."

Ailsa couldn't help but drink in the image before her, even as her revulsion threatened to untether her.

Before she could scream, the Brollachan reared up in front of her, coiling as it launched itself down her throat.

Chapter 5

Angus's shout of dismay was far away as she was pushed back into her own mind, making room for the new master of her body. The Brollachan took up so much space, she was suffocating. She knew it would be only a matter of time till she was squeezed down so small that she ceased to exist.

The monster's hissing thoughts were so loud, they eclipsed her own. The Brollachan was exulting in the luxury of its new host, she could feel its glee as it spread out.

I haven't had a real body for hundreds of years.

It would take a bit of time getting used to the movements this body could make, but it hoped it could learn how to move it before it died of hunger and thirst. If it could just get the arms and legs working, it could climb out of the trap it had laid.

Ailsa listened as it paused, calculating.

The other mortals will be a problem, though. They will want to try to save the one I have stolen. Well, I will just need to show them that there was nothing left to save.

Ailsa could hear it willing her toes to move first.

The Brollachan reached down, pulling on the muscles, willing them to work. At the same time, it thought of all the places it would bring this new body to.

New places with new bodies, it reminded itself.

It needn't stay just in this one. Who knew who else it might encounter on its travels?

Besides, after a while, this one will be useless; the decay of death will start sinking in after a few weeks. That is the inconvenience of this life, that the possession of a host starts to eat away at it. This body is only half human, so it will last a bit longer... but if I can find a true immortal perhaps I can go months, years even.

The Brollachan poked at Ailsa's memories, pulling out her name and her thoughts, chuckling at the absurdity. She had been planning to find the Faerie Queen.

Well, the Brollachan supposed, *I'm saving the girl from a worse fate. But if I can follow through with the girl's plan, maybe I could find a sturdier body in the Unseelie Court...*

Somewhere at the back of her mind, Ailsa shuddered as her lips twitched without her permission. The Brollachan swelled in joy.

A small triumph but a fine start.

It was so preoccupied with its puppetry that it didn't feel Ailsa uncurl herself from her hiding spot.

She had listened to the Brollachan's thoughts, waiting until she knew the monster thought it had won. She slipped along the prison it had made for her and peered through the bars. Looking out through her own eyes, she saw Angus fighting with Gris, trying to climb over the lip of the basin himself.

Iona was staring at Ailsa's body, her mouth opening and closing in disbelief. *I'm still here*, Ailsa wanted to shout. Slowly, she opened her hands and released the power she had been holding since she had called it down from the sky.

The Brollachan had managed to work from moving the toes, all the way up both legs. Soon, it would have the arms and head moving, and it could climb out of the pit. The shouting from up above had stopped.

The girl's friends must have given up.

It had begun to work on the fingers when a strange feeling had it pausing. It waited, trying to work out the source, but soon it decided that all new bodies had strange senses, and so it began again.

Ailsa forced her way forward, blasting the smallest, furthest parts of the monster with her magic. She turned a corner, recoiling a little as she beheld the full mass of it, squatting there.

"You have a body," Ailsa whispered to it. "Now you can die."

The Brollachan didn't see the first wave of electricity coming as the energy blasted into its back. It reared in pain as the shocks blistered its swirling hide. Abandoning its control, it lunged for Ailsa, but she was there again, reaching out a hand and releasing another wave of power.

To Angus, Ailsa had looked like she could be sleeping. She had been lying still where she had fallen in the clearing, save for a few twitches of her face and legs. If he hadn't seen that thing possess her, he would have expected to hear her gentle snores. But now, she was no longer still. Her whole body was jerking as if in pain.

He struggled harder against Gris's arms. "We need to help her!"

"She's been taken," the Fear-Laith grunted, holding him tighter. "Unless you want to end up the same way, we have to go."

"Come on, Angus," Iona urged, her gaze darting around the darkening forest. "We have to run."

"Like hell I will," he shouted, trying afresh to launch himself from Gris's hands. But the Fear-Laith was too strong, pushing him to the ground. Angus continued to watch Ailsa's body thrash around from where his face was pressed into the dirt.

Then, all of a sudden, the movement stopped. Angus was about to start screaming again, when a wave of light blasted from her body, hitting the sides of the Brollachan's lair. All was quiet for an instant. Even Gris seemed to be holding his breath as they stared down at her. Then, Ailsa's eyes shot open, revealing not blue, but white. Her skin glowed golden as she sat up from the ground.

"Ailsa?" Angus asked tentatively. Gris had relaxed his hold, giving the prince the opportunity to wriggle free; yet he did not jump down the hill the way he had planned. He watched as his friend stood, glowing brightly. She turned her face upwards, just as the clouds parted, allowing the sun to shine down upon the clearing. Ailsa smiled. "Not quite what you had in mind, I know Gris," she said. Then she doubled over, throwing up on the mud the bile she produced was black and sticky. Where it coated the ground, steam rose and Angus was able to smell the decay from where he knelt. A few heaves, and Ailsa had expelled all that was left of the Brollachan.

Chapter 6

"Stop your clucking, I'm fine," Ailsa said for what felt like the hundredth time.

"You passed out." Angus tried to grab her pack as they walked, but Ailsa snatched it back.

If being possessed hadn't put her in a bad mood, Gris's reaction had managed it just fine. She had climbed out of the Brollachan's lair, sore and sick, expecting to at least get a clap on the back for defeating it. Gris had just grunted and said they had to get moving. Angus and Iona seemed impressed though—and terrified. Their faces had taken a full half hour to turn from ashen back to a healthy colour.

As they marched through the forest, the rain fell from above, but Ailsa couldn't find it in herself to control it. It thundered through the leaves overhead; the noise only drowned out occasionally by a strong gust of wind. Iona, without a word, created a barrier, sending any drops of water which should have hit them bouncing off into the brush.

Angus tried to speak again, but he gave up with a look at Ailsa's glum face.

It was Gris who broke the silence. "We'll need to find a place to camp to wait out the storm."

"To wait out my bad mood you mean?"

"I wasn't going to mention it, but yes," he grunted.

Ailsa narrowed her eyes. "I thought I was supposed to be controlling earthly powers, not making it rain?"

"You just haven't learned how they work yet," Gris said. "You'll get there."

"What if I'm not Nicnevan's daughter?" The question had been bubbling on the surface of her brain for days, and it burst from Ailsa without her control.

Gris groaned, clearly loath to have this conversation. "It would be a big coincidence if you aren't. A half fae baby goes missing and a week later I find a half fae baby in the woods? What are the chances?"

"Do you see any resemblance?" Ailsa grabbed his arm, making him stop. "Do I look like her?"

Gris appraised her face. "Nicnevan looks like a Faerie Queen. I doubt many people look like her."

Beautiful he means, Ailsa thought with an internal groan.

"Ailsa, you're a changeling," Iona said gently. "Your appearance was changed. How much, we don't know, but we can't assume you'd look anything like Nicnevan."

"Here," Angus interrupted. "There's an old bothy up ahead. We can stay there for the night."

Sure enough, a rundown building squatted in the

woods ahead, looking barely watertight, but it would be better than sitting in the elements. Gris reached the door first, opening it with a creak. Inside, something squeaked as it was disturbed by the light.

"I'll catch us something to eat," Iona told them as they threw their packs down on the stone floor. "Angus, would you help Ailsa start a fire?"

Look after Ailsa, is what she meant.

Gris grunted something about scouting the area and then Ailsa and Angus were left alone. The rain pattered off the tin roof, drowning out the noise of Angus stacking old wood in the grate. He struck a match from his pack and threw it on the pile, blowing it until it caught into the start of a fire.

"So," Angus said, staring into the flames. "Do you want to talk about it?"

Ailsa blew out a breath and took a seat next to him, warming her chilled skin. "I don't know. Yes?"

"What's on your mind?"

Nothing. Everything. "It seems like my whole life has been a lie, but it's only gotten worse since I found out." Even her reflection was a mystery.

It seemed so obvious now, but she'd never thought of it before. Her mother had had similar blue eyes, the same brown hair, though it was curly instead of straight. The resemblance had been near perfect... which meant that it couldn't be real. Ailsa's stomach plummeted.

"Someone made me look this way." She gazed up at Angus, who's pale colouring was so like her own. Like most Eilanmòrians. "They made me the way I am so I would fit in. So that I could hide."

"What do you mean?"

"Gris told me he had found me in the forest, after I had been stolen away. I have a changeling mark, so I've obviously been *changed*."

What would she have looked like if she had been left alone? Like some golden-haired Faerie Queen? Or would she have taken after her father? The tales hadn't said much about his identity, only that he had been a brave Eilanmòrian warrior, who had been in love with Nicnevan until he had trapped her in her own kingdom.

"I feel like something has been stolen from me... or is about to be stolen. I don't know whether to mourn the face that I'll never know, or if I even want to know." Ailsa shook her head. "Does that make sense?"

Angus nodded. "You don't know whether you want Nicnevan to be your mother or not."

"If she is, then I'll be met with a new image of myself and the old Ailsa will be gone."

Angus stared off into the shadows. "What if... Nicnevan is your real mother... and you have the chance to return to the way you would have looked?"

"I don't know. But Nicnevan... She may be my birth mother, but she didn't tuck me into bed at night, or protect me from danger, or hold me when I needed comforting. Heather MacAra was my true mother."

"That doesn't mean you can't get to know this one," Angus said. "Besides, we have to go anyway. Harris is counting on us."

"This is becoming a bit of a theme." Ailsa shucked off her damp cloak with a groan, revelling in the heat the roaring fire was producing. "We should start charging him."

"Maybe," Angus said with a grin. "If we weren't also always getting into trouble ourselves." He flicked his gaze to the door and laughed. "Speaking of trouble."

Ailsa turned to find something huge and antlered blocking the doorway. Only when the creature grunted in annoyance did she realise it was Iona, trying to drag a limp, dead deer through over the threshold.

"Don't you think that's overkill?" Ailsa went to help the selkie pull the animal into the bothy, tugging on its coarse fur until it was in front of the fire. "There's only four of us."

"I'm going to turn what we don't eat into jerky," Iona huffed, brushing off her dress. "Besides, Gris said he found it with a tree branch through its neck. Seems like a gift from the gods to me."

"Fine," said Angus. "But we should skin it outside, so we don't have to deal with the smell while we're trying to sleep." He reached into his pack and produced a short knife, before picking the deer up and slinging it onto his shoulders.

"Show off," Iona grumbled as he strode out of the bothy. She shed her cloak and arranged it on the ground in front of the fire, sinking down with a sigh. "So, how are you feeling now?"

Ailsa kicked at the pile of wood with her foot. "The rain's stopped, hasn't it?" Ailsa folded her body down beside the selkie. "I'm just worried. Every day we get closer to Ephraim and I'm no better at controlling my magic. And Gris isn't exactly filling me with confidence."

"He's a bit of a task-master, isn't he?"

Ailsa grimaced. "I suppose that's what he was used to. Did you know he used to be a soldier in the Edessan army? He's good at training people. He trained me."

"Yes," said Iona gently. "But you're not a soldier. Marching into Ephraim, as bold as brass, isn't going to win you any favours."

Ailsa threw her hands up. "And what is?"

"Knowledge," Iona said. "Knowledge is your best weapon."

"Why do I even need a weapon?" Ailsa asked, staring at the edge of the flames. A tiny spider crawled out of the unburnt wood, scared from its hiding place by the heat. It scuttled across the flagstones, taking its time, the cracks between hard to navigate like deep valleys. Ailsa felt suddenly exhausted. "Surely, if I am Nicnevan's daughter, I'll be welcomed with open arms?" She brought her gaze back to Iona, who looked dubious.

"Maybe," said the selkie. "But I'm afraid it won't be that easy. Ephraim isn't the friendliest of places."

"Go on then, fill me in."

"When we get to the faerie court, you may see some things that are... unfavourable." Iona shifted, tucking her feet under her. "There's a reason that it's the Unseelie, the evil fae, who are loyal to Nicnevan."

"So she's evil," Ailsa grumbled. "Great."

"Nicnevan is…" Iona's mouth twisted. "She does what she wants. It is all a game to her. It just so happens that the Unseelie are best at playing."

"You said she's been trapped for years, maybe it's mellowed her out?" Ailsa asked hopefully. She was starting to get a stomach-ache.

"Maybe…" Iona gave her a sidelong look. "The only thing she has ever cared about is her daughter. Perhaps you are what is needed to change Ephraim. Turn it to good."

"So basically..." Ailsa said, "you're telling me I need to save the world again? Can we just focus on finding Harris please?"

"That's why we're going." Iona bit her lip and reached to grab Ailsa's hand in her own. The selkie's palm was surprisingly warm, despite the evening chill. "But, Ailsa, I don't want you to put my brother before yourself and your happiness. I know that you... felt something for each other. But if finding out about who you really are is important to you, then it's important to me."

Ailsa was silent for a moment. "Iona... did you know that I wasn't human? When you met me?"

"Yes," Iona admitted, giving Ailsa's hand a squeeze. "Though I just assumed there was some fae ancestor you didn't know about. We can't tell how fae someone is, just that they're not human. So many people have fae lineage, I didn't think it really mattered. I certainly didn't think you had any magic. I'm sorry."

Ailsa closed her eyes. "I think Harris knew. About my magic I mean. I think he knew before I did. But he didn't say anything."

"My brother plays his own games. Who knows what he was thinking."

"He's so hard to read," Ailsa agreed. "I could never tell whether he liked me or if he was just messing around. One minute I'd think he liked me, the next he was off talking to someone else."

The selkie *tsked*. "Harris has never been very constant. Listen, Ailsa, I don't want to tell you what to do, but I care about you as much as a sister. Harris is immature. He might have lived for several decades but he's still a little boy at heart. He cares so much about people, and he's a loyal friend, but he gets distracted easily, especially by lovely things."

"Ah well, that counts me out then."

"You are a lovely thing, Ailsa." Iona bumped her shoulder into hers. "He cares about you, but are you willing to wait until he is mature enough to stop chasing all the other lovely things of the world?"

"It doesn't matter anyway," Ailsa said, raising her chin. "I'm going to save him because he's my friend."

Iona lifted their clasped hands to her mouth and gave Ailsa's a swift kiss. "And that's why you're too good for him. My brother is an idiot. But a pretty lucky idiot to have us all."

"Done," announced Angus, from outside.

Both women stood from their place by the fire. Ailsa dropped Iona's hand and immediately felt the loss of warmth. "Would you mind if I go find Gris?" she asked. "You're a better cook than me anyway."

"Of course," Iona said. She gave Ailsa a pat on the shoulder, then she was striding outside, giving Angus orders on how she wanted the food prepared.

Ailsa had to stifle a laugh as she passed. Poor hen-pecked man.

The mist had burned off, revealing a sky of burnished golds and reds through the trees. The evening smelled of pine and rain, so thick Ailsa thought she could taste it on her tongue.

The sound of wood splintering echoed from the tree line and it wasn't long until she found the source.

"I thought we should replace the firewood we're using. For the next people," Gris muttered. He was standing with his feet spread and a chunk of wood in his hands. With a growl, the Fear-Laith tore at the piece, muscles bulging, until it was ripped in half. He dropped the two bits into a pile and stood panting with his hands on his hips.

"How are your wounds?" Gris grunted as Ailsa got closer.

Ailsa pulled out her axe from her waistband. "I'll live. Do you want some help?"

"Would you take over? My legs aren't what they used to be. Here, I'll pass them if you split them."

Good. It was always easier to speak to him when they were doing something.

Ailsa swung her axe down on the log, failing to crack it down the middle. She just had to find the right place to hit it. She swung the axe again, splitting it, and kicked the smaller bits out of the way. "Gris," she began, flexing her shoulders. "Would you tell me more about when you found me? I just can't imagine it, coming across a baby in the woods."

Gris placed another stump in front of her. "I had been out scavenging when I came across you and the dead faerie woman. At first, I thought she was sleeping, but then she didn't move when you cried. I remember dropping everything when I heard you. It was the talk of all the fae—Nicnevan was imprisoned and her child had been taken—so I knew exactly who you were. The faerie had been some sort of messenger, ferrying you away from Ephraim. I couldn't tell what had killed her, though I guessed some sort of curse. I can imagine Nicnevan having a protection on you."

Ailsa swung again and this time her axe split the wood in half on the first time. "Weren't you worried you'd be cursed?"

"I already was," Gris replied with a shrug. "I'd been living in the forests of Eilanmòr as a Fear-Laith since the start of the Mirandelli war. In my youth, I'd thought to come here to fight for peace."

Fight for peace? "So what happened?" Ailsa kicked the wood to the side and nodded for another one to take its place.

"Same as the faerie, though not as final at least. I was cursed."

"By who?"

"You're not going to like the answer."

"Nicnevan." Ailsa stared at the new piece, feeling suddenly how tired her arms were.

"Wrong place, wrong time," Gris said. "That's what I get for wandering through the Forest of Frith instead of being down south where I should have been. When I found you, I had been living like this for years. It felt like I had nothing to lose."

"Then you took me to my—to Heather MacAra."

"Not at first." He scratched at his beard. "At first I didn't really know what to do with you. Then I heard another baby crying. I thought if I brought you to someone who was already a mother then you'd be safe. It wasn't until I found the house that I realised that baby was dying. Once it had gone, I swapped her for you and took her away. She was buried near the house, beside a flower bush."

Ailsa couldn't help the way her lip curled. "Gris, that's awful. What if she'd wanted to mourn her baby?"

He fixed her with a steady stare. "She *had* a baby. You. Anyway, your mother knew you were a changeling, but she treated you as her own all the same."

Needing something to do, Ailsa lifted the axe above her head and brought it down upon the waiting wood. It cracked in a corner, but the blow hadn't been strong enough. "Did you put the changeling mark on my face?" she asked in a small voice.

"No, it was already there. You'd already been changed by the faerie. I suppose she just tried to make you look as Eilanmòrian as possible."

Brown hair, blue eyes. Just like everyone else.

"Ailsa, I regret having to leave you. I know if I was human, I could have looked after you, raised you knowing what you were. But my place is in the forest. I couldn't raise a baby there."

"I wish you'd told me or let me know you were around. All those years being scared of you—of being alone—could have been avoided." She pulled the blade out and readied to try again, sweat prickling along her back.

"I tried, but you kept running away."

"Until you were human again."

"Fear-Laith's have such a short time as a human, I was desperate to make it count. That's why I was so hard on you, why I pushed you in your training."

"If you hadn't, I wouldn't be here today." Ailsa threw her weight into the swing and the wood split cleanly. She straightened, holding her axe in both hands in front of her; the axe that Gris had given her. The handle was smooth with use.

Gris nodded. "I think that's enough," he said, bending to retrieve the pile. "I'll go take this in."

Ailsa replaced her weapon in her belt, enjoying the cool breeze on her hot skin.

"You know," Gris called over his shoulder. "You could have used magic to split all of this."

"I know," Ailsa said. "But you taught me to survive, without magic, and for that I'll always be grateful."

With a half smile, Gris shuffled off and then Ailsa was left alone in the woods.

Chapter 7

Harris hated the ceasg.

They were too much, with their damned riddles and their cold hands. It didn't help that they fancied themselves to be as beautiful as the faeries they were serving. Arrogant. Self-absorbed. Brainless.

A day into his capture, one of them had actually tried to drown him. He held her gaze under the water, smirking, counting down the time until she recognised her mistake. It took a lot longer than it should have. Never try to drown a selkie.

As much as they infuriated him, he was relying on their dim-wittedness. In a pack they were a formidable force, too aggressive really to fight. But if all went his way, he wouldn't be fighting his way out. He would be strolling.

They had travelled inland for a few days, sticking first to sea water lochs, then wide rivers. Sometimes he would change into a seal, but they didn't like that very much. Confused and enraged, they would pummel him until he changed back. It didn't matter anyway, if this was going to work, he would need to appear human.

He would need to do it soon, the proximity of the forest told him they were close.

Stuic-iasg, the ceasg's leader, prowled around her sisters up ahead, snapping her teeth at them if they got too close. Her name meant *stab-fish* in ancient Eilanmòrian; they all had stupid names like that. *Murder-fish, Bite-fish, Rip-fish.* They obviously thought it made them sound fierce, but Harris had pointed out to them that it's only really threatening if you're a fish.

His current jailer was a softer creature than the others. Harris sensed that Pog-iasg was a bit of a social pariah. Her name meant *kiss-fish* after all. Her comrades had stuck him with her, so she could prove herself. She kept her eyes on him at all times, though from the glaze in them Harris knew her mind was wandering. As much as a ceasg's mind *can* wander.

It was getting to twilight, and the others had swum off in search of food. It would have to be now.

"Excuse me," said Harris carefully. "Do you know how long it will take us to get to Ephraim?"

Pog-iasg's eyes lost a bit of their glaze as she studied him. "Why do you want to know?"

He smiled lazily. "I want to know how long I have to escape."

The ceasg tilted her head, unsure.

"I'm just joking, of course," he laughed. "Though, who could blame me?"

"We need to take selkie to Nicnevan," was all she answered.

"I know." He ran a hand through his copper hair, the ceasg watching his every movement. "But it's a real shame."

"What is shame?" she asked.

"We didn't really get to know each other."

"I don't need to know selkie. All selkies are same."

"But not all ceasg are," Harris lowered his voice. "You, Pog-iasg, are very different."

"Different is not good." She sank her fingers into the silt and pouted.

"No, different is very good. I've been watching you for a while, and I know what the others don't."

"What?"

"You've been waiting. Waiting until you can strike down the ones who have mocked you." He ducked his head, like he was fighting for his words. "I've... given you a new name... in my head."

"New name?" Her face lit up.

"Cradh-iasg," he whispered, filling his voice with wonder. Roughly translated, *torture-fish*.

"Cradh-iasg," she repeated, her smile showing razor-sharp teeth. "A fine name." Her smile fell. "No one else will call me that name."

"But they will," he told her, "you just need to stand up to them."

She stared at the water, twisting something around in the sand. *Eyes back on me*, he thought.

"What do you have there?"

She hissed. "Can't have it."

"Is that…" he smiled conspiratorially, "…your egg?"

"Mine," she said, holding the thing to her body.

"It's just…" he faltered, "I have never seen a ceasg egg before. I bet it's as pretty as you are."

"Pretty?"

"Has no one ever told you, you're the prettiest ceasg around? I bet the egg you came from is the best too."

The ceasg appraised him, the slow cogs in her head turning over. Harris fought the urge to roll his eyes. If he waited until she came up with a thought of her own, the others would come back.

"May I see your egg?" he asked, tilting his head.

She hesitated, regarding him warily. Then, with maddening slowness, she pulled out the pearlescent orb that had been under her palm.

Ceag were asexual, producing their eggs by themselves, making perfect clones. It was likely that Pog-iasg had not only inherited her mother's looks but also her low-ranking status. It would take something momentous for her to change her position in the ceasg pack. A position that her own daughter would inherit.

High stakes, thought Harris. *High enough that she would risk everything?*

"Your egg is lovely," he told her honestly. Shame that it would hatch one day and grow into one of those infuriating creatures.

Pog-iasg continued to watch him, though now with an insipid grin lighting her face. Oh, this will be too easy.

"I have an idea to help you," Harris began, sitting back on the silt of the riverbank. "If you want a new name, then you'll have to earn it."

"If I want to be Cradh-iasg, I will have to find fish to torture."

"Hmm, it's not very flashy though, is it? Fish are so small, if you try torturing one it'll probably die fairly quickly..." Harris tapped his chin, pretending to consider. "You need something bigger... like... a selkie?"

Pog-iasg's smile glinted in the fading light, no doubt imagining the words '*torture*' and '*selkie*' together.

"Ah but," Harris laughed. "I'd rather you didn't torture me, of course." He thought for a second, watching her hungry look. "How about Sealg-selkie?"

She sniffed, clearly disappointed. "How will I '*hunt-selkie*' when you have already been hunted?"

"What if, you let me go—just briefly. Then you could sound the alarm that I'm missing, and come after me? We could meet upriver, where there's a curve. I'll wait for you, and then you can find me in front of the other ceasg."

"What does the selkie want for this? How do I know you will not run?"

"I could give you something very precious to me, so that I will have to come back?"

"What does the selkie have?"

Harris watched her warily. "You must promise you will give it back to me when I am back. I couldn't bear to be without it."

"What is it?"

Harris screwed up his nose. "Close your eyes so you don't see where I keep it."

To his surprise, the ceasg obeyed. With a grin, Harris scanned the riverside, trying his best to find what he needed in the low light. Then he spotted it, tucked underneath the grassy bank. He leaned as far as he could without getting up, doing his best not to rustle too much before he turned back to face Pog-iasg, the object safe in his hands.

"You can look," he said.

The ceasg opened her eyes, her gaze flicking to his closed palm.

Biting his lip, he opened it, revealing a smooth, grey river stone.

"This is my egg."

"Selkies do not have eggs…" argued Pog-iasg, though there was doubt in her face.

"We do, we just never reveal them to anyone. They're very special to us." He bit his lip. "If we give our eggs away then we turn into seals and we can't turn human again until we have them back."

Pog-iasg stared at the stone in his hand. "It is not as nice as mine."

"No," Harris allowed. "I am very jealous."

"Do we have a deal?"

"Give me your egg."

Harris brought the stone to his lips, kissing it, before handing it over with a shaking hand. As soon as Pog-iasg lifted it from his palm, he shed his human skin, shifting into a seal.

She made a sound of shock, a smile dawning on her face when she saw the evidence of his story.

"I could keep selkie's egg," she mused, turning it over in her hands. Then her smile faded. "But I need selkie's help for my name." She clacked her teeth together as she thought. Harris resisted the temptation to just bite her with his sharp seal teeth.

"Fine," she said. "Selkie will go to bend in the river and wait there. I will tell others you have gone, then I will come find you." Pog-iasg smiled again. "I will have to scratch and bite selkie to show I am strong."

Harris gave a huff, as if in acquiescence, and Pog-iasg nodded. She took the stone and her egg, and hid them away in a pouch on her abdomen. Then, with a growl, she motioned for him to go.

Harris ducked into the water, swimming against the current. He hoped that Pog-iasg would think to give him a head start. It wouldn't matter soon anyway.

The water was dark and murky, but that had never stopped Harris before. He slithered over the pebbles at the bottom of the river, fighting against the current, feeling with his whiskers. Up ahead he could just make out a dark wall, signalling the turn in the river where he had said he'd meet Pog-iasg. But when the ceasg found her way to their meeting point, she would be sorely disappointed. Harris banked to the left, following the river's course, sweeping past the bend with strong flippers.

Once he felt sure he had gone a reasonable distance, he allowed himself to float back to the surface, poking his ears up into the night air. He paused. Had they found him gone yet? Sure enough, a moment later, above the burbling of the water, he heard the piercing screams of frustration. Pog-iasg had told her sisters that Harris had disappeared. No doubt she would be punished before they could even set out to look for him. Harris didn't have it in him to care. Any minutes spent reprimanding the stupid ceasg would be time he could make his escape.

Harris swam on, until he reached the bank of the river, hastily changing back into a human when he reached dry land. *Selkie eggs indeed*, he laughed to himself. Ceasg really were idiots.

He slunk through the grass, keeping close to the ground, listening to the now distant wails of ceasg. It was almost too hard to contain the laugh that bubbled up inside him. Wait until he told Ailsa this story! He supposed she was probably sick with worry, ready to mount some rescue attempt. Well, no need! He had gone and rescued himself.

When he reached the trees, he allowed himself to pause in the shadows and look back towards the river. He could just make out the marble-like bodies of the ceasg swimming around, unable to step out of the water. One of them was clawing at the bank... Pog-iasg he realised. He let out a guffaw as he thought up a final name for her: Caill-selkie. *Lose-selkie!*

Harris sucked in some air after his laugh and blanched. What was that smell? It was like something had died nearby.

A snort from behind him made Harris turn. What he saw froze the grin on his face.

The head of a gigantic horse was inches away from his nose. No—not a horse—but perhaps something that used to be one. The creature's skin had been pulled away from its muscle, leaving raw and shining flesh behind. Harris could see its veins and arteries spidering across its great head. It looked like an animated corpse. The creature snuffed warm, putrid air in his face and Harris had to fight to stop from vomiting.

"What the…" Harris began, but his voice faltered when he saw what was riding the undead-horse before him.

The rider was a man, or what looked like one. But like the horse, it was skinless and awful. It seemed like its lower body was fused to the horse, like they were one creature. In its mutilated hands it carried two sharp knives.

A nuckelavee. Harris had heard of the undead-horse fae before, but had never seen one. This was the sort of monster his mother would have told him about to scare him from going into the woods.

Harris turned to run, but then the smell became unbearably foul. Distracted by the roiling in his stomach, he tripped, his chin hitting the earth with a crunch. He could hear the nuckelavee get closer and closer, the heavy hooves of the horse clicking across the ground.

Harris struggled with a wave of dizziness that washed over him, but the smell only got stronger until he was blessedly unconscious.

Chapter 8

Ailsa woke with the dawn. Through the window, she could see grey morning mist clinging to the trees, making the sun's direction difficult to pinpoint. In the low light, she did her best to make out if her companions were awake. They hadn't spoken much as they'd eaten their venison, and afterwards had decided to call it an early night. Gris had fallen asleep leaning against the far wall, as if he had stayed up late to watch over them. Iona and Angus were sleeping back to back, sharing heat. No one stirred when Ailsa pulled her cloak around herself. She left her pack and her axe sitting beside Angus so he would know she was coming back soon.

As she trooped through the woods, Ailsa steeled herself, rolling her shoulders and inspecting the dirt underfoot with resolve. An early morning practice session was what she needed. Maybe her attempts at magic had been so useless because someone had always been watching her.

Ailsa found a clearing far enough away from their camp that she was sure they wouldn't hear whatever noises she made. The trees above swayed, rustling their leaves together. She breathed in deep and listened, allowing the sound to ground her.

Now that she was alone, Ailsa was able to feel the magic as it sparked to life under her skin, like striking a match. It hummed through her bones, ready to be used.

Just do what feels natural first, she told herself. Then you can try to do what Gris said.

Raising a hand, she allowed the power to reach out into the air, pulling the particles into a gentle breeze at first. Ailsa concentrated, flexing her fingers, until the wind picked up, whipping around her body. She sent it around the treetops, sweeping away the fog, allowing the sun to shine down onto the forest floor where she stood. Ailsa smiled, basking in the heat.

See, that wasn't so hard.

Ailsa thought she heard a sigh of contentment follow her thoughts, but she brushed it off, assuming she had made it herself.

Now I just have to work out how this relates to faerie magic. Gris had said she had to find some way to focus her power on the earth. Ailsa searched around her. The dirt in front of her was covered in leaf litter. With half a thought, she sent the wind at it, swirling the debris up from the ground, leaving a blank canvas for her to experiment on.

Ailsa bent down to examine the soil. She reached out with one hand, feeling for an answering pulse of power from the earth. If only she could feel it, like she could feel the air, maybe she'd be able to get control.

But the soil was cold and packed together tightly. Ailsa grimaced, placing her other hand on it. If she could just push herself…

She wrinkled her nose. A pressure was starting to build in her head, but she ignored it as she continued. She could feel something between the particles of dirt, calling out to her.

You're feeling the trapped air, she realised. Maybe this was how she could control the earth.

She felt around for the particles of air, rocking them back and forward to make the pockets bigger.

So slow. The dirt was pressing down on them—a weight she felt become heavier and heavier the more she concentrated—like her own body was becoming buried in it. She growled as she felt something trickle from her nose.

This is not your magic, a voice in her head whispered.

She winced and tried to ignore it as she dug her fingers into the dirt.

"Come on," she grunted. "Do something."

Above, the clouds grumbled with electricity, rolling over themselves in her frustration.

You have to do this, she told herself. *People are counting on you.*

Her fingers were aching from where she had them

buried. She closed her eyes and focussed on the feel of every grain of earth.

You know how to make your pain stop, the voice said again. *Just let go.*

Her scalp tingled from the change in air pressure as the storm grew overhead.

Let go, or I'll make you, said the voice, louder.

With a snarl, she lifted her hand towards the sky. The relief was immediate. Lightning crackled around her fingertips, kissing her skin.

But in her euphoria, the voice was replaying in her head again. *Let go, or I'll make you,* it had said. *Who, or what, had said that?*

The voice was different to her own, now that she thought about it.

"Who are you?" she asked it out loud. This was too much, too close to when she had been possessed by the Brollachan yesterday. Had it somehow stayed inside her? But that couldn't be right. With slow dread, she remembered she'd heard it before, when she'd almost destroyed all the Avalognian ships and all the captives on them.

She paused, her hands still in the air, as she waited for an answer. Just when she thought she had imagined it, the voice spoke again.

I'll show you your true potential.

Then Ailsa's body was not her own. Her hands came

down on the ground again, and the magic she had built up pulsed into the dirt, to the cracks in between the grains. With a jolt, the air between forced itself out, causing the ground to explode.

The soil launched into the air, like a wave. The sound was deafening and Ailsa tried to brace herself for the impact. But then there was a wall of swirling air around her and the soil was bouncing off, landing again where it should have been.

"Stop!" she shouted. The air crackled with electricity. A shot of lightning speared down from the sky, hitting the tree in front of her, setting it on fire.

Ailsa's body jumped and she took the opportunity to wrestle back control. She fell to the ground and curled into a ball as she felt the aftershocks of her magic.

She listened for the voice again, but there was thankfully only silence for several minutes. It was back to being dormant somewhere inside her brain. Ailsa sat up, surveying the damage. The place where she had been standing was untouched, but around her the soil had been churned up. The tree was still on fire. Ailsa felt the heat from it; allowed it to warm her numb bones.

What had happened? She blew out a breath when she realised she was back to hearing her own voice inside her head.

"Thank the gods," she mumbled, running a hand over her face.

Then a voice answered, and Ailsa gave a start. *Was whatever it was back?* But this was a male voice, and the other had been decidedly female.

"Get up," the new voice repeated.

Ailsa whipped round, to find a man leaning over her. In his hand, he held a dagger.

"Get up," he said for the third time.

Ailsa peered around him, her stomach sick with dread as she saw there were twenty or so others behind the man, each holding some sort of weapon.

A woman to his left spat in Ailsa's direction. "You trespassed in the wrong forest, changeling."

Chapter 9

Iona looked up from the book she had been reading and stared. "Say that again," she breathed.

Then Alasdair McFeidh, Prince of Eilanmòr and third of his name, smiled at her and said, "Marry me?"

Iona allowed herself a pause to memorise the moment. Alasdair was sitting on the end of the couch, her slipper-clad feet in his lap. He had a book in his hand too, some sort of adventure story, when hers had been romance. It was cold in the little cottage by the sea, so both were swathed in jumpers and blankets, all in mismatched tartans. A fire crackled lazily in the hearth, trying to combat the roaring wind outside. They had been reading by candlelight, the glow of which was bathing Alasdair's grinning face in warmth. He had a little stubble on his cheeks—he'd been too relaxed to bother shaving. After a day of collecting seashells, they'd had a cosy dinner of warm soup, and the bowls were still sitting on the table behind them. Everything was far from how it had been when she'd first met Alasdair in Dunrigh. She'd been at a ceilidh when he'd asked her to dance, charming, polished, and elegant. She much preferred him this way.

"Yes," she answered, beaming back at him. "Yes, I'll marry you."

Except, that wasn't how it had happened. Iona held on to the dream as long as possible, but it crumbled around her as she struggled. This was how she'd wished it had happened. Instead, the real Alasdair hadn't looked up from his book. She remembered watching him that night, wishing he would ask her that question, but he never did. He'd told her he'd loved her, of course. But they had both known it wouldn't last. A month after Iona had been sitting in their little cottage by the sea, reading books and hoping for wishes to come true, Alasdair had told her his father had died and he had to go back to Dunrigh for his coronation. And his wedding.

Outside of her sleep, Iona could hear the faint shufflings that usually preceded her companions' wakening. She scrunched her eyes closed and clung to the feeling from her dream.

"Iona." Angus's voice threatened to wake her. When she didn't respond, she felt a hand shaking her shoulder. "Iona," he said again, louder this time.

"Yes?" she answered groggily, throwing a hand over her face.

"Ailsa's gone."

The selkie stretched and sat up. "She's probably out doing something useful."

"Except we have more than enough firewood and

plenty of food and water," the prince pointed out.

"Where's Gris?" asked Iona. "Maybe she's with him." She watched Angus pull on his boots with a furrowed brow. *Well, I might as well get up too.* It wasn't like she could return to her dream.

"I just have this bad feeling…" Angus said. "Will you come and help me look?" He turned his earnest gaze on her, and Iona's heart stopped. It wasn't often that Angus reminded her of his grandfather, but when he looked at her like that, Iona couldn't ignore the resemblance.

"Yes," she managed to choke out. "Go on, I'll be there in a moment."

The prince smiled and made to stride out of the bothy, but before he reached the door, it banged open by itself.

The sight of the Fear-Laith shouldn't have filled Iona's heart with dread. He wasn't a monster after all. But the look of horror on his face was enough to tell her something was wrong. Behind him, it was beginning to rain and a great gust of wind rattled the trees overhead.

"I can't find Ailsa anywhere," Gris said. "I've been searching for a few hours. She got up at dawn, but I didn't bother to follow her. I thought she needed some space. But she's gone."

"We'll all go and look for her," said Angus. He reached behind his pallet for his pack. "Look," he said. "She's left her axe here."

"Ailsa wouldn't have left that behind if she was going

to be gone for a while." Iona bit her lip. "Okay, I'm getting worried."

Outside, the wind picked up, slamming the door shut and then whipped it open again. They took that as their cue to grab their things together as quickly as possible.

"This will seem silly when we find her exploring," Iona told them half-heartedly as they stepped out into the beginnings of the storm.

The trio searched all day, but Ailsa was gone.

"We're going to have to look for shelter soon," said Angus. "Maybe we should go back to the bothy and she'll find us there."

"And what if something *has* happened to her?" Gris barked. Though he had been pressing them onwards all day, Iona could tell his legs and feet were causing him pain.

"We'll keep looking for her tomorrow, when we've had a rest," Angus insisted.

Gris's face shuttered. "Another hour." Then he marched ahead, leaving no room for argument.

They'd only gone another hundred paces, however, when Angus stopped. "Do you hear that? It sounds like someone crying."

Iona listened intently. Indeed, forlorn wails drifted from somewhere up ahead. They were sorrowful but melodic, almost like a chant. They rose and fell in their pitch and strength, like waves.

"Come on," Angus said, starting towards the crying. "Maybe it's Ailsa."

Iona caught his arm as he rushed past her, holding him in place. "It's not Ailsa," she told him in a hush. "There's a Bean-Nighe somewhere close."

Chapter 10

Ailsa threw herself against the door of her cell again, willing that this time it would collapse under her weight. Nothing. *I hope these villagers paid their craftsman well,* she thought bitterly. The door was utterly impregnable.

Her gaze turned to the source of light in the room—a single skylight, barred to prevent escape. Ailsa could tell her jail was underground because she could see the shadows of people passing by the window up on ground level. Every now and then someone would poke their ugly noses into view, and she would growl at them. She did not appreciate having an audience to her break-out attempts.

Rolling her shoulders, she sunk to the straw floor to take a break. *Any moment now, Angus, Iona, and Gris will come storming through the door to save me,* she kept telling herself. Unfortunately, it had been a whole day and she was yet to hear the tell-tale screams of stupid villagers up above, which would signal her companions' arrival.

After she'd been ambushed, they'd shoved a bag over

her head and made her walk until her legs were aching. She had tried desperately to throw her power out so she could save herself, but then she'd heard a whisper of that voice and she'd had to give up. When the blindfold had finally been removed, the world was in twilight. Ailsa had just been able to take a glance at stone buildings and curious eyes before she had been kicked inside a door, down some steps and into her jail.

She rubbed a hand over her face. How did she get into this mess? She'd come up against superstitious villagers before, but then she'd been sure that they were wrong about her. But she was a changeling, like they feared.

Maybe they should lock you up. If there was something inside her, trying to control her, trying to destroy and kill and rage, then maybe she was better off in a prison.

As soon as Gris had told her she was Nicnevan's daughter, Ailsa had had a nagging thought that she couldn't push away. It had only worsened as Iona had described Ephraim. Nicnevan was evil, or she had done some evil things, at least. So if she was Nicnevan's daughter, did that make her capable of evil too? Ailsa thought of herself as a good person, but then memories began surfacing which were making her doubt that. Within the last few weeks, she'd killed people—had wanted to kill more people. She could explain some of those instances away as self-defence, but what about all those innocent people on the ships?

Destroy, the voice had commanded.

She'd gained back control, but barely. How long would it be before *the thing*, whatever it was, got its way?

Ailsa gave herself a shake. It was no use moping and imagining what could happen. That sort of thing could come later. For now, she had to get out of the village and find Harris. He was counting on her.

First step, she told herself, get some rest. You're not going anywhere if you collapse from exhaustion. The rest she'd work out when she was out.

"I've never seen a changeling before," someone said from up above. Ailsa saw the face of a scrawny, gawking, teenage boy staring at her through the skylight. She hissed at him and his face disappeared, followed by a curse as he hit his head in his hurry to get away.

This is going to be a long day. Ailsa turned her back from the window and curled in on herself so as little of her body as possible could be seen from above. With a groan, she shifted into a more comfortable position, and tried to fall asleep.

Chapter 11

"Ou have to choose."

Ailsa blinked and found herself in a dark room, lit only by torchlight. The room was bare, except for a wooden table and a large, ornate mirror. She stared at her reflection. This wasn't what she had been wearing before. Instead of her ruddy travelling clothes, she wore a dress of deep, midnight-blue silk. Just like the night sky, it was covered in glittering stars. She touched the fabric reverently, then tore her gaze away to look up. What she saw in the mirror made her start. Where her face should have been, there was only black.

"You have to choose your face," said a voice. She knew she'd heard it before.

Ailsa looked down at the table and found it was covered in masks. Some were decorative, like the ones she'd seen Mirandelli nobles wear. Others looked more lifelike.

Her first instinct was to reach for a beautiful, ornamental half-mask, dark blue like her dress. She put it over her face, tying it behind her head and raised her gaze to the mirror. There, she could see the mask, but underneath, she had no eyes.

"Next one."

Ailsa removed that mask and placed it to the side. This time she tried a full face made of white porcelain. It was a little small for her, and when she examined herself, she saw only blackness staring out of the eyeholes.

"Next."

Ailsa moved down the selection, trying any that she admired. But each time, she found the same problem. The masks were lovely, but none would restore her face underneath.

She moved on to the more realistic ones, frowning when she came across that of a man with a beard. She brought it to her face, and gasped—it was Angus's face. The mask was contorted into a shriek, looking so lifelike except for the hollow black where their eyes should be.

She quickly took it off. The next mask was familiar too, but it wasn't until Ailsa tried it on that she recognised Iona's face. Her mouth was open wide, like she was shouting.

Ailsa worked her way through the pile. Gris's face, human—like she had known him once—was next. Half of his face was a normal brown, but the other half was covered in red welts, like he'd been burned.

Harris's face was screwed up with confusion. Then there was her mother's, looking so tired. Her brother, Cameron's, was young like she remembered him, and carried the exact same expression he had worn when he'd been dragged out of their cottage that final time.

Each time, she expected to see eyes through the masks, but there was only dark.

Finally, she came to the end of the pile, to a mask so beautiful, she felt she dared not try it on. This mask was not contorted in a sneer or cry; it was smiling. The woman's skin was almost glowing in the low light, as if it was made of pale gold. With shaking fingers, Ailsa placed the mask over her face and tied it behind her head. She flicked her gaze to the mirror.

At first, it looked like this mask also didn't work. But then, eyes materialised in the holes. She sighed with relief. But then, the irises were not blue like her own, instead they were a luminous green. The mask moved, the smile becoming wider and wider. Ailsa reached behind her head to untie it, but she couldn't feel the ribbon. Around the new face, her hair turned blonde, tumbling around her shoulders. She scrabbled desperately at the corners of the mask, trying to pry it off, but it was stuck, melded to her skin.

Her new face raised an eyebrow and laughed. "You're just like me now," it said, and the voice was the same as the one that had instructed her at first. The same one she had heard in her head when she had been using her power. The voice that had commanded her on the Avalognian ships to "destroy" them all.

Ailsa tried to scream, but the mask wouldn't let her. Her arm lifted in front of her at the mirror, out of her control, and she was only able to watch in fear as electricity pulsed down her skin, to her hand and out towards the glass. With a boom, it shattered, shredding the candles and plunging her into darkness.

Chapter 12

Ailsa's chest heaved as she was pulled out of her dream. She moved her eyes wildly around her surroundings, trying to calm the shaking of her body. She was still in the jail cell, but it was dark through the window. How long had she been asleep?

There seemed to be a crowd overhead; the sound of people chattering was indistinct but loud enough to have woken her. Ailsa sat in the dark, trying to make out what they were saying. Every few minutes someone would shriek, but she couldn't tell if it was from fear or part of a game.

Abruptly, the talking ended and Ailsa braced herself. Sure enough, a few seconds later, there was the sound of keys rattling and then her cell door was thrown open.

Two men Ailsa recognised from her capture came striding in, daggers out in front of them, and hauled her to her feet. She kept her mouth shut as they tied her hands behind her back with rope and pushed her through the door.

They emerged into a corridor lined with many other portals. *Pay attention and be ready to run*, she told herself. Now that there wasn't a bag over her head, she could look for ways out.

"Keep moving," the man behind her grunted, nodding towards a set of narrow stairs that climbed up towards another level.

To Ailsa's surprise, another two women were pulled from nearby cells and pushed on in the same direction. One was petite and covered her face with green hands, her shoulders shaking with sobs. The other had quick darting eyes and a strange gait, and it wasn't until Ailsa looked at the bottom of her dress that she knew why. The creature walked on hooven feet, like those of a deer.

They reached the top of the stairs into what appeared to be someone's house. Ailsa had just enough time to notice a neatly made bed beside a crackling fire before she was thrown through the front door into the street.

Here was the crowd she had heard before. Groups of people stood facing the building they emerged from, watching the captives' every move like one would watch a spider. Ailsa met the gaze of a little girl who was peering out between her mother's skirts, mouth open in terror.

I should be the one that's afraid, Ailsa thought. She tried to imagine what they looked like to the children watching from the safety of their parents' arms. A parade of freaks.

They were pushed on down the street, until they came to what must have been the village's square. In it, a large bonfire raged, bathing everything in flickering orange light.

"Stop here," said one of the men behind her. The other two women were brought beside her, so they were in a line, ready to hear their fate.

An older woman stepped forward to address the crowd, her voice strong despite her frail body. "A ghillie-dhu, an urisk, and a changeling. They're far too dangerous to keep around."

"What shall we do with the fae monsters?" asked the man who had told Ailsa to stop.

"Burn them!" shouted someone from the crowd.

Ailsa grimaced. Of all the ways to die, she'd rather it wasn't that. Even drowning would be better. She cast her magic out, feeling for a storm up above.

A woman with a baby in her arms *tsked*. "The ghillie-dhu and the urisk are hardly dangerous."

"All fae are dangerous," shot back the man beside her.

"I say, blindfold them, stick them in a wagon and drive them out into the forest as far as we can go. Get them so confused that they can't find their way back."

"You do realise they aren't animals? It's not like they don't know where they are."

"Well, what do you suggest?"

"A quick knife to the chest."

The deer girl, an urisk they had called her, was shaking, her body brushing against Ailsa's arm with every vibration. A raindrop landed on Ailsa's scalp, trickling down her neck , and she bit her lip in concentration.

"That's an easy way to anger the gods."

"The gods have long since abandoned us, I don't care what they think."

"I'll remind you of those words when we're not only trapped but we've also run out of food."

The woman who had first spoken stepped forward and regarded the three of them with a puckered scowl. The crowd instantly stopped their bickering and waited. "Do you promise to never return if we set you free?" she asked.

The ghillie-dhu and the urisk nodded; hope almost making them jump. Ailsa didn't allow herself to join them. There had to be a catch.

"If we see you again, we'll shoot you on sight," the woman cautioned with a growl. That stopped the two fae's giddiness.

"Let these two go," the woman said, nodding her head to Ailsa's companions.

"What about the changeling?" came a shout from the crowd.

Ailsa held her breath, refusing to open her mouth in case she was tempted to plead. If she was going to die, it would be with some dignity. From far away she heard the distinct rumble of thunder.

Come on. Faster.

The woman lifted her chin. "We're going to kill two birds with one stone. We need a sacrifice for this month."

Oh, she did not like the sound of that. Sheets of lightning flashed, illuminating the faces around her. They were no longer terrified. Instead they looked almost eager.

"What—" she began to ask, but she was plunged into darkness as the bag was shoved over her head again.

"Don't worry," said the voice of the woman. "This won't be as bad as being burned."

Suddenly, Ailsa felt something hard hit her back and she pitched forward, sprawling in the dirt.

"We have to bleed her first," said a woman. "It draws the monster."

Ailsa screamed as her shoulder was held and something sharp sliced into her. The wound was shallow, but she could still feel blood blooming along it.

Then she heard it, the voice from before.

Kill them all, it whispered. *You can do it.*

No, she told it. There were children in the crowd.

"Knock her out, it'll be easier to transport her," someone said.

Too late, said the voice.

Ailsa could only groan before something came down upon her head and she lost her grip on her surroundings.

Chapter 13

Angus followed as closely as he could behind Iona, almost stepping on her heels until she had hissed at him. He held his sword out in front, ready. He knew it wasn't much—his companions were much more powerful after all—but it was better than nothing.

Bringing up the rear, Gris's crunching footsteps echoed through the forest. There was no way to sneak around with the sound, but Angus supposed Gris didn't care. They were on the hunt for something that wouldn't be frightened off easily.

"What if we can't find it?" Angus asked Iona's back.

The selkie gave him a brief, withering look over her shoulder. "We'll find *her*."

Feeling the blood warm his cheeks, Angus bit his lip. It wasn't long, however, until his anxiety pulled more questions from him. "But what if we can't? Should we really be wasting our time looking for a faerie tale when Ailsa is missing? What if she's injured? Or dead?"

"This is the best way to find her," Gris grumbled. "The Bean-Nighe will know what happened to her. Especially if it's bad."

"I know you're worried," Iona said. "We all are. But Ailsa's tough."

Angus sighed. "She shouldn't always have to be. I'm sick of seeing her in danger."

Iona slowed, reaching behind her to find Angus's arm and give it a squeeze. "I hate it too," she agreed.

Gris sniffed. "It's just the card she was dealt. Same as the rest of us. With the extraordinary, comes sacrifice."

"Well, when we rescue her and Harris, I'm locking everyone up in Dunrigh castle for at least a month and we're just going to eat sweets and nap." Angus chuckled, though it was strained. "Even you Gris. We'll grow you a forest in the greenhouse."

The Fear-Laith just growled.

Iona had increased her pace again, her dress whispering along the ground as she glided through the trees. "There's a river up ahead. That's where we'll find her," Iona called.

Angus followed, but couldn't help feeling something was wrong. The closer they got to the river, the more he wanted to turn back. It took everything in him to keep his feet moving behind Iona. When he voiced his discomfort, she just nodded.

"It's because you're human. The Bean-Nighe wants to keep you away."

The sound of water crashing grew louder as Angus's legs strained from the effort of moving. He watched as

Iona raced on ahead, getting further and further away. Even Gris managed to overtake him. Angus stuck his tongue out at the Fear-Laith's back as he passed. It was petty, but it made him feel better.

Finally, Iona stopped, waving her hands to her two companions to hurry. When Angus reached her, she gestured down a hill towards the thundering river. At first, Angus couldn't see what she was pointing at. Then, as a feeling of dread settled in his stomach, he saw her.

An old woman, dressed in a tartan arisaid, sat beside the water's edge. Her head was bowed as she stared at the river, but her body shuddered as she wept quietly.

Angus lowered his sword, and went to step around Iona, towards the woman. Something terrible had obviously happened, and he wasn't about to stand around staring like his companions seemed to be doing. Before he could pass Iona, she threw out an arm to stop him.

"Wait," she said.

At the sound of the selkie's voice, the woman lifted her head to reveal her face. Though the hair around it was silver with age, her face was unlined. The tears she was crying glowed in the twilight, lighting up her eyes, which were sharp and intent as she watched them.

Iona walked down the hill gracefully. When she reached the woman she sunk into a deep curtsy. At Iona's cough, Angus and Gris followed suit.

"My lady," Iona greeted the Bean-Nighe.

The old woman nodded. "You seek me out?" Her voice crackled with age and despair, though, as Angus watched, her tears flowed from her smooth cheeks back into her eyes.

"Yes," Gris said. "We are in need of your knowledge."

"And what will you give me in return?" said the Bean-Nighe, her gaze turning baleful.

At once, Iona's hand went to her ankle, producing a wicked knife.

Angus almost choked on his own breath, but instead of throwing it at the hag, the selkie grabbed a piece of her own hair and used the blade to cut off a strand. The hair glinted copper in the moonlight as it fell to the ground.

The old woman made no move to collect it. Instead she sniffed loudly, but smiled. "What is your question?"

"A friend of ours has gone missing," said Iona. "How do we find her again?"

The Bean-Nighe blinked. "It is best if you do not. I suggest you go home."

"What do you know?" Gris growled. When the Bean-Nighe just stared at him, he folded his arms and huffed a "*please.*"

Satisfied, the old woman turned back to Iona. "Are you sure you want to know? You can't unknow it again."

"Yes," said the selkie.

"Very well." The Bean-Nighe picked up a piece of fabric

from the river in front of her. Though it was soaking wet, Angus could tell it was heavily embroidered. The Bean-Nighe ran her hands over it, inspecting it and Angus thought she didn't mean to answer them after all. Then she raised her head, her face paling. "I see two paths ahead of you three. In one, you return to your homes and forget about the Faerie Queen you are seeking. In this path, I do not see your deaths for a long time."

"My brother and our friend are waiting for us," answered Iona. "We can't just turn around."

"Then you'll choose the other path. There are a lot more deaths there," The Bean-Nighe said.

The hag pulled out another bundle of cloth from the water. She separated it with deft fingers, into three black shrouds. "Family, friend, lover. But which loved one belongs to who? One will die saving theirs. One will watch theirs die. One will betray the whole world to save them, yet it will be in vain."

They looked at each other, trying to guess the meaning of the Bean-Nighe's prophecy.

"Can we do anything to stop this fate?" asked Iona, finally.

"Turn around," the Bean-Nighe said simply. "Choose the other path."

Gris shook his head. "Well, if there's nothing to be done, we had best continue."

"How do we find Ailsa?" asked Angus.

Up until that moment, Angus hadn't realised the Bean-Nighe hadn't looked at him. Then she turned the full force of her gaze on him, and for a moment, he could see infinity in her eyes.

"A few miles from here is a village, hidden deep in the woods. Humans can go there, but they cannot leave again. Not until the curse is broken. If you break the curse, you'll find your friend."

"But what if we can't break the curse?" said Angus. "I'll be stuck there and then I won't be able to help save Harris."

The Bean-Nighe set down her washing. "She'll break the curse," she said, nodding to a stunned Iona. "Something waits for her there, in a lake near the village. She will need it to save her brother."

"A monster?" asked Angus.

The Bean-Nighe threw back her head in a watery laugh. "Silly boy," she answered. "It is your salvation."

Chapter 14

The first thing Ailsa felt when she drifted out of unconsciousness was the dull ache of a rattled skull. Every time she had woken on the journey, her captors had knocked her out again. The bag on her head had been removed. Keeping her eyes closed she took inventory. She could smell pine and rain. The old fear of dark forests and monsters that lurked, came unbidden to her mind, but she shoved it down. The Fear-Laith, Gris, was her friend. The forest was no longer something to be afraid of.

But what about the other monsters? Asked a small, rasping voice inside her.

From above her head came a steady trickle of water, probably water the leaves had collected. It landed with a drip, drip, drip on her shoulder. With each droplet of rainwater she opened her mind to a new sensation.

Pain was the dominant feeling. Pain from her arms which were twisted behind her. Pain from her wrists that were rubbed raw from the rope that bound her to... a tree? Pain from the cut on her shoulder that those damn villagers had given her.

A sacrifice they had called her. Not the first time she had been given that title. Why did everyone seem to think they would gain things by killing her? *Next time someone tries to sacrifice me*, she thought, *I'm taking them with me.*

She groaned at the banging in her head and leaned back against the trunk. So where was the thing she had been sacrificed to? The villagers had not struck her as the most sensible of people, maybe this was all just superstition?

Or maybe you'd better start getting yourself out of this before you find out.

Finally, she opened her eyes, taking in the leafy green clearing she was in. The trees around the outside made a perfect circle, but it was not them that attracted her attention. In the centre, about three feet from where she was tied, was a collection of small stones standing upright, covered in carved symbols. A memory tugged at her mind, forcing it back to an evening when she had seen something similar.

They had been on the way to find the Stone of Destiny—was it only a few weeks ago? She had been annoyed at Angus and Harris; she hadn't wanted to go into the forest. Then she had heard the steady footsteps of the Fear-Laith, and they had run.

Ailsa mentally shook herself and studied the boulders, thinking hard about what she remembered. Before the soft crunch of the Fear-Laith, there had been other signs of life in the forest. The stones with their intricate carvings had obviously been left by someone. Then there had been... a handprint...

Her head whipped up to scan the surrounding trees, the task becoming harder in the fading light. They had found a handprint near the boulders, burnt into the tree trunk, as if someone had etched out the mark with a torch. But how could someone do that? She breathed a sigh of relief when she found none of the similar marks. Whatever had done that was not something she wanted to meet.

The sound of distant thunder cracked in the air and she cursed. It was why she was in this mess; she hadn't been able to control herself. How she wished she could grow some flowers instead, like Gris had been trying to teach her. How exactly could a storm help her?

The silence fell like a blanket on the clearing, dulling everything except the beating of her own heart. She stared out into the dawn light and a breath of wind licked over her skin, raising gooseflesh.

Something was there, watching her.

Her lips formed a snarl and she fought against the bonds holding her. If only she had her axe.

"You're only going to hurt yourself," said a deep male voice somewhere behind her.

She went still, even her heart stopped for an instant.

"That's better," the voice praised. "Why are you tied up in my woods?"

My woods.

Ailsa's throat constricted. Was this the creature they'd left her for? She counted her breaths a moment, waiting for it to say something else but it soon became clear it expected an answer.

"Apparently, there's a monster I'm being sacrificed to," she croaked, hoping she hadn't given it any ideas.

The voice muttered something in a foreign tongue, though she somehow understood it was a curse.

Ailsa squared her shoulders and growled, "But I'm afraid I'm actually a monster myself." Even now she was calling on that ancient power within her. The power that had killed.

A pause. "You are?"

She tilted her chin. "So wherever this monster is, it had better think twice before taking me."

"What type of monster are you?"

She thought of the Avalognian raiders whose ship she had blown apart. "The kind people underestimate."

"I'm beginning to realise that." He gave a low chuckle. "Just as well the monster you're being sacrificed to isn't here."

Ailsa smothered a scoff. This was some attempt at trickery. "And who are you?" she asked sweetly.

"Just someone who was passing by who thought you

might need some help."

"Oh?" She tried to strain her head, to catch a glimpse but gave up quickly when her shoulder- wound twinged. "Well, what are you waiting for?"

The creature laughed—the sound almost human. "You just told me you're a monster. I'm worried that if I help you, you'll attack me."

She licked her lips. "Maybe we should make a pact then, not to hurt each other?"

He paused. "We could promise to try?"

"I suppose I don't have much choice…" Ailsa ground out.

Then she felt warm hands near her arms. Not warm—hot. Hotter than any human had a right to be. *This is no human, stupid girl,* she told herself. But neither was she. Her muscles coiled as he began to release the rope keeping her in place, ready to fight as soon as she was free.

First one rope fell to the ground, heavy. Then another. Ailsa's hands itched as she felt the strength of the storm overhead building in her body.

Was he using a knife? She couldn't hear sawing; it must have been incredibly sharp.

The last rope around her midriff went taut and then it fell. She whipped her body away from the tree and the creature, ready to face it.

The evening had darkened and, at first, she could

only see an outline. The outline of a man. Maybe he was human after all? But then her eyes travelled down the silhouette, noticing a faint gleam coming from his hands. It was almost like his skin had been cut by fissures of light. Lines of red crossed his flesh, glowing from within, as if underneath he was made of molten lava. A quick assessment of the smouldering ropes at her feet confirmed her suspicions, he had incinerated them. That was what the heat had been.

"What are you?" asked Ailsa.

The shadow stayed where he was. "Just a passer-by."

Noting that he hadn't attacked her yet, she nodded. "Thank you."

He held one of his hands out, glowing less than before, and said, "Don't thank me yet. I'm afraid you are *my* sacrifice, after all."

A bolt of fear shot through her. The panic called to the sky, bringing it down around her. She felt it, using it to give her strength, even though it made her dizzy. "And I'm afraid I'm still a monster," she growled.

Lightning crashed into the tree he was standing beside, setting it on fire and illuminating his form. He stumbled away from the tree, as the flames licked across the wood.

Ailsa sucked in a breath as she beheld what was in front of her. Indeed, he had all the shape of a man: arms, chest, and legs were all there. His skin was darker than most Eilanmòrians and there was plenty on show. His torso was completely naked, though he wore a cape around his shoulders. The skin on his arms was even darker, like it was covered in soot, reminding her again that he had reduced her bonds to ashes. Her gaze travelled up his body to take in his head and there the illusions of humanity ended. Sprouting from his black hair were two delicate, gold antlers, just like the deer's they had eaten in the bothy. His heavy eyebrows and strong nose would have made him handsome—if not for his eyes. There were no whites or irises; his eyes were pitch black.

Ailsa gave in to her body's terror and screamed as the demon stalked towards her.

Chapter 15

The demon cringed. "Please be quiet. I'm not going to hurt you, but if other things hear you screaming, they might come and do just that."

She strangled the scream, looking frantically around the trees for a way out.

"You're bleeding…" he said, and she snapped her eyes back to his. She couldn't really tell where he was looking, those black eyes betrayed nothing of his vision, but she could feel them on her.

With every step forward he took, she took one back, always keeping him in her sights.

"How did you do that?" he asked. He kept his hands by his side, turned face up to show he held no weapon. But Ailsa knew creatures like this didn't need weapons.

"I told you I was a monster," she answered, her heart hammering as she tried to think of the best way to escape. "It's why they captured me and left me here. They hoped one of us would kill the other." If she could just keep him talking…

"I'm afraid you wouldn't stand a chance," he sighed. "Demons are very powerful."

"How do you know I am not?"

"Well, for one, I know you couldn't really control your power there. You are new to it."

"And how long have you been using yours?"

A look of sadness played across his face and he stopped his steps. "Since the last great war."

So he must be as old as me, thought Ailsa, though she had somehow thought he was much older than that. There was an... *ancient-ness* to him.

"Well what now?" he asked. "Are you going to fight me?"

"That depends on what you do. If you plan to eat me, then I'm afraid I'll have to fight you."

"Ah..." he breathed sadly, "because I'm a demon you think I'll eat you?"

Had she offended him? Something in his expression had her wishing she could take back her question. "I suppose it's not a very polite thing to ask, but you can't be too careful."

"I'm not going to eat you. I just want to have a look at your wounds. Did you know your nose is bleeding?"

Ailsa's hand flew to her top lip where there was a crust of dried blood. "My nose *was* bleeding. It's stopped."

"Why did the villagers attack you?"

"Most people in Eilanmòr don't really like me. Aside from the obvious..." she gestured to her face, but his expression remained blank. "My mark," she explained, "it means I'm a changeling."

"It just looks like a birthmark to me," he said, coming closer still.

She willed her feet to stop moving. Now that the shock had worn off, she didn't feel like she was in immediate danger from the demon.

But would be ready to run just in case.

"*Are* you a changeling?" he asked, peering at her with those ink-dark eyes.

She swallowed. "Yes."

He nodded to himself, seeming to have confirmed something. "You said '*aside from the obvious*'. What is '*aside from the obvious*'? Did they have another reason to attack you?"

"They saw me using my... powers."

"And they decided to sacrifice you…"

"They debated really long and hard whether to just kill me outright." She looked him up and down. "I'm still deciding whether being burned at the stake would have been less scary…"

"Than being sacrificed to me? Out of the fire and into the flame," he murmured. He seemed upset by this. He turned away from her abruptly. "You're going to have to come with me."

"Why?"

"Well, one, I need to see to your wounds," he regarded her over his shoulder. "And two, you have been sacrificed to me. I'm afraid that's some deep magic." He started walking towards the thick tree cover. "You're stuck with me."

Indeed, the further away he moved, the more she felt compelled to follow. She dug her heels into the earth, fighting the impulse, but then it wasn't an impulse anymore. It felt like a wall of... *something*... was pushing her from behind.

At first, she pushed back against it, so she was leaning all her weight on the air but then her feet were sliding forward under her, leaving two lines in the mud and leaf litter.

"What the hell is this?" she shouted at his back. "Make it stop!"

"I can't. I told you, you're stuck with me."

Ailsa turned so she could push the force with her hands, but it was relentless. Her muscles groaned as she heaved a shoulder into it, but still it pushed her back, towards the demon.

"Why are you doing this?" she barked, still trying to resist the constant advance of the hard air.

"I'm not doing it," he said.

Then, the wall gave way from under her hands. Or rather, it moved back a few inches. Ailsa's body had been pushing hard against it and so she toppled over, the side of her face bouncing off the barrier, until she landed hard on the ground. Somewhere along her shoulder one of the gashes ripped open, pulling a shriek from her mouth.

"Oh gods, I'm sorry," the demon said, jogging over to her. "I started walking back to you and I didn't realise the bond would move that fast."

From where she lay on the ground, she watched the approach of his boot-clad feet. Then he crouched down beside her, and those monstrous eyes came into view.

"Please," she croaked. "Just leave me alone." All of the pains from her beating were made worse by the fall, and she could feel where her tunic was soaking up the blood from her open wound.

"You need medical care," he told her. "Can you stand?"

She tried to push herself up, but was hit by an instant wave of dizziness. The demon's face swam in front of her. His face tightened in... assessment? It was so hard to tell when they were all black.

"I just want to help," he explained, as if to a frightened animal. Which Ailsa supposed she was. Then strong arms were turning her over and she was being lifted. She watched the forest canopy get measurably closer as it spun around. She knew she should be fighting, kicking, and screaming, but it was all she could do to keep the nausea at bay. So far pure adrenaline had kept her on her feet and moving, but the pain was catching up to her. She was in no state to fight back. Better to wait until the demon lowered his guard, then she could escape.

"Hold on tight," he muttered.

Ailsa closed her eyes as she felt the swinging of his footsteps. She tried to imagine a new face for the stranger, a human face, but really that was no better.

Human or demon, it didn't matter. They could be just as deadly.

Chapter 16

The walk through the forest passed in a blur of pain and nausea. Would the demon be more likely to kill her if she threw up on him? Harris would laugh at that, she was sure. Thinking of Harris brought both comfort and misery. If she was killed, who would save him? She was sure Iona and Angus would be able to do it, if they didn't waste time trying to find her. How long would Nicnevan keep him alive? As long as it would take for someone to give her information on her daughter. But what was she doing to him while he was her prisoner?

Night had fallen, made even darker by the storm up ahead which was following along like a lost pet after its master. It ate up the stars in its path, ravenous, ready and waiting. Ailsa blinked blearily up at it and wished she had the strength to use it.

The demon stepped up and over a rock or log, the movement jarring her in his arms. She gritted her teeth against the pain.

He pursed his lips. "Sorry," he said gruffly.

"Why are you doing this? Why couldn't I get away from you?"

He exhaled. "You were sacrificed to me. It means you're bonded to me. It's old magic. But believe me, I'd rather you weren't."

"What does that mean? I'm your slave?"

"It means you have to serve me until it is deemed you have fulfilled your contract."

Ailsa's stomach turned. "Have you ever had anyone else sacrificed to you?"

"I haven't, no, but I know of others."

"There are other demons?"

His face darkened. "There are many."

"I can't just stay here and hex people with you. I need to get to Ephraim—"

"Nicnevan's court?" His eyebrows climbed into his hair. "Have you got a death wish, girl?"

"My name is Ailsa," she muttered.

"Maalik," he grunted. "We're here."

Here seemed to be right in the darkest part of the forest. Ailsa craned her head to the side, cringing again when her shoulder twinged. They were standing in front of a small cottage. *Not where I expected a demon to live*, she thought. The roof was covered in moss, like the forest was trying to reclaim it. Light flickered in the one window. Ailsa debated telling the demon he shouldn't leave candles burning when he wasn't in. *Ridiculous.*

He paused. "I... I've got supplies inside. To tend to your wounds I mean," he said hesitantly, his lips twisted in a frown. "Would you believe me if I told you not to be afraid?"

"From what you've told me, I don't have a choice anyway," she grumbled.

Did she believe him? He hadn't harmed her yet. Aside from shifting that wall of air so she smacked against the ground. But since then he had been careful with her. *Unless he's just keeping you intact so he can eat you inside.* Well, she'd thought the same about Gris and he was nothing more than a grumpy giant with a lot of patience.

"Lead on," she gestured with the hand that wasn't pressed against his chest.

He walked them down the worn path to the door which, to Ailsa's surprise, opened before they reached it.

He can move things with his mind too, she noted, filing the knowledge away for later.

The inside of the cottage smelled like campfire and smoke. Indeed, the ceiling above the lit fireplace was covered in ash. How long had the fire been going? Judging by how long she had been with him, at least half an hour. Why hadn't it died down yet?

The room was occupied by a wooden table, a small kitchen, and a couch. In the corner was a single bed, its sheets pristine, folded neatly. On this, the demon carefully laid Ailsa so she was nestled against the pillow.

"I'm just going to grab some supplies," he told her, turning to the kitchen. Opening a cabinet above the sink revealed shelves packed with bottles and bags. "I think calendula for your wounds. I'll add some garlic as an antibiotic."

She scrutinised his back suspiciously. "An anti-what?"

"It will stop your cuts from getting infected."

"Oh." Was he helping her? She had thought he might just let her lie down for a while, but as he collected bottles from the cabinet and dumped the contents into a small bowl, she had to wonder what he was making. He grabbed a pestle and began grinding the contents, one corner of his mouth quirking into the ghost of a smile.

"Oh," he exclaimed, seeming to remember something. "I have a little crystallised willow left which should help the pain. Muck, would you boil some water for me?"

Who the hell is Muck? Wondered Ailsa as she struggled to sit up. *Hopefully not a new nickname for me...*

Her hand brushed something fuzzy at the side of the pillow and she whipped her head around, her heart in her throat. There, staring up at her, were two wide, purple eyes. She forgot to breathe as they loomed closer, the creature they belonged to flew off the bed to regard her at head height. It was about the size of a potato, with a head larger than its body. Its tiny moth wings should have been too small; they seemed to lift its body into the air by pure determination. The creature's whole body was covered in brown fluff, like a baby duck's, and sprouting from its head were miniscule antlers like those of a deer.

Below its violet eyes was a tiny pink cat-nose and two fangs poking from its eager smile.

"What the hell is it?" asked Ailsa.

"That's Muck," explained the demon, not looking up from his work. "She won't hurt you." To the fuzzball he whistled. "Come on, boil me some water."

It made a chirping noise and whizzed across the room to the fireplace. Ailsa watched in astonishment as it lifted a pot of water twice its size and hung it on a hook above the flames.

Not for the first time in recent weeks, Ailsa felt like a rug had been pulled out from under her. She really should be getting used to surprises like this by now.

"And what is Muck?"

Maalik turned to her with a slight smile playing on his lips. "Didn't your mother ever tell you it's impolite to ask what things are?"

Wrong thing to say. Ailsa snapped her mouth shut and sank further into the pillows. Her mother had certainly not been very forthcoming about what *she* was. A wave of guilt accompanied that thought. Maybe she hadn't known what she had let into her house. What had been left to replace the baby she had loved. Her real child.

The demon frowned at her silence. "Muck is a brownie. She helps me around the house. She found me a few years ago and decided she liked it here, since there's always a steady supply of blood."

Blood? Ailsa turned to gape at the demon but her fear faltered when she found his expression. It was hard to decide what it was... was he teasing her?

The brownie made another chirp, signalling the water was ready, and lifted the steaming pot off the fire. She flew around the demon's head like an annoying house fly.

"You'll have to ask her nicely," he said to her and she zipped off back to where Ailsa lay.

"Brownies take their pay in blood, but she won't hurt you."

Ailsa studied the creature with suspicion as she came closer, landing beside her on the bed. With tiny paws she padded over the mattress and came to stop beside Ailsa's shoulder. Ailsa's tried to pull away, noting the little fangs poking from the brownie's mouth, but she was pinned against the wall. The ball of fluff approached, her gaze never leaving Ailsa's, and stuck out a delicate pink tongue. Before Ailsa could scream again, the brownie found the still bleeding wound on her shoulder and licked.

Ailsa could only make a whimpering noise as she watched with disgust as the brownie withdrew her tongue from her wound. The creature gave a satisfied grin before flying off to sit on a shelf in the corner between two books.

"What just happened?" Ailsa's voice came out too high as her heart hammered in her chest.

The demon approached carrying the bowl and a mug. "Brownies like to taste blood, think of it like collecting stamps—"

"She *collected* me?!"

"It means she likes you."

"Will she do it again?"

"Only if your blood changes." He sat on the bed beside her and placed the mug on the floor. "I've made a poultice for your wounds. Either you assist me, or I force feed you the tea first and when you're unconscious I do it anyway."

She looked at him sullenly as he waited for her answer. The truth of the matter was, if she'd been able to stand, she'd have already been out the door, but she was much too weak. He seemed like he wanted to help. If she was going to escape, she would need to be stronger—she would just have to risk it.

"Fine," she answered. "What should I do?"

"Start by telling me where it hurts."

"My shoulder," she began, trying to distinguish the sources of the pain. Now, they all blended into one. "I was... I was hit in the head."

His face was solemn as he lifted a hand, feeling around the top of her skull. When he reached a particularly tender part, she winced, and he withdrew.

"The willow will help with the bruising. I'm going to treat your cuts first." He stirred the contents of the bowl, before lifting out a brush and painting it on her shoulder first. She had expected it to burn, but aside from a dull ache it went on easily.

"It smells like food."

"That'll be the garlic. You'll stink for a few days. A small price to pay for not dying of sepsis."

She rolled her eyes. "You know I don't have any idea what you're talking about? What are you, some kind of healer?"

"Trying to be," he murmured, moving on to the little cuts around her chin. "So since you've been very impolite and asked Muck what she is, why don't you tell me what you are." He quirked an eyebrow. "Aside from being a 'monster.'"

Her mouth tightened into a grim line. "I'm half-faerie."

"Well that's interesting," he muttered as he continued to smear on the poultice.

Her eyes snapped open. *Interesting?* "I've killed people with my magic." Her face became hot.

"What, the rainstorm? I'm sure you could grow a lot of plants with rain powers."

Her lip curled. "Well, *yes*, but that's not the poi—"

"I mean when you said you were a monster, I thought you'd at least have had some sort of super strength or something."

Her lip curled. How dare he? "I'll have you know, I

am Nicnevan's daughter."

That gave him pause. "Are you?" he said, appraising her. "I would have thought the infamous Faerie Queen's daughter would have been a little braver. I mean, you've been screaming and worrying about poor Muck licking you. I bet you're even too scared to drink this tea." He held the mug out in front of him, meeting her gaze with dead eyes.

She took the cup. "I know what you're doing."

He smiled pleasantly. "And what would that be?"

"Trying to goad me into drinking this without a fuss."

He had the grace to look abashed. "Did it work?"

Who was this man? He looked like a demon but behaved like… he wanted to care for her. She searched his face for any sign of malintent and found none. She took a sip; the liquid had turned lukewarm, and in a fit of courage she downed the whole lot in three gulps.

"Happy?"

"Very." He took the cup from her. "Maybe you are brave after all. I'll see you in the morning."

"What do you mean?" she started to ask, but then she felt it. Spreading from her toes, her body was shutting down. She blinked up at him blearily. "You poisoned me. I thought it was just for pain?"

He sighed. "I mixed in some valerian to help you sleep. You're welcome."

Her head was swimming and it was an effort to stay

alert. "Bastard," she slurred, and then she succumbed to unconsciousness.

The last thing she saw was the demon's teeth bared in a triumphant smile.

Chapter 17

Ailsa fought a wave of dizziness as she woke from her sleep. She remembered exactly where she was, what had happened last night, but the remembering was little comfort. *At least I'm still alive*, she supposed. A small miracle when she had been unconscious in the home of a demon.

Something landed on her chest and she cracked open an eye. Muck was sitting on top of her blankets, making soft chirping sounds as she waited for Ailsa's attention. As soon as the brownie saw that she was awake, she gave a trill in her throat.

"Have you come to suck my blood again?" Ailsa asked her with a groan.

The brownie just wriggled, as if it were a dog wagging its tail. Ailsa had to grudgingly admit that she was somewhat cute.

"Ah, you're awake," a voice stated from the other side of the cabin. The demon was no less terrifying in the early morning light, his dark eyes unblinking as he watched her from his space beside his work bench. He rustled around with some tools, and Ailsa fought the panic that crept up her throat. He had played nursemaid fine enough last night, but for what purpose? Would he heal her only so he could carve her up when she was whole again?

"How are you feeling?" the demon asked.

"Like I was drugged," Ailsa ground out in return.

The demon—Maalik—looked like he was about to smile, but then his lips trembled and curved back into a scowl. "I have to go out today. You'll have to decide whether you'll come with me or you'll stay here."

Ailsa pulled the blankets up higher. "I'll stay here."

He regarded her briefly. "Be sure you do; I think you learned enough last night to know what will happen if you don't. You are bound to me or my home."

"Why?" she asked again, feeling the panic that had her heart rate speeding. If she couldn't get out, how would she find Angus, Iona, and Gris again? How would she rescue Harris? No, she'd find a way, and perhaps it would be easier if he wasn't around...

"I'm sorry," was all he said.

She lay back down on the bed, listening to him shuffling around the kitchen. Finally, he cleared his throat and she looked up again. He had shouldered a satchel and had slung a cloak around his still naked torso. The brownie was bumbling around his head, pausing on his shoulder every few seconds like a fat bird.

"I'll be gone all day," he told her.

"Fine," she answered.

"There is food in the cupboard, take whatever you like."

She would indeed, and anything else she could carry before she escaped.

"Please stay put and try to rest," he said, glowering like he could already tell her plans.

"Right," she said.

He took one last look at her, as if weighing if it was worth his going, before shaking his head and stepping out the door. Ailsa bit her lip and listened to the sound of the portal closing and Maalik's steps as he stalked into the woods. He did not lock the door.

Ailsa counted her heartbeats as she lay within the warm bed. It was so tempting to do what the demon had said, to sink down further into the comfortable pillows and flirt with sleep for a few hours more.

We're counting on you, Angus had said. But why? He was a prince, accompanied by a powerful selkie and a man who was not only a Fear-Laith, but a trained soldier. Surely, they could save Harris by themselves? She imagined the path ahead of her, what she would find if she did make it to Ephraim, to the Unseelie Court. She would be a princess, but more importantly, the heir to a throne. Ailsa knew that saving Harris would be only the start of what her friends had hoped from her. It had gone unspoken this past week, since they had set off with Gris, but she knew they hoped for far grander, save-the-free-world things from her.

She imagined the other path then, the path that would take her back to home, back to her beach. Alone again, but with far less responsibility. Whichever path she decided to take, it certainly did not involve spending years as a slave to a demon in the woods. *So start from there*, she told herself.

She rose slowly from the bed, her head still swimming from the drugs the demon had given to her. She still had her old clothes on, for which she was thankful. She didn't like the thought of the demon stripping her in her sleep. A quick search and she found her boots. She put them on and stood, wishing that she could feel the weight of her hatchet at her side once again. Perhaps the demon would have a weapon she could steal, she mused as she searched around the kitchen for food. She grabbed a couple of apples, some bread, and hard cheese and tied them in a towel she found hanging near the sink.

It was then that Ailsa noticed the door in the corner. It was a very fancy cabin indeed if this was the bathroom, she'd had to make do with an outhouse growing up. At the thought, the fullness of her bladder became suddenly apparent. Ailsa strode to the door, hoping that the toilet was as clean as the rest of the cabin.

The door opened with a creak. *The demon needs to oil his hinges*, she thought absently, opening it further so that she could see inside. But what she found was not a bathroom. Instead, Ailsa came face to face with a set of razor-sharp teeth.

With a gasp, she swung her gaze up from the huge mouth to find a pair of eyes watching her. Ailsa watched as the creature sniffed through a large black nose before the face rose even higher, as the monster got to its feet.

Ailsa scrambled back, tripping in her haste to get away, until she fell, sprawling on the floor in front of the beast. Its paws, the size of dinner plates, shifted over the wooden floor, as if it was thinking about running at her. Ailsa was eyeing the cabin's door, wondering if she would be able to make it out before the creature, when it threw its head back and howled, the sound raising the hairs on the back of her neck.

Ailsa threw herself, half running, half crawling, away from the beast and at the door, her only thought of escape. Panic clutched at her chest as she thought the demon might have locked it, but it mercifully swung open when she pulled it. Behind her the creature howled again, as she scrambled out of the portal. Then she was up and running, away from the animal, away from the demon's lair, back to her friends. Thankfully, the thing didn't seem to be following her.

She made it ten paces before she smacked into something solid.

She fell, startled by the impact. But what had she run

into? It looked like there was nothing there. Reaching out a hand, she felt through the air, until again she came across something stopping her. Ailsa desperately ran her fingers along it, rising to follow the invisible wall. *Come on, come on*, she thought, looking for an opening. She circled the cabin, but it seemed the barrier was surrounding her. Abandoning her search, Ailsa ran instead for the tiny shed around the back—the real outhouse—finding it gloriously empty except from a toilet and sink. She launched herself inside and locked the door behind her, just in case the creature decided to follow her after all.

Marvelling at how she had managed not to pee herself when she saw the creature, she hastily did her business and then slumped on top of the toilet lid. Now that the adrenaline had worn off, she felt her whole body vibrate with every hard heartbeat.

She peeked through the slats in the wood back at the cabin. The creature seemed to have remained inside. She replayed again the moment she had opened the door. Huge teeth, a black nose, yellow eyes. Her brain finally caught up enough to supply a name for it. *Wolf.* But it was bigger than a wolf ought to be—at least three times the size—when it had stood up.

Ailsa had run into wolves before. They were often used to caution children against running off by themselves, but the truth was they were only dangerous if you were a sheep. They tended to stay away from humans unless they were starving. So why did the demon have a wolf in his cabin? Had it been there all through the night, when she had been sleeping only feet away?

She had to escape - but something was stopping her.

"You are bound to me or my home", the demon had said.

Ailsa groaned. She hadn't thought he'd meant it literally. But it seemed that something like the bond she'd felt last night was keeping her here. She'd have to get the demon to drop the barrier next time he was out. Or maybe she'd have better luck if she went with him.

The sun was sinking through the trees when she heard footsteps nearby. She watched through the cracks in the wood as the demon returned to his cabin, and went to walk inside. Something inside her made her want to shout out a warning—*there's a wolf in that house*—but she bit her tongue. *Maybe the wolf will eat the demon and then I can get out.* Surely the barrier would vanish if the demon was dead?

There was talking coming from inside the cabin, and Ailsa strained to hear it. Then a light emerged, carried by the black arm of the demon, as he peered around the sides of the house. Ailsa tucked her head down and held her breath as the man's footsteps came closer and closer. She pulled her legs into her chest, trying not to make any sounds. But she could feel the bond from last night, going slack the closer the demon came, pinpointing exactly where he was. Ailsa had no doubt that it was showing him her hiding place. With a growl, she unwound herself from her seat. If she was going to be found, she'd rather it wasn't cowering on a toilet in the half-dark. She unlocked the door, and it swung open, revealing the demon exactly where Ailsa had felt he would be.

"Hello," he said, his lip curling. "I see you found the toilet."

Ailsa straightened. "Well it seemed the only safe place to be, after I found out you had a house guest."

"Wulver said that he'd met you."

"I suppose Wulver is the massive wolf you have lurking inside your spare room?" she folded her arms in front of her, wishing she had an axe handle to grip.

To her annoyance, the demon actually laughed. "Yes," he chuckled, turning back towards the cabin.

Ailsa followed at a distance, scanning the clearing for the creature. "And why do you have a huge wolf for a pet?"

"He isn't a pet," said the demon. "He's a forest guardian."

Oh, of course. "Is there a reason he's in your cabin?"

Maalik reached the door and held it open for her. "I thought you might try to run away."

Ailsa planted her feet outside the cabin. *No way am I going in there with that thing.* "How was seeing a giant wolf supposed to stop me from running away?"

"He was watching out for you," Maalik said. "I wanted to save you the pain of running into the boundary."

"Well, he didn't warn me," Ailsa gritted out.

"He should have told you not to, but it seems you caught him off guard. He's mostly nocturnal, you know."

Something zipped around between Ailsa's and the demon's heads, alternating between speakers. Muck seemed to grow more excited with every word they shouted at each other. The demon was studiously ignoring her, but Ailsa couldn't help but watch the brownie's progress warily, remembering the feeling of her little tongue as it tasted her blood like an oversized bumblebee.

"He said you've been out here for hours," Maalik said, looking genuinely sorry for her.

Ailsa squirmed under his gaze. "Well I wasn't about to go back into the house where he could eat me."

"You must be cold?" said the demon. "Would you like to come inside and meet him properly? I can start a fire."

Ailsa still didn't move. *I just want to leave*, she thought for the hundredth time that day. Harris, Iona, Angus, and Gris were relying on her.

"Don't worry, he won't do you any harm. Come on." With that, the demon turned on his heel and made his way back round the front of the house. Ailsa stood in the almost-dark for a few moments, weighing up her options. She could spend all night out here, but he was right, she was cold. She knew all too well that even in the summer, it wasn't good to sit outside overnight in Eilanmòr. She'd also meant to eat some food, before she'd come across the wolf. Her stomach rumbled painfully after hours of being ignored.

Finally, after trying one more time to press against the barrier that surrounded the cottage, she gave up and went inside, hoping she had made the right choice and wasn't about to be wolf food.

"*He won't do you any harm.* So says the demon," Ailsa muttered.

The wolf was lying next to the fireplace, taking up the whole hearth. He opened an eye when Ailsa walked in but quickly closed it again with a sniff. It seemed he wasn't impressed by her earlier reaction.

"See," said Maalik. "Everyone's friends."

Ailsa gave him a dark look and sat down at the small table.

"Do you like falafel?" Maalik asked from the stove. "I've got all the stuff to make them, I just need to fry them up."

Ailsa wiped a hand over her face. "What's a falafel?"

"Vegetables and flour, deep fried together."

"Like a tattie scone?" Ailsa asked, thinking of the potato cakes her mother had always made.

"Kind of, but not just potato. It's got chickpeas, onion, leeks, celery—"

"Sounds healthy," Ailsa commented in an exasperated tone.

"It's got everything you'll need for coming out and working with me tomorrow."

"Working with you?" Ailsa leaned forward in her chair. "Who says I'm doing that?"

Maalik tilted his head. "Do you want to stay here with Wulver?"

Ailsa looked at the wolf, who had fallen asleep again. For all she knew, he could just be pretending. "Fine," she relented, throwing her hands up. "But I'm not helping you."

Maalik just went back to his cooking. Soon, the kitchen was filled with the sound of sizzling and the smell of garlic. Ailsa's stomach was almost painful from hunger. Still, when he set the plate down in front of her, she paused.

"This isn't going to knock me out, is it?" she said, thinking of the night before.

"I would never dare." The demon sat down opposite her and took a bite of his own food. When Ailsa couldn't bear it anymore, she copied.

"What do you think?" asked Maalik.

It was one of the best things she'd ever eaten. "It's okay," she answered, her mouth stuffed with food. "Can all demons cook?"

"It depends if the demon was once human, I suppose," Maalik said, with a faraway look.

From then on it was silent as they ate. Ailsa watched the demon surreptitiously. Not for the first time, she thought he looked more sad than menacing. The deep dark circles under his eyes made him look exhausted too. *It depends if the demon was once human.* Well, that meant *he* had once been human. Perhaps that was why he was so sad. *Imagine being turned into a monster*, Ailsa thought, but that was too close to her own truth.

After dinner, Maalik pottered around the kitchen and Ailsa crept into the bed. She meant to sit up and watch him and the huge wolf. But a full day of feeling terrified was draining and soon she felt sleep tugging at her. That night she dreamed of the masks again, but this time it was Maalik that was trying them on.

Chapter 18

harris hated the nuckelavee more than the ceasg.

At least the ceasg didn't smell like rotting flesh. They were easier on the eye too. And easier to trick.

Unfortunately, it was rather hard to make an escape attempt when you were unconscious, which was how Harris found himself in Ephraim.

Harris awoke to find his head being jostled with every step the nuckelavee's horse made. From the ache in his temple, he imagined this had been going on for a while. He suppressed a groan and took a quick inventory. The nuckelavee hadn't bothered tying him up. Probably because he could just knock him out with the supernatural stench again if he tried to run.

"Through here," someone called out and then the horse was cantering down a steep path. Harris clung to its back, feeling the wet muscle underneath his hands and shuddering. The sound of water got closer and then they were ducking behind a waterfall into a dark corridor.

"I'd really rather—" Harris began but then he was shoved off the nuckelavee's back and onto the floor. He landed hard on his side, the fall knocking the wind from him.

"Enjoy your stay," someone shouted and then a wall of branches and thorns grew up in front of him, creating a living cage.

He launched himself up, wrapping his hands round the foliage, receiving a few cuts in the process. The branches were wound tightly around each other, but allowed whoever was inside, or outside, of the jail to look through. Outside, several dark figures watched him. *My jailors,* Harris presumed. The nuckelavee made a sound somewhere between a scream and a grunt and trotted away. *At least I don't have to worry about the smell anymore.*

"Don't bother trying to escape," a voice said from the back of the cell.

Harris barked a laugh, turning to look for the owner of the voice. "Where's the fun in that?"

Sitting alone, huddled against the stone wall, was a young man. He was hunched over and holding himself at an odd angle, wrapped fully in a woollen blanket. "Being punished is no fun," he said in a tired voice.

Harris blew out a breath and crossed to the man's side, sliding down the wall so he could sit beside him. Harris offered him a hand to shake, but the man didn't move. "How many times have *you* tried to get out?" Harris asked.

"Three times. I'd rather not try again." The blanket slipped from the man's head, revealing vibrant purple hair and a pained expression.

Harris was silent for a minute. He could see a puddle of illuminated ground through the gap in the branches. Drops of water were spotting there every now and again. It was probably from the waterfall, but they reminded him of rain, which reminded him of a certain person. But it was best not to dwell on those thoughts when she was so far away. "So," he said, "what stupid thing did you do to get locked up in a cell in Ephraim?"

The man beside him sighed. "I went looking for it."

Harris snorted. "Yeah, that was stupid."

"And you?"

"It was a series of stupid things really. First, I was born a selkie. Second, I tried to save Eilanmòr. Third, I tried to save a girl." And there he was thinking about her again.

"A girl? She better have been worth it?"

Harris didn't hesitate when he replied. "She is."

The man shifted, causing the blanket to pool around the back of his neck. He was a lot younger than Harris had first thought, perhaps only a little older than Angus or Ailsa. His nose had a slight hook, and a piercing, which Harris couldn't help but admire. A dusting of stubble was coating his jaw, probably from being in the cell for a while.

"So a selkie?" said the man. "Why have they locked up one of their own? If you're just here to torture me more, I'm afraid I'm too tired."

Harris frowned. What had happened to this guy? "I'm nothing like the monsters that dwell in this court," he answered with a little more vehemence than he'd meant. "Selkies are Seelie folk: pure and kind and incredibly attractive, if I do say so myself," he finished with a wink.

Finally, a smile on the man's lips. "I can't argue there, but you're not my type."

Harris stretched his legs out and surveyed the walls of the cage. "So, how are we going to escape?"

The smile on the man's face disappeared. "Did you not hear me about being punished? Should I show you?"

The stranger pulled the blanket off his body, letting it fall to the ground around him. The light in the cell was dim, but it was enough for Harris to see the left side of the man's body was misshapen and stiff. He held out his arm to reveal darkened veins snaking around underneath his skin. The prisoner lifted his shirt gingerly to show the lines ran down his chest and side.

"Are you poisoned?" asked Harris.

"No, not poison," the man said with a wince. "Worse."

He held out his arm for Harris to touch. Harris's fingers skimmed the surface where the veins were, feeling them to be hard.

"What is it?"

"Wood," the prisoner shuddered. "I'm growing a tree inside me. Instead of veins, I have twigs. Every time I disobey, Nicnevan adds some more branches. They grow through my skin sometimes, but I snap them off, so they don't catch." He dropped the edge of his shirt to cover the skin again. "Have you ever had a splinter? How do you think it feels to have wood growing inside your veins and arteries, tearing at your skin with every inch?"

Harris felt a wave of nausea sweep up from his toes. "That's barbaric."

The man leaned his head back against the wall. "It goes from my fingertips down to my waist on this side. I can just about sit down comfortably. Next time, perhaps she'll start on my right side. I'd rather not find out."

"How are you still alive?" Harris breathed.

"Magic, I suppose," the man answered, his voice breaking on the last word.

Harris turned his face to stare back out of the jail. "Well, thanks," he said numbly. "If I didn't already have a million reasons to get out of this place, you've given me plenty more."

The man looked at Harris sadly, then turned away to huddle against the cell wall again. "Don't say I didn't warn you."

Harris stood up and walked to the door of branches. He rested his forehead against the plaited wood, being careful of the thorns, and ran through his options. His first instinct was to charm his way out; it had worked in the past after all. But something told him that Nicnevan wasn't as easily fooled as a common ceasg. He could wait until he was brought out and paraded around before the Unseelie, but he had no guarantee he wouldn't just be left to rot for a few years first. Maybe even decades. The world would have moved on. He pictured his sister, with a brood of pups and a husband to boss around. She'd have looked for him, but in the end, she had her own responsibilities that always pulled her back to Struanmuir.

And Angus. There might be grey hairs in his beard, and he might have injured a hip from dancing too vigorously. That would be a real shame.

Harris's mind strayed, as it always did, to Ailsa, and immediately he wished it hadn't. She would be as beautiful as the last time he saw her on that ship, her newly found powers electrifying her face. Unlike Angus, she wouldn't have aged—whatever fae blood she had running through her veins would have preserved her youth. Maybe her hair would be shorter though. She was always hiding behind it, but perhaps time had given her confidence. Would she still want to carry on their conversation from the inn? It had felt like a beginning, but they had been interrupted before any real assurances had been made. What would it feel like to run his hands along her skin again? Or to taste her lips? Would she even let him? No. In fact, he hoped she wouldn't. Someone like Ailsa was too special to wait around for the likes of him. He hoped that she would find another in that time. She deserved to be happy and cared for, and he didn't like the idea of her being alone for however long it took him to escape. Then again, who knew? Maybe she'd see him again and decide to leave her perfect lover…

Harris gave himself a mental shake. *Pull yourself together,* he admonished. *You've only been gone a week, at most. It's far too early to start worrying.*

What he needed was a plan.

Chapter 19

Ailsa woke to the sound of scraping. Peeling one eye open, she found the demon sitting on the couch, leaning over something on his lap.

"What time is it?" she asked, her voice rasping from sleep. She found a line of dried drool on her chin and surreptitiously tried to wipe it away with the back of her sleeve.

Maalik continued to move his hand over the object. Whatever it was glinted in the dawn light seeping through the window. *A knife*, Ailsa understood with a jolt.

"The sun has been up almost an hour. I'm running late," he grumbled, as if somehow this was her fault.

"You could have woken me up." She ran a hand over her hair as she sat up in bed, trying her best to pat down the tangle. "What exactly are you late for?"

"I told you last night. I've got work to do."

"And what work is that?" *Being a pain in the backside,* Ailsa answered in her head.

He gazed at the blade and grimaced. "If you had come with me yesterday you would know."

Ailsa blinked. Could it be that the demon was in a bad mood? He had looked exhausted yesterday, but in the morning light he looked almost dead on his feet. *Maybe he hasn't slept well and it's making him grouchy.* If he was in a foul mood, he might not let her go with him. On one hand she wouldn't have to find out what horrible things demons did for a profession. On the other, she'd be left here with the huge wolf again. She thought of how Harris would have handled her in a similar situation. Gentle humour and teasing.

And then when he takes you outside, you can start to look for a way to escape.

The silence was stretching on, the knife in his hands getting sharper.

Ailsa tilted her head. "Were you planning on butchering me in my sleep?"

The demon fumbled with the blade, sending it scattering to the floor, barely avoiding his foot. "What makes you say that?" he demanded with a scowl.

"Well, I woke up to find you sharpening it, not even a foot away." Ailsa shrugged. "And after yesterday I wouldn't blame you if you decided it would be better to chop me up and throw me in your stew."

"I don't know where this obsession with me eating you has come from." Was that a pout on his lips? "I'm a vegetarian, you know."

"Hmm." Ailsa let her mouth tilt into a smile. "I knew

there was something strange about you."

Maalik's eyes widened, displaying black orbs. "I don't really see what's strange about—"

"No," she cut him off. "I don't think we can be friends if you're a vegetarian, our interests are far too different."

He stared at her, speechless, as she inspected her nails.

Ailsa tossed her hair back. "And who has ever heard of a vegetarian demon anyway? How are you supposed to terrorise villagers on a diet of carrots?"

She looked up at him from under her eyelashes, his utter bemusement almost making her snort.

"I mean, I don't know how you ever get your 'work' done, whatever it is. Look at you…" She waved her hand in his direction. "… you're practically skin and bones. No, I think if I'm going to be here anyway, I'd better help you." She stood from the bed and bent to pick up the knife he had dropped. He was looking at her like she had grown three heads, but let her grab it and stick it in her belt all the same. The blade should have made her feel she had the upper hand, but being a breath away from the demon had her heart racing.

"Come on, lazy," she said with forced bravado. "We better get to it."

She waited an agonising moment as he stared up at her, those black eyes flickering. Finally, he lifted a hand, palm out.

"Lead on then, girl."

Ailsa huffed her way up the path behind Maalik, doing her best not to twist her ankle on the tangle of roots criss-crossing the path.

Maalik was setting an unrelenting pace, but with the pull of their bond, Ailsa had no option but to jog behind him. She was desperate to stop, but didn't want to give the demon the satisfaction of knowing he was tiring her. Instead, she pulled a flask out of the pack she was carrying and tried to take a drink without spilling it down herself.

Somewhere down the hill the noise of a river thundered by, but the water was obscured from view.

"It isn't much further," Maalik called back to her.

Ailsa flipped through a few choice curses in her head. "Can't you just remove this bond thingy?"

He turned his head, raising his chin. "So you can escape?"

"Well," said Ailsa with a huff, coming to a stop. "In the last few days I've been possessed, captured, beaten up, sacrificed to a demon, poisoned and almost been eaten by a wolf. Now I have to follow you about? Wouldn't you try to escape?"

Maalik paused too. "I'm sorry you're trapped like this, but so am I. Do you think I want some vagabond attached to me?"

"Listen, this isn't about me. I have to leave, someone needs me," Ailsa said, putting her hands on her hips.

He looked her up and down. "Really?"

"Yes," Ailsa gritted out.

The demon tilted his head. "Tell me about it."

"What?" Ailsa said, taken aback. "Why?"

"We're stuck together. I'm making conversation."

"Fine." Ailsa flopped down on the path, not caring if the damp ground seeped into her clothes. "A friend of mine got captured by some ceasg and taken to Nicnevan."

"Your mother?"

"That's what they tell me."

"I can't say I know much about her." Maalik took off his pack and absently rooted around in it. "Lives up north, hates humans, bit of a bitch." He looked up quickly. "No offence."

Ailsa sniffed. "Well I'm hoping I will be able to appeal to her maternal side."

"Good luck with that. So this friend of yours, why is it up to you to save him?" Maalik produced an apple from inside the bag and threw it for her. She caught it reflexively and her heart gave a tug. Memories of Harris eating apples and doing tricks with a little boy before they set off for the Stone flashed in her mind's eye.

Ailsa had to clear her throat before she answered. "He was trying to save me when he was captured."

"Sounds like neither of you are great at rescue

missions. He got captured trying to save you, you got yourself sacrificed to a demon trying to save him." Maalik rubbed the back of his neck. "You must have known him for a while then."

"Only a few weeks," Ailsa realised. "But we've been through a lot. We saved the kingdom, and, by proxy, you." She bit into her apple, savouring the sweet flesh. "You're welcome by the way."

"And how many times did you almost get yourselves killed doing that?" When she didn't answer, he sank down on the ground in front of her and fixed her with those fathomless eyes. "Is he worth it?"

Ailsa almost choked on her apple. "Of course he is. He's my friend."

"Oh? Is that all?"

What was this? *Are all demons such gossips?* She thought about replying with a snarky remark but then, wasn't that exactly the question she had been asking herself before? The way she and Harris had left it, that wasn't all they were. But was that still what she wanted? "I don't know," she answered.

"Sorry, I shouldn't have pried," Maalik said.

Ailsa shrugged. "So, tell me about you."

The demon's face instantly shuttered. "No."

"Go on, I was almost spilling my guts to you there."

"How about this." Maalik paused, sucking on a tooth. He waved a hand towards himself. "Tell me what you see when you look at me."

"A demon," Ailsa answered immediately.

Maalik looked disappointed, but not surprised. "Is that it?" He shook his head. "Don't answer me now. We'd better get going."

Ailsa followed as he set off again, watching his back all the way. She couldn't help but feel she had failed some sort of test.

Ailsa felt her stomach sink as they approached a lone, little house in the woods. There were no sounds or signs of life coming from inside, except a lazy stream of smoke puffing from the chimney. Ailsa hadn't been sure where Maalik had been leading her, but she had imagined it would be somewhere sufficiently dark and scary. So why was the demon here?

"Maalik—"

He placed a finger to his lips in a command to be quiet. Ailsa wasn't sure whether to obey this order or to scream a warning to the people inside the cottage, but then it was too late as Maalik strode right up to their door and knocked.

Don't open, don't open, Ailsa thought hard at the people inside. For a second it seemed they had heard her. Maalik knocked again. This time, though, there came a very faint voice from inside the cottage.

"Come in."

The demon opened the door and stepped inside. Ailsa felt the answering pull of the bond to follow Maalik into the dark interior. It took a moment for her eyes to adjust. The fire was on its last life in the grate, giving out little heat. The room was covered in stuff: pillows and blankets and old knick-knacks clearly collected over many years. It felt lived in and homely. But when Ailsa looked more closely, a layer of dust had settled on the possessions, as if they hadn't been used or touched in a long time.

Ailsa joined Maalik in the corner of the room.

"Hello, Mrs Malcolm," Maalik said. At first, Ailsa wasn't sure who he was talking to, until the pile of blankets in front of him shifted, and she saw the tuft of white hair. Curled up inside the quilt was a tiny old lady. Her skin looked as thin as paper and underneath she was all bones. But when she heard Maalik say her name, her face transformed into a grin.

"Maalik," she said weakly. "I wasn't sure you'd be coming today."

The demon fussed over the old woman's blankets, making sure they were tucked in around her. "I couldn't stay away. Mrs Malcolm, I have a friend with me today. This is Ailsa."

The old woman searched the air near Maalik's head. "Hello, Ailsa. I'm glad Maalik here has some help. He works too hard."

"She's blind," murmured the demon.

Probably for the best, thought Ailsa looking the demon up and down.

A little louder, he said, "Ailsa, would you mind going and putting some hot water on? I need to give Mrs Malcolm her medicine and then she can have some tea."

Ailsa gaped at Maalik, who had gone back to straightening out covers that had bunched up around the old woman's feet. How could this be the demon's job? There had to be some sort of trick.

Still, she thought, nothing wrong with heating some water. She had to bring the dying fire back to life before she could get the kettle onto it, but soon it was steaming away. From the corner of her vision she watched Maalik feeding the woman something. Then he raised the back of his hand to her forehead. He took her wrist in his hands and became very still. Then there was a lot of movement when he lifted her off the couch she was on, but Ailsa quickly understood he meant to help her to the toilet and averted her gaze. The water began to bubble so she rustled up a mug and some milk.

"Two sugars, please," Maalik called from the corner.

Ailsa carefully carried the mug over to them and placed it down beside the couch. She watched in silence as the demon blew on it then held it while the woman sipped the liquid. After every drink she smacked her lips, revealing toothless gums.

"We need to go, Mrs Malcolm," Maalik told her once she'd finished. "I'll be back tomorrow to see how you're doing."

The old woman nodded, her eyes already closing as she sunk back into her pile of blankets. Maalik collected up all his belongings and motioned for Ailsa to follow him out. She got one last glimpse of the dusty room before he closed the door quietly behind him.

"So that's your job?" Ailsa asked as Maalik strode away. "You look after old, blind people?"

"I try to heal people, like I did with you the other night. But it's not always possible. Sometimes I just need to try to make them comfortable."

Ailsa watched the demon's retreating back. His broad shoulders were slumped and he was almost dragging his feet along the leaf-strewn ground. Black hands clutched at the straps of his bag, as if it was a heavy weight. Peeking out from his black hair, his golden antlers caught the sun's light.

Defeated, Ailsa realised. *He looks defeated.*

The rest of the walk back to the cabin was done in silence. As soon as they entered the small dwelling, still with a fire crackling in the hearth, Ailsa peeled off her boots and jacket.. Her clothes were starting to become brittle with sweat, but she did her best to clean her face in the sink in the kitchen.

Beside her, Maalik began tipping food into a pot. The

demon sniffed in her direction and gave a wince. "I don't suppose you want a change of clothes?" he asked.

Ailsa pursed her lips. "What are you trying to say?"

"There are clothes in that chest over there. They might be a bit big I'm afraid."

Ailsa paced to drawers beside the bed and pulled them open while the demon went back to his cooking.

"You asked me earlier what I see when I look at you," she said as she selected a top and trousers. "What I see are impossibilities. You're trying your best to look fierce and terrifying, but what you do, your actions, are the opposite. The way you comforted that woman—"

"—but it's never enough." Maalik stopped stirring and stared at the wall in front of him. "I can't save them."

"You're doing your best," said Ailsa. "Sickness, old age, death; they're inevitable, but I bet she finds a real comfort in knowing there is someone looking after her."

The demon rubbed his temple with a black hand. "Maybe."

Ailsa nodded. It was enough for now. "I'm going to get changed and washed in the outhouse."

Maalik took a deep breath, unlocking his body and began to cook again. For a moment, before Ailsa walked out the door, the sun shone through the window in front of him bathing him in light, and he looked a little less demonic than he had the day before.

Chapter 20

Ailsa had been here; Iona could feel it. The shadow of her magic still clung to the air, even after a few days.

The village was quiet, its residents probably still sleeping. But all around, the air sparkled with another presence. Countless fae had passed through here. But whether they had left again, Iona couldn't tell.

Angus followed close behind her, one hand on his sword. They'd decided, as a human, he was the best companion to have around. The Bean-Nighe had said the villagers were wary of fae. Gris had stayed away for that exact reason. Iona didn't want to think what they would do if they saw a towering, hairy grey man stomping into their village. Besides, leaving the cover of trees was hard for him.

Iona on the other hand, was adept at appearing quite the lady. She had prided herself on charming even the most sullen humans in the royal court. What hassle could a few superstitious villagers pose?

As they wandered further into the town, it looked like someone had been in a rush to get away. Bags and tools were left lying on the ground. A bag of fruit sat propped against a well. The hairs on Iona's neck rose. The villagers weren't sleeping after all. They were being watched.

"Hello?" Iona called out. "We're not here to hurt anyone. We're looking for our friend."

Then, there was the sound of doors being thrown open and they were surrounded by the villagers. There were at least a hundred of them, young and old and everything in between. Many of them were wearing hostile expressions, but underneath that was the distinct feeling of fear. Iona felt her mouth hanging open as she looked around.

"I'm warning you now, leave this place or we'll be forced to fight," demanded a squat man brandishing a rake in front of him like a weapon.

"We're just looking for our friend," Iona answered, raising her chin.

"She's short, bad-tempered, and has a birthmark on her left cheek," Angus added.

A middle-aged woman with a torch stepped forward with a scowl. "The changeling. Yes, she was here yesterday."

Iona's heart gave a lurch. "Where is she now?"

"Sacrificed to the forest," said the first man. "The same will happen to all of you if you don't leave now."

Angus lifted his sword in front of him looking murderous. "Do you mean you killed her?"

"No," said the woman, quickly, with an eye on his blade. "We know we can't kill fae. It's much easier to let you all kill each other."

"I'm not fae, I'm human just like you," Angus growled at the same time that Iona ground out a haughty, "I demand to know where you took her."

The man sneered at Iona, looking her up and down. "And who are you?"

Angus stared and barked a laugh, sheathing his sword. "This is Iona of Struanmuir, advisor to the crown of Eilanmòr, who could literally drown you in your own spit if you piss her off. Which you already have, by the way, since you took our friend." He strode up to the man. "So tell us where she is, and we'll be on our way."

"Who do you think you are?" spluttered the man.

It was Iona's turn to step in. "Prince Angus of Eilanmòr."

Then the villagers did the last thing Iona expected. One by one, they began to cheer.

"We've been trying to contact Dunrigh for so long," a middle-aged woman was saying as she led them into the largest dwelling in the village, where a fire burned warmly, chasing away the cold from outside. Iona fought the itch to remove the water droplets soaking them all.

The villagers were unwilling to trust fae, so she wasn't about to rub their faces in her magic. It would serve them right too, to remain wet. The woman quickly busied herself with setting a pot on her fire. The rest of the village appeared to have given up, dispersing quickly as soon as they realised they weren't all going to fit inside the house. "Thank the gods," muttered the woman. "Our letters must have got through to Dunrigh."

Iona pulled out a chair at the worn wooden table. "What letters?"

The woman laid out some mugs. "About the curse."

"What is going on? What curse?" asked Angus with a frown. Iona knew what he was thinking. She just wanted to find Ailsa too. The thought of helping people who had harmed her did not sit well. "We just want to know where our friend is."

"We'll tell you where she is if you help us." The woman stopped making tea and turned, her eyes wide. "Please, we're desperate."

Angus crossed his arms. "We're not about to help people who have taken our friend."

The woman sighed. "We thought your friend was going to hurt us. I'm sorry, but we've had to be so careful. She's alive and well, I can promise you, but please, *please*, help us before you go find her."

Angus sunk into a chair beside Iona, reigning in barely controlled irritation. "Fine," he grumbled. "We'll listen and then you'll tell us what happened."

The woman nodded and poured the boiling water, handing them steaming cups of tea. "A year ago, something changed in the forest. Fae showed up more and more frequently. At first, it was only the Seelie. We would let our children play in the woods with the pixies and ghillie-dhu. But then, we started seeing more and more monsters. The forest became unsafe and we were trapped here. We tried sending messengers out to call for aid from Dunrigh, but they never returned."

"What's bringing them here?" asked Angus. "You said something about a curse?"

The woman gave them a dark look. "There is something evil in the river. It draws fae near, like a magnet."

Iona crossed her arms. "I didn't feel anything…"

"You think you didn't feel anything. But yet, you're here."

Iona frowned. "We're here to find our friend."

"Listen, I don't know, I'm not fae." The woman threw up her hands. "But for some reason we've seen a huge increase in fae of all kinds passing through."

"So that's the curse?"

"No, that just seems to be a part of it." The woman rubbed her hand over her face. "Something much worse is happening. Anyone who goes into the woods alone, comes back with some sort of sickness. Their skin turns black and their bones are broken."

Iona froze, memories of death and disease flashing across her mind. She had waited in Dunrigh for Angus, Ailsa, and Harris to find the Stone of Destiny because King Connall had been sick like that. She had read to him, nursed him, heard his stories, and watched his rages until the morning that the trio returned with the Stone and he had lost his fight. Was it only two weeks ago since she'd gone to his funeral, watched his funeral pyre burn?

"We've seen that before," Angus choked. He had gone pale.

Iona reached out a hand and squeezed Angus's knee. He hadn't made it back in time for his father. "What can we do?" she asked the woman.

"If the evil is removed, our forest will be safe again. We just want to live as we used to, without fear."

"We promise to take a look," said Iona. "But you must tell us where our friend is. You don't know it, but she saved all of Eilanmòr only a fortnight ago."

"We'll tell you what happened to her when you've seen the whirlpool. We'll travel out at first light. Until then, you can sleep here."

"I'd like to see the sick people first, see if it is the same disease," Angus said.

The woman gave them a dark look. "We have to tie them down, so they don't kill themselves."

Three beds stood against the far wall, as far away from the door as possible. Quiet groans pierced the silence.

A woman and two men. It was impossible to tell how old they were underneath all the bruising. On their cheeks and around their noses, the skin was blackened with disease. Lips were cracked. Eyes were reddened and staring at nothing. Each person was bound to their bed with lengths of rope. As they approached, Iona could see their skin had been rubbed raw around their bindings.

The man closest to them gave a rasping cough, almost bucking off the bed. Once he was done, he sunk back into the mattress, gnashing his teeth at nothing in particular.

"You said you thought you'd seen this before?" said the woman from behind them.

"My father," murmured Angus, staring at the moaning figures. "He died from the same sickness."

"We've already lost two men to this. They escaped and the next day we found them dead, seemingly by their own hands."

"And they didn't travel outside of Eilanmòr?" asked Iona. *This can't be the same thing.* But the evidence was hard to ignore.

"They didn't travel outside of this forest. Why? Where did the King get the disease?"

Angus reached out a hand as if to touch the person in

front of him. Iona caught it up in hers before he could, bringing it back down to his side. "He had been on a voyage, exploring the island of Nerebus," she said. "He looked like this when they found him on the beach."

"Will they recover?" asked the woman.

Iona frowned. "The King didn't. He had moments of clarity though."

"It's part of the curse that calls the fae here." The woman's gaze became hard and she turned away from the three invalids. "I don't know why, but they're linked somehow."

"I don't think so," Iona said, pushing Angus to follow her out the door. "This is something else. Something unrelated."

The woman dropped back into her seat by the hearth. "Well," she said. "Will you help us?"

"Yes," Angus spoke first, breaking his silence, "but then you have to tell us where Ailsa went."

The woman nodded. "You can stay here tonight; get some rest. We'll go to the river in the morning."

Iona didn't speak as they were led upstairs and given rooms, but she stayed alert. She felt like there was still something the villagers weren't telling them. She was desperate to speak to Angus alone, but the woman, who had since told them her name was Brighid, was alway lurking around somewhere.

Iona's room looked like it had once belonged to a child. Dolls lined the shelves around the walls, their little porcelain eyes following them as they walked. *They'll be getting turned around when I'm alone*, Iona vowed. A small desk was littered with pencils and paper. The child had drawn mostly houses and families, though when Iona shifted the pile surreptitiously, a drawing of a horse with a horn coming from its head was revealed.

The woman pointed to a chest, where she said Iona could find towels and blankets. Iona eyed the small bed frame. *That'll be interesting later.*

Angus's room was much grander. A large bed filled the space, covered in a crocheted bedspread. Several antlers decorated the walls, but it was the stag's head above the bed that caught Iona's attention straight away. The glassy eyes reminded her of the dolls in her room. *I don't know which is worse.*

"We can stick the stag in my room and I'll come share a bed with you, if you like?" Iona muttered to Angus, earning a frown from Brighid.

"No," Brighid shook her head, "you should really stay in your own rooms. It'll be more comfortable. Now come on, you've come a bit late for dinner, but there should be some food next door," she said, before whisking them out of the house.

It seemed that the whole village was also in the next

house. When they arrived, many were seated at long tables, enjoying their last pints of beer of the night, alternating between sipping and yawning. Gone was the hostility from earlier. Now they just looked exhausted.

Iona was surprised to still see children running around the room, probably woken from their beds by Iona and Angus's earlier arrival and unwilling to go back just yet. A couple of little boys darted forward, playing a game of chase. They didn't even notice they had strangers among them until one slammed into Angus.

"Oof, sorry," he said, giving his head a rub with one eye shut.

Brighid swatted her hands at him. "Get away to your mother."

The little boys ignored her, staring wide eyed up at Angus. "You're the prince," one whispered in awe.

Angus crouched down so he was at their level. "Not the one that matters," he said with a wink.

One of the boys turned to look at Iona, pulling on the other's sleeve. "Are you a princess?" he asked.

Iona smiled. "I'm just a lady."

Angus mock whispered into one of the boy's ears, "She's a magical selkie."

He turned to grin at her and Iona fought the urge to roll her eyes.

"A selkie?" one boy squealed. " I've never seen a selkie before."

The other boy tugged on her skirt with a little plump hand. "Will you turn into a seal for me?"

They aren't scared. "Maybe," laughed Iona. "If we come to an agreement."

"Ciaran and Connor, that's enough of that," said Brighid. "Go home now."

The two boys were unrepentant as they skipped off, giggling with glee.

"We're trying to keep the children's spirits up. They're doing so well," murmured Brighid. "Ciaran's brother went missing a few weeks ago."

Iona's stomach twisted. "I know how that feels."

They ate their leftovers quickly, feeling eyes on them the whole time. Brighid stuck to them like glue, talking at them all the way to their rooms. Angus and Iona exchanged a glance before wishing her good night and shutting their doors. Iona listened to Brighid shift on her feet for around five minutes until she appeared satisfied that they had indeed gone to bed. The stairs creaked as the woman descended and at last the house was quiet.

"*Psst,*" a voice said at Iona's door. "Let me in."

Angus rushed in when she opened the door, and collapsed on the tiny bed. He made a face before reaching underneath his back to pluck out a stuffed cat toy. "I really don't like this," he said, throwing the cat across the room. "What if they're trying to do to you what they did to Ailsa?"

Iona sighed, dropping down gracefully onto the floor. "We don't really have much choice. They know what happened to her and they aren't going to tell us until we help them."

Angus scratched his beard. "Can't you just threaten to drown them?"

Iona wrinkled her nose. "I don't think that will ingratiate me, somehow."

"I just wish we could find her now," he groaned. "First, we lose Harris, now Ailsa. This is the opposite of what should be happening."

"Oh really?" Iona said. "What should be happening?"

He closed his eyes. "You, Harris and Ailsa should be with me in Dunrigh. Gris can even come too, if he likes. I'll let him stay in the greenhouse. You and Harris can be permanent ambassadors for Struanmuir, and Ailsa can be a knight. I'll teach her. We'll go to ceilidhs every week and we'll eat the best food. Sometimes we'll go on adventures, but we'll always be back for dinner."

"Sounds nice," Iona said gently. "But Ailsa left Dunrigh, remember? She wanted to go home."

"That was only because she thought she didn't belong." Angus sat up. "I'll make sure she does."

"And what about those people downstairs? They were sick, just like your father. Don't you want to know why?"

Angus's gaze flicked to the door. "Yes," he said. "Yes, I want to know."

Iona reached on a hand to squeeze his leg. "The first step is finding out why they're sick and finding Ailsa is helping this village."

Angus bobbed his head in a tight nod. He placed a warm hand over hers, giving her a squeeze back. "We'd better get some sleep," he croaked. "Big day ahead."

Iona stood, bending so she could give the prince a hug. He turned his head into the crook of her neck, and she let the embrace last a moment longer. When they finally separated, his eyes were glassy. *It's been a long few weeks*, thought Iona as she shepherded him back into his room. The stress was beginning to take its toll on her companion.

Suddenly, the loss of her brother and Ailsa was almost unbearable. They would know what to do. If Harris had been there, he'd have charmed the whole village within an hour. And Ailsa would have known how to cheer Angus up. She shut the door behind her and climbed into the narrow bed, allowing herself to imagine Angus's dream of them all together in Dunrigh.

Chapter 21

Sometimes, when she was young, Ailsa would wake up in whatever barn or hovel she had found for the night and listen to the silence outside. It rarely stormed when she was sleeping, the night was peaceful and so were her dreams back then.

She would peer into the dark and wonder what had woken her, if there was no thunder. The only sound was the beating of her own heart. Then, as it often did in the pitch black of childhood nights, her heart would beat faster and she would swear the sound wasn't coming from her, but from outside. A relentless *thump, thump, thump*, getting faster and faster. Somewhere out there was a monster, its footsteps getting closer and closer. It couldn't be the forest monster—she never went near any woods anymore—it had to be something else. Her skin would prickle, sure there was something there, in the dark, watching her.

Some nights the wisdom of childhood would have her pulling her cloak up over her head and she would sing a song under her breath, willing the whatever-it-was to go away, until she fell asleep.

Other nights she would be in a state of total paralysis, unable to move, unable to scream. A shape would move in the gloom and inside she would be crying but no sound would escape. She would watch the thing, tears leaking from her unblinking eyes, as it came closer and closer.

Then all of a sudden, she would be released from the waking dream, able to move once again, and she would see there was no monster. She would stay awake for the rest of the night, her back pressed against whatever wall she could find and she would wait for daylight.

In the light she could pretend it would never happen again.

Until the next time.

Ailsa's eyes opened instantly, a feeling of dread filling her as she stared ahead into the dark, completely unable to move.

It had been years. Years since she had experienced the bloodcurdling terror of being totally paralysed, waiting in the dark for whatever monster would materialise.

Her breath came in quick pants, trying its best to keep up with her pounding heart.

Inside her head was blank with fear, she could only think of one word, over and over again, as she waited. *No, no, no, no…*

Then, a shape formed out of the corner of her eye. The dark thing came closer, seeming to cock its head, watching her as she fought in vain against her body.

"Are you awake?" a voice whispered from the creature.

She wrestled with her tongue, but it was a weight in her mouth. The best she could do was a gurgle in her throat, which died as the thing reached for her.

"Gods, come on, wake up. You're dreaming."

A clawed hand grabbed her shoulder and a white-hot horror screamed inside her head.

"You're ok," said the creature. "I have you."

It has me.

The monster's arms came around her, bringing her body towards it.

Bile rose up in her throat.

"I won't hurt you," it said and then instead of eating her, it began to stroke her back. She expected any moment for those claws she felt to gouge into her flesh.

Then, the creature sighed—she felt it through her whole body—and whispered her name.

"Ailsa."

She sucked in a breath like she was breaking the surface of some water and suddenly her limbs were unlocked, and she was flailing and screaming and, *oh gods*, she was awake, and the creature was still holding her. It wasn't disappearing like it had when she was young. She thrashed harder, willing it to drop her.

"Shh," it murmured, holding her closer. "Calm down, before you injure one of us."

Her brain was finally catching up with her body. She knew that voice.

She turned her head and above her, Maalik's face came into view. She stilled her body as she took in those golden antlers, the dark spots where the whites of his eyes should have been visible. The skin on his cheek was cracked, revealing something glowing underneath. She hadn't been wrong; she was being held by a monster.

"You can let me go," she croaked.

Immediately he lowered her back to the bed, though he kept one hand on the back of her neck. "Are you alright?" he asked. She felt his gaze searching her face, an interesting sensation considering she couldn't see where he was looking.

She breathed in deep, savouring the feeling of being free from her caged body. "I think so."

"What was that?" he asked. "You started breathing so fast, it was like you were hyperventilating."

"A waking dream. I used to have them a lot when I was young. I couldn't *move*..." Her voice broke on the last word.

"You're fine now," he said, and she wasn't sure if it was a reassurance or a question, but she nodded just the same.

He hovered beside her bed a moment longer, like he

wanted to say something more, but before she could ask, he rose and made his way back over to the couch. He folded himself back against the wall and slipped into a silence that sent a shiver along Ailsa's back. There was little light in the room. Was he still watching her?

Turning her gaze towards the window, she lifted a hand and gathered her wavering strength. Slowly, very slowly, she dragged a finger across the sky, willing the clouds to part. It was hard work, like dragging them through syrup. She was so tired. But eventually, she pulled the wisps aside, allowing the moon to shine through the window and into the room.

She turned her head to look at Maalik again and found him huddled over, his face turned, staring outside.

"That was impressive," he murmured. His mouth quirked up at one side in a sardonic smile. "Trying to scare away the demons?"

"Only trying to see what the demons are up to," she replied, sitting up like him.

"Well, as you can see, I am not planning on how I will eat your soul," he bit out.

She studied him solemnly as he watched the stars outside. In the dark he was something of nightmares, though there was something beautiful about him too. The moon's glow turned him varying shades of grey, like a statue to a fallen god. Or devil.

"I'm sorry I woke you up," she muttered.

He turned his face to her then, his fathomless gaze raising gooseflesh on her arms.

"I don't sleep," he replied.

"Never?" Now that was a worrying prospect. Lying unconscious in a room with an alert demon…

He sighed. "Rarely. An hour at most."

"Is that all you need?"

Silence met her question and she waited, holding her breath.

After a long moment, he answered, "I need to sleep as much as you, but my mind won't let me."

She felt it then, the subtle change in the room, the weariness that emanated from him. The sadness.

And she knew then, because she had been the same once.

"You're afraid to sleep," she guessed.

"Yes," Maalik said quietly.

"Have you slept tonight?"

"No."

She paused, considering, warring with her thoughts. She couldn't believe she was doing this, making this offer…

How often had she wished someone would do the same for her?

"Move over," she finally commanded.

A low growl came from his chest. "Why?" he asked suspiciously.

She stood from her bed and began pushing it across the small room towards the couch he was on.

"What are you doing?" Maalik asked, sounding a bit panicked.

The shirt she was wearing slipped from her shoulder and she pulled it back up impatiently, standing tall and straight, ready for the fight she knew she was about to get into.

"Give me a hand."

"With what?"

She sniffed. Wasn't it obvious? "I'm pushing the bed and the couch together."

"Why?" he questioned, but he stood from his spot, hesitating.

"Sometimes it can help to have someone nearby when you're sleeping. Now, stop fussing and help me move the cot."

To her surprise, the demon came around the side of the bed and bent down, pushing with her until it was flush with the couch he had been sitting on. Ailsa climbed on, settling herself into the cushions and held out an arm for him.

"Come on then, lie down."

He blinked at her in disbelief. "Not still worried I'm going to eat you?"

She wrinkled her nose. "That would be extremely rude of you."

He watched her a moment later before heaving a sigh and lying down, as close to the edge and as far away from her body as he could. "I don't see how this is going to help…"

She relaxed a little, and scooted closer. "Just try to sleep," she said, reaching out a hand. He jumped when her fingers first touched his hair. It was like trying to pet a particularly angry kitten, though she would never tell him that. She didn't want to get scratched.

"What are you doing?" he whispered.

"My mother used to stroke my hair when I couldn't sleep. It helps…"

She tangled her fingers into his dark locks, marvelling at how a demon could have such soft hair. She could feel him tensing at first, but then slowly, as she stroked his head again and again, he relaxed, allowing her ministrations to pull him into sleep. She knew the moment he was unconscious because his breathing started to come in soft snores. And still she massaged his head, moving from his hair to those golden horns, feeling their ridges, and then down to his forehead. She watched, marvelling at how her pale hand looked against his dark skin. She ran a finger over one thick eyebrow and watched as his face twitched in a dream.

In his sleep, he nuzzled closer and her stomach jumped. Holding a sleeping Maalik was like taming a very cranky dragon.

Chapter 22

Angus couldn't sleep. Every time he tried to close his eyes, he found his father's face, shrivelled and blackened, as he had been before death. What was causing this illness? It was nothing like he'd ever seen before, even in the army when sickness managed to run rampant among the weak. He was inclined to agree with the villagers: it did seem like a curse. He hadn't thought much of it before when he had assumed it had come from Nerebus, but now it was in Eilanmòr? A small part of him wondered if it was best the village was cut off from the rest of the kingdom. Wouldn't that stop the spread? But no, Iona was right, they had to help these people. They had captured Ailsa and were now holding her whereabouts to ransom, but it was because they were frightened and desperate. Would he act any differently in a similar situation?

A noise from outside had him sitting up in bed, straining to hear it again. What was that? He held his breath, counting his heart beats. Nothing. *You just imagined it*, he told himself, lying back down.

There it was again. A faint tinkling, that sounded just

too strange to be natural. He swung his legs out of bed and grabbed his sword and boots, choosing to go out into the cool night without his cloak.

The moon overhead gave enough light to see no one was around. Whatever the source of the noise was seemed to be becoming more and more worked up. The tinkling became louder and louder as he crept down the street. He wanted to tell it to be quiet, so it wouldn't wake everyone else up, but a part of him knew no one else could hear it but him. He rounded a corner, keeping to the shadows. He imagined the windows of the houses were eyes, watching his progress through the village. He was nearing what looked like the town centre. Rustic signs pointed to shops which, during the day, would probably be bustling with people. A child's tricycle lay abandoned in the middle of the street, the sight making Angus's hair stand on end. What was it about abandoned children's things that were creepy?

He almost passed by a large building tucked away from the main thoroughfare, but something about it caught his attention. Creeping forward, he spotted it, around the side of the building. The door was glowing.

Angus held his breath as he approached the unassuming wooden door. He reached for the handle and it was warm in his hand. Angus opened the door and was blinded by the light inside at first. Once his vision had adapted to the brightness, he gasped at what he saw. Inside the barn sat creatures of every size. Green hounds seemingly made of grass began to bark as soon as they spotted him at the door. They strained against chains around their necks, trying to get to him. A cat made of stardust prowled inside a cage, glowing as galaxies collided on its fur. In the corner, a little boy with pointed ears was shaking. He lifted his head to look at Angus, revealing he didn't have a mouth.

"Oh gods," Angus whispered. Had this been where the villagers had kept Ailsa when they captured her? Had she been locked up like these fae, waiting to meet their fate?

Angus wished Iona was with him; she would know what to do.

"Free us," said a voice to his left.

Angus turned to find the speaker, but only saw the side of a horse. The beast was huge, and Angus was sure he would have noticed it first, had it not been curled in on itself, with only its brown side to the door. He stepped forward warily, looking around the horse for the mystery speaker.

"Who said that?" he asked.

The horse lumbered upwards, revealing its massive size. It swung its head round, into the light and Angus gasped. Above its cream muzzle and its intelligent eyes, a pure white horn protruded from its forehead. A unicorn, Angus's brain supplied.

The voice spoke again, and now it was obvious it was coming from the beast in front of him, though her lips were not moving. The voice was strong but calm. Somehow, it reminded Angus of his mother. "Please free us," it said. "We've been trapped here for weeks."

"How do I know you won't seek revenge on the villagers?"

"We were drawn here by the power in the river, then captured by these villagers. They were scared, and did not know what we were, only that we were fae. We just want to be free."

The unicorn stamped her huge foot impatiently. "You have my word, human. Not a single fae here will harm a villager."

Angus looked into the face of the unicorn, searching for a lie. The unicorn stared back unblinking and mysterious.

"I'm going to regret this," he muttered. Then he swung his sword on the lock of the nearest cage. The celestial cat broke free, darting out the door into the night. Angus hacked at the bindings, freeing one fae at a time. He wasn't scared until he got to the elf boy in the corner, who regarded him unblinking with large round eyes. He didn't move when he was freed, until the unicorn hissed at him and he slunk off out the door.

Finally, with sweat pouring down his back, Angus turned to the unicorn. It tossed its head impatiently, when Angus approached, but with a few swings of his sword, it was free.

The unicorn did not leave like the others had. She sniffed at the air around her and raised her gaze towards the door.

"The villagers are waking up. They'll know soon you set us all free."

"Yeah, well, I don't exactly care what they think."

"Thank you," said the unicorn, bowing her head. She still towered over him.

"You should go before anyone catches you and tries to lock you up again."

"I owe you a great debt. If you ever have need of me, I will endeavour to repay it. My name is Laire. Just whisper it to a silver birch tree, and I'll hear it." The unicorn then rose on her hindlegs, and gave a whinny, before thundering out the door.

Angus fought to keep his eyes from rolling. *Fae and their drama*, he thought as he trudged back towards his bed.

Chapter 23

"Don't you ever have a lie-in?" Ailsa asked as she watched Maalik wander about the small cabin, stuffing things into a pack.

The demon didn't look up. "I've got stuff to do. And I did have a lie-in, it's already eight." He looked much better rested than he had last night.

Beside the bed, something furry lurched upright and Ailsa fought back the scream behind her lips. Wulver had been sitting beside her, though for how long she couldn't be sure. She caught the wolf's eye as he stretched and Ailsa gave a start as he looked as if he winked at her.

"Wulver is heading out today too," Maalik said from the kitchen.

Ailsa threw the blankets off and stretched. "Why? It's not like you can't scare people off by yourself."

The demon sniffed. "He has his own job to do. If you're lucky you might catch him at it. Here, carry this basket for me."

Getting out of the warm bed was a battle in itself. *You're getting soft,* Ailsa told herself. *You were never this lazy when you lived by yourself.* She stumbled up to the kitchen, rubbing the dried sleep from her eyes. Overhead, something whizzed by and Ailsa caught a glimpse of a fat hairy body and buzzing wings.

"Is Muck coming too?" she asked. She wasn't sure which was worse: the hulking great wolf or the tiny bloodthirsty faerie.

Maalik handed her a woven bag, filled to the brim. "That's up to Muck. She never tells me if she's going to follow me; she just does whatever takes her fancy on that day."

"So you're saying Wulver does tell you?"

Maalik's brows knitted together. "Can't you hear him?" He shouldered another, bigger bag and went to kick on his boots.

Ailsa sucked on a tooth, sure that the demon was messing around with her. Not once in the last few days had she ever heard the wolf talk.

It was blowing a gale outside, and for once Ailsa felt like it had nothing to do with her. As soon as she stepped out, her hair whipped into her face, obscuring her vision. Even Wulver was having difficulty. The wolf dropped his head to protect himself from the wind, and Ailsa felt a little sorry, despite herself. *Wolves can't raise their hands to their faces to block out the wind.*

Ailsa closed her eyes and felt the air flowing across her skin. With a deep breath, she concentrated, imagining the wind slowing and turning into a breeze.

Calm, she thought at it.

The air gentled, turning from a roar to a whisper. The sound of the wind buffeting the trees quietened, replaced with noises of the forest at peace.

I did it! Ailsa opened her eyes to find Maalik staring at her.

"That was you?" he asked.

Ailsa nodded. "I'm a monster, remember?" she said, thinking back to their first meeting.

Maalik's mouth quirked. "What else can you do?"

"I'm not entirely sure," Ailsa said, wrinkling her nose. "I'm still trying to figure it out." She raised a hand to the sky, focussing on a cloud high above. With some effort, she pushed the puff over to the left, allowing it to collide with another cloud. They gave a satisfying crackle of electricity but then dissipated into a thin fog.

"Interesting," Maalik muttered.

Ailsa grimaced. "What?"

"It seems like you have some sort of power over the air particles. You make them rub together and charge, funnelling the static into lightning."

She snorted. "I have no idea what you just said."

"Here, give me your hands," Maalik reached out expectantly, but Ailsa gave him a dubious look.

He shook his head. If his eyes weren't black, Ailsa was sure he would have rolled them.

With a sigh, she extended her hands. Maalik's fingers

171

circled her wrists, turning them so that her palms were pressed together, like she was praying.

"See, imagine your hands are the air." He placed his own on either side of hers, pushing them so they moved together.

"If you rub the air together, like this, it causes friction. Do you feel how your hands are getting warmer?"

Ailsa nodded her agreement, watching their hands move. Maalik's were so much bigger and black as soot.

When he finally let go, she examined her skin, incredulous that the black had not transferred. She looked up to find Maalik watching her.

She coughed, taking a step back. "I think I understand a little better, but I'm not sure how a faerie could get these powers."

"Maybe you're just special? Perhaps it's a mutation?"

Her mouth twisted. "You're using words I don't understand again."

Maalik's lips looked like it wanted to copy hers. "Come on, we'd better get going. We have to swing past Mrs Malcolm's first, then I have a few people to make deliveries to." He stalked off and Ailsa watched after him for a moment before following. She flexed her fingers, still feeling them tingle.

A noise beside her gave her a start. Wulver was regarding her unblinkingly.

She fought the urge to stick her tongue out.

Ailsa followed Maalik into the forest, brushing her fingers through the lavender bushes that grew on the edge of the clearing. She raised her fingers to her neck, rubbing the fragrance of the plant into her skin. Hopefully, it wouldn't be too long until she could have a nice bath back in Dunrigh.

What have you become? She admonished herself. *A spoiled princess who can't stand a bit of dirt or a plunge in an icy river?* She wrestled with her pride. If she was truly honest, she'd sell her soul for those plushy palace beds and the food they served in Dunrigh.

Soon, they were back at the same little cottage from yesterday. Ailsa felt dread in the pit of her stomach. What state would the old woman be in now? She had been so frail the day before.

Maalik gave the door a knock before entering.

"Maalik, dear," croaked the old woman from inside. "You came back to visit."

She certainly appeared to be doing a little better. Ailsa peered around the door after Maalik and found the old woman sitting up on her couch. She was still tiny amidst all her blankets, but there was now some colour in her paper-thin cheeks.

Maalik smiled down at the woman. "Of course I did, Mrs Malcolm. I couldn't stay away."

And then the old woman gave a gummy grin. "Oh you."

"Mrs Malcolm, my friend from yesterday is still here helping. Is that okay?"

Ailsa stepped forward. "Hello."

"It was Ailsa, wasn't it?" said the old woman with a frown, as if she was trying to remember something from a long time ago. "I hope you're keeping young Maalik here on task, he's such a gossip, I can never get him to be quiet."

"Oh, erm..." Ailsa looked to the demon for help, but he just shrugged as he began to root around in his bag for something.

"She sounds pretty, Maalik," Mrs Malcolm said with a chuckle. "I hope you're not getting distracted from your duties."

Ailsa felt the tips of her ears heat. Yes, the old woman certainly was feeling better.

"Of course not," Maalik replied, reaching out to place the back of his hand on the woman's forehead. "Now, how's your chest?"

"Better now, thanks to you."

Ailsa hovered for a while behind Maalik, before giving up and going to the kitchen to make tea. The demon had brought some more milk and sugar along with him, so she made the tea extra sweet.

Behind her, Maalik was murmuring soothing words

to the old woman, every now and then letting out a chuckle when she said something funny.

Finally, Ailsa delivered her tea and Maalik stood up. "You're doing much better. We'll be back in a couple of days," he told her.

Mrs Malcolm pouted. "But I'll be lonely."

"Isn't your neighbour's son visiting tomorrow?" he asked.

The old woman grinned, slyly. "But he's not a handsome young man, like you."

Ailsa couldn't quite tell due to his darker skin, but she was fairly sure Maalik blushed. "You can't even see me, Mrs Malcolm."

"I can still tell," she said, settling into her blankets. "Ah well, I can wait a couple of days."

Maalik ducked his head. "Take care, Mrs Malcolm."

"Goodbye, dears."

They stepped out, and Ailsa shut the door after them with a click. "So…" she began with a smile.

"Don't start," Maalik cut her off.

"What?" asked Ailsa. "She's nice." She bumped him on the shoulder. "And she has a crush on you."

The demon pursed his lips. "Come on, we still have a lot more houses to visit."

Ailsa laughed, trying to come up with a tease, but someone came running through the forest. A young boy, barely ten-years-old, raced towards them. His face was red and covered in tear tracks and when he skidded to a halt in front of them, he had to take a few lungfuls of air before he could speak.

"Please... I've been looking for you all morning... my grandfather..." he choked on the last word, looking like he was going to cry again.

Maalik stood up straighter. "Lead the way," he said.

The boy turned around and half walked, half ran, back through the forest. Maalik followed behind, the bond tugging at Ailsa to do the same.

Ailsa felt dread pool in her stomach. Something told her that what she was about to see would not be happy.

Chapter 24

"What were you thinking?" asked the man with the pitchfork.

Angus did not back down. "You were keeping innocent fae against their will. I merely set them free."

From the moment that Iona had woken to muttered curses outside her room, she had been trying to catch up with the situation. It seemed that the prince had not had a restful night, instead choosing to walk around the village in the dark saving fae. Some of the villagers, upon realising this, had come calling for his blood. By the time Iona had dressed and made her way downstairs, Angus was already leaning against the kitchen table surrounded by a group of angry people. Brighid, for her part, was doing her best to be the voice of reason.

"We should never have kept any of them in the first place. It's a relief they're gone," she said.

The man with the pitchfork beat it against the ground once. "That wasn't up to him. They trespassed on our land and they were our prisoners."

Angus shot him with a cool look. "I am a prince of Eilanmòr and these creatures are my responsibility as much as you are. I was not about to let them continue to suffer because you're all superstitious idiots."

The man almost choked on his anger, sticking a finger in Angus's face. "You're not even in line for the throne. You're just some spare who will be forgotten about in a few years!"

Angus paled underneath his beard. *Time to intervene,* Iona thought.

"Enough," she said, stepping between the man and Angus. The villagers backed up away from her quickly. "We're here trying to help you," she continued, raising her chin. "We could just leave you to it, especially after kidnapping our friend. I'm sure there are other ways we could find her, that don't involve helping you."

Brighid held up her hands. "Please, don't listen to Tam and the rest. They're just scared."

"They're just eejits," replied Angus. "But luckily I care less about my ego than I do my friend. We'll help you but then we're done."

Brighid nodded, then rounded on the group of hecklers. "Out! Before you ruin everything."

Once they'd left, grumbling all the way, Brighid set about ladling some porridge into bowls for them. "I am sorry about that. And I'm sorry about keeping those fae. We had just seen so many of them and whenever we let them go, they just came back again. We didn't know what to do. I'm sorry to say they got off lightly."

"Did you kill any Unseelie that you found?" asked Iona. She already knew the answer.

Brighid sighed. "We killed any fae that tried to attack. I have no idea what makes one fae Seelie and another Unseelie."

Iona poured some milk on top of her porridge, drowning it. "You would if you just observed them instead of killing them straight away." How many good fae had they killed because they were defending themselves?

Angus stirred his porridge thoughtfully. "I wonder if the other fae know what's in the river? I really should have asked the unicorn last night."

"Unicorn?" Iona almost spat out her food. "I didn't know there was a unicorn."

"She was the one that convinced me to break them all free."

"Unicorns are extremely rare," Iona said. "And they're very particular with who they choose to speak to."

Angus gave her a grin. "Must be my animal magnetism."

"Now," said Brighid, dropping into a chair. "Once you've had some breakfast we'll head out. It takes about half an hour to get to the river."

"Will it just be us?" asked Iona with a frown. "How many people are coming with us?"

Brighid shrugged. "A few."

Chapter 25

This is what death sounds like, Ailsa thought. The old man was gasping for breath. She tried to block out the sound, but it was impossible.

Maalik was murmuring something to him as the demon rubbed a wet cloth on the man's forehead. "Would you hand me my bag?" Maalik asked, not taking his eyes off the man.

"Will he be okay?" asked the boy.

Ailsa handed Maalik his bag and he pulled out a bottle of something. "This will help for now," he told the boy. "But it's only going to get worse."

The boy hung his head, unwilling to look at his grandfather. So young, Ailsa thought again. He shouldn't have to go through this.

"Go get your mother," Maalik told the boy. "She'll want to be here."

Ailsa watched the lad nod, then sprint out the door. The flash of view of the outside revealed it was starting to rain.

"This is horrible," Ailsa whispered.

"This is life," Maalik replied, going back to mopping

the old man's forehead, now that his breathing had calmed. "All life comes to an end eventually. It's how you go that matters."

"I wish he wasn't in so much pain."

"Me too," Maalik said quietly.

In the end, the decision was made. The old man's daughter arrived, clutching her toddler in her arms, followed by the teenage boy. Her face was pale but resigned.

"Do whatever you need to, to end his suffering," she said.

And so Maalik did.

By the time it was over, the rain was pouring outside. Ailsa bit her lip and tried her best to move the clouds away so the family wouldn't be soaked through as they made their arrangements. She followed Maalik out the door and through the forest blindly, not caring where he was taking her. Finally, they reached his cabin, but instead of going inside, Maalik slumped down underneath a tree facing the house and put his head in his hands. His skin cracked, revealing glowing molten flesh in the fissures.

"Are you okay?" Ailsa asked the demon.

Maalik wiped his face and looked up at her. "It never gets easier."

Ailsa took a deep breath and then went to sit beside him, between the tree roots. They were silent for a while, listening to the raindrops drip onto the leaves above. The sky darkened with twilight though not a single star peaked through the thick clouds. Slowly the demon's skin knitted back together.

Maalik was so still, Ailsa thought he had fallen asleep. It was so hard to tell if his eyes were open in the dark. His arm was within reach, so she hesitantly stretched out her fingers until one brushed his smooth skin. He shivered. It was like holding her hands out to a fire. Ailsa shifted, so her whole body was closer to his, stealing his heat.

"Is this alright?" she asked.

He only gave a grunt in answer, but Ailsa took it as an affirmative and settled in closer to him.

"That was hard for you today," she said, not a question but a statement.

He grunted again and Ailsa felt his shoulders shift. She chewed on her lip. *Say something*, she told herself. She had never been adept at cheering people up. When her mother had died, it had been her brother who had comforted her.

Just say something.

"So what's the deal with demons?" Even to her own ears that sounded idiotic.

Maalik sighed. "What do you wish to know?"

"Do they all go around healing people?"

"Playing the Grim Reaper, do you mean?" He shook his head. "How do you feel about what I did?"

"He was suffering. You put him out of his misery."

"That's right. But that's the opposite of what most demons want." His mouth twisted. "They feed off evil deeds, but it can't be their own. Demons feed off the evil deeds of humans. We are parasites." He spat the last word out like a curse. "So if I was following my base nature, I would have tempted the youth in the cottage to kill his grandfather himself.

"Though the act itself would have had the same outcome—the old man would have escaped his pain— the boy would have spent the rest of his life in anguish over what he had done. This might have led him to wallow in remorse, or he might have found that he could kill again."

"People do evil things all the time," Ailsa said quietly.

"Which can sustain us for a while. But soon, the scales start to tip towards good deeds and demons find they have a little less life force. In that case, we must become a bit more direct. Wars are started, mass murders are committed. But then, there are less people and so fewer evil deeds. We must get the balance right. Most demons prefer to play the long game. Tempting a few souls to evil deeds over a long period is far more sustainable."

"But you killed the man before the boy had to."

Maalik balled up his hands and tilted his face to the sky.

"I will do anything I can to stave off evil. Unfortunately, that in itself is a balancing act. I can't be so obvious that I am caught, for one. I also can't stop all the evil deeds at once, or, like I said, war, mass murders, and so on. So I must work like the demons, except I prevent the evil deeds one at a time, so no one notices. It might not be much, but I'm trying."

Ailsa felt a pang of pity but also respect. It would be so much easier to just be what you're supposed to be. But here was Maalik, fighting his nature to save others. "What makes an action evil, anyway?"

"It can't be an accident. It must be done with malice in one's heart." He held out his hands in front of him. "For example, there are many reasons why you might kill an animal, and all fit along a scale. Perhaps it broke its leg and will never heal. If you killed it, you are saving it from a slow death from starvation. Though killing something is never to be taken lightly, that deed has come from a place of mercy. Now, if you were to kill an animal because you were defending yourself against attack, this would be neutral. You were acting in self-defence, and if you hadn't killed it, you would be dead. However, if you killed an animal for sport, or for a trophy, you have ended a life for your own glory and selfishness. This would be considered an evil act, and this is what would feed the demons."

"It seems like it's open to interpretation," Ailsa said.

"Who judges it?"

"Sometimes actions come down to debate. In these times, no one wins."

Ailsa considered this. "Are angels the opposite then? Do they feed on good deeds?"

Maalik's jaw tightened. "Yes, but what makes a good deed? Is killing a murderer good? Is stealing money from a shopkeeper to feed your family, even if they go hungry, a good deed? It's all about the motivation."

"It sounds complicated," Ailsa told him.

They lapsed into silence again, and Ailsa fought for something to say to break it. Finally, it was Maalik who said, "Let's go back to the cottage. I've got to make some medicine." He pushed off the ground, unbending his body. His shoulders still curled inward, as if he was carrying a huge weight on them.

Ailsa rose and followed behind, into the cabin. All was quiet inside; not even Muck was flying around making noises. While Maalik stumbled to the kitchen and started looking in his cupboards, Ailsa surveyed the room with a frown. How many times had the demon returned from a day like this to the cold and hush of his lonely home? She knew all about being alone, yet during her isolation, she had never had to deal with the same tough decisions. She had never once looked out for someone else. Maalik had probably met with more resistance at first than she had as a changeling, but he had obviously worked so tirelessly and been so unselfish that he now had a small community of humans who trusted him. How long had that taken? And still, he returned to his cabin every night and had no one to look after him.

Ailsa watched his back as he began to grind some herbs together. *Well*, she thought, *as long as I'm here, I'm going to look after you.* Hopefully, that wouldn't be for too long, but at least it would be something.

She strode to the fireplace, setting out kindling as she made a mental list of things to do. Once she had a fire crackling in the grate, she filled the kettle and hung it up over the flames. Next, she laid out two mugs and threw some tea leaves inside.

As she busied herself, she noticed that Maalik had stopped what he was doing, following her progress around the room.

"What are you doing?" he asked.

She came up behind him, and grabbed his arm. "Go and sit down," she ordered. "There's plenty of time for that later."

He didn't even fight her as she pushed him towards the couch and threw a blanket over him. Maalik eyed her carefully as she tucked him in and gave him a book she'd seen him reading the day before.

"I don't suppose I have a choice in this?" he asked.

She smiled at him sweetly. "Not if you know what's good for you."

She handed him a cup of tea. Muck chose this time to whizz out of her hiding space and tuck herself into Maalik's shoulder, where she snuffled his neck. Ailsa sipped her tea while leaning against the kitchen counter. She could feel the demon's black gaze on her.

"Thank you," he finally whispered. "You're being so nice to me. I never expected anyone to."

She blushed and raised her mug to him. "Here's to secretly and quietly preventing evil, and being nice when people don't expect it."

Maalik gave a chuckle. "Hear, hear."

Chapter 26

Iona eyed the crowd lining the riverbank and gave a *tsk*. '*A few*' had turned out to be most of the village, including the children. Many of the older adults were watching the water, looking worried, while the younger ones played and lounged on the grass like they were at a fayre.

"All we need now are some picnic baskets," she mumbled, rolling her eyes.

Angus gave her a sympathetic look—because he wouldn't need to do anything. It was going to be up to her to sort out this mess.

She turned towards the river. When Brighid had told them about it, she had pictured barely a stream with water lazily flowing, as if into a drain. The actual river was so wide and turbulent a human would have struggled to cross it, even if it had been gushing normally. But right in the middle, the water churned round and round into a huge whirlpool.

"Can you tell what's happening?" Brighid asked her over the thundering of the water.

Iona cast her power out to the swirling water, testing

it for resistance. It was so bizarre; she couldn't seem to control any of it. She could only watch and wonder as she felt the river being sucked down, down, down. To where, she wasn't sure.

And yet, she had a strange feeling. Whatever was causing it, whoever was causing it, it didn't mean her any harm.

"There's only one way to find out," she said firmly.

"I don't like the look of it, Iona," Angus murmured beside her.

"If I get rid of the thing, then the villagers will tell us what happened to Ailsa. If you've got another way, please enlighten me." She softened slightly. "I'm a selkie, Angus; it's not like I'm going to drown."

"You don't know what's down there. It could be a trap."

Iona kicked her shoes off. "The Bean-Nighe said I'd break the curse. You can trust a Bean-Nighe. Washer women don't lie."

The woman's words drifted through her head. *Family, friend, lover. One will die saving theirs. One will watch theirs die. One will betray the whole world to save them, yet it will be in vain.* But which one was she? A small, selfish voice told her she would do anything as long as Harris wasn't involved. But the Bean-Nighe's prophecy was a worry for later. Now she had to concentrate on navigating the whirlpool in front of her.

The water thrummed with power.

"I guess I'll see you on the other side," Iona said to Brighid as she stepped up to the raging river. A hush fell on the riverside as the villagers stopped their chatting.

The first step caught her off guard. It was surprisingly warm. Iona concentrated, willing her body to change shape to one more used to the water. She imagined her skin changing, becoming furred, yet sleeker. Her hands would turn into strong flippers, perfect for moving through water. Her eyes would darken, ready to see in the gloom.

But the change wouldn't come. Iona's long human legs were still standing in the river. She tried again.

Turn, she willed her body.

But there was nothing.

"I can't change into a seal," Iona growled in frustration. "Whatever it is won't let me."

"Can you still swim?" Brighid asked with a crease in her forehead.

"Of course." Iona sucked on a tooth. "My clothes will get wet, that's all." She hated being in the water when she was human, but it would have to do. Iona pulled her tunic over her head and threw it onto the riverbank, leaving her just in her undershirt and leggings. She pulled a piece of leather from her pocket and used it to tie her hair back. Her actions were tight and savage.

This body was not as skilled at swimming or holding

a breath, but she was still a selkie. She could do this. She waded in further until she was waist deep, then, taking a deep breath, ducked under. Immediately, the water changed from warm to biting cold. Pins and needles snaked up her fingers, but she pushed away at the sensation and swam further down. The pressure in her ears was building until she cracked her jaw, popping the bubbles.

You have seven minutes, at the most, she told herself as she swam. If she spotted the source of the whirlpool and needed more air, she could always resurface and swim down again.

Iona pumped her arms, descending further into the murk and gloom. The deeper she swam, the less light, but also the less debris floated in the water. Luckily, her vision was well-adapted to the dark. They scanned the river, looking for any disturbance. Sounds of water rushing filled her sensitive ears, but she was able to pick out something different up ahead. A faint chime of magic. Iona followed the noise, until she found the whirlpool.

The column of water condensed into a single point. Iona squinted her eyes to get a look at the origin. It was then that she felt it. The object called to every particle in her body, like a siren song.

"I belong to you," it said.

Iona paused a moment, cautioning herself. This could

be a trick; part of the curse that had the villagers trapped. But somehow, she knew it wasn't. Whatever was making the whirlpool was meant to be hers.

The selkie swam closer, feeling her lungs beginning to burn. You don't have long, she reminded herself. Yet, when she spotted the object, all thought of drowning went out of her mind.

It was vaguely bowl-shaped, yet irregular, roughly hewn. The outside looked to be made of dull rock. Two holes had been scraped into the sides, looking much like hand-holds. Three stone feet stuck out underneath, making it look sturdy in the swirling water. A pot. It looked like it could feed a whole village, it was so gigantic.

Iona felt she could easily fit inside. It wasn't until she was right beside it that she could look within. Her heart shot into her throat. Instead of the rough stone, beautiful pale blue crystal lined the sides. It had been polished until it was smooth and gleaming, looking almost like glass. Layers of periwinkle and gold agate shone in the dull river water.

Again, Iona had the same feeling: she was meant to have this. She reached out to touch it.

Something flashed white out of the corner of Iona's eye, but when she turned her head there was nothing there. She reached out again, fingers almost brushing the rim of the vessel, when something bashed into her side, knocking her out of the way.

Iona fought to keep the little air she had left from escaping her lungs. She looked up towards the pot, bewildered. Floating there was a woman.

A kelpie? Iona wondered, at first. But no, while the woman was beautiful, she was far too strange looking to pass as human. Her blue hair swept up from her head, revealing large protruding gills. The creature flickered between opaque and translucent, half water wraith, half ghost. *An ashray*, Iona realised. She had heard of these phantom water-fae, but had never seen one. They only lived in freshwater, well away from selkies.

It circled the source of the whirlpool, manoeuvring using thin filmy skin which joined her arms and legs together, like the wings of a skate. It growled, digging its fingers into the silt of the riverbed.

"Go away," Iona tried to tell it, speaking through her mind like all selkies did under water. It didn't seem to understand her. *Or*, Iona thought, *it isn't complying.*

The cauldron is mine, she spoke again, even if just to herself. Cauldron? Her mind had supplied the word, but now she knew that this was exactly what it was.

As she stared at it, it whispered its name. *The Cauldron of Life.*

Iona bared her teeth at the ashray. This vessel belonged to her; she could feel it. And she would fight for it with all the breath left in her body. Which was admittedly not much. She wouldn't let the ashray know that though.

The creature circled the cauldron, regarding Iona with pinprick eyes. Then, all of a sudden, the ashray launched herself at Iona, tackling her to the riverbed. The selkie was pinned down against the gravel for a moment, until she turned her head and bit into the arm of the other fae. It gave a metallic shriek as it wrenched itself away. With disgust, Iona noticed she still had a piece of the creature's oily flesh in her mouth. She spat it out and snarled at the ashray, waiting for its next move. But the ashray appeared to re-evaluate her. It tilted its head, treading water. Then, with a flurry, it darted off back into the gloom.

Iona ignored the burning of her lungs as she swam closer to the cauldron. *Mine*, she thought as she reached out towards it. *Yours*, she thought she heard it whisper to her as she touched the rim. Then it shook in her hands. Iona tried to break her grip on it, but she was stuck. Now, she could feel the unmistakable burning that signalled her breath was running out.

Let go, let go, she thought desperately. She thrashed and bucked against the cauldron, but it wouldn't let go. The more she pulled, the tighter its hold was.

I'm really going to die from drowning, she thought incredulously. A sad excuse for a selkie she was.

Her vision was beginning to blacken, but still she struggled on. The need for air was torturous. She felt her human body trying to force her to breathe, a deadly reflex. She knew it would only be inhaling water.

Then, the cauldron began to bubble. With a rumble, it shot towards the surface, dragging her by the hand. She watched as the light above got closer and closer, but everything was fuzzy and she was so deep still. With a groan, her body finally took over and water surged down her throat.

Chapter 27

Her brother was cuter when he was like this, thought the girl as the fluffy white seal pup snuffled about in her arms. He couldn't talk for one thing. As a human toddler, he loved to babble away, not quite making sense. He had learned a new word this week: "no". Everything she offered him was "no" even if he did want it. She'd caught him a perfectly good fish just half an hour ago and he'd told her "no", so she'd thrown it back. Now he was whining because he was hungry.

"You have to look out for him," their mother had said. "He doesn't have the power you have."

As far as the girl saw it, it wasn't her fault her brother had been born defenceless. Why did she have to look after him?

"I could teach you to swim," the girl said to the seal pup. He hadn't been in the water yet, but that didn't mean he couldn't. After all, wouldn't their mother be pleased when she saw that he was swimming for the first time? A selkie who couldn't swim was just a nuisance.

The girl slid the seal pup off her lap and transformed, changing her body so that it was lithe and strong and made for the water. Gone were her red hair and freckles, though she still had spots littering her fur.

The seal-girl inclined her head to the pup and slid gracefully into the water in front of them. She could feel the cold around her snout, but her fatty layers were thick and kept her warm. Her brother hadn't followed her in, so she poked her head back out to see him perched on a rock watching her.

"Come on," she told him. The seal pup could hear her in his mind, even if she couldn't say the words. Her voice was familiar and comforting, and so he dipped his nose towards the water. Unsure of what to do he leaned closer and closer, until he lost his balance on the rock and fell in with a splash.

The seal-girl tried not to laugh. She had enough humility to know she probably hadn't been any more graceful on her first venture into the sea.

Her brother licked his lips, tasting the salt for the first time.

The seal-girl nudged him towards the surface. "You have to come up to breathe. Like this," she said, showing him how to stick his nostrils in the air to suck in a breath. "You hold it and then you can swim."

It took a few minutes for him to get all his flippers under control, but it was faster than learning to walk. Once he'd learned to coordinate, he twirled and circled beside her, obviously enjoying himself.

That wasn't so hard, thought the girl. *I don't know why mother hadn't taught him sooner.* And now that he could swim, she wasn't stuck on the rocks babysitting him. She could go where she wanted, and he could just tag along.

It wasn't the best day to learn, she supposed. The waves were choppy, churning up the silt below, making the water murky.

"Stay close," she told the seal-boy. Keeping one eye on him, she swam further down and away from the rocks. He followed with a little difficulty, but did his best to stay by her side. Yes, she definitely preferred him in this form.

"Okay, why don't you try popping up to breathe by yourself?" she asked. He would need air before she did, and this way she could watch him try it on his own.

"No," he said, but began to swim upwards. She snorted, giving him a nudge in the right direction. The seal-girl watched with pride as the little white body floated towards the surface. She couldn't wait until her mother found out.

Then, she felt something in her whiskers—a vibration through the water. She stared into the murky sea, watching for movement. At first, there was nothing. Then, to her right she saw it. The distinct marking of an orca.

"Harris!" she screamed, swimming as fast as she could towards the baby seal. "Go!"

But the seal pup didn't know what she was saying. Up

above he had spotted a fin and watched, mesmerised as the big black thing came closer.

The huge body swam on the surface, spouting water in a huff through its blowhole. Its powerful tale pounded up and down, gaining on the baby seal. The girl rocketed after the whale, swimming as fast as her flippers would propel her.

Her brother watched, terrified, as the whale's jaw opened to reveal sharp teeth. The girl's heart leapt into her throat as it got close enough to swallow him with one gulp. Just as she thought he was going to be eaten, the seal pup shouted a definitive "no!" and dove down into the water. The orca wasn't quick enough, and its mouth closed around sea water.

The baby seal swam down and down, and the whale followed, gaining again. But the distraction had worked. The seal-girl managed to reach her brother, and before the orca could eat them both, she changed her form back into that of a human. Her red curls spread out around her in the water like seaweed and she pushed it away hurriedly as she struggled to see with her new eyes. It was so much harder to see like this. She was also so much worse at holding a breath. She rounded on the whale and raised a hand. Immediately, her powers rushed forwards, creating a rip tide. The whale screamed as it was pushed backwards, away from the girl and her baby brother, and far away from Struanmuir.

The seal pup nudged her back in thanks, but the girl's vision was getting fuzzier. It was only then when the whale was gone that she noticed how deep she was. She struggled to hold on to the last pockets of breath as she kicked her legs out behind her, too oxygen deprived to even think of turning back into her seal form.

This is it, she thought to herself.

But then her brother was there, pushing her up towards the light above. She managed to wrap an arm around his silky body as he swam upwards, more powerfully than she could as a human. The world was starting to go black at the edges of her vision, but then with a final heave, the baby seal pulled her above and into the air.

The woman drank the oxygen into her lungs greedily, coughing and spluttering all the liquid she had swallowed.

Her fingers found something hard and she grabbed onto it, too tired to keep herself afloat. Her brother had managed to bring her back to the boulders, jutting up from the sea floor.

A slapping sound beside her told her Harris had jumped out of the water. Big black eyes full of concern met hers.

She put her head down on the rock. "I'm okay," she wheezed. "But I'm never swimming underwater as a human again."

Above, the baby seal flopped down beside her with a huff. "No," he agreed.

Chapter 28

A wave crashed over Iona's face and then she was coughing up water. Her fingers gripped something sturdy as she spluttered. It took a long moment to realise where she was. Air flooded into her lungs between coughs. Air. That was impossible if she was still at the bottom of the river. Iona looked up to see that, indeed, she had made it back to the surface. But how did she get there? The answer became apparent when she studied what her hands were holding. They were grasping the lip of something made of mottled grey stone.

I'm inside the cauldron, she realised.

Iona uncurled her body, nestled inside the cauldron, which had grown since she had found it under water. It was floating in the river, yet staying in place where it had surfaced, instead of being swept away with the current.

"Iona!" someone shouted. She looked up to see Angus splashing through the water towards her.

"I'm okay," she croaked, trying to right herself within the cauldron. She managed to tip it enough that she could slide out, keeping one arm around the lip, feeling too tired to swim unsupported.

Angus reached her and grabbed her shoulder. Feeling Angus's hands on her made Iona realise how cold she had become.

He began pulling her back towards the bank. "What is that thing?" he asked, nodding to the cauldron dragging along behind Iona. As they moved, it appeared to shrink, getting smaller and smaller until she was able to tuck it under her arm.

"It was causing the whirlpool," she said. They'd made it close enough to the river's edge that she felt gravel underfoot. With shaky legs, she stood up, allowing Angus to take her weight. Now the cauldron was even smaller—the size of the bowl she'd had her porridge in that morning.

Up ahead, along the side of the river, the villagers were watching her progress with fascination. They chattered loudly, pointing to the middle of the water where the whirlpool had been.

"This belongs to me," Iona muttered to Angus, indicating the cauldron in her hand. "I don't want anyone taking it."

Angus frowned but opened the pocket in his trousers. "I'll hide it for you, if you like."

Iona gave him a relieved look and turned her attention back to the vessel. "Smaller, please," she told it. The cauldron shrunk again, until it was no bigger than a thimble. Iona felt a pang of possessiveness before she tucked it into Angus's pocket. *You'll get it back in a bit,* she admonished herself.

As soon as they reached the water's edge, the crowd cheered. Iona fought to control her shiver as she stepped out of the river. What she needed now was some dry clothes and a hot drink.

"Thank you," someone shouted.

"You've saved us," said Brighid with a smile.

"You don't know that," said Iona. "I just got rid of the whirlpool; it doesn't mean the curse has been lifted."

Brighid's jaw became tight. "Keep your voice down. Everyone is hoping that we're free. If we're not, then we can find that out later. For just now, let them celebrate."

Iona looked around the faces of the villagers, at the awe and gratitude she found there. Only a day ago they had looked at them with fear and suspicion. And they hadn't even known she was fae. How had they looked at Ailsa, with the changeling mark on her face?

"Tell us what happened to our friend and we'll be away," Angus grunted.

Brighid bit her lip. "She was left in the forest as a sacrifice to a demon who lives there. It was a day north of here."

Iona's jaw fell open. "A demon?!"

"It had been hanging around in the woods for months," Brighid explained, wringing her hands. "We hoped that if we gave it the girl, it wouldn't venture further south. We already had enough trouble with kelpies and doonies. We didn't want to have a demon to deal with too. We've had other demons in our forest before and they can wreak havoc on a town."

"So that's it then," Angus murmured. "She's dead."

"Ailsa won't be dead. It's the demon you have to worry about," Iona said fiercely.

"She'll be alright," Brighid said. "This demon that we sacrificed her to is a bit strange. We heard it's been healing sick people. I don't think it will harm her."

Angus shook his head in disbelief. "We have to find her!"

"We left her a day's ride north. That's a good place to start." Brighid looked behind her at the celebrating villagers. They didn't seem at all concerned about what they had done. "I'm sorry. I truly am. For so long we were tormented by fae, it just seemed like all of them were evil."

Iona snarled, "I hope you've learned that lesson, because if I ever hear of a good fae dying by the hands of anyone here, you will see how dangerous selkies can be." She smiled then, showing all of her white teeth.

Chapter 29

Ailsa woke to the dawn chorus of chirping birds and groaned.

"Come on," called Maalik from the kitchen. "We've got work to do."

Ailsa rolled over and mumbled into her pillow, "You know, I assumed demons would want to be out at night, not first thing in the morning." The bed dipped, causing her to roll into Maalik's side. "Ooh," Ailsa groaned, nesting in deeper. "Stay there, you're nice and warm."

"We need to go," Maalik said, giving her shoulder a shake. "And Wulver is coming with us today. He has to go to the same place."

Ailsa cracked open one eye, seeing that, sure enough, the great wolf was standing beside the door. "Fine," she relented. "But he better not be going to eat anyone."

Maalik snorted. "You're obsessed with eating people."

Half an hour later, Ailsa was up and dressed with a stomach full of oats. She had to admit that Maalik was a skilled cook. It still didn't make up for how early it was.

"Even the squirrels are still asleep," she moaned, stepping out of the cabin. Immediately, a cloud rolled across the sky to blot out the sun.

Maalik looked up and gave a chuckle. "You're already getting better."

Wulver ran ahead, then doubled back, as if he was waiting for them but had too much energy to walk at their pace. As Ailsa watched the wolf pad about the forest, she couldn't help admiring his sleek body and the power in those long limbs. She'd seen wolves before but never this close. *And never this big.* The packs she had come across on her travels had scarpered as soon as they'd spotted her. People were too dangerous to hunt. Wulver, though, was big enough to take down a human easily.

"What exactly does Wulver do?"

Maalik's forehead furrowed. "Aside from eating people?"

"Oh shut it," Ailsa said, going to push the demon's back. However, Maalik ducked out of the way before she made contact and grimaced.

"Sorry," he said. "I have a back injury."

Ailsa felt her ears go hot. "Oh, sorry," she replied awkwardly. *Stupid*, she admonished herself. He doesn't want you to touch him. Just when you were getting on well.

They walked in silence the rest of the way, which, thankfully, wasn't long. Soon, they came to a river and Maalik stopped. His smile had returned and seeing it,

Ailsa felt a little better.

"Take a seat," he told her, folding his legs under him on the grass. "Wulver's about to go for a swim."

"A swim?" she asked as she complied. "I didn't know wolves could swim."

"Technically he's not a wolf, he's fae. Anyway, you'll see."

Wulver loped down the bank, picking between the roots of the trees that overhung the water. He didn't pause when he met the river, just waded in until it was halfway up his legs.

"Watch this," said Maalik.

Ailsa thought for a second that Wulver was just going to stand in the fast-moving water. He was so still, he looked like a statue, carved from rock. But then, with a tensing of his muscles, he pounced and the water erupted in a giant splash.

"What just happened?" Ailsa asked.

The wolf continued to splash around, then he turned and emerged from the river, clutching something in his mouth. It was a huge salmon. The fish flopped around, gasping its dying breaths. Wulver trotted back to them, as if he was pleased with himself, and deposited the fish at Maalik's feet.

"He goes fishing?" Ailsa frowned. "Is that it?"

The demon took the fish and chucked it in the basket he'd been carrying, while Wulver ran back down to the river. "You'll see," Maalik said again with a grin.

Ailsa was getting a cramp in her leg from being crouched in the bushes for so long. Beside her, Maalik peered through the branches at the little house, holding a pebble in his hand.

"This is so stupid," Ailsa said with a huff.

"I'm just giving him a hand," Maalik muttered.

Wulver had run to the doorstep of the cottage with the basket of fish and dropped it there. Now, he ran back to their spot and ducked down beside them with a *flump*. He lay there, panting with his tongue out.

"Okay, ready." Maalik launched the pebble at the door with a smile.

Almost immediately, the door opened and a tiny blonde girl with pigtails stuck her head out. She looked around for whoever had knocked on the door before finding the basket.

"Look, mama," called the little girl. "Wulver left us some fish."

A tired looking woman appeared with a baby on her hip. "Well, you'd better tell him thank you."

"Thank you!" shouted the girl, then she ran inside with the basket, almost tripping over her feet in glee.

The woman paused for a moment, her gaze scanning the trees. Ailsa sunk down further into the bushes.

"Thank you," the woman finally said with a smile and went back into the cottage.

"And why," Ailsa asked, "couldn't he just wait at the door to give them the fish himself?"

Maalik stood, dusting himself off. "It's more fun this way. Usually he has to just leave the fish at the door, but I wanted you to see the family finding it."

Wulver gave a yawn and a stretch before standing to his feet too. From the spring in his steps, Ailsa could tell he was pleased with himself.

"There are so many families that Wulver helps every week. He has a knack for picking out the ones most in need. So," said Maalik in Ailsa's ear, "still think he's all big and scary?"

Ailsa huffed a laugh, despite herself. "About as big and scary as you."

Chapter 30

An angry Fear-Laith was a frightening sight.

When Iona and Angus found Gris and delivered the news of Ailsa's capture and sacrifice, Angus thought he was going to explode. Underneath all the grey fur, he could almost see Gris turn red.

"We have to find her. Now," Gris growled out, fixing Angus with a stare that told him the Fear-Laith somehow blamed him for this.

Nothing new there then.

"Well, there's no point marching off all willy-nilly into the forest," Iona admonished when Gris looked like he wanted to do just that. "The villagers told us they left her a day's ride north. Since we do not have a horse, it will take longer."

That stopped the Fear-Laith in his tracks. "What do you mean, *'we do not have a horse'*? Why is she here then?" He motioned a large hand towards some ferns and Angus felt his heart stop.

The plants shook and then snorted, and then the unicorn was rising elegantly to her feet. She was larger than Angus remembered. Not a delicate creature like all the faerie-tales said; she was muscled and sturdy, like the draught horses they kept back in Dunrigh. Her chestnut fur was gleaming in the morning light, and right in the middle of her white forehead blaze was an ivory, swirled horn.

"What happened to whispering to trees?" Angus asked her weakly.

"When I left the village, I came upon your friend here." Laire tossed her head. "He explained that you're looking for someone. I thought I would help."

"Oh my gods," Iona breathed, stepping forward as if in a trance. "I've never seen a unicorn in the flesh."

"I rescued her from the village," Angus explained. "Her name is Laire."

Iona blinked. "You named her?"

"She named herself."

"How do you know that?" asked Gris.

Angus frowned. "She told me."

"You can hear her?" Gris curled his lip.

"Can't you?" Angus laughed. Surely they were messing with him. "She said you told her about Ailsa."

Gris nodded slowly. "Well, she just appeared and then she didn't go away so I started talking to her. I did wonder if she could understand me..."

Angus turned towards the unicorn who regarded him with her huge brown eyes. "Why can only I hear you?"

But it was Iona who answered. "I've heard of this.

Unicorns can choose a human to ride with. It's rare. Usually they choose women."

Laire nodded her head. "I liked you."

"So this unicorn belongs to the prince?" Gris grumbled.

Laire stamped her feet towards the Fear-Laith, startling him. "He belongs to me."

Well great, Angus thought to himself as the unicorn settled herself to sit beside him. *Looks like I have an admirer.*

"So anyway, we have a horse." Gris tensed, watching Laire out of the corner of his eye. "Or, at least, a horse-like creature. We can get there quicker."

Iona shook her head. "Laire won't let anyone but Angus ride her. We still have to go on foot. Which means," Iona said, looking up at the morning sky. "We should get going as soon as possible."

"I know where the demons are found," Laire told Angus. "You just have to follow the hand-burns."

"Hand-burns?" But then a memory came into focus. He'd been far away, in a different forest, trying to find the Stone of Destiny with Ailsa and Harris. Ailsa had just told them the story of the footsteps that haunted her through the woods—which turned out to be Gris watching out for her—and they'd found a burn mark on a tree. In the perfect shape of a hand.

"I've seen one," Angus breathed. Then to Gris and

Iona, he said, "I know how we're going to find Ailsa.
Let's go."

He only hoped they wouldn't be too late.

Chapter 31

"So what are we up to today?" Ailsa asked as they picked their way through a particularly thick tangle of trees.

"We're looking for hawthorn trees. They grow mistletoe," explained Maalik.

"Mistletoe?" Ailsa laughed. "Are you planning on catching someone for a kiss?"

Maalik pursed his lips. "It's really useful. If I mix it with ivy it can be used to slow heart rate. Add it to skullcap and it can reduce anxiety."

"Isn't mistletoe poisonous?"

"All the best medicines are a little poisonous. You just have to get the balance right." Maalik wiped his forehead with the back of his hand. The day was getting hotter, with the sun beating down.

"It seems dangerous." She pulled at the air with her fist, bringing a cool breeze to blow over them.

"It's the only thing I have. So far, I've always erred on the side of caution. I'd rather I didn't kill my patients with the herbs. I wish I could do something more, but without magic..."

"I don't imagine that's a gift many demons have," Ailsa said casually. As soon as the words left her mouth, she knew it was the wrong thing to say.

His face darkened. "No. It isn't."

The silence stretched on after that. Ailsa tried to reason it was because the path was ascending steeply uphill, but she knew Maalik was absorbed in his own thoughts. *He can be so melancholy sometimes.* She was starting to develop a habit of putting her foot in her mouth.

"You know," Ailsa said, her breath huffing from the incline. "You'd never run out of your herbs if you grew them. It's not like you don't have room."

His jaw clenched. "I'd have no idea where to even start."

"I could help you get it started, if you want?" Ailsa offered. "I used to have a garden."

Maalik looked sideways at her. "Yeah, that would be great. I think I have a book that might be useful somewhere..." He reached out a hand to steady her elbow as she fought up an especially steep part.

"A gardening book?" she huffed.

"Yeah, do you want to have a look?" A smile was beginning to play around his lips.

He's being kind, she reminded herself. *He doesn't know.* "I can't read, I'm afraid," Ailsa told him.

His eyebrows creased together and Ailsa waited

for the pity, the derision. It was obvious Maalik loved reading, the cabin was packed with books.

Instead, he just shrugged. "We can have a look together then. I'll read and you can tell me if any of it is wrong."

Ailsa felt her mouth pop open. "Oh, yeah. I'd like that."

Maalik smiled, and it was like a cloud had gone from his face. "Maybe when we're back this afternoon, we can start having a look at planting?"

Ailsa couldn't help returning the grin. "You'd better get those muscles ready, then. Gardening's hard work."

It took longer to find the mistletoe after that, because Ailsa kept stopping to point out shrubs. Maalik didn't seem to mind though. They collected seeds from those varieties they could, and clippings from others until the demon had a pack full of potential plants.

He never lets up, Ailsa thought with a chuckle as they sat down to have their lunch. Maalik had peppered her with questions the whole walk, and was now talking animatedly about which herbs he would find useful. Ailsa had the feeling he was like this with every new piece of knowledge. Despite being pitch black, there was a lightness behind the demon's eyes now that he was absorbed in learning.

Ailsa realised she had been staring at him when he blushed.

"What?" he asked, with a self-conscious laugh.

"Sorry." She felt her own cheeks heating in return. "You look happy."

Maalik considered this. "I guess I am. It feels rare these days. Thank you for the distraction." Then he grinned, his teeth white against his dark skin.

Ailsa felt her stomach flip. "You're welcome. I'll try to distract you more in future."

"The ground is too hard at the moment. We need to dig it all up, put some air into it, before we can add the seeds."

They had arrived back at the cabin mid-afternoon and Maalik had immediately begun pestering Ailsa for ideas. He had a notebook in one hand and was writing notes as he sat on the ground, listening to her advice.

Ailsa kicked at the dirt to the south of the house, where she'd picked out a spot to get started. "At the beach I had to add some mulched leaves to the soil, but this stuff should be okay. Since it's in the forest, it's probably a lot richer than coastal soil."

"How did you learn all of this without books?" Maalik asked in amazement.

Ailsa just shrugged. "Trial and error mostly. I learned a little from my mother when I was younger. She grew vegetables in our garden."

"I wish I'd learned something so useful," Maalik said

wistfully. "Should I grow vegetables too?"

Ailsa couldn't help but laugh at his enthusiasm. She didn't think she'd ever seen him so wondrous. "Let's start off small for now. A few herbs would be good."

He added something else to his sketchbook, sticking his tongue out between his lips. Ailsa watched his mouth, mesmerised, until something small and furry came zipping past.

"Hello, Muck," Maalik said without looking up.

The brownie flew to his shoulder, inspecting what he was drawing, but she quickly grew bored of that and began darting between the flowers around the clearing's edge, chasing fat bumble bees and butterflies out of the blooms.

Maalik sighed, and mumbled something that sounded like "*I can't take her anywhere.*"

One bumble bee buzzed lazily around his head and he watched it in thought. "I've always toyed with keeping bees," Maalik said as it flew off. "Did you know honey is a natural antibiotic?" When Ailsa didn't answer, he looked up, finding her confused expression. "It stops disease," he explained.

"Oh, yeah, I did know that," said Ailsa. *Just use simple words.* "My mother was a beekeeper. She used to sell honey in local markets. I spent my whole childhood with cuts covered in honey."

"Sounds... sticky," he wrinkled his nose. When she

ducked her head and didn't answer, he backtracked. "Sorry, I didn't mean to make fun. You said your mother *was* a beekeeper. Has she retired or…?"

"She died."

Maalik nodded. "I thought so. You have this weight around you. I know what that feels like. Was she your only family?"

"I have a brother, but I don't know where he is." She took the spade he'd provided and chopped a divot into the soil. Anything to keep her hands busy. "For so long I was alone, and I thought I liked it. But then Harris and Iona and Angus came into my life. I guess I finally understood what I was missing."

"I don't blame you for being so desperate to find them again."

She was reaching the harder undersoil, so Ailsa drove the shovel in with her foot. "What about you? Do you have any family?"

"Long dead. And far away from here. Distance and time are great healers. Do you want some help?"

"Nah, I'm just testing the soil further down. I want to see what the drainage is like." She gave him a half smile. "Keep talking, it'll make the work go faster. What was your favourite food as a child?"

"Candied dates." He stuck his pencil behind his left ear. "What's your favourite colour?"

Ailsa shrugged. "It changes. Sometimes it's blue like

the ocean, sometimes it's bright pink."

"And now?"

She hit a clump of rocks and had to grit her teeth as she answered. "Am I allowed to say black? Is that a colour?" Black like the night sky. Black like the sea in the dark. Black like—

"It doesn't matter, if that's what you like," he answered.

"What's yours?"

He raised his head, taking in his surroundings with obsidian eyes. "Forest green. When's your birthday?"

"September 5th. I'll be twenty." Ailsa paused. "Though, I suppose it isn't really."

Maalik frowned "What do you mean?"

Ailsa spoke slowly, puzzling it out herself. "I'm a changeling. So much—my birthday, my family, my appearance—is stolen from the child I replaced." She looked up at the demon feeling suddenly very lost. "I don't know who I am anymore."

Maalik beckoned her over. "Come on, take a break."

Ailsa dropped the shovel and came to sit beside him, basking in his heat as the sun began its descent.

"There is so much of you left after those things," Maalik murmured. "Your knowledge, your interests, the friendships you've made."

"I guess."

He reached out an arm, wrapping it around her slender shoulders. "Why don't you choose a new birthday?"

She snorted. "Just like that?"

"Why not? It can be just yours. I'll give you one, if you like?"

She smiled tentatively. "Okay."

"Let's say it's the 15th of July. That's a month from now. And by then, you'll hopefully be free from this curse, you'll have saved Harris and you'll probably have a big party in Ephraim to celebrate. You can wear a big pink dress. Or a black one if you'd rather."

"Will you come along?" Ailsa asked, licking her lips.

Maalik frowned and dropped his arm. "In spirit, yes. It's too far away to be there in body. My soul is trapped. I can't go that far from it."

"Where is it?" Ailsa asked.

Maalik's face shuttered. "Hell."

Hell? He couldn't possibly be serious?

"I think we're done for today." He rose, stretching his legs. "Come on, Muck," he called to the brownie. She flew after him as he went inside the cabin without a backward glance.

Idiot, Ailsa cursed herself as she stood to follow. *Where else would a demon's soul be?* She hadn't thought demons would have souls, and yet... Maalik wasn't how she'd imagined other demons. Of course he would have a soul.

"Maalik," she asked quietly as she entered the house. "Is Hell a real place?"

He had his back to her, beginning to shop some vegetables for dinner. "Unfortunately, yes. And it's closer than you'd think."

"Then can't you just steal your soul back?" she whispered.

"It's being guarded by other demons." He turned to her then and lifted a corner of his lips, so she knew he wasn't angry at her for asking. "And believe me, they're not all as nice as me."

"And you truly are terrifying," she tried to joke, with an answering smile.

"Funny," came his sarcastic reply. Yet, when she sidled up beside him, he handed her a potato and a knife silently. "Thanks, Ailsa. Not just for helping with the planting. It's been a long time since I had someone to talk to."

At this, Muck zoomed around his head, her buzzing reaching a higher pitch.

"Someone that isn't a tiny annoying brownie or a wolf who sleeps all day, I mean," he chuckled.

"You're welcome," Ailsa replied. "I know what it's like to be alone."

Chapter 32

Sunlight streamed in through the small window, illuminating the kitchen in a soft glow. Maalik was pottering around, still with bed-mussed hair. It curled around his golden antlers like ivy. Ailsa watched him move around the cabin, unwilling to interrupt the peace of the morning.

"I know you're awake," he finally said with a smile.

Ailsa stretched and swung her feet out of the bed. "Sorry. What time is it?"

"An hour after sunrise. I made eggs."

Ailsa dropped into the seat at the table and Maalik placed a plate in front of her. She shovelled a forkful into her mouth before muttering a quick thanks.

"No problem. You'll want to eat up. I don't have any call-outs so we're spending the morning training."

Ailsa swallowed. "Training what?"

Maalik smirked. "Training you. If you're going to walk into Ephraim and not get your ass handed to you, you're going to need to practise using your magic."

The food turned sour on her tongue. "My friend, Gris, was trying to train me before and I was rubbish at it."

"I've probably been around a lot longer than your friend has," Maalik said. "Let's just give it a try, alright?"

"Fine," Ailsa mumbled. "I'll try not to zap you with some lightning."

Once they'd finished food, Ailsa scrubbed at the plates until they were sparkling. Then she made the bed and folded the previous day's clothes. But too soon all the chores were done and Maalik was pushing her out the door and into the forest beyond.

Ailsa had expected to begin practising in the clearing outside the cabin, but it appeared that Maalik wanted her further away from his house.

"Tell me something else about you," he asked as they hiked through the foliage. "Just about you."

She huffed, giving him a sidelong glance. "What do you want to know?"

"What did you want to be when you were older? When you were little I mean?"

"A cat."

"I'm being serious," he snorted.

"So am I," Ailsa laughed. "Okay, I guess I wanted to be like my mother, making something useful. Though if you'd asked me when I was eight, I'd have said a princess."

"Ironic."

She gave a grunt in affirmation.

Maalik pushed a branch to the side so she could pass. When he let it go, it snapped back into place, making the leaves shiver. "And now?"

"Happy," Ailsa said without hesitation. "I want to be happy. What about you?"

His forehead wrinkled below his gold antlers. "It was so long ago. I'm afraid that you're looking at an old man."

That brought Ailsa up short. "You look my age."

"This was the age I was when I... died," he said, gesturing down to himself.

Ailsa was beginning to see a pattern. Every time she asked Maalik about being a demon, his face would shut down completely. Yet, she couldn't help but ask: "Is that how you got like this?"

Indeed, his cheeks drained of colour. "More or less." With a cough, he changed the subject. "I think I wanted to be a doctor. I remember seeing them helping people in my village and I really looked up to them."

"Well, you're doing that now."

He sighed. "I'm trying."

"You said you're from Kemet? I've always wanted to go there." Her brother had kept a map of Ossiana above his bed in their mother's house and she had spent hours with him imagining adventures in far off lands. From the pyramids of Kemet to the icy tundra of Visenya, they had planned a world trip. Ailsa had always been fascinated by stories of the lush rainforests of Edessa, while Cameron had wanted to see their inventions. It had never occurred to them to see Eilanmòr first. *Well,* Ailsa thought, *I'm seeing it now. Maybe one day I'll get to see the rest.* "Will you teach me some Ancient Kemetian?" she asked.

His forehead creased. "What do you want to know?"

"Start with the basics."

"*Khére* is hello."

"*Khér-e,*" Ailsa said slowly.

"Maalik *pe pa-rán,*" he said, gesturing to himself. "You would say: *Ailsa pe pa-rán.*"

"Oh gods." She shook her head. "You've already lost me."

"It's okay, it's tricky. People in Kemet speak the common tongue of Ossiana now."

"Well, I think old languages are cool. I tried to teach myself some Eilanmòrian, but it's hard when you don't read. Sometimes my words aren't exactly right."

"Have you ever wanted to read?"

She shrugged. "I'd rather have someone read *to* me."

"Well, if you ever want to learn—" Maalik cut himself off. "I'm sure there are plenty of people that'll teach you."

"Would you teach me one day?" she prompted.

"Soon the curse will be over, and I wouldn't blame you if you never wanted to see me again."

Ailsa snorted. "Don't be daft. You're not that ugly." When Maalik ducked his head and frowned, she reached out a hand to grab his arm. "Sorry, it was a joke."

"No, I know. I just wish I wasn't like this. I do think I

was pretty handsome, you know, before all this."

She tsked. "You're not exactly disgusting."

"I don't agree," he replied, before lengthening his strides. She had to half-run to keep up after that, unable to carry on their conversation.

Finally, Maalik was satisfied they were far enough away that she wasn't about to explode any of his belongings, then turned to face her. It looked like he'd pulled himself out of his thoughts for now, which Ailsa was extremely glad of.

"This'll do." He gestured around the glade. "Whenever you're ready, go for it."

Ailsa bit her lip. "Should I be, I don't know, stretching or something?"

Maalik's thick eyebrows raised above his black eyes. "Do you usually stretch before doing magic?"

Instead of answering, she stuck out her tongue before turning away. Around the clearing, bluebells waved lazily in the breeze. She felt the wind in her hair and imagined it picking up, rustling the trees until the noise became deafening. But that wasn't useful. Gris had taught her that.

Instead, she looked down at the earth and tried to feel its power under her feet. She held out a hand, willing it to obey her command like the wind always did.

She could feel the particles of air between the grains of rock and dirt, but they were trapped under the weight.

Come on.

"What are you doing?" Maalik had come closer, peering at her with confusion.

Focus. Ignore him. "I'm trying to call on my power?" Ailsa told him through gritted teeth. *Can't you see I'm trying to concentrate?*

"I thought you could control the weather? Shouldn't you be looking up?"

Ailsa groaned. "Apparently it's not very faerie-like. Gris said I had to channel it in a better way."

He gave a short laugh. "And how has that been going for you?"

"Not well," Ailsa gritted out. "You said you'd help me." Her cheeks burned.

Maalik must have noticed that she wasn't in a joking mood because his voice became soft. "I can't help you be something you're not," he said.

She finally raised her head up from the ground and looked at the demon. "What does that say about me, though?"

"Worry about that later. For now, just think about staying alive when you get to Ephraim." He pointed up to the sky. "I know you can control the wind, so focus your attention up there first." Maalik gave her a half smile. "Show me what you've got."

Ailsa huffed at the rolling clouds. It wasn't hard to imagine a storm closing in, she felt like it was already happening. Her annoyance was crackling in the air. Time to show the demon what she could do.

She raised her arms to the skies, concentrating, feeling the answering pull of the air. Using this power was getting easier and easier. It was hard to believe that she hadn't even known she'd had it until a few weeks ago. Something inside felt lighter as the wind rushed around her, answering her call. With one hand she pulled a gust down so that it swirled at her feet, then let it fly up into the sky.

"Can you move the clouds up there?" Maalik called.

Ailsa grinned and sent the air to the mist above. With a flick she sent it towards one cloud, chasing it across the sky. She used her other hand to push another one in the opposite direction.

She was starting to get giddy. Ailsa felt her laughter building up inside her as she pushed the air around above. She pulled a gust down and then let it spring back up towards the puffs of white.

"Now," said Maalik. "Try grabbing those two big ones."

A couple of darker clouds were floating on opposite sides above them. Ailsa reached for each with a hand and felt the magic tingle down her arms. These clouds crackled with static, ready to storm when given the right pressure. Ailsa pulled them together, the energy thrilling down her spine.

Yes, whispered a voice.

Ailsa felt dread wash over her. *That voice.*

The control she had on the power slipped her grasp.

The clouds above lost their momentum, but it was too late. They crashed together with a boom. Lightning crackled above, building between the vapour.

"Get down!" Ailsa shouted, grabbing for Maalik's arm. Just in time, they hit the floor, as a fork of electricity crashed into the tree above, slicing through the bough with a crash. It tumbled to the ground, right where the demon had been standing.

Ailsa waited for her heart to start beating again as she surveyed the damage. Dust and leaf litter floated in the air, like a bomb had gone off. Maalik lifted his head beside her, his mouth popping open in surprise.

"Are you alright?" Ailsa asked him.

"What happened?" the demon gulped.

"I... lost control." She sat up and wiped a hand over her face. "How am I going to defeat the most powerful Fae in Eilanmòr, if I can't even control myself?"

"What did it feel like?"

"What?"

"Well, we have to know how it felt to lose control so you can recognise it in the future. "

"It just…" She sucked on a tooth. "There's this voice."

"A voice?"

Ailsa could feel Maalik's gaze darting all over her face

in confusion. "I'm not crazy. It only happens when I'm trying to use magic."

"Interesting."

"What?" she asked, her voice giving a slight growl.

Maalik sat back. "You have a spirit guide. Another consciousness linked to your power."

"Like a parasite?" She couldn't help remembering the insidious feeling of the Brollachan possessing her body.

"Is that what it feels like?" Maalik asked. "As far as I'm aware, they're supposed to be helping you. Most people would say having a guide is a real gift."

"Well, she is completely bloodthirsty. She wants to destroy everyone. I almost killed three boat loads of captives a few weeks ago."

"Sounds like you just have to agree what the boundaries are. At the end of the day, it's your body, your magic. You have to learn to control it so she can't control you." Maalik scratched his chin, sizing her up. "I think that's the first step—let's talk to her."

"There, that should do it," Maalik said, placing the candle on the ground between them.

Do what? Ailsa wanted to ask but she couldn't quite get the words out.

Maalik regarded her for a moment, then reached out and lifted her chin with a crooked finger. Ailsa's heart missed a beat as those black eyes stared into hers.

"Can we talk a moment?" he murmured. "I need to speak to whoever else is in there with Ailsa."

"Yes?" said a wheezing voice, to Aila's shock. Her gaze darted around for the source, but the sound didn't come from around them. It came from Ailsa's own mouth.

Maalik's grip on her chin tightened. "What's your name?" he asked.

"Ishbel," it replied, using Ailsa's mouth.

She tried to shrug off Maalik's hand, but Ailsa realised, in a panic, that she couldn't control her own body.

Too much, she thought. *Too much like the Brollachan.* But she had no control, no way to tell Maalik this. And with the gleam in his night-dark eyes, she wasn't sure he would listen anyway.

"Ishbel," he repeated back to the entity.

"Why have you called me, boy?" the voice asked.

Maalik let out a breath. "Ailsa wanted me to. She hoped that you could be a little less bloodthirsty in the future? It seems like you've been putting her off."

"I do not understand."

"She said you tried to wrestle control. She almost killed some innocent people."

"No one is innocent."

There were children on that boat, Ailsa tried to shout back, horrified.

"Ishbel," Maalik fixed her with an even stare.

"Why are you here?"

"To protect," replied the voice.

Maalik frowned as he seemed to think about this a moment. "Really? And what about if I use this?"

To Ailsa's dismay, she watched as the demon produced a wicked looking dagger from behind his back.

The voice inside her hissed. "You do not touch her," it said through gritted teeth. "I will kill you."

"Oh yes, and how will you do that?"

One of Ailsa's hands raised jerkily off her knees and reached towards the sky. "Her power is my own. I will kill you before you can hurt her."

"I'm not going to hurt her, but you are hurting her, whenever you take control."

"You do not touch her," repeated the voice.

Maalik stabbed the knife into the dirt between them as thunder cracked somewhere in the distance. He raised his hands in a show of defeat, watching Ailsa's face the whole time. "I will not touch her," he agreed.

Ailsa's hand lowered again, now that the danger had passed. Inside, Ailsa thrashed against her body, willing it to obey her command again.

"She can protect herself," Maalik said.

"She is just a child."

"Then teach her," Maalik said. "Teach her to use her power. But she has to have control."

Ailsa waited, counting her body's breaths as they went

in and out. She felt her own nose wrinkle without her command. Her hand raised again, as jerkily as before, but this time it found itself to the side of Maalik's face. Her palm cupped the skin on his cheek, but she couldn't feel it.

"You despair," the entity croaked out.

Maalik froze.

"Poor little bird lost its wings," the voice crooned as Ailsa's thumb rubbed back and forth over the demon's stubble. "But don't worry," it said. "It'll get them back soon. Stick close and you'll see."

The demon gaped at her, his jaw working to form a sound, almost like he was possessed himself.

The entity forced Ailsa's lips into a smile. "Fishes are not attractive. Try harder."

Maalik's mouth closed with a snap. "Will you let her have control in the future?" he gritted out.

"I'll try," said the entity.

Ailsa watched as her hand slid from Maalik's face, and then the world tilted backwards.

Ailsa stared up into the leafy canopy as she felt her body slowly come back to her. The thing—Ishbel it had called itself—had retreated. It was still there, though, somewhere in the back of her mind. Ailsa groaned as she tried to sit up again, finding her body foreign at first.

When she had finally righted herself, she looked across the forest floor to where Maalik was sitting. He had his legs tucked under himself, almost like he was getting ready to run. He stared at the knife still stuck into the ground in front of him, completely still except for the muscle ticking in his jaw.

"Maalik?" Ailsa whispered.

It didn't seem like he had heard her.

Ailsa tried again. "What was it?"

The demon scrubbed a hand over his face before replying. "One of your ancestors, I assume. That's who the guides usually are. A powerful one, too, since she was able to use your body so easily."

"Could she do it again?"

"It seems like she just wants to protect you. I don't think you have to worry about her." Maalik got to his feet and dusted the twigs from his trousers. "We should probably start heading back."

"And what did she say about birds?" asked Ailsa, rising to follow him. "And fish? She sounded crazy to me."

The demon raised his head towards the leaf canopy ahead. "Meddling," he murmured, before setting off through the trees.

Ailsa looked down, realising Maalik had walked off without the candle. She picked it up and blew it out before feeling the tug of their bond pulling her behind him.

Chapter 33

If I don't do something soon, I'm going to die in this cell.

It had been days—*days*—since he'd arrived in Ephraim and been thrown in with the strange prisoner. Aside from when they delivered a couple of meals a day, he hadn't seen a guard. His companion hadn't spoken, except to inform him when he needed to relieve himself in the bucket, and he didn't look very well either.

I need to get out of here.

It was midday and they hadn't had their morning meal yet. Just when Harris was about to begin shouting, the sound of footsteps echoed down the corridor outside the cell.

"I want to speak to the Queen," Harris said as soon as the guards came round the corner.

His cell companion jumped at the sound of his voice, then curled up further on the ground, trying to make himself as small as possible.

With a groan, the intertwined branches around the door peeled back, leaving a gap that revealed the grotesque faces of the Unseelie courtiers. The one in front, possibly the ugliest, ran a thick tongue over the surface of one of the tusks peeking through his bottom lip. "You first," he growled.

Harris did his best to fix a charming smile upon his face. "I hope the Queen won't mind how I look," he said, gesturing to the tattered clothes hanging from his body.

"The Queen won't be seeing you today," grunted the faerie in front. "She's busy."

"Then where am I going?" asked Harris, hopefully. Maybe I'm getting cleaned up?

"Interrogation," answered another fae. It stepped forward, making a clacking sound. As it moved into the torchlight, Harris got a glimpse of its back, which was completely covered in rattling shells. A shellycoat, he realised. The creature resembled a human, but its limbs were slightly too long. Huge protruding ears would have given its face a comical look, if not for its wide, manic grin that sent a shiver up Harris's spine.

He tried to calm his racing heart, aiming for a nonchalant demeanour. "Interrogation for what?"

The shellycoat laughed. "We want to know where the princess is and we're willing to do anything to get the answer." It came closer, extending a long finger at Harris's chest. "Unless you're willing to tell us where you took the child now?"

"What child? Nicnevan's? I've told the ceasg and the nuckelavee: I have no idea what happened to her. I was too young when she was taken, no one told me anything."

I can't believe I'm getting blamed for this.

"That is what the Queen thought you would say. So until you confess, you'll spend your nights in this jail cell," said the shellycoat with an evil grin. "And you'll spend your days with us. We can be *very* persuasive."

Harris looked between his captors. None of them looked particularly pleasant company. "Let me see the Queen myself. I had no part in her daughter's disappearance."

"Her daughter's *kidnap*," growled a jailer from the back. A huge cloaked figure stepped forward, illuminating its ghastly face in the torchlight. It was covered in thick yellow fur and had no nose, just a hole where one should be. It opened his jaw wide as it spoke, revealing a snaking tongue. "The princess was stolen by you selkies. She was ours, our future queen, and now she's gone because of you. Even if you don't have a hand in her kidnap, it was your family who planned it, and I will happily let you rot in hell."

With that, the group of jailers surrounded Harris and dragged him upwards and out of the prison. The guards at his side kept their bruising holds on him throughout the walk up from the earthy cell to the gloom of the forest. Harris tried his best to summon enough bravado and charm as he was pulled further into the Unseelie Court.

The company Nicnevan kept was far from savoury.

Harris tried not to stare at the fae as he was led through them, but he couldn't switch off his other senses. The smell of rot and decay cloyed around his nose. He shivered as he was led through hot and cold spots, the temperature change like being pelted with buckets of water. Even for a selkie, it was terrifying. He thought briefly of the human back in the jail cell and wondered how he'd managed to keep his sanity.

At least I might still manage to meet Nicnevan, Harris told himself. She had to be around here somewhere. The Queen was supposed to be chained to an old willow tree, deep within her court. If he could just get to her and explain, surely he'd be able to make her see sense.

I could always offer to go and find her actual daughter, Harris thought. It couldn't be that hard to find a changeling hidden somewhere in Eilanmòr. He'd briefly entertained the idea that Ailsa could be the lost faerie daughter when he'd met her, but he doubted someone so important would be left to fend for themselves for so long. No. Nicnevan's real daughter would be looked after; guarded. It would be hard for an Unseelie to get to her, but a Seelie like Harris? He would be able to explain everything.

And then what? He asked himself. If he found Nicnevan's daughter, what if she didn't want to meet her mother? What if she was corrupted, like his family had thought all those years ago? Everyone deserves to have that choice. If the princess wanted to meet Nicnevan, he would escort her to Ephraim. Maybe she would convince her mother to kick out all of the Unseelie. On the other hand, if Harris couldn't convince the girl to come, he could just disappear for a bit. A few years lying on a beach would do him some good after all of this. Perhaps Ailsa would join him too…

His captors pulled him into a clearing, which at first looked empty. It wasn't until Harris looked up at the trees that he realised he was surrounded. Faeries of every shape and size were waiting silently in the boughs.

"We've brought the selkie," said the shellycoat.

Harris's legs were kicked out from under him, sending him sprawling on the moss. "Steady, lads." He put his head in one hand, as if he was reclining there on the ground on purpose. "I don't suppose any of you lot would let me speak to the Queen?" he said, looking up at the faeries in the branches.

"The selkie thinks he's funny," the shellycoat growled. "I can shut him up any time you like."

"That won't be necessary," said a soft female voice.

At first Harris's heart gave a leap. Was this Nicnevan? But then she dropped from her branch and he saw no chain attached to the woman. She was too plain to be the beautiful Faerie Queen anyway. The faerie was a little too thin and jagged. Underneath the wisps of gossamer she wore, Harris could see the limbs on her legs bent the wrong way as she walked towards him.

"Where is the princess?" asked the woman.

Harris's forehead creased. "I've already told my jailers: I have no idea. I was too young when she was taken."

The faerie woman shook her head. "But I think you do know. I bet the selkies all crow about how they stole her from us in Struanmuir."

Harris was beginning to feel a tingling in his left hand. He gave it a shake absently as he gawked at the woman.

"Well," she said. "No matter. We'll just need to convince you to tell us."

Now the skin on his hand was starting to burn. He stared at it, looking for whatever magic was touching it. "What—" he began.

"Changed your mind?" she asked.

"I don't kno—" But then his hand was on fire. Harris clutched it, howling as pain flared under his skin, especially in his thumb. The agony crested and he screamed. "Stop!"

And it did. The pain subsided so that it was only a tingle. But when he looked at the skin on his thumb he balked. It had turned to grey stone.

"So," said the faerie woman as Harris panted. "Let's try again. Where is the princess?"

Chapter 34

They'd only been up for a few hours, but in that time Maalik and Ailsa had already been to three houses. Mrs Malcolm was well enough to get outside for a bit. Ailsa had made sure to chase away the rain clouds, so the sun shone on the little old woman. Mrs Malcolm had laughed as she titled her face into the light. Ailsa sat beside her, listening to the woman's thin voice weave stories together while Maalik busied himself inside the cottage, giving it a clean.

Inside the next house, a toddler was tossing and turning from a fever. Maalik had been there before for another child, so at least the family weren't shocked by his looks. The parents just watched as he pressed a wet cloth to the toddler's forehead before setting about making up a herbal concoction for him to drink. The child grumbled and Ailsa bit her lip before pulling a cool breeze in through the windows to soothe the toddler.

"Well done," Maalik said, and quickly the parents seemed to realise what she was doing.

Ailsa expected them to kick her out—she was a changeling after all—but instead they murmured their gratitude.

The toddler eventually settled down and Maalik and Ailsa moved on to the next house. A foul stench of vomit and alcohol came from inside, but Maalik didn't seem to mind. While Ailsa hovered at the door, he strode in and began opening windows and washing glasses and plates. The house's owner, a young man, watched balefully from his bed, looking green.

"You just have a really bad hangover," Maalik told him. "You'll be fine by tomorrow. Drink lots of water and don't drink so much next time."

They left the man with some dry toast and peppermint for his stomach.

Finally, there were no more houses with patients. Maalik announced that they should have some lunch and led Ailsa to a spot beside a loch, where Wulver was already waiting. Maalik threw down a blanket and opened his bag to produce flatbread and some sort of paste. Ailsa eyed it suspiciously at first, but it was actually quite tasty.

Once they'd done eating, Ailsa stretched out on the blanket, allowing the sun to warm her body. A soft breeze blew across her skin, keeping it from overheating. Absently, she thought about the possibility of getting burnt, but it was so lovely that she couldn't find it in herself to care yet.

"It's a nice day," Maalik said. Something about the way he'd said it had Ailsa opening her eyes. Sure enough, his face was twisted into an amused grin.

"What are you getting at?" Ailsa replied lightly.

"You like this. Helping people," Maalik clarified. "It makes you happy."

"And nosey demons make me unhappy," she grumbled.

Maalik's shoulders shook and Ailsa swore he was laughing. *I don't think I've ever seen him do that.*

In a lot of ways, Maalik reminded Ailsa of how she used to be, not too long ago. She'd been a recluse, after years of rejections and fights. A sullen demeanour and a snarl had been her weapons as much as her axe had. It wasn't until Harris and Iona had come along that she had been pulled out of long-learned habits.

Maalik, on the other hand, had responded to his lot by trying to help people. Though he was as much of a recluse as she had been, he had responded with kindness when she had been bitter.

But underneath it all, all the caring and gentleness, Ailsa could sense a deep anguish that she couldn't begin to fathom. To see him smile, even a little, eased her heart just a little.

Maalik nudged her shoulder, ending her train of thoughts. "Do you want to go for a swim?" he asked, looking out at the water. "You can swim, can't you?"

"Yes..." Ailsa answered carefully. It was so nice lying here, she wasn't sure if she wanted to get up.

"Look, Wulver is enjoying it."

Ailsa chewed on her lip, watching the wolf paddle jumping on the waves, trying to catch the light reflected there.

But it was Maalik's face, so hopeful and open, that finally convinced her. "Fine," she answered with a sigh.

"Should I go first?" he asked.

"Tell me how cold it is."

"You know you could cut the breeze and it wouldn't be as cold?"

Ailsa concentrated. This was the opposite of what she usually did, and it felt like a muscle being used backwards. With a hand, she felt for the air, whispering across her skin. She took a breath and held it, letting her heart slow.

"That's it, good. Now follow me." He stalked down to the water's edge, chucking off his shoes and dipping a foot in.

Ailsa followed, watching as he sunk further into his waist and stopped, turning back to wait for her. "Aren't you going to take your clothes off?"

Maalik's face fell. "I'd rather not."

He's shy. "Fine, but I'm not getting my stuff wet." She pulled on the hem of her shirt, tossing it to the side. Maalik quickly faced the other direction and ducked under, as if he was trying to give her some privacy. Why did her heart sink a little? She finished pulling her trousers off until she was just in her undershorts and vest. Dipping a toe into the loch, she fought back a yelp. It was as cold as it looked. She had no idea how Maalik had got in so fast. Sucking in a breath, she counted down in her head. Three... two... one. Ailsa almost didn't follow through, but at the last moment she turned and allowed her body to plunge backwards into the cold water. Her body immediately began to shiver, so she pumped her arms, following after Maalik. The closer she got, the warmer the water became.

Ailsa reached him and wrinkled her nose. "Did you pee?"

Maalik's jaw dropped. "What? No!" he spluttered. "I'm a demon, I'm hot! I must have warmed the water around me."

Ailsa fought to control a laugh that bubbled up inside. "Oh great, come here then." She was so cold that the heat coming from his body was pulling her in, like a moth to a flame.

She grabbed his arm and he jumped at the contact. "What are you doing?"

"Getting some heat," Ailsa said through chattering teeth.

Maalik stared down at her, black eyes fathomless. "Just... don't touch my back, okay?"

"Fine." Ailsa put her hands on Maalik's shirt covered shoulders and sighed with relief at the warmth she felt there.

She felt Maalik's body relax a little as he realised she was doing as she was told. "You know, you'd get used to the cold if you just swam around a bit?"

His face was so close that she could see a dimple on his chin threatening to come out. She surged up and pressed her nose to his collarbone, eliciting a shiver. "Too late now, I'm stuck here."

"Here, turn around," he said hoarsely. "This will be easier."

She turned as best she could while still being close to the heat of Maalik's body. She shivered as her front suddenly met the cold water again.

Maalik held out his hands beside her. "May I?"

"You had better get your arms around me, right now," she growled.

Maalik's arms wound their way around her, one across her chest and shoulders and the other under her ribs. "Happy now?"

It was like wearing a huge hot water bottle. "Yes. Though, my legs are still cold."

Maalik wrapped his legs around hers and she hummed in contentment.

"You could always just get out," he muttered.

"I'm in now. And it's nice. It's been a while since I swam in water that wasn't salty." She sank down a little, allowing her chin to go under water. The cold stung her skin there, but it wasn't so bad now that the rest of her was warm.

"I don't think you can exactly call this swimming." Still, Maalik tightened his arms around her. The skin of his cheek brushed her neck, the stubble scratchy.

"Well, we could float around a bit at least."

They watched as something caught Wulver's attention underneath. Then, with a splash, he dove underwater and emerged a moment later with a fish flapping in his jaws.

This must be where he gets the food for everyone. The wolf emerged onto the bank of the loch and shook himself off, spraying water everywhere. He deposited the fish in the basket he carried around and lay down in a sunbeam, his chest heaving.

That could have been their cue to get out too, but Ailsa wasn't ready yet. In the light of day, touching Maalik was completely different from when they shared a bed, somehow. Having him wrapped around her was comforting and thrilling at once. *It's because he's a demon*, Ailsa told herself. Yet, she couldn't help but wonder if he felt the same way. He had spent so many years with only a wolf and a brownie for company, and though Ailsa was sure they had been nice to have around, having close contact from another human-type being was different. She tightened her hands on his arms and allowed herself to sink into the embrace. "Want to play questions again?" she asked.

"I feel like one of us always makes it sad," came

Maalik's reply. She was so close she could feel it rumble in his chest.

"I guess that's what happens when you're a changeling and a demon."

"Tell me something happy then. Where would you love to visit in the world? Maybe I can tell you about it?"

"Where would you recommend?" asked Ailsa.

"Well, I know that I'm trapped here, but I do think Eilanmòr is one of the most beautiful places in Ossiana. Maybe one of the smaller islands?"

"I think I'd like to go to Edessa so I could see all the inventions. My friend Gris was an Edessan warrior and he told me all about these things called hot air balloons. They use hot air to lift you into the sky," she said wistfully.

Maalik tensed behind her. "Would you be afraid? Of heights I mean?"

Ailsa looked up to the wisps of clouds above and imagined floating up there into space. How would they feel if she touched them with her fingers, not her magic? "I don't think I've ever been up high like that, so I don't know."

Maalik was silent for a moment. Ailsa thought she could almost feel him withdraw. "No, stop it," she said, gripping him tighter. "Stop getting sad. I can tell you're doing it." Ailsa pursed her lips, desperately thinking of a distraction. "How about this: would you rather lick a stranger's toes or never be able to read again?"

Maalik startled. "What? What sort of question is that?"

"One that's supposed to make you laugh." *Come on, cheer up.* She poked him on an elbow. "Now, what's your answer?"

He was silent for long enough that Ailsa worried she hadn't managed to divert his attention. Then, he answered slowly. "How long do I have to lick the toes?"

Yes, thought Ailsa. "A solid minute I'd say. Get right in the crevices." She stuck her tongue out for good measure.

"You're disgusting," he snorted.

Ailsa grinned. "Well?"

"I suppose it would have to be the toes."

"Yuck, no way!" she snickered.

"I like to read," he muttered sullenly. "Okay, how about this: would you rather always be sweaty or always have a runny nose?"

"Sweaty. Having a runny nose is annoying. Would you rather only be able to whisper for the rest of your life, or only be able to shout?"

"Whisper. I'd scare my patients. Would you rather marry an ugly person who is smart, or a handsome person who is stupid?"

"Neither," said Ailsa. "I'd rather not get married."

"That's not the game."

Ailsa groaned. "Well, then I'm sure me and my handsome husband will be very happy together."

"Really? Is that what you'd choose?" He sounded disappointed.

"I don't know," she said with a shrug. "Looks or intelligence don't really matter much, do they? If you love someone, it's because they're kind or funny or caring."

"Is that why you like Harris?" Maalik asked quietly. Ailsa felt his arms come around her a little tighter.

She was silent for a beat, choosing her words carefully. "Harris is a good friend, but I'm not sure he's the sort of person I would want to spend my life with."

"And yet," said Maalik. "You're working to save him."

"That's what friends do," Ailsa replied.

He cleared his throat behind her. "He's lucky to have you as a friend." Then his arms relaxed and he pulled away. The cold on her exposed skin felt like needles. "We'd better get out now."

"Yeah, quit slacking off. You've got people to save," Ailsa joked around chattering teeth.

Maalik didn't laugh. Ailsa thought he was about to swim back to the bank without her when his arms took up their former position on her body.

"I'll help you," Maalik said in her ear. "Can't have you freezing to death."

"Thanks," said Ailsa with a smile. "You're a good friend, Maalik."

Chapter 35

"So, how did that work out for you?"

Harris groaned and lifted his head from where he had landed in the jail cell. The human was still in the same place as before. "I'm working on it," Harris said, pushing himself up gingerly. "Just wearing them down."

The other prisoner looked at him with concern. "You're hurt."

Harris sighed, wiping his undamaged hand over his face. "No more than you." He inspected his arm, turning it over. It wasn't painful anymore, and for that he was thankful. The whole hand from the wrist down was now pale, grey stone. He shivered, remembering the moment the skin on his palm had turned hard. He tapped his fingers on the ground, making a dull dunking sound. Solid.

Well, this was going to be a mild inconvenience.

"Our only hope is to try to escape," Harris stated.

The man in the corner gave a weak laugh. "Good luck with that."

Harris smirked at the other prisoner. "I don't think you heard me. *Our* only hope is to escape. You're coming with me."

"But I can't move." The human gestured to his body, slumped over at a strange angle.

"Then I'll carry you," Harris told him.

The human smiled sadly. "You should escape by yourself."

"Nah," said Harris. He stood, cradling his stone arm to his body. "If I have you along, I can always leave you behind as a distraction." He winked at the man and sat down beside him. "How did you end up in Ephraim anyway? I didn't think humans could find it by themselves."

The man scratched his beard like he wasn't used to having it. Now that Harris was closer, he could see where the prisoner's purple hair was beginning to grow out, revealing brown roots.

"I didn't find it. I was brought here," said the man. "I was looking for it though."

"Looking for a faerie to grant you wishes?" Harris chuckled.

The man frowned. "I'm a cartographer. A map maker for the Eilanmòrian army. I was trying to place Ephraim on my map."

Harris whistled. "Wonderful idea. Then all humans would know where not to go on their holidays." The selkie studied his cell-mate, noting the nose piercing and his nails, which had been painted black once but were now chipped and peeling. "You don't look like a soldier," he said.

"Thanks," said the man. "It wasn't my first choice of career."

"Nevertheless, can you fight?" Harris asked.

The prisoner shrugged. "I've had the same training as anyone else in the King's army."

"Good," said Harris. "Because you may need to if we get caught running. Let's try to avoid that though, eh?"

"So you have a plan?"

Harris tapped his hand on the ground again, making the same dull noise. "We just need to wait for the right moment." He looked at the man beside him, and gave him a nudge with his unimpaired arm. "Don't look so sad. I've been in worse binds."

The prisoner snorted. "You must be pretty unlucky then. Maybe I don't want to join up with you after all?" He shook his head. "What's your name anyway?"

"Harris of Struanmuir," said the selkie, holding out his hand for the human to shake. "And you?"

Up until the other prisoner gave his answer, Harris's brain had been half listening, half whirring away working on a plan. But the human's next words brought all his thoughts screaming to a stop.

The man grimaced and took Harris's hand in his own. "Cameron," he said. "Cameron MacAra."

Chapter 36

"Slow down. You don't always have to go in hard all the time."

"What do you mean?"

"Try holding the power at half strength. It'll help you learn to control it. Like using a muscle."

They'd been training all day, and Ailsa had to admit that Maalik made a lot more sense than Gris had. Still, sometimes she could feel herself tire from all the magic use and that made her feel grouchy. Ailsa eyed the growing shadows between the trees—an old habit. *It's late*, she thought. Still, she didn't voice her concerns for the time. As much as she was tired, she was determined to keep going.

"I don't see how this is going to help me," she groaned out. The power fizzed in her veins like pins and needles. "Surely I need to be ready to go in as hard as possible."

"There are other ways to use your powers. Don't underestimate a gentle breeze," he said, circling Ailsa. "Directed in the right way, it can give you valuable information."

"Like?"

His mouth twisted. "It can tell you when someone is nearby. You can use it to pick up their scent."

"How am I even supposed to know what someone smells like?" She threw up her hands. "Surely a scent isn't really that distinct?"

"Yours is," Maalik said.

Was it her imagination or had his voice come out deeper when he had said that?

She tilted her head. "What do I smell like?"

He watched her a moment, assessing whether she was joking. She met his black stare with her own, unflinching.

"Well," he began, taking a step towards her. "When I first met you, you smelled like blood. It was how I knew you were hurt." He wrinkled his nose. "Then, of course, you smelled like the garlic I used to heal you."

Ailsa's face felt hot. "And now?"

"Now..." He closed his eyes. "Now... you smell like the lavender that you run your fingers through every morning when we leave the house. You smell like days spent in the woods. But above all else you smell like the world after a rainstorm."

It felt like the appropriate response would be to laugh, but she couldn't quite work the sound up her throat. She watched him in muteness as he shrugged, running a hand down the back of his neck.

"I mean I suppose that's to be expected," he mumbled. When she didn't answer, he gave a nervous chuckle. "It's called petricor, you know. The smell of rain…"

She cleared her throat and his gaze snapped to hers again.

"Maybe," she said, biting her lip. "I should make sure I have your smell memorised. You know, so I can practise."

He swallowed. "That's a good idea."

She hesitated, before taking a step forward. "It'll be easier if I'm closer. You don't mind, do you?"

"Ailsa, we've slept together—" He paled. "—in the same bed, I mean... I don't think you need to ask."

She closed the gap between them, her heart thumping harder in her chest. *It's just Maalik,* she told herself, though she wasn't sure why.

She reached out and touched the fastenings on his cloak, allowing it to anchor her to his body. Ailsa searched his face for regret or disgust as she leaned in. When she saw neither there, she closed her eyes and pressed her face into his neck, inhaling. His body was so warm, just like...

"You smell like… fire…"

He stiffened, but she carried on.

"… like a campfire on a cold night…"

Why had she said that? To make him feel better?

"… and like the spices you use in your healing…"

She breathed him in again, and she felt him shiver. One of his hands came up to touch her hip, like he needed something to steady him, too.

This was a dangerous game they were playing.

"... you smell like something else too, I just can't put my finger on it..."

Her hand brushed down his arm, taking his own fingers in hers. She raised them, turning her head to smell the source of the other fragrance.

"... paper?" she wondered. "No... books." She nodded, inhaling again. "That's it. Campfire, spices and books."

Finally, Ailsa opened her eyes and looked up into his own. She wasn't expecting the expression she saw there. His jaw was set, his nostrils flared. It was enough to have her drop his hand and step back.

"Sorry, I got carried away."

He released the hand on her hip, angling his body away from hers. "It's getting late, we should head back home."

She nodded, following him as he pulled on his pack and stalked through the trees.

What was that? she wondered, watching his retreating back.

By the time they returned to the cabin, Ailsa was flagging. All the magic use had left her body sore and exhausted. Maalik had walked on ahead, but then she stumbled and his arms were around her, keeping her upright.

"M'sorry," Ailsa mumbled.

Then she was being lifted into strong arms. She allowed the rocking motion to comfort her and thought absently that she had been right about his smell.

The door banged open and then her body was being laid down gently onto something soft. She snuggled in, ready to drift off.

The demon was sitting on the edge of the mattress and a small movement pulled Ailsa up from the sleep waiting to consume her. A hand stroked her cheek softly and she felt Maalik lean closer.

He's going to kiss me, Ailsa thought. But would that be such a bad thing?

The mattress dipped more, and she felt the demon's breath on her forehead. The fingers on her cheek drifted up to tuck the loose strands of hair from her face.

Ailsa kept still.

What's a kiss between friends? Ailsa wondered absently. No, it wouldn't be bad at all.

But then Maalik leaned away from her, tucking the blanket up to her chin.

"Sleep well," he whispered, before rising from the bed and moving away.

Ailsa cracked an eye open, feeling her face burning. *You're in trouble now*, she told herself as she rolled over.

Chapter 37

I can't believe I've found Ailsa's brother. Harris chuckled to himself, imagining Ailsa's face when he next saw her. He gave himself a little shake. *You're not going to see her if you don't focus on the task at hand.* Which happened to currently be flopping around on the cell floor, keening loudly.

"Help," Cameron shouted beside him. "The seal's dying."

It was the middle of the night, so there was only one guard on duty. They'd been watching their shifts for a while, counting out the length and frequency. It was a particularly ugly troll on duty. He stuck his face in between the bars and narrowed his yellow eyes.

"What do you want?" he snarled, his grey mouth contorting, showing rows of rotten teeth.

Cameron pointed to Harris, writhing on the floor. "Something's wrong with the selkie."

Harris picked up his shouts, cracking an eye open slightly to watch the troll.

Their captor gave a huff. "He'll be fine."

"Wait," Cameron said. "It seems like he's under some

sort of spell. It's killing him."

"Good riddance," said the troll. He turned to walk away from the cell.

Harris flopped over, clutching his side with his flippers.

"He said something before he changed, though," Cameron insisted. "Something about knowing where the princess is?"

This stopped the troll in his tracks. His ugly face reappeared through the branches that created their jail door. "What did you say?" he asked slowly.

"The selkie said he knows where the princess is, then he turned into a seal and started screeching."

Harris picked up his cries an octave at this. From the corner of his eye, it looked like Cameron was trying to fight a smile.

"Do you think someone put a spell on him so that if he revealed he knew where the princess is, he'd die?" Cameron asked the troll.

Their captor scratched his chin. "Maybe..."

Now it looked like Cameron was trying not to roll his eyes. "Don't you think you'd better find out what he knows before he dies? I heard Nicnevan is desperate to know where her daughter is."

The troll watched them for a moment, listening to Harris's cries. It looked like it was taking quite a while for his brain to process Cameron's words. Finally, he gave a growl. "I'll take the selkie. You stay where you are, human."

Cameron nodded, and scooted himself away from the seal.

The troll waved a hand and the branches of their jail unwound themselves. Harris howled louder as the creature stepped into the cell and bent to pick him up. With a grunt, the troll threw the selkie over his shoulder. Harris gave a few barks in protest.

"Wait," Cameron called after the troll's retreating back. "I don't feel very well now, either. Has the spell rubbed off on me?"

The troll turned around towards him, swinging Harris's body round too. Except, now their jailer was holding a pair of legs instead of a tail. He didn't seem to notice until Harris's arm, now longer than a flipper, managed to snake down to the troll's waist and pull out his sword.

"What—" the troll began, but it was too late. Harris spun round and smashed the hilt of the sword down on the back of the troll's head. It wasn't enough to knock him out, but in a daze, he dropped the selkie. The troll stumbled towards Cameron, who threw out a leg, causing their jailer to trip and fall onto the cell floor.

"Quick," Cameron said.

Harris raised the sword again, bringing the end down on the troll's head once, twice, three times, before the creature's eyes rolled back into his head and he passed out.

"Step one, success," crowed Harris with a grin.

Cameron frowned in a way that was so like his sister, that Harris stared, confounded. How had he not seen the resemblance before?

"Hello?" Cameron said. "You alright?"

"Yeah," he said, coughing. "Fine. I've got something to tell you after we've escaped, but it can wait."

"Fine. Help me up."

Harris reached down to tuck his shoulder into the other man's armpit. With a groan from both of them, he pulled Cameron to his feet. "We'll also need to get you a shower," Harris huffed.

"I apologise for not washing when my veins have been turned to wood and I've been trapped in a jail cell," Cameron said, sucking on a tooth.

The two men hobbled towards the gap in the branches and out into the stone corridor. Though it was night, someone had lit torches along the path, so it was easy to find the exit behind the waterfall. A fine mist clung to their skin and clothes, and Harris felt Cameron shiver in the evening air. *Humans*, he thought. *So delicate.*

Whether from the hour or from luck, there was no one in sight. They slunk up the path, ducking behind trees when they thought they heard a noise. The further from the waterfall, the darker it got until they were only finding their way by a sliver of moonlight. It soon became clear that Cameron could no longer see, so Harris had to mutter instructions to him as he dragged him along.

"Careful, there's a root, lift your feet. One, two, that's it."

"Harris," Cameron whispered. "I hear something."

"It's just a little further," Harris muttered back. "Keep quiet and hurry up."

Something was shimmering up ahead, through the trees, and Harris could feel instinctively that it was the end to the magic which hid Ephraim from the humans. As they got closer, Cameron tensed up, like he was being repelled by the wall of power.

"It's okay," Harris reassured him. "It's the way out."

The glow emanated from a clearing up ahead, containing five standing stones in a circle. *This must be it*. They pushed through the forest, until they were twenty feet, ten feet, five feet away from the stones. Harris reached out his hand, almost touching the largest of them, covered in carved symbols. "We're here," he told Cameron.

And then the magic disappeared.

"Are we out?" Cameron asked hopefully.

Harris felt a pit in his stomach. It hadn't felt like they'd crossed through. He'd expected a tingle at the very least.

All of his fears were realised when he heard a voice behind him.

"I heard you wanted to see me, selkie? Big mistake."

Harris couldn't turn around in time to see who spoke. Fire erupted under his skin, in his veins. He doubled over in agony, hearing Cameron's screams meet his own.

No, he tried to say. *He had nothing to do with this.* But he couldn't turn his wails into words.

Chapter 38

Ailsa wasn't sure what disturbed her, but she was pulled from her sleep like wading through syrup. She drifted into consciousness, noting first that it was still dark outside the window, and second that candles were glowing softly around the room.

She blinked blearily, shifting a bit in the bed. The blanket Maalik had placed on her was still up beside her ears and she was too hot. Maybe that's what had woken her. She scrubbed a hand over her face, pulling the blanket down so that she could feel the cool night air.

That's when she looked up to find a figure perched on a stool near the fire. He was bare from the waist up and was rubbing something on his shoulders.

"Maalik?" Ailsa asked sleepily. Her gaze moved to the figure's back.

The demon jumped from his seat and turned towards her, but it was too late. She had seen what was on his body, what he usually kept underneath his shirt.

Oh gods...

"No," Maalik whispered. "You weren't supposed to see this. I thought you were sleeping." His back was a tortured mass of scars and metal, as if someone had poured molten silver on his skin.

Ailsa pushed herself up from the bed "What are those?" she whispered.

"Please," came his anguished reply. "Forget you ever saw them." He tried to cover up his body with his hands. His clothes lay discarded on the couch beside her.

"Did... did someone hurt you?" Ailsa asked. It looked agonising. She stood from the bed, coming closer to where he hovered. "You can tell me, Maalik." She placed a soothing hand on his arm, turning him a little so that she could see his back in the firelight again. "Oh gods," she whispered.

He didn't move, waiting tensely for her verdict with wide, black eyes.

Ailsa reached out to touch the gnarled skin but hesitated. "I could rub some salve on your skin if you want?" The metal gleamed wickedly in the firelight. "They look like... wings…"

A shudder ran through his body, but he didn't reply.

What had done this to him? Who had spent time carving him up and then filling the holes with the metal shards? It almost seemed a joke that they had placed them there in that pattern, on a demon.

And then the answer came to her.

"Maalik?" she said in a low voice. "You haven't always been a demon, have you?"

A sob echoed from his throat; a sound so wretched that it cleaved a wound into her heart. She placed a hand on his arm, where there was no wound and rubbed it as he shook. She hadn't cried in so long; it was hard to know what to do.

"You were an angel," she stated. Because she didn't need to ask, it was so obvious now. Healing others, almost like he was trying to repent. How the other demons shunned him. His low moods, like he had lost something.

"How does an angel become a demon?" she asked, unsure if she really wanted to know the answer.

Maalik took a heaving breath. "You do something so horrible, so reprehensible, that the gods themselves cast you down to Hell."

Ailsa stroked his arm. "You're not in Hell."

"This is hell," he said, gesturing to his back. "To become a monster. To lose the ability to heal those in need. To never fly again…"

The horror of Maalik's loss was starting to dawn on her. He used to fly?

"Is there nothing anyone can do?" she asked.

He gave a short, mirthless laugh. "I've never heard of any demon becoming an angel."

Ailsa looked him over, from his shaking legs to his clenched fists. She wracked her brain for any clues, any indication that Maalik had been hiding this secret all along. He had never removed his shirt in front of her, but Ailsa had assumed he was just modest. But to have been an angel, to be carrying around this weight on his back… Now that she was able to piece it together, it was starting to make sense. What had made him like this? "Maalik," she breathed. "What did you do?"

He dropped his head into his hands. "If you knew, you would never be able to look at me again."

Ailsa wound an arm around his shoulders and squeezed. Her lips desperately tried to form the right words. *It doesn't matter. You could never have done anything to make me hate you.* But how could she know that? The silence stretched on, punctuated only by their breathing and the crackle of the fire.

"I'm sorry I never told you," Maalik finally said. "You deserve to know who I really—"

A knock on the door cut his sentence short and Ailsa jumped.

"Maalik," called a silky male voice. "Come on out, I know you and the girl are in there."

Chapter 39

Maalik's nostrils flared. "Stay with Wulver," he bit out, the emotion in his voice still raw.

"Who is it?" Ailsa asked as she watched him stride across the room to the door.

He looked over his shoulder, his mouth in a grim line. "I'm sorry, Ailsa. I want to tell you to hide, but you need to be seen."

Wulver growled beside her but pressed himself close to her side, allowing her to reach out and stroke the thick fur on his back. She looked up at the massive wolf, but his gaze was on Maalik, while his muzzle wrinkled, revealing sharp canines.

Maalik took a deep breath, squaring his shoulders, and then closed his hand around the door handle. A cold draft swept inside as the portal was opened, revealing the world, as black as ink outside. For a moment, Ailsa blinked, unable to see who exactly had knocked in the dark. Then, from out of the gloom, a person appeared. Not a person though, she realised, feeling the wrongness of him as he sauntered forward. This was another demon. And, unlike Maalik, this demon had never been an angel. Now that she could compare them, she could feel how wrong, how evil, a real full-blooded demon was. Maalik was a shadow of this, a flickering candle beside an inferno. The demon smiled wickedly, his teeth gleaming white in the dark and Ailsa shrunk into Wulver's side. Deep in her gut, Ailsa knew that if it had been this demon who had found her in the woods, she would be long dead by now.

"Maalik," the demon began, his voice slithering into the frigid air. "It has been a long time, brother."

"Bram." Maalik did not return his smile. "State why you're here." He gripped the door handle tightly, ready to slam it shut at any moment. Only Ailsa and Wulver behind him could see that his hand was shaking.

The demon *tsked*, smiling wider. "I've been sent to check up on you..." he paused, and Ailsa could feel those black, featureless eyes flicking to where she sat, "... and your friend here."

She gripped Wulver's fur tighter, knowing her hands were sweating but unable to release him.

"As you can see, she's still here," Maalik ground out.

"Ah, but a lot more comfortable than I expected." The demon, Bram, stepped forward so that the light from the fire kissed his head and revealed more of his features. He was paler than Maalik on his face, though Ailsa could see that, like Maalik, his hands were black with ash. Instead of the golden antlers that grew out of her friend's hair, his horns corkscrewed from his skull. The place where the bone burst from skin was easily spotted as his hair was almost completely shaved.

Maalik angled his body as subtly as he could, so he was blocking the entrance to the cabin.

Bram snickered. "Playing house, are we, Maalik?" He inclined his head at each of them in turn. "Father... Mother... and their pet hound. Nice and cosy." The demon chuckled. "Do you kiss her cheek when you leave for work in the morning? Does she massage your feet and feed you cakes when you come home? And..." he gazed lazily at Ailsa, "... does he satisfy you in your marriage bed?" His voice became conspiratorial. "You know, you could always find another husband, if you grow bored with him. I could pleasure you in ways—"

"Enough!" Maalik growled. "She assists me in my work every day, as is demanded by the sacrifice. I don't need to treat her like a prisoner the rest of the time."

"But that's what she is, isn't she?" Bram's lip curled. "She cannot leave this cabin without you. Therefore, she is imprisoned. Don't pretend you are anything but her master."

Maalik remained silent, his whole body almost vibrating in rage.

"I'll keep this short, since I am clearly unwelcome," the other demon drawled. "You've been summoned to the Nest. The council wants to see her for themselves."

He winked at Ailsa before continuing. "It's not often that a slave survives this long."

"Can't you tell them yourself she is here and fulfilling the promise?"

"Where is the fun in that? No, you will attend tomorrow night, with her. If indeed, all is as it should be, you may return here with her."

Ailsa shuddered. To be in a room full of demons like Bram... she clamped her lips shut as she felt the bile rising in her throat.

"However," he said. "If they find out you are misleading us, that you are in any way cheating, she will be stripped from your possession."

He smirked again at Ailsa. "I could always use a slave. Though I doubt you'd prefer me over Maalik here. We'd have fun though, for the time that you are alive."

Maalik was glowing with anger. "Get out."

"I am out." Bram slipped his hands into the pockets of his black tunic. "Tomorrow night," he repeated, before turning and walking back into the woods. Maalik held the door open, watching his back until he was swallowed by the dark.

Ailsa stared after him. She had expected him to disappear in a thunderclap, walking was so... *human*. But, she realised, if he could dissolve so easily into the blackness of the forest, he could be out there at any time.

Chapter 40

Ailsa waited until Maalik had slammed the door and stalked over to the sink to rise from the table. Wulver, gave her a pointed look before padding through the door to his den and shutting it behind him.

She bit her lip, returning her attention back to the demon. *Angel,* she corrected herself in awe. Indeed, he looked like one now, his head bowed, hands braced on the tile. How could she have not seen what he truly was?

Worried as she was about visiting the demon council, it seemed that Maalik was more upset. She couldn't bear the silence that stretched on in the aftermath of the visit. He was staring unblinking at the tap when she came up behind him and touched his arm.

He jumped a little and sniffed. "What are we going to do?"

"I don't really see that we have a choice. I'll just have to go to the demon Nest with you."

"You will not," he told her, turning. His jaw tightened as he watched her. Well, if he wanted to throw a tantrum, then two could play at that game. An angry Maalik was much preferable to a scared one.

"What the hell is wrong with you?" Ailsa asked, stepping closer. "You've been training me all this time, helping me get ready to face Nicnevan, yet you won't let me help you. It's clear that if I don't show up, it'll be your neck on the line…"

"But that's the problem." His voice became quiet, measured, like he knew she was trying to get a rise from him. "All this time I've been helping you. Don't you think that is slightly against the rules? Do you think that it's normal for demons to allow sacrifices to sleep in their beds? To make them food and treat their wounds." He angled his head, biting his lip. "If they realise I haven't been treating you badly, they'll start looking into the other things I haven't been doing."

Causing misery, tempting humans to evil.

"Well then, maybe you should be making my life miserable, just like the other demons want." Ailsa shot back. "Is it worth risking their wrath?"

"Yes," he growled. "You are worth it."

Ailsa swallowed, her voice soft. "Maalik, don't you see? You think you're a monster, but every day you prove that you're not. Please, let me help you."

His gaze raked over her, but she refused to back down.

"I don't want you to get hurt," he finally said.

"Don't you trust me?"

A nod.

Good, she thought. Now she would just need to

convince the other demons as easily. They would need to pull off one hell of a trick if the demon from earlier was already reporting back to the council. She imagined Harris, what he would do and allowed some of his swagger to loosen her body. "Right," she smirked. "Let's put on a performance. The other demons think you're not torturing me, let's make them believe that you are."

Maalik frowned. "How?"

"Something you didn't know about me is I'm a fantastic actress." She winked. "Though, it would help if I had a few cuts and bruises…"

His jaw clenched. "I'm not injuring you."

"Fine, do you have any potions that could do it?"

He made a noise, halfway between a laugh and a growl. "I only have medicine. Not something that could cause you harm."

Ailsa's eyes darted around the room. Before Maalik could react, she sprinted to the door and out into the cold night. She could hear his footsteps, his huffing breath behind her as she ran, heading for the nearest tree. If he wasn't going to help, then she'd do it herself. A tree could cause some nice scratches, maybe even a bruise if she hit it quick enough.

A foot away from the tree and her body was anticipating the pain. The tree's branches were low and sharp. She closed her eyes, readying for impact. With a thud she collided, not with the wood, but with a warm body.

Arms wrapped around her back, and she blinked up at Maalik's face, thunderous even in the low light.

Ailsa cursed. *Stupid demon speed.*

"Let me be clear," he said, his jaw tight. "You will not harm yourself for me."

She swallowed, and Maalik lifted a hand to cup her neck, that midnight glare flicking across her face. "I'm sure that we can put some ochre under your eyes and you'll look battered enough."

"Fine," Ailsa said, her words lacking the bite she had intended. She stepped out of his arms with a shrug and he followed her movements with a frown.

"Did you notice how far away you got from me when you were running? The distance you can go is increasing…"

"Why?" she breathed.

His eyebrows pinched together. "I don't know…"

"Maybe my sentence is reducing?"

"Maybe… You'll have to stick close tomorrow though. We don't want the other demons to be aware."

Ailsa nodded. "So what do I do?"

Maalik wiped a hand over his face. "Keep your head down, speak only when you're spoken to and you'll be fine. I'll do the rest." A shadow passed over his features. "I may need to act cruel at times. Please know it is just that—an act."

"I know."

Apparently deciding that she could be trusted not to inflict injury upon herself, Maalik pushed off the tree and started walking back to the house. The familiar tug pulled Ailsa forward, though now that Maalik mentioned it, it wasn't as strong as it had been. How far would she be able to get in a few days? A week? Surely Maalik would be pleased not to have her tied to him anymore; he'd said as much when they had first met. Though now... Was she stupid to think things had changed between them? *We're friends*, she thought. Friends weren't usually bonded together by an evil sacrifice, to be fair. Would they ever see each other again if they no longer had that connection?

"Maalik," Ailsa called as he reached the door.

The light from the fire inside illuminated his body, casting his face into shadow as he turned. She knew though, that he was watching her, knew that his face would be lined with worry and concern.

She took a deep breath and shook the image from her mind, staring instead into his shadow. "What happens if the sacrifice is fulfilled? If we don't have the bond between us anymore?"

Maalik's face shuttered. "You'll be free."

"And what will you do?" Ailsa pressed.

He paused, weighing his answer. "I suppose everything will go back to the way it was before you came."

She hesitated, tasting the words on her tongue. "Will

I... will I ever see you again?" Before he could answer, she pressed on. "You could come with me." She hated the waver in her voice as she sounded her hope, even as she continued. "I may need to be a hero for a turn, but then you could come with me back to Dunrigh. Or somewhere else, if you prefer. The capital is not the most tolerant of places to outsiders."

His head tilted, the firelight glinting on his antlers. "Like I told you before, the council of demons has my soul. When I became a demon, it was taken from me." He rubbed his chest with a black hand.

She remembered back to their conversation from a few days ago. It made a lot more sense now. Losing your soul; she couldn't even begin to comprehend how that would feel.

"As long as the council has it, I have to stay where they want me."

Not an outright no, Ailsa told herself.

"What if..." she wondered, stepping closer to the house, "what if we were able to get your soul back?"

Maalik became perfectly still. "How?"

"I have a plan."

Chapter 41

They had talked through the night—though arguing was a better description—propped up on either side of the narrow bed, with Maalik's legs bracketing Ailsa's for warmth. Despite the shining hope that had crossed Maalik's face when she had first suggested the rescue, he did his best to convince her against her plan.

Too dangerous, he had said. But he was being ridiculous—worrying about her safety when something like this was at stake. She had argued, again, that he had been training her all this time and now had no faith in her. Wulver had stuck his head out at their shouting and growled at Maalik, shocking the demon into silence.

If only I could have a five-foot wolf behind me in every argument, Ailsa thought. He would certainly be a strong ally when she went to Ephraim.

"Remember, stay silent," Maalik instructed her again. "You won't even know I'm there."

"And don't look anyone in the eye."

"There's nothing to see anyway," Ailsa muttered.

Maalik turned, his lips a thin line. "I'm glad you find this funny. If this doesn't go well, I'll be dead, and you'll be tethered to some sadistic prick."

"That would be a shame, since I like the sadistic prick I'm currently tethered to." She smiled sweetly.

His lips quirked into a grin. "Have I ever told you that you're insufferable sometimes?"

"No," Ailsa answered, shrugging. "But plenty others have."

"This isn't funny."

"I get that. I mean, basically both of our souls are on the line." She reached out a hand, extending an olive branch. "I'm just trying to distract you."

He allowed his chest to brush against her palm, so she could feel his thundering heartbeat. Outside, thunder cracked.

"We'll be fine," Ailsa murmured, soothing Maalik and herself. She took a sip of her tea without tasting it. "You were about to tell me how you became a demon, before Bram showed up."

Maalik ducked his head. "That conversation feels so long ago now. I'm sorry for the way I reacted. I never wanted you to know."

"That you were an angel?" Ailsa prompted.

He closed his eyes. "I was turned twenty years ago, here in Eilanmòr. I did something against the rules, and I was punished for it."

"What?" Ailsa whispered.

"I murdered someone."

Ailsa blinked at him in shock. "I mean, I've killed people befor—"

"—how many of those you killed deserved it?" he asked, cutting her off. "I bet you killed them in self-defence, or in defence of someone else. Or maybe you even killed out of mercy?"

Ailsa shut her mouth, waiting for him to continue.

Maalik sighed. "I killed someone in cold blood. He was a good person and I ended his life for selfish reasons. It was against the vows I took when I became an angel, and I did it out of greed, without a thought. So I was turned into this by the gods as punishment. And I deserve every moment."

"No," Ailsa argued in a low voice. "You don't."

He looked as if he was about to argue, before giving a sigh and scratching a hand into his hair. "You should probably get some sleep before tomorrow. You'll need all the energy you can get." He kicked his legs out of the blankets and stood up. "I'm going to go for a walk around the cabin," he told her.

Ailsa hesitated, wanting to offer him some company, but thinking better of it. He needed to be alone, she sensed. She ducked down deeper into the bed, which felt colder now that Maalik was gone and watched as he slipped his boots on. "Don't stay out too late," she finally told him.

He gave a nod and then slipped out the door.

Ailsa turned onto her side, facing the window. With a pull of her hand, she sent a warm breeze after him and did her best to chase the thunder clouds away.

Chapter 42

"**A**re you sure you want to do this?"

Ailsa fought her eyes as they tried to roll. *He means well,* she told herself. It didn't make it less annoying. If he kept asking her, eventually she would yell, *No, Maalik, I am about to walk into a nest of demons who would eat me as soon as look at me, I am not sure.* But then where would they be? Bram would probably come looking for her and she would definitely be demon food then. Or worse. If she could just be brave for a few hours, they could see she was unable to escape from Maalik and they'd send them on their way.

Of course, that was if Maalik could keep himself together.

She looked at the man beside her. Shoulders hunched, teeth worrying at his bottom lip. "You know, for a demon, you aren't very menacing," she said, elbowing him in the ribs.

His lips pursed. "I can be menacing if I choose to be."

"And right now you don't choose it? Maybe I need some scaring. Don't slaves need put in their place?"

His lip twitched. "Would you like me to scare you?"

"Well, you could try," she laughed, swinging her hands by her sides. "I think when you regularly watch your captor drooling in sleep, or find him holding baby kittens, it tends to take away the fear..."

She paused, waiting for him to defend himself against her mockery. A second passed. Then another.

"Maalik?" she asked, turning back to where she thought he would be following. Nothing.

"Very funny," she called, continuing through the trees. Well, she would just keep walking until he decided to sneak up on her. He couldn't be far after all. A faint tug around her belly button told her he was somewhere behind.

Ailsa followed the rough path, winding her way through the trees in the fading light. It was almost laughable, Maalik was trying to frighten her, yet only a few weeks ago, her mere presence in a forest would have been enough to scare her witless. Now she could wander in the sea of trees, smelling the pine resin and smoky earth. It was a shame she had been scared for so long.

And yet, just because she found one monster to be harmless, didn't mean all of them were. She didn't know how far she would need to walk until she found the demon Nest. Any step could reveal it. She slowed her pace. Surely, Maalik would end the ruse before she stumbled upon it?

But then there were the other creatures, both mythical

and natural. Hadn't she met a kelpie on the edge of woods like these? She wondered briefly what one would appear like now. Would he have curling bronze hair and a cheeky smirk? Or would his lips be soft and brooding, his skin golden and his eyes black. Ailsa's cheeks heated. What had come over her? A kelpie was much more likely to tempt her transformed as a warm bed and a chocolate cake. Still, it would almost be worth seeing one for her to know for sure.

An owl hooted up ahead, breaking her daydreaming and making her jump. Where was Maalik? Did he intend to follow her all night? She peered through the trees, looking for his silhouette. It had gotten much darker, and she had to squint to see the spaces between the trunks.

"Maalik?" she shouted, turning around. "You've made your point; you can come out now."

Nothing. Only the rustle of the branches swaying in the wind up ahead.

But then, there. A movement to her left caught her eye.

"Oh good, there you are," she sighed. He had gone further than she had thought, but now his shadow was walking towards her. Except... was Maalik standing on something? He seemed taller...

A hand over her mouth had her heart leaping into her throat, but she could barely make a squeak before she was pulled behind a tree and crushed by a warm body.

She looked up into Maalik's worry-lined face as they listened to the shadow stalk nearer.

Ailsa's heart was thundering in her chest, matched in rhythm with Maalik's beneath his thin shirt. The shadow crashed through the foliage, snuffling as it went. Maalik's eyes were darting around, behind the tree trunk Ailsa was pressed against, obviously watching whatever it was rumble about. The lines of his body were tense, telling Ailsa everything she needed to know: don't make a noise, or you'll be dead.

The creature scraped something against a nearby tree. Its claws? It huffed a few breaths and Maalik froze. Then he let out a long breath, the hot air fanning over her forehead. A moment later, the crashes were getting fainter and he dropped his head, allowing his lips to rest in an almost kiss upon her brow.

"That was close," he whispered against her hair.

Ailsa let her shoulders relax. "What was it?"

"A bear."

Ailsa couldn't quite squash the nervous laugh that bubbled up inside her, the sound coming out almost like a sob. A bear? After all the talk of demons, of kelpies and witches... and she'd almost been eaten by a bear?

She could feel Maalik's mouth quirk. "I'm glad you find it funny."

They had walked through the forest for hours, until Ailsa was completely lost. The arches of her feet were aching when Maalik finally stopped before a gnarled old oak, and gestured for her to sit. Panic had been bubbling under her skin for a while now, and her eyes continued to dart to the sky—watching for the sun's first rays—as Maalik studied the tree.

"I suppose demons don't expect punctuality?" Ailsa mumbled, biting her lip.

Maalik wrinkled his nose. "What do you mean?"

"We've been walking all night; it's almost sunrise." Ailsa looked again to the sky, sure that it was getting lighter.

Maalik just shook his head, a chuckle escaping his lips.

Ailsa's mouth popped open. "What?" How could he be so blasé now, when yesterday he had been terrified?

"I just forgot," he said, rubbing his chin. "You think we've been walking all night?"

"Yes." She had the blisters to prove it.

"It's one of the tricks of the Nest. If anyone but a demon tries to find it, they'll think it's taking them too long and give up."

When Ailsa's mouth twisted in confusion, he shook his head again. "We've only been walking half an hour. You just think it's been all night because, one—the demons want to confuse you, and two—they want you in a weakened state when you enter."

"Are you telling me that my legs are aching, and I've been bored following you all this time and it wasn't even real?"

"Welcome to Hell," was all Maalik said, turning back to the tree.

She watched as he pulled something from his pocket and extended his other hand. Before she could shout, he had scraped a dagger over his arm.

"Why did you do that?"

"The entry demands payment."

"Demons really are barbarians," she muttered. When she heard Maalik's soft laugh, she allowed the corners of her mouth to lift slightly in return. After spending the previous night fretting, she was glad that he could find humour now. He hadn't slept, a fact she knew because neither had she. Instead, they had lain awake all night, neither wanting to say anything. What was there to say? They had planned their course of action in detail, they just had to wait to enact it. That morning they had risen, bleary-eyed, from the bed. Ailsa had been unsure what to say, and felt relieved when Maalik had decided to spend the day gardening.

Now, she rose from her seat, and curled her shoulder inward, trying her best to look like a cowed and meek servant. She stepped up behind Maalik, who was flicking his arm at the tree's trunk, splattering his blood on the wood.

She held her breath for a beat. Two.

Just when Ailsa thought nothing would happen, the tree twisted, and as it did, it spiralled out of the earth like a corkscrew. It grew out of the ground until the whole trunk was clear, balancing on the thick roots like some sort of spider. Where the tree had been, there was a hole.

"Don't tell me," Ailsa breathed.

Maalik sighed. "Down we go."

Chapter 43

hell was colder than she had expected. The Nest, Ailsa corrected herself. As they descended a narrow staircase, the temperature plummeted until Ailsa could see her breath. Noting her shivering, Maalik had placed his hands on her shoulders to warm her. She would have preferred to have his arms wrapped around her, but she guessed that would have looked a bit too cosy. She was supposed to be a slave after all.

A cacophony of screams and laughter rose from the halls below, and Ailsa sucked in a breath.

"Get in and get out," Maalik whispered. "Those are the two important things. If it turns bad, we run and take our chances."

"We'll be fine," Ailsa murmured back. *Please let us be fine.*

They reached the bottom of the stairs and the sounds stopped at once. Ailsa fought back a yelp as she saw hundreds of faces turn towards them. In the low light, their black eyes made them look like skulls.

The crowd parted as Maalik pushed her forward. His fingers pressed into her shoulders like claws, but he kept the strength out of his grip.

"Now, now everyone," called a familiar, silky voice. "Nothing to see here." Bram stalked out of the crowd, who tore their gazes away from the newcomers when he passed. He gave Maalik a wide smile as he approached and extended a hand. "I'm so glad to see you, Maalik."

Maalik looked at the offered hand but made no move to take it. "Just show us to the council," he muttered.

Bram shrugged and then came to stand in front of Ailsa. "You're looking a bit rougher than the last time I saw you," he said with a grin. "Has Maalik been acting out his frustrations on you?" Then, the demon came closer and leaned in so that his mouth was near Ailsa's ear. She fought the shiver she felt coursing up her spine. He smelled like flowers and decay. "Or..." he murmured, loud enough so that Maalik could hear him too. "... did he make it seem like you'd been mistreated to cover his ass?"

Ailsa wished she had her axe with her.

The other demon straightened up and laughed. "The council will find out, anyway. Come on, let's go." With a wink he turned and began slinking back through the crowd.

Maalik pushed Ailsa forward. The cavern they were in was so packed with bodies, they had to fight through them. The cold Ailsa had felt when she'd first entered was completely gone now. Heat and sweat pressed in from all sides as they pushed past burning hot demons. Some, like Maalik and Bram, had golden horns or antlers on their heads. Others had open, festering wounds where they should be.

"A punishment," Maalik whispered into her ear. "They grow back eventually but it's very painful."

All the demons, though, had the same black eyes. Ailsa couldn't tell, as she walked through the crowd, whether any of them were looking at her out of the corners of their vision. She had a nasty feeling that all of them were.

They snaked their way through the first cavern and out into a much higher and wider one. It too was crowded with bodies. Openings lined the sides, looking as if they led to tunnels. Bram led them through the second one, which branched off into three others. By the time they had gone through the fifth portal, Ailsa was hopelessly lost. *It's probably what they want.* She felt her throat squeezing and couldn't help but imagine the low ceilings pressing down on them.

Finally, they came upon a door. Its wood was scratched and rotting, and there was a faint screaming coming from inside.

Bram turned round, and spread his arms wide. "Well, we're here. Ready for your trial?" He didn't wait for their answer before knocking twice on the door. The noise seemed louder than it should have been; the booms shook the hinges, making Ailsa jump.

Maalik squeezed her shoulders but couldn't say anything to comfort her with Bram still watching them. The screaming had stopped, replaced with a waiting silence.

Then, someone shouted from within.

"Enter."

Chapter 44

A group of five demons sat around in low chairs around a crackling fire. Unlike the others, who could have passed for human on a dark night, there was no mistaking these creatures for what they were. The five demons wore clothes only on their bottom halves, revealing large swathes of skin on their arms and torsos, which were covered in sores and scabs, as if they had been burned over and over again. Of those that had their backs to them, only one had the same melted metal wings as Maalik. *Another fallen angel*, Ailsa realised. Their teeth had sharpened and elongated so that they protruded out of their mouths like fangs. Despite their nightmarish bodies, they all possessed gleaming golden horns and antlers, polished and bright.

Bram bowed deeply before the group. "I present to you all, the demon Maalik and his current sacrifice."

Behind the group of five, another demon stood. She was so small she had been completely hidden by the others. This one wore robes of deep red that swamped her child-like body. She tilted her head, regarding them with huge black eyes. "Why is he here, Bram?" she asked in a clear, high voice, despite her huge teeth.

Ailsa gave a shudder. *Creepy.*

"I've been keeping an eye on Maalik here since he joined our ranks. At first, I thought he was an informant for the angels." Bram gave Maalik a little shove and grinned. "But then, that's silly, isn't it Maalik? They don't want you."

The little demon girl did not return the smile. "How long have you been one of us, Maalik?"

Maalik raised his chin. "Two decades."

She nodded. "And yet, we've never had any cause to distrust him before."

Bram shrugged. "He does a good job, our friend, of slipping through the cracks."

The girl sighed. "Well, get on with it then, Bram," she said with a wave of her hand.

Ailsa turned to look at Maalik. He had explained this to her, how they would try to find them out, the specific skills that Bram would use. Maalik took his hands off her shoulders and held one out for Bram to take.

The other demon took Maalik by the wrist and chuckled. "Let's see what you've been up to."

Maalik closed his eyes and furrowed his brow as if something unpleasant was happening. It only took a minute for Bram to release him, but Ailsa couldn't help holding her breath the whole time.

"Death, disease, dull," Bram concluded with a sniff.

"What I expected, obviously. Maalik is pretty good at controlling his thoughts." He rolled his eyes. "But you're so boring. If you could provide some more exciting viewing material for next time, it would be much appreciated."

Then, Bram turned to Ailsa and held out his hand. "This should be more interesting," he said, curling his lip.

Ailsa bowed her head, fighting the urge to run at him and claw his eyes out. She lifted her hand towards him and allowed the demon to take her wrist.

The violation was subtle. If Ailsa hadn't been bracing for it, she might have missed it. Something, other, foreign was looking into her brain. Waiting for her memories to betray her.

Maalik had warned her that Bram could read minds, but she had prepared.

"Now, little girl, what has dear Maalik been doing these last few weeks?"

She schooled her thoughts, choosing one to place in the front and display for the demon. She felt him watch as she focussed on the horror of seeing Maalik for the first time, of the feel of the sacrifice locking into place. She remembered the shock of seeing his eyes, lit up by her lightning.

Bram smirked. "She was truly terrified of you."

Ailsa could think of how Maalik had carried her back

to his cottage, how he knocked her out with a sleeping draught. She selected another memory: when she had gone with him to do his work.

"Interesting," Bram said. "She watched him kill an old man." He snorted. "Bit of an easy mark."

Ailsa tried again, conjuring up memories of Maalik tackling her to the ground, of him catching her before she could run away, waking up to find him standing over her.

Bram's forehead was creasing in worry as he watched these memories play out in her head.

"Well, Bram? Has Maalik been doing anything punishable?" asked the little girl demon.

Ailsa was running out of memories. She felt a bead of sweat slide down her back.

Bram peered into her face now, as she tried desperately to think of other times Maalik had behaved like a demon.

But instead her other thoughts escaped the place she had filed them away, bubbling to the surface. Maalik tending to her wounds. Maalik smiling at her. Maalik passing her food.

The feel of Maalik's lips on her hair as she was falling asleep.

No!

Bram smiled now, triumphant. He turned to the demon on the throne, ready to out them, and Ailsa did the only thing she could think to do. Reaching down to her boot, she pulled out the knife she had hidden there. She had slipped it from Maalik's kitchen before they had left, just in case.

Thank the gods, she thought to herself.

Before any of the demons could react, she jumped on Bram's back and plunged the knife into his neck. It sank in far too easily.

"Ailsa!" Maalik shouted.

Almost immediately, the handle of the blade became too hot to hold and Ailsa fell to the floor in surprise. She watched as Bram turned on her, eyes wide as he clutched at his wound.

"She—" he tried to speak but it ended in a gurgle as blood bubbled from his lips.

A hush fell over the group of demons as they watched Bram stagger to the side, then collapsed as his knees gave way.

Then it was chaos.

Chapter 45

"Maalik!" Ailsa screamed.

"No!" came a shout to her left.

Ailsa felt her shoulders pop as her arms were wrenched behind her back.

The five demons around the table were shouting and hissing but it was the demon girl who sent a shiver up Ailsa's spine. She seemed completely and utterly unmoved by the sight of Bram's gurgling body in front of her.

"Take them away," said the girl serenely. Then Ailsa was being dragged away and down a hall, deeper and deeper into the depths of Hell. Close behind her, she could hear a commotion and she tried to strain her neck to see. If Maalik got into trouble for what she did, she'd never forgive herself. Still, it had felt like the only thing to do at the time. If they'd known how he'd been treating her, they'd both be in grave danger. Now, hopefully, he'd be able to pass off her actions as human panic.

The demons stopped in front of a jail cell but instead of throwing her in, they pushed her to the floor in front of it. The rough ground tore the skin on her hands as she was forced forward.

"Bring him in," someone shouted and then Maalik appeared beside her. Before she could say anything, he was thrown inside the cell and the metal door slammed shut behind him, sealing him in.

"What—" Ailsa began to ask, perplexed. Why was Maalik being jailed and not her? But when she met her friend's eyes, he gave a slight shake of his head. Her mouth snapped shut.

"You'll be called for your trial in the morning," one of the demons told her with a growl. He punctuated his words by spitting at her feet and then their captors turned and left.

"What—" she tried to say again, but Maalik held up a finger.

"Wait. Wait till we're sure they're gone."

Ailsa stared at her feet as her ears thumped to the beat of her heart. *Calm*, she told herself. *Focus. You won't be able to get out of this if you lose your head.* She looked around the room, taking stock of their situation. The front of the cell was made from metal pipes, which looked like they had been welded into the walls. She crawled forward, peering through the gaps. Maalik's cell was little more than a hole in the wall. If he was to lie down, either his feet or his head would be forced to lean against the stone. Outside, where she had been left, was no more hospitable: a dank and dark tunnel.

But why am I out here while Maalik is in there, she wondered, eyeing the demon through the bars.

"Okay, I think we're safe," Maalik murmured. His black fingers threaded through the pipes, as if to touch her.

"Well," she said weakly, slumping against the metal, "this is a nice change of scenery." Ailsa reached out a hand to him, suddenly feeling very tired. "Why are you in the cell and not me?"

"They know you can't go anywhere because of the bond. If I'm trapped in here, you can't leave."

Ailsa closed her eyes. "I'm so sorry, Maalik."

"I'm going to save you," Maalik ground out.

Ailsa gave a low chuckle. "Really? How?"

"We'll sort it out."

Images of the metal bars being blown open, of electricity surging from her body, crossed Ailsa's mind. She knew exactly who they had come from.

That's not exactly helpful, she thought back to the voice inside her head. The voice that belonged to her guide. "We're so far underground, I can't even see the sky to find a storm."

You don't need to find a storm, Ishbel told her. *You can make your own.*

Ailsa rolled her eyes. Maybe if she had a year and a lot more training. But right now, time was of the essence.

Maalik finger rubbed hers through the gap. "I can't

believe you killed Bram."

"He had it coming," Ailsa growled.

She could feel Maalik inspecting her face. "He saw things, didn't he? Good things."

Ailsa sighed. "I couldn't help it. I'm sorry. I didn't have enough memories that could be construed as bad."

Maalik snorted. "Are you telling me off for being too nice?" Then, a little softer, he said, "Don't be sorry for thinking those things. Please."

She nodded, biting back all words on the tip of her tongue. *We should have run. You shouldn't have been so nice to me. I shouldn't be your burden.*

Instead, she asked: "So what now?"

"You'll be brought before all the demons tomorrow, and put on trial. If they decide your actions were selfish or evil, they'll let you go."

"But I'm fae." She gestured to the mark on her cheek. "I thought demons could only feed off the actions of humans?"

He shrugged. "You're half human. But you were protecting yourself, Ailsa. That's neutral. So they'll probably just tell me to punish you."

The sound of a pebble skating across the rough floor was the only warning they had that they weren't alone. The demon easily blended into the shadows, but then when he opened his mouth his smile showed glowing white teeth against the dark. "I'm afraid it's worse than that," said the stranger. "It wasn't self-protection, was it, girl? You were trying to save Maalik here."

Ailsa's mouth went dry as she took in the newcomer. He was dressed much finer than any of the demons she had seen so far. His muscular body was clothed in billowing purple trousers and a tight black jacket over his bare torso, which was covered in tattoos in thick dark lines. His hair was shaved short on one side, but hung long and waved over his other shoulder. Golden ram's horns curled around his ears.

The demon sauntered forward. "No need to look so worried. I come in peace."

Ailsa had thought she recognised the demon's accent but now she realised it was similar to Gris's. Not an Edessan, his skin was lighter, though just as tanned as Maalik's. An Akrosii then. Or, at least, he had been an Akrosii once.

"Well?" The demon laughed. "Aren't you going to introduce us, Maalik?" Then he reached out a hand towards a gap in the bars of Maalik's cell.

Maalik smiled. "It's good to see a familiar face," he said, taking the offered hand to shake in his. Then he turned back to Ailsa. "This is Calix. He's a friend." When Ailsa didn't relax her shoulders, he gave her fingers another squeeze with his other hand. "He's a fallen angel, like me."

"Don't say that so loud. I've built up my reputation

as best I could. You don't need to remind everyone I'm an outsider like you. Unlike our friend Maalik here, I've forgiven myself for my shortcomings." Calix sat down and leaned back against the bars, looking more like he was on a beach than in a jail. "Oh, my friend. You are in serious trouble."

"Oh really," said Maalik, looking around himself. "You don't say. What's the word?"

"It's not good," said Calix, tilting his head in Ailsa's direction. "Bram was one of the council member's sons."

"He tried to kill me first," Ailsa ground out.

The demon laughed without joy. "You're a fool if you think they care about that. Any excuse they can find to kill you, they'll take it."

"So what do I do?" Ailsa asked.

"The only way they'll let you go is if they're too scared to execute you. I don't suppose you've got some fangs hidden in that pretty mouth?" he asked slyly.

A growl from Maalik had the other demon rocking to the side. "Gods, Maalik, it was a joke," laughed Calix. "You're getting a tad territorial."

"I'm not going to let anything happen to her." Maalik ran a hand over his face. "She's in this mess because of me."

That's enough of that, Ailsa thought. "Hardly. You didn't exactly drag me into this hellhole like your pal Bram did. And before that you didn't ask that I get sacrificed to you. I suppose Nicnevan kidnapping Harris was your fault too? Stop being so self-deprecating and use that energy to get us out of here."

Calix slapped his leg and whooped a laugh. "Ooh, I like her. Exactly what you need, Maalik, is a woman who isn't afraid to tell you to stop whining."

Maalik gave the other demon a dark look, before turning back to Ailsa. "We're going to have to fight our way out, but we can make you seem a lot scarier than you are first."

"What do you have in mind?" Calix asked.

Ailsa could feel Maalik's eyes moving over her, even if she couldn't see them.

"Not only is the woman before you in possession of strong elemental magic, she's also the daughter of the Faerie Queen," he said.

Calix cast an appraising gaze over her. "Nicnevan? Interesting."

"Maybe," Ailsa muttered, her cheeks growing warm. "It hasn't been proven."

"It doesn't matter if it hasn't been proven, you just have to make the other demons believe it."

"So what do I do?"

Calix chuckled. "Try to be as terrifying as possible."

"I can try."

"Trust me," said Maalik fond look. "She can be terrifying when she wants to be."

Calix stood, satisfied with the plan. "I'll be back in the morning to collect you and I suggest you have a plan sorted by then. I'll do some eavesdropping, try to find out what the others are saying about the trial." He turned to Ailsa and bowed. "*Mi señora*, until we meet again."

Ailsa watched as Calix swaggered out, feeling rather glad that she had been sacrificed to Maalik and not him.

Chapter 46

She'd tried pacing. She'd tried sleeping. She'd even tried counting the stalactites on the ceiling above. Nothing could quiet Ailsa's mind.

Maalik, on the other hand, was sitting cross-legged inside his jail, eyes closed, looking as if he was a thousand miles away. His black hands rested gently on his knees and he was breathing slowly and deeply.

Ailsa leaned against the bars and tried to do the same, but she just couldn't switch off. She wished she could see outside, to find out if it was still nighttime or if they would soon be collected for their trial. She felt like a piece of thread holding a heavy weight, fraying and fraying, ready to snap at any moment.

"I know you're scared," Maalik suddenly said, still with his eyes closed. "But you can't do anything about it right now."

"Yes I can. I can worry," Ailsa grumbled.

"That's not helpful." He sighed, rolling his shoulders. "Try picturing yourself somewhere else. Somewhere you love."

Ailsa closed her eyes and thought. The first place that

came to mind was her beach. She imagined the fresh salty air and the sound of waves crashing on the sand. Then she remembered a scream. A seal with a bloody gash in its side. Raiders with skull masks and sharpened teeth.

Well, that's no good.

She cleared the image and instead thought of her childhood cottage. Bees buzzing happily outside the windows. The crackle of a warm fire. Buttery toast and snuggling under blankets with her wriggly big brother and her mother. Except, she wasn't her mother. Ailsa had been an intruder. This should have been someone else's memory.

Ailsa's eyes snapped open. "I can't think of a place. Would you tell me about yours?"

Maalik frowned. "I don't really have one either. I just imagine one that isn't real." He ran a hand through his hair, stopping his fingers when he got to the golden antlers. "I'm high up, on a mountainside, looking down over fields and valleys and rivers. The sun is setting but I can still feel the heat on my wings—" He stopped, failing to hide the sadness on his face. "It's bittersweet, but it's how I imagine being happy again. Maybe one day, it won't just be a dream." He looked like he didn't believe his own words.

Ailsa's heart clenched for him. "You never told me how it happened. How you became a demon. Sorry, if it's too painful—" she hastened to add.

"You'll never be able to look at me the same."

"No, because I'll know you better after. Help me understand. How did this happen?"

He paused considering for a moment. Something in her eyes must have convinced him because he uncrossed his legs and sat back against the stone wall, facing her head on. "How much do you know about Eilanmòrian history?"

"Very little."

He nodded. "In truth, I was the same when I first came here from my homeland of Kemet. Kemet was one of the few places holy enough to make angels. There was a collection of deities so concentrated that it wasn't unlikely that you would come across one in the street."

"Make angels?" Ailsa breathed. "How do you make an angel?"

"They are made from the souls of children who die too young."

She thought of a different child who had died, the one who she had replaced. Why wasn't she turned into an angel?

"I don't remember much from my early childhood, except fear. Kemet was under great upheaval. The pharaoh had turned his back against the gods, declaring himself to be the true master. So the gods sent plagues down to teach him a lesson." A fissure cracked down the skin on his cheek, revealing the fire underneath. "It was the Kemetian people who suffered. First there were droughts, then thundering hail wrecked our homes. But the gods had never been heartless. They provided food and shelter for anyone who would leave the main cities and pledge themselves to a deity. They wanted to show the pharaoh they had the real power. They expected him to see the hordes of people denouncing his divinity and for him to find humility."

His jaw tightened. "They were wrong."

"The pharaoh, instead, sought out the magic of the shaitan—evil spirits. He gave them leave to chase after the dissenters, to kill them."

A thousand questions whipped through Ailsa's head, but she pursed her lips together, keeping them inside. The story was pouring out of Maalik and she didn't want to make this any harder for him.

"My father had left Raqote, the capital, to pledge our family to Nebt-het, the goddess of mourning. She had come to him after the passing of my mother, and he had been her servant since. With us was my grandmother and my three older sisters. I remember they had nagged at me for being too slow.

"We were a mile from Nebt-het's temple when the shaitan came. I'll never forget the screaming of the other families behind us in the desert. It was like a wave was sweeping through the sand, getting closer and closer. We ran, but I couldn't keep up. My grandmother stopped, telling me to run ahead and not to turn around to look for her. Her screams told me she had sacrificed herself to buy me time.

"The doors of the temple were open. My father reached it first, with my sisters close behind them. I remember being so close I could see the horror on the faces of the other people inside the temple." Maalik clutched a black hand at his chest, lost in the memory. "Then a shaitan caught me."

"Dying was painful, but it was quick. Like snuffing out a candle. The next morning, my soul stood over my mangled body, watching as the blood slowly baked into the sand. It was a sad sight.

"On the horizon, the fields of Heaven materialised, calling me home, but a hand on my shoulder stopped me. The goddess Nebt-het had found me outside her temple. She offered to grant me a body again, if I would serve her. I was a young boy, not ready to leave the world, so I accepted."

His face cleared and a soft smile pulled at his lips. "I was given new flesh—stronger, faster—and best of all: wings."

Then he barked out a joyless laugh. "Little did I know that she didn't change me out of pity. The gods were building an army, and we were their soldiers. They trained us, equipped us with divine powers and in return we took our vows: destroy the shaitan, heal the injured and don't harm any humans. The army of angels swept through the cities, healing and cleansing until, finally, there was only one place we hadn't been—the capital.

"The ensuing battle left hundreds of angels and shaitan bleeding into the dust. Neither side won. The gods, seeing there would be more bloodshed if they continued, decided to call a truce. The pharaoh could have Kemet but none of his followers could go to Heaven when they died. The gods were tired of living amongst mortals, so they left. The angels were instructed to keep the peace, quietly and secretly.

"A few hundred years passed, and I'm afraid to say I became bored with my life. Healing minor injuries and delivering messages wasn't as exciting as war had been.

"I hadn't seen any of the gods for many years, but I was desperate to prove myself. If I could only be noticed by the upper circle of deities, perhaps I could ascend to archangel and be deployed outside of Kemet. So I started seeking out larger dwellings, bigger calamities.

"There was a disease ravaging the Western lands, many people were dying in agony. It took me two weeks to cure the sick, and then the disease was eradicated. Surely, I thought, now I will be noticed. But I heard nothing.

"Finally, I crossed the border and left my homeland behind on my own.

"I travelled first to the cities of Akrosia, which had been hit by earthquakes, then down to the islands of Edessa which had been battling hurricanes. It took decades to heal the injured and help rebuild. Still, I wasn't visited by a single god. Then I heard there was a war breaking out between Mirandelle and Eilanmòr and I travelled west."

Ailsa gave a jolt of recognition. Up until this point, everything had seemed so fantastical and far away. But now she could get her bearings in his story. She had heard about that war; it hadn't been that long ago. Certainly before she was born, but not by much. If Iona was here, she probably would have remembered it.

"I landed first on the island of Nerebus, determined to learn more about the politics involved," Maalik continued. "I wanted to be sure I was helping the right people. Unfortunately, it wasn't as clear cut as I had hoped. The monarchs of the two countries were cousins. Queen Luciana had sent her youngest daughter from Mirandelle to Eilanmòr for a summer. On the way, Princess Marissa went missing. The Eilanmòrians said she had never arrived, but Mirandelle was sure she had been murdered. I prepared to fly to Eilanmòr, to look for the girl. If she was alive, the Eilanmòrian's deserved my aid first, then I would help the wounded Mirandellis when the war had been won.

"However, before I could leave Nerebus, I was finally

contacted by a goddess. She confirmed that the girl had indeed been killed, and worse, the Eilanmòrian king was intending to use the skirmish as an excuse to invade Mirandelle. He hoped to release horrific monsters from the forests of Eilanmòr, to win the war and declare himself master of all."

Ailsa blinked in shock. "I've never heard of any of that."

Maalik gave her a dark look. "That's because it wasn't true." He sighed. "But I'm sure you can see the similarities between the story of this new king and the pharaoh from my childhood? I didn't even question the lie. To me, history was repeating itself, and I was the only one who could stop it."

"The goddess told me she would reward me if I helped end the war and of course I accepted the mission. We flew to the borders of Eilanmòr, to where the battle was raging. I remember circling overhead, watching as young men and women met their gruesome ends. The sun dipped below the horizon, drenching the battlefield in an orange glow, as if it were on fire. Bodies were split open, their wounds too much to heal.

"And then, out of the woods, stalked another army. Just like the shaitan of my childhood, they came in all manner of shapes and sizes—some with huge fangs, some with wings and some that rent the earth as they walked. I had seen enough. I believed I was seeing evidence of the goddess's story. An army of demons.

"I was about to fly into battle when the goddess stopped me. '*You are but one,*' she said. '*You cannot fight all of them. It is better to choose your opponent wisely.*' She led me to the largest Eilanmòrian tent. Inside, was an injured man, being tended to by a young woman in battle gear.

'*This is the king of Eilanmòr,*' the goddess told me. '*If you kill him, you put an end to his tyranny, and you will save countless lives.*' She gave me a spear and told me to plunge it into his heart—" Maalik's voice cracked on the last word and he closed his eyes.

Ailsa sucked in a breath, waiting for the inevitable. Because she knew where this story was going.

A black hand came up to cover his mouth, as if he was watching this happen all over again in his mind's eye. "I had been warned not to kill a human, but now I had the chance to save two countries, and ascend to a higher calling. In my head, I argued that it was for the greater good, but really, I was allowing my ambition and fear to cloud my judgement.

The armoured woman saw me first, and charged. One blow from the spear was enough to pierce her heart. Then I was standing in front of the king. He didn't plead, like I thought he would. Instead he looked me in the eye and told me his dying words. '*Please, tell my son, Connell, that he did the right thing.*'"

Oh gods, Ailsa thought as she finally put the pieces together. This was King Alasdair, Angus's grandfather.

Maalik breathed out through his nose. "What a strange final thought for someone so monstrous, I thought. Perhaps he had finally realised the error of his ways."

He took his hand away from his face and looked Ailsa in the eye. "Then I plunged the spear into his chest."

She felt a pain in her own chest at his words. The damage that one act had done, for all parties, was unimaginable.

"Afterwards," Maalik said. "I stood over his body, ready to feel the wave of righteousness wash through me. I had ended a war after all. Yet, I couldn't shake the feeling that I had done something irreparably wrong."

His voice grew thick as he said, "And then my wings became heavy. *Destroy the shaitan. Heal the injured. Never harm a human.* Those had been my vows, and I had just disregarded the last.

"Sometimes, people call us fallen angels, but it didn't feel like falling. Instead, it felt like flames were flying up my body, burning me from the inside.

"I clawed at my skin, trying to get the inferno out, but my hands became blackened with ash and my body turned molten inside. The fire burned through all the healing magic I had. Worst of all, my wings melted to my back, becoming heavy and unyielding.

"My second death was worse than the first. It lasted for hours. Finally, the pain abated, and I looked through my new eyes at the carnage that had been wrought. Not only had I been burned, but the tent had caught alight, leaving nothing but a crater of ash behind. Then, from out of the smoke, came the goddess.

'*You succeeded,*' she said, smiling benevolently. '*The war has ended with the death of the King and his daughter. The Mirandellis have retreated and the Eilanmòrians are burying their dead.*'

'*But look at me,* I croaked, lying on the baked ground. *I'm a monster.*'

'*You sacrificed yourself for the greater good. You should be proud.*'

'*Will you allow me into Heaven now?*' I asked the goddess.

The goddess shook her head. '*Heaven is only for angels and gods. It does not allow demons within its gates.*'

"*Demon,* my mind echoed, struck with horror."

Maalik stared down at his hands. "I remember her suddenly smiling. '*Do not worry,*' she said. '*You can come back to Nerebus and serve me.*'

'*Will you not be returning to Heaven yourself,*' I asked.

Then the full weight of what I'd done came crashing down on me. '*Oh dear little demon,*' she laughed. '*I am also forbidden. You should not blindly follow every god you meet. Someone will take advantage of your faith.*'"

"She used you," Ailsa breathed, feeling cold rage lick down her spine.

Maalik nodded. "It would seem so. And in my naivety, I believed her." He fixed her with a hopeless look. "So now you know."

Ailsa growled and reached out a hand through the bars. Maalik jumped when she placed it firmly on his leg and gave a squeeze. She pushed the anger down, replacing it instead with total acceptance and understanding, letting it burn brightly in her eyes, so he would make no mistake about how she felt. "Now I know," she agreed.

And somewhere inside Maalik a chink of darkness crumbled.

Chapter 47

Ailsa realised she'd fallen asleep when she startled awake with her face pressed against the metal bars. One of her hands was in Maalik's, who had moved closer so she could steal his heat.

"It must be morning," Maalik told her, giving her hand a squeeze.

She surreptitiously rubbed the dents in her face and peered around the jail. It was as dark as it had been when they'd been brought here. "How do you know?"

"I just feel like it's morning. Must be my circadian rhythm. My body clock," he corrected himself when she arched an eyebrow at him.

There was an echoing of footsteps in the corridors and Ailsa's heart leapt into her throat. "Maalik—"

"It's okay," he soothed. "It's Calix."

Sure enough, the Akrosii demon sauntered around the corner and chuckled. "Well, you two look cosy."

Maalik dropped Ailsa's hand and she gave it a flex. The frigid air bit against her skin so she tucked it under her armpit.

"Is it time?" Maalik asked.

Calix discarded his smile. "Almost. I've come to collect you both."

Maalik stood, clutching the bars for support. With a flick of Calix's fingers, the door swung open, allowing him to stumble out. "I think we're as ready as we'll ever be."

Ailsa uncurled herself from her spot on the floor. "Actually, I was wondering if I could speak to you before we go?"

Maalik tucked a stray strand of hair behind her ear. "What is it?"

She felt her cheeks heat. "Actually, I was hoping to speak to Calix."

The other demon barked out a laugh. "Tough luck, amigo, the ladies can never resist." To Ailsa he said, "How far does your bond stretch?"

"Enough that Maalik could go ahead a little." She tried not to look at Maalik's face, but she couldn't help but notice his whole body had gone rigid.

He coughed once while Ailsa stood awkwardly against the cell. "Fine, just don't be too long. I had hoped not to let on how far I can get from you." Maalik paused, as if he would say something further but then seemed to think better of it, stalking into the dark of the tunnels.

Ailsa could feel the tug of the bond pulling at her as he moved further away but it wasn't enough to unroot her from her spot. *I'm sorry*, Maalik, she thought. *This is for your own good.*

Half an hour later, Calix led her out of the jail. She could feel the bond getting slacker as she shuffled through the dingy tunnel, until they passed by an alcove and a hand snapped out to grab her elbow.

"Shh," Maalik whispered. "I've been waiting for you here. It's best if we go in together."

"I'll announce you're here," Calix said with a wink at Ailsa, squeezing Maalik's shoulder as he passed. He disappeared into a chamber ahead.

"Are you going to tell me what that was about?" Maalik whispered as he led Ailsa forward, not taking his hand off her elbow.

"Yes," said Ailsa. "Later. If we ever make it out of this alive."

The sounds of chatter echoed from a red door up ahead, which was illuminated by the flickering of firelight. Calix appeared at the door again, and motioned for them to come through. "You can go in now. I'll wait out here till you're done."

"Deep breaths," Maalik muttered, rubbing a thumb up and down her arm.

"You could still run," Ailsa murmured back. "You should get out of here while you can."

"I'm not leaving you," he said as they marched towards their fate.

They crossed the threshold of the room they'd be tried in and Ailsa's breath left her. Every other place in the demon's Nest was closed and claustrophobic, but this room was the opposite. A towering fire roared in the middle, creating a warm glow on the marble floor. The room was so huge that the back walls were shrouded in blackness. In front of them, though, Ailsa couldn't help but see the thousands of demons, crowding together to get a look at her. They clawed over each other, fighting to get closer. The only thing that kept them at bay were the red ropes slung up between the ornate columns as a barrier.

As wide as the room was, it looked doubly tall. The high vaulted ceilings seemed impossible underground. But right at the top, a circle of stained-glass windows allowed slivers of daylight in. There was the world above. There was freedom.

"So this is the sacrifice that killed a demon?" came a rasping voice.

Maalik strode forwards, but was quickly blocked by two demons acting as guard. One gave Ailsa a push towards the centre of the room and she made her own way, legs shaking. In front of the fire, the six demons from the night before sat in thrones of metal. The chairs looked like they had been melted and then solidified again, over and over. In the middle, on the largest throne, sat the little girl. *Their leader*, Ailsa thought. It had been clear by the reverence everyone paid her.

The demon closest to her twirled a glass in his hand. Its contents looked uncomfortably like blood. "Let's begin," he said, as if he was bored.

The crowd renewed their frenzy, trying desperately to launch themselves forward over the ropes. But none could cross the barrier. *It must be enchanted*, Ailsa realised.

"This girl is accused of killing a demon to save another," shouted a different demon over the rabble. "Bram was clearly about to reveal secret memories she had, and she killed him for it."

"Now hold on," the girl said, holding a hand up. Immediately the room hushed. "I'd like to hear it from her. Why did you kill Bram?"

Ailsa squared her shoulders, even as her stomach roiled. "I felt like it."

"Oh? Do you often kill for pleasure?"

A single bead of sweat trickled down her back. "Never before, but I've wanted to."

The girl ran her small tongue over her teeth in a motion that looked too mature for someone so young. "I think you're lying. I think you did it to save your friend."

Ailsa gritted her teeth. "Prove it."

"I don't need to," snarled the demon girl. "I just *feel* like killing you."

"No!" Maalik shouted. A demon beside him punched

him in the gut making him double over in agony. Another kicked him when he was down, taking advantage of his prone position.

This is it then. Ailsa braced for whatever torment they had planned.

"I wouldn't do that if I were you," someone called from behind her. The Akrosii demon sauntered forward with a wild smile on his lips.

Ailsa lifted her chin and he gave an almost imperceptible nod in answer.

"Leave off it, Calix," the demon girl said. "I'm resetting the balance. She killed Bram. I'm taking revenge."

The Akrosii chuckled. "I didn't know you cared so much."

"He was a demon. She is a human."

"No, she isn't."

"Calix…" Maalik warned.

"Shut up, Maalik. No, this girl is half fae. See that mark on her cheek?" He reached out with a finger as if to tilt her chin up, but then twitched it away at the last moment. "Dear Ailsa, is a changeling. And a very important one at that." With a flourish, he turned to the crowd. "This is Nicnevan's lost daughter."

"Queen Nicnevan?"

"Now, Nathaira, don't we have an interest in Queen Nicnevan's Unseelie Court? If you let this girl go, she will bring more death and destruction than Bram ever could." Calix waved Ailsa forward, still not touching her. "Show them what you can do."

The demons gazed to her, interest and hunger in their eyes. They weren't going to give up watching her die for a mere story. But as Calix had been talking, Ailsa had been throwing her powers up high towards the vaulted ceiling.

You know what to do, Ishbel told her.

Ailsa raised a hand, and the wind from outside answered her call, breaking through the stained glass of the windows, sending it showering over the crowd of demons. They erupted in panic, pushing and climbing over each other in a bid to get away. Ailsa's heart leapt as she realised she could see the sky in the gaping holes where the windows had been. Behind her, she raised a shield of impenetrable air over Maalik and Calix, and got to work. With a shout, she pulled the energy down from the clouds, sending a gale into the hall. It swirled around the room, ripping apart benches and tables, with her body as the eye of the storm. Up above, lightning crackled through the gaps, threatening to arc down to the floor.

She'd left the demon council unharmed so far, but now she addressed them. "Let Maalik and me go before I destroy all of Hell and you with it." Her voice had become deeper, more commanding. Almost otherworldly.

But the little girl who was their leader only gave a

delighted smile. Then she threw her head back, clapping her hands together as she laughed. "Brilliant. Absolutely brilliant. Look at the destruction. Well done, Calix."

"So you'll let her go?" asked Maalik.

The demon girl grinned again. "Fine, fine. I'm sure she'll be a valuable asset to our cause, especially by Nicnevan's side. Once the sacrifice has been fulfilled, send her on her way. I can't wait to see what she'll become."

Ailsa loosened her grip on her power. *We did it*.

"You on the other hand," the girl said darkly, staring at Maalik. "Need to learn a lesson." She raised her hand, revealing long black claws. With a swipe, she brought them down through the air. Maalik gave a gasp as deep gouges appeared on his cheek, exposing the molten flesh underneath. Then the girl struck again, doing the same to the other side.

Ailsa growled, building the charge again faster than light. The electricity erupted into the chamber, heading straight at the council of demons. Just before it could reach the little girl, Calix pushed Ailsa over. He gave a yelp as some of her charge shocked him. The energy crashed into the ground, a breath away from the demon leader. She didn't flinch.

"Leave it," Calix whispered to Ailsa, helping her up. Surreptitiously, he managed to slip a hand into the pocket of her jacket, leaving something heavy behind.

"Impressive," the girl told her, sounding a bit out of breath. "You can go now. But Maalik? We'll be watching you."

Her demon was dazed but as Ailsa reached him, she managed to get his arm around her. Despite the power that she could still feel in her body, he didn't jerk away. "Come on, let's go," she told him.

Then, against all odds, they walked out of Hell together.

Chapter 48

"I really am okay," Maalik grumbled as he pulled his arm back. For the first part of the journey home, he had leaned heavily on Ailsa, but then, after a while he'd pulled himself together enough to walk unaided. Not that she was letting him.

"You've stumbled twice in the last ten minutes."

"I'm just tired. Sleeping in a cramped jail cell will do that to you."

"Hmm," Ailsa regarded him coolly. "So you don't have any injuries from when you were punched and kicked in the gut?" She poked a finger at his midsection, and he scowled.

"It wasn't important. Nothing a bit of rest won't fix."

"You're unbelievable," she huffed. "You never look after yourself."

Maalik avoided her eyes. "I'm not worth it."

"You are," she growled, offering no room for argument.

They had arrived at the cabin, the return journey taking much less time than the departure. Ailsa wasn't sure she liked that. It made the demon Nest seem too close.

Ailsa strode ahead of Maalik, opening the door for him and almost tripping over Wulver in the process, who had been lying at the entrance. Now he stood, greeting the demon as he stepped inside with a nuzzle. Something came whizzing towards Maalik, licking at the wounds on his face affectionately.

"Hello, Muck."

"Well," Ailsa said, closing the door behind her. "If you won't look after yourself, I'll just have to. Go sit down and I'll make you some tea."

Maalik sank into a seat, nudging his foot into the side of the wolf's heavy body. The brownie, content with her blood-meal, settled herself into Wulver's fur so she could lick her wee paws clean. "Are you going to nurse me better?"

She filled a pot with water and hung it above the fireplace, glancing at Maalik for some help. He rolled his eyes, then, with a snap of his fingers, the tinder sparked in flame. Ailsa gave the wood a poke in the right direction, then came to sit on the floor in front of the demon. In her hand, she carried a cloth and a smaller pot of water.

"It depends whether you're going to be a good patient." She caught his chin with one hand, raising the wet cloth to his cheek with the other.

"That depends whether you're going to *be* patient with me."

Giving the skin a dab, the fabric came away reddened

with the dried blood Muck had missed. Luckily, the scratches underneath were healing quickly. "I'm being serious, Maalik. How are you going to cope when I leave?"

His smile dissolved. "What if I asked you not to? Leave I mean."

Ailsa stopped cleaning. "You know I have to," she answered quietly.

Maalik nodded. "And that's why I like you."

"There. That's you," she said, cheeks heating. She placed the pot of now murky rust-coloured water to the side. "By the way, I have something for you."

All this time, she'd felt the thing in her pocket wriggling gently. With a deep breath, she reached her hand inside and cupped the precious cargo, bringing it out to show Maalik.

The demon gasped when he saw it. "Is that—"

It was a small thing, a soul. Much smaller than Ailsa had imagined it. From the moment Calix smuggled it to her, it had emitted a comforting warmth. She had worried the faint glow would have alerted the demons to its presence, but they had been so distracted by all the electricity that they hadn't noticed.

Ailsa had wondered if you could tell who a soul belonged to, but now, she was sure you could. This glowing orb was distinctly Maalik, but lighter somehow. She could almost feel how he would have been before.

Before he had become a demon. Before he had been betrayed. Her heart broke a little, but imagining how he would react when he realised what she had done was enough to keep her strong. Now, watching him take the soul into his hands, tears glistening in his eyes, she was not disappointed.

"How did you get this?" he asked.

"It's why I asked Calix if I could speak to him. He knew where it was and promised to get it for me. It was pretty easy for him to steal it then pass it over when we were causing such a scene."

Maalik shuddered, pressing the luminous sphere to his chest. "Ailsa... I don't know what to say."

"It doesn't give you your wings back—"

"But now I can leave," he said wondrously. "I'm not trapped here."

"You're right. You could go back to Kemet. Or anywhere really."

"I could come with you?" His large black eyes were unblinking as they stared at her, almost as if he was terrified of her answer.

Ailsa beamed. "I'd like you to come."

Then his arm was around her, enveloping her in a warm hug. "I've been here so long," he said into her hair. "I don't even know what the rest of Eilanmòr looks like."

"Well, Dunrigh is pretty nice. I'll show you the castle, if you like."

Maalik let her go, hesitating before allowing a faint smile to form again on his lips. "And will you stay there? Once you've rescued your friend."

"I don't know." Ailsa shrugged. "I was heading back to my beach when he was captured, but I don't know if I belong there anymore. I used to be frightened of so much, the forest, other Eilanmòrians. But now that all seems a bit silly."

"What about Ephraim? Perhaps you'll want to stay there, with Nicnevan."

Her nose wrinkled. "I doubt that. From what I've heard, it isn't a place you'd want to stay. Maybe we could decide together?"

"Yes," said Maalik. "I'd like that."

Ailsa ducked her face. Something was squirming in her stomach. She looked down at his chest, watching as the little orb squirmed in his hands. "Shouldn't a soul be inside you?"

The demon sighed. "It was ripped out by magic. It has to be put back inside."

"How?"

"I have no idea. I've been reading books on the subject, but it requires great power. Only a very powerful fae would be able to do it."

Ailsa blinked. "Like a Faerie Queen?"

"Perhaps? I know that I could have done it as an angel. But I can't exactly ask them for help." He chewed on his lip, staring at the glowing sphere. "I have heard of a powerful object that could do it: The Cauldron of Life. It's an Eilanmòrian treasure, lost for centuries, that restores things damaged by magic back to their original state. I've been looking for it for years, but there was only so far I could go."

She patted him on the knee. "Sounds like the next adventure after saving Harris."

"You'll help me find it?" Maalik asked.

"Well, it can't be hard to find something like that; Eilanmòr isn't very big."

"Maybe..."

Ailsa stood, looking around the cabin. "Where are you going to put it in the meantime?"

Maalik poked at the brownie sitting on Wulver's fur. "What do you think, Muck? Will you hide it for me?"

She gave a cheep before zipping into the air to hover in front of his face.

"You're not to eat it though, eh?" he told her sternly.

Another chirp, which Ailsa hoped was an affirmative, and the demon handed off the ball of light to the brownie. Her little bee's wings whirred as she lifted it across the room and up onto the bookcase. On one shelf, sat an old hat and some baubles that she used as a nest. Muck placed the soul inside, then sat her fuzzy rump down on top of it as if it was an egg, squeaking in contentment.

Ailsa didn't think there was a safer spot for a soul to be.

Chapter 49

For someone who spent their days nursing others, Maalik was not a very good patient.

"I need to go out again, people aren't going to feed and heal themselves."

"What you need to do is sit down in that chair and drink your tea."

Insufferable, Ailsa thought as Maalik huffed and sat back on the couch. The worst of it was he reminded her of herself when she was injured.

"I can make myself food, you know," he muttered.

Ailsa stirred the contents of the pot with her wooden spoon, trying to stay patient. "I'm sure you can, but you're still recovering." The truth was she wished she was tucking into one of his meals—he was a much better cook than her. But he was her patient. And the gods knew he deserved to take a load off for a little bit.

"Fae heal faster than humans," Maalik moaned.

"I don't."

"You're only half fae."

Ailsa tried to fight the smile from her face as she watched his lips pull into a pout. "Here you are. Now eat your soup like a good wee demon." She brought two bowls over and handed him one before curling up on the opposite end of the couch with hers. "Don't worry, it's vegetarian."

"Thank you." Maalik lifted his spoon, blowing on it. His jaw was darkened with days old stubble. Ailsa cast her mind back, trying to remember ever seeing him shave.

"Everything okay?" Maalik asked with a frown.

Ailsa's cheeks flushed as she realised she'd been staring at him. "Yes. Yes, I was just waiting to see if you liked it."

He smiled, bringing the spoon to his lips and she watched as his tongue darted out to check the temperature. It must have been manageable because he tipped the whole thing in his mouth. "Hmm, not bad."

"Really?"

"I suppose I'm pretty lucky to have you nursing me back to health."

"Well," Ailsa said, tucking her hair behind her ear. "It's only fair you're looked after."

Maalik sat forward suddenly, and laid a hand on her knee. "No, I mean I'm lucky to have *you* nursing me back to health."

Ailsa's heart thudded in her chest. How black eyes could ever convey emotion was a mystery. But the way he was looking at her made her feel like she was standing on the edge of a precipice. This was it, the thing they had been tiptoeing around for weeks now. The culmination of every hand squeeze and shy glance.

She didn't know if she was ready.

She didn't know if she could wait until she was.

"Maalik, I—" Ailsa began, leaning towards him.

A whistle cut through the air from somewhere outside. Ailsa would have ignored it if not for Maalik's reaction.

The colour drained from his face, leaving his usually tanned skin ashen. His mouth twisted into a snarl. "Stay here." Then his long limbs uncurled themselves from the sofa and he was up, racing towards the exit of the cottage. The soup he had been holding tumbled off the couch, splashing the contents all over the floor.

"What is it?" Ailsa leapt up after him and tried to grab his arm, but he shrugged her off. "Is something wrong?" *Is it something I did?*

"Please." It was almost a shout and the silence it left was deafening. "Please," he repeated, turning back from the door to look over his shoulder at her. "It's dangerous. I'll be back soon."

She watched incredulously as he left, closing the door quietly behind him. What the hell could be more dangerous than gatecrashing a demon meeting? She was sick of people trying to protect her.

But Maalik looked... scared.

Then he needs me to help him.

Hadn't her powers been getting stronger? She wasn't a weak human anymore. She could hold her own in a fight; she had proven that when she had broken them out of Hell.

She would have to be quick if she wanted to follow him, or she'd be trapped in the cottage. What if he never came back? Would she be trapped there forever?

She kicked on her boots and wrapped a cloak around her shoulders. *I wish I had my axe*, she thought for the hundredth time as she grabbed a knife from the butcher's block in the kitchen, strapping it to her belt. Her hand was on the doorknob when she heard a growl from behind.

Ailsa's hand flew up to her heart. "By the gods, you scared me!"

Wulver was in the doorway to his room, the shadows curling around his fur. His blue eyes were unblinking, and he moved not a muscle. She could sense the disapproval emanating from him.

"Shouldn't you be out feeding people?" She nudged the door open slightly and his eyes snapped to the movement, all predator. She wondered if he would stop her.

A sigh rumbled through his huge body.

"I'm not running away," she told the wolf vehemently. Of course she wasn't. *Though*, whispered a voice, *it's only been two weeks since he caught you trying exactly that.*

She raised her chin. "Maalik needs me."

He dropped his body to the floor, crossing his heavy paws and giving a whine as if in resignation.

"I'll be back with him soon," she vowed.

The wolf nodded his head once as she closed the door behind her.

Ailsa crept through the woods, the incessant press of the sacrificial wall behind her. She had been just in time to escape the cabin before the magic pushed in on her. Now there was no turning back. She would need to follow Maalik until he returned home.

It was easy to track him. If she turned the wrong way, the barrier would push against her, until she set course in a different direction. She picked her way carefully through the forest, letting her power build up inside her. She wanted to be ready to fight, just in case. The clouds overhead followed her at a distance. To anyone else, it would seem like they were drifting naturally. The wind caressed her back, licking at her skin, willing her on. It waited patiently to do her bidding, circling back around like a devoted hound. It brought with it smells of pine and fire.

Maalik must be close.

Up ahead, she could hear voices and she deftly sunk into a crouch so she could creep between some boulders, unseen.

"You can tell her that when she speaks to you," came a rough voice. "If you dare."

"She doesn't have anything to hold over me anymore," was Maalik's reply. "Let her do her worst."

Deep in the woods, Ailsa peered through the ferns in front of her hiding spot. Maalik had his back turned to her, and in front of him was a surprising sight. There were people, around twenty of them, in a circle. They were identical yet wholly divergent; their features and clothing showed them to be from all different places. Eilanmòrian, Avalognian, Visenyan, Edessan... even some she couldn't place.

But they were all alike in their haunted stares, their gaunt faces, the claw marks that ran over their faces and arms. They looked like animated corpses and Ailsa could not tell if they were even breathing. The figures stood hunched over, each bearing the weight of a massive crystal in their arms without a flinch. Something about them was familiar, but she couldn't quite put her finger on it.

A man was waiting—it must have been him that had spoken before. His blonde hair and armour betrayed him as Mirandelli. A soldier? He was unmarked like the others, breathing and intact.

"That is what everyone thinks," he said, before turning to the circle of people. "Oh beloved goddess, I have brought you the demon." Light blazed from the crystals.

At the front of the group, Ailsa could see that Maalik flinched. He looked frightened but resolute. Ailsa had the feeling he had seen this before. If she had been in his position, she would have been shrinking away from the walking dead and their rotting skin.

In the centre of the ring, the air shimmered, distorting its surroundings. Ailsa watched with bated breath as it became milky and something moved inside its depths. Then it cleared and standing amongst the leaf litter was a figure. Ailsa's eyes snapped to where Maalik was, but he didn't seem surprised.

The figure was dressed in pristine white armour, which did nothing to hide the curves of her body. Like her clothing, her hair was moon-white, though her skin was ashen grey. Black lips stretched across pointed teeth. The only spot of colour on her was the golden crown on top of her head. She was unnatural, like nothing Ailsa had ever seen.

"My love," said the being. "It has been too long."

"What are you doing here, Dolor?" snapped Maalik.

He knew this... woman? Ailsa watched in shock and revulsion as the thing in the circle of crystals pouted in mock hurt.

"I have missed you and this is the greeting I get?" The woman lifted a hand as if reaching out to him. Ailsa watched in horror as Maalik's cloak was pushed to the side—just like it had been moved by the woman in the circle. She mimed gripping something and Maalik's chin snapped up.

She's touching him, realised Ailsa. *Even though she's not beside him.* The fear was boiling in her stomach, but it was also mixed with something else: rage. How dare she touch him!

"I could make you bow to me," said the woman. "Is that what you want? Would that…" she smiled, "… excite you?"

Maalik's hands were clenched in fists. "Just tell me what you want so I can leave."

She pouted again. "No fun. But, very well, I want you to join us, my love. We need a being of fire, and you're the perfect candidate."

"As I have told you many times before, Dolor, I won't make the mistake of doing anything for you ever again. So you can go and find someone else."

The woman's eyes darkened. "Listen here, you insolent mortal. You would be dead if it weren't for me."

"If it weren't for you, I'd still be amongst the ranks of my kin, healing people." His voice broke. "My life is miserable because of you. I wish you had let me die."

"You're not living up to your full potential," she hissed. "Running around, playing a healer when you know you have the power to influence the world… for me."

She raised the talons on her right hand, and brought them down, leaving red scratches across Maalik's chest.

He shuddered, trying his best to stay still.

Ailsa had had enough. Raising her fist in the air, she brought the storm thundering upon the clearing. The Mirandelli soldier looked up first.

"What's happening…?"

Dolor halted her clawing, and raised her gaze to the sky, a smile spreading across those lips. "Is this some sort of trick, Maalik?"

Ailsa stepped out from between the boulders and called the power from the tempest into her body. The electricity crackled in her veins, in her voice. "You have five seconds to get out of here before I fry every last one of you alive."

The woman regarded her a moment before bursting into laughter. "Oh Maalik, it seems you've caught yourself an admirer. And a powerful one too. Thank you, my love, she is perfect."

Frighten her, Ailsa thought. She directed a zap of lightning at the earth two feet from where the nearest person held their crystal. It sizzled the air in its wake, but the almost-dead people didn't even flinch.

The Mirandelli however, made a noise deep in his throat and launched himself at Maalik, holding a blade to his throat. "Stop it," he shouted, "or I kill the demon."

"Don't you dare," seethed the woman in the circle. "I have a better way to deal with this."

Suddenly, Ailsa's body was in agony. It felt like all her

bones were being twisted, ready to crack. The pain was burning, and she writhed, falling to the dirt, the storm forgotten.

"Now, Maalik." Ailsa could barely hear the woman over her own pain. "Are we going to agree, or do I need to hurt her more?"

Ailsa twisted her head to the side, suppressing the scream building inside her. Maalik was fighting against the hold of the soldier, shouting curses at the woman.

The creature in the ring shrugged a shoulder. "Suit yourself."

Blinding pain. Ailsa had never felt anything like it. Not when she had been beaten by villagers or thrown around by the Brollachan. The centre of the agony was in her right arm. She hugged it to her body as a whimper left her lips unbidden. The pressure increased until she couldn't think around the pain and then, with a sickening crack, a bone in her arm snapped.

Ailsa couldn't stop the scream ravaging her throat.

"No!" shouted Maalik, fighting harder against the Mirandelli.

"It's such a shame I'm not there in the flesh," chuckled the woman. "It would be so much better."

"Leave her alone!"

The pain around her bones was pulsing now, as if the creature was increasing and decreasing the pressure, allowing her to feel it more than if it was constant.

345

She shrieked and writhed on the ground, the agony intensifying again around her chest until, with another snap, one of her ribs broke.

"Please!" Ailsa shouted. In her haze, she wasn't sure whether she was pleading with the woman to stop or with Maalik to end it.

"I need you," said the woman to Maalik. "Say you'll join me, and I'll put her out of her misery."

Ailsa didn't miss the threat. This would end in her death.

"Don't let her—" Ailsa started to shout, but another shockwave of torture turned her words into screeches.

Maalik's eyes were haunted as he met hers for a brief moment. "I will never kill anyone for you again," he seethed.

"Too bad."

Ailsa's body reverberated with the sickening crunch as a bone in her spine was shattered. The world was pulsing in and out, unconsciousness biting at the sides of her mind. Through the haze of pain, her stomach plummeted as she realised something was irreparably wrong.

"Maalik," she choked. "I can't feel my legs."

The growl that ripped through the air sounded like it belonged to a beast.

"I will never kill anyone for you again," he repeated with burning hot rage. "But I'll gladly kill for her."

Ailsa watched, paralysed as his skin began to glow. It cracked, exposing molten flames beneath. The Mirandelli screamed as Maalik grabbed his arms, refusing to let go. The soldier's body caught in flame, until the places Maalik held him became ash. With a final howl, the servant died, and the demon dropped his charred corpse.

"I'll just find someone else," warned the woman. Behind that unnatural face, Ailsa could swear there was a hint of fear.

"Go to Hell," Maalik growled. "Ailsa, look away."

The people holding the crystals started to moan, their voices rising higher and higher. The bodies closest to the demon began to sway, but their faces remained impassive.

Maalik's body became ever brighter, until Ailsa could no longer focus on him. She closed her eyes and waited as the earth shook with his power. Then, with an almighty boom, a tidal wave of heat erupted from where he had been standing.

The outer air from the blast punched Ailsa in the side, and she gritted her teeth, riding it out. Even from where she was laying, the heat was almost too hot to stand. Where her clothing wasn't covering her skin, the blazing wind felt like sandpaper.

Somewhere ahead, a female voice screamed but the cry was cut off by the noise of stone shattering. The people carrying the crystals didn't make more than a moan as the fire burned them alive.

Just as the heat seemed almost unbearable on Ailsa's skin, Maalik let out an almighty roar and the air changed direction, as if it was being sucked back into his skin. Her body was flipped to the other side, like a rag doll. She felt the aftershocks only on her upper body.

And then, all was still.

Ailsa's ears were ringing from the explosion. She peeked an eye open to find that the woman was gone, and the crystals had been destroyed, along with half of the bodies holding them.

Now that the woman was no longer influencing them, it seemed like the power keeping the people alive had shattered too. Those who hadn't been ripped apart in the explosion, jerked around like fish until one by one their bodies stopped twitching.

Ash rained down from the sky, cloaking the air in a thick, noxious mist. Some of it got stuck in her throat, making her cough and tremble as she was unable to get away.

Oh gods, my legs.

"Ailsa?" shouted Maalik, emerging from the fallout. "We need to get you out of here."

"I can't move, Maalik," she whimpered. "I think she broke my spine."

He cursed before bending to scoop up her broken

body. "You'll be fine," he murmured into her hair as he lifted her.

She took a shuddering breath as he broke into a run through the forest, unable to feel the lower parts of her body. She would never be fine again.

Chapter 50

Maalik crashed through the trees, thoughts screaming through his mind. *Your fault,* they repeated, over and over. If he hadn't gone when the goddess had called... if he had told Wulver to keep an eye on Ailsa... Maalik shook his head. It all came back to the same thing: if he hadn't been so reckless and naive all those years ago, he never would have worked for Dolor. This was just another consequence of that decision, another thing he would have to live with. When would he ever again be able to look in a mirror and not loathe the reflection, he wondered.

With his every step, Ailsa's body shivered with the ghost of pain. He tried to keep his breathing even as he ran but a sob was threatening to escape his lips. Ailsa drifted in and out of consciousness and for that he was thankful. If she wasn't looking at him, he didn't have to hide the devastation on his face.

The light from the cabin shone through the woods and Maalik managed to will his legs on faster.

Wulver was waiting at the open doorway, as if he had sensed something was wrong. He asked no questions as he moved aside from the portal, though Maalik felt the reproach in the wolf's eyes.

"I need to get her lying down," he told the wolf. A few steps in and he gently laid Ailsa's body on the bed, trying his best not to jostle her. Her eyes flickered open, pain glazing the blue like ice.

"Maalik…" she croaked, trying to reach a hand for him, but failing to lift more than a finger.

"Shh," he whispered, stroking her hair. "I need you to lay still."

"Am I… am I going to be paralysed forever?"

"No," he said. "I'll fix you. I promise."

She blinked at the tears forming along her lashes, refusing to let them fall. "I can't, Maalik… I can't—"

"You won't have to."

"Please." Her lip trembled. "You have to find my friends… they need to know I can't go with them anymore…"

"Hear me now," Maalik growled. "You will be fine. I am not going to let you stay like this."

But she had already slipped back into unconsciousness.

Chapter 51

When Ailsa next woke, she was weighed down by some unknown force. The pain was gone, but in its wake, there was... nothing. It was almost worse.

She kept her eyes shut as she tested her body, trying to wiggle her toes like the Brollachan had done. She envied the monster now; if only she could find another, working body to inhabit she could walk right out of this cabin and kill the goddess who had done this to her. Her mind whirled with the repercussions—ways she needed her body, things she would now be unable to do—*but later,* she told those thoughts. Those things could be worried about another time. For now, she would concentrate on every toe, every nerve, until she felt some flash of... something.

The slam of a hand on a table caught Ailsa's attention and her eyes snapped open, blinded for a moment by the honeyed light. "Holy gods," she murmured as she took in what exactly was in the room with her.

It was like a scene from a painting, where Heaven and Hell were fighting over her destiny. Which of these creatures would claim her soul, she wondered, stunned.

The demon with the sad eyes or the angel whose anger was radiating from his divine body. Because, sitting at Maalik's kitchen table, sat someone who could not be anything other than an angel. The figure glowed in celestial light, though in his face was righteous judgement. But it was his wings that had Ailsa gasping. The ivory feathers fanned out from behind his back, taking up most of the small workspace, even though they were tucked in tight. If the angel heard her noise, he didn't acknowledge it. Instead, he stared down the demon before him.

Maalik's jaw was tight as he met the angel's disdain. Like the angel, his body glowed. The same cracks had appeared in the skin of his arms and chest, giving a glimpse of the hellfire underneath.

"I don't see why," the angel was saying. Even his voice was beautiful.

"I have been punished, over and over again," Maalik hissed back. "And rightly so. But this is not about me. My actions have yet again put an innocent at risk. But you can heal her. It would take but one thought."

"Even coming here was a breach of the sacred laws. Doing the bidding of a demon—"

"This is what you were made for," Maalik continued. "I don't know how you can sit there—"

"*I* don't know how you could follow the orders of that monster," the angel thundered. "How did you not see that you were doing the most despicable thing?"

"I thought I could end the war," Maalik rose from the table, his skin glowing brighter. "I thought if I sacrificed a few, I could save thousands."

"Well, perhaps if I sacrifice this one, you'll finally understand your folly."

Maalik brought his hand to his face and was silent for a moment. When he removed it, the devastation on his features had Ailsa choking.

"Please, Vasilii. Please, heal her. She is... the one light in my darkness. She deserves to be whole and away from me. Please, let her walk out of my life."

The angel regarded the demon for a moment, before blowing out a breath. "And what say you, girl?" His eyes found Ailsa's in the dim light and she gasped.

Maalik's head snapped round, finally realising that she was awake. In the space of a heartbeat he was across the room and on his knees before her. "Ailsa, how are you feeling?"

She bit her lip, remembering again the wrongness in her body. "I... I still can't..." Her throat choked on the hateful words, closing around on them as if to erase them, make them untrue. She was paralysed.

Maalik squeezed her hand, and Ailsa tried to lift the corner of her mouth for him.

A movement to the side caught her attention. The angel, Vasilii, had come closer, his eyes never leaving

Maalik. They were opposites, yet both had the makings of nightmares. When she had first met Maalik, his black eyes had frightened her, but now she had learned to read his other features. The way his nose wrinkled, or the way his lips quirked when he was holding in laughter. Even his golden antlers were more of a faerie tale than a horror story now.

The angel, however, was severe in his radiance. Where Ailsa expected divine benevolence in his face, she found only cold disdain. Was that because of her or Maalik?

She cleared her throat, trying to bring his attention to her, if only to protect Maalik's back from the harshness of his gaze. With reluctance he looked to her, coming closer to where she was on the bed.

"It has been a long time since I was this close to a human," he mused. "I don't often make visits anymore."

"So why are you here?" asked Ailsa, though she knew the answer. *I need to hear him say it.*

"This demon wants me to heal you," he said.

Ailsa's heart jumped into her throat, but she pushed the hope down. The conversation she had heard did not seem to be going favourably. She forced herself to control her features, offering up a cool, "He's nice like that."

"He seems to think you deserve this intervention." He almost looked bored as he sized her up. "What do you think?"

"You don't want to hear what I think," Ailsa mumbled.

For some unknown reason, this seemed to pique the angel's interest. Where his gaze had been flicking between her and Maalik, now she had his full attention. He stepped forward and crouched beside her feet. "Why don't I want to hear it?"

She sniffed. "Because I'm trying very hard not to tell you to piss off, but I'm afraid that would offend those sensitive, holier-than-thou sensibilities of yours."

Shock registered on Maalik's face, but the angel's features didn't even twitch. This close, she could see the irises of his eyes were an unusual shade of dark amber, like liquid bronze. Were Maalik's eyes like that once?

"Why would you tell me to 'piss off'?"

"You're offending my friend and I don't care for it."

The side of the angel's lip twitched. "Your 'friend' is a fallen angel, disgraced by the gods."

"All I know is, he was the first demon I ever met, and he's been kinder to me than most people have. You're the first angel I've ever met, and you seem like a complete bastard." Ailsa blew out a breath, turning her gaze away from Vasilii towards the ceiling. "So if you're not going to heal me, then I suggest you get out."

Though she wasn't looking, she could feel Maalik's mouth fall open. She also felt the subtle creak of the floor indicating the angel had walked away.

Good, she thought as her eyes danced over the roof beams. If she was going to suffer her body breaking, then she'd rather not have strange winged men around to add insult to injury.

The bed dipped beside her, and she looked to the side, expecting to find Maalik.

She flinched when instead she found Vasilii had walked towards her, not away.

"Who are you?" he asked, peering down at her with those burning eyes.

"A girl who has some severely bad luck," she croaked out in an attempt at a joke.

It was Maalik, speaking from behind the angel, who answered the question properly.

"She's a changeling and the suspected heir to Queen Nicnevan's domain. She's a woman who risks her life for those in need." His forehead creased, his voice thick with emotion. "She's a friend who is the bravest person I know."

"Impressive," said Vasilii. "So you're the key to Eilanmòr's future?"

She wrinkled her nose. "Perhaps."

"Then I suppose healing you could potentially save the lives of thousands of people?"

"Well I can think of at least one person whose life, right now, is counting on me not being paralysed..." *Who knows what state Harris is in by now.*

The angel looked her over for a moment, taking in her defiant expression and the tears threatening to spill from her eyes. Finally, he sighed. "I must warn you—both of you—something strange is happening. The balance of good and evil is being tipped, people of great power are being tempted into making bargains that they should not make. If you indeed are Nicnevan's lost daughter, you will have your part to play in what is to come."

"What is to come?"

"War," the angel said simply. Then he turned to the demon beside him. "How much do you care, Maalik? What would you do to heal her?"

Maalik's face lit up. "Anything."

"You stole back your soul. Would you give it up again?"

Ailsa looked at him in horror. "No, Maalik—"

"Yes," he answered.

"You can't do this!" Ailsa shouted at Vasilii.

He just ignored her. "Where is it?"

"In the hat on the bookcase," the demon said.

"Maalik, it's not worth it!"

He looked at her sadly. "You're worth it, Ailsa. Please, I can't heal you myself, but this is the next best thing. This is what I was meant for."

The angel stepped towards her, raising his hands. "Now, hold still and take a deep breath. This will feel strange."

"You bastard!" Ailsa struggled harder, willing her body to get up off the bed. "Stop. I don't want it."

But there was a tingling in her skin, starting around her chin. Ailsa whipped her head back, willing it to stop, but it was no use.

She screamed as the angel healed her, and the demon wept for his soul.

Chapter 52

The only sound in the small cottage was the steady patter of rain hitting the window.

Maalik was slumped against the wall, with Wulver curled up beside him. Ailsa watched his chest rise and fall through a veil of tears she wouldn't let spill. Her toes buzzed dully under the blankets, not quite under control but getting there. Though she was relieved by the feeling, she cursed it silently. Now every time she used her healed legs, she would remember what the demon had lost.

"Why?" she croaked. "Why did you let him take your soul? After we fought so hard to get it back."

The demon shuddered. "It's not like it changes what I am."

"But you could have left. You could have come with me."

"I don't deserve to leave this forest."

"You do," Ailsa told him vehemently, sitting up. "How many people do you have to save before you realise you deserve more than this?" She scrubbed a hand over her face, feeling the rage simmering inside. "This is the fault of that goddess. She tricked you." When he didn't respond, she slammed a hand down on the bed. Outside, thunder rumbled. "Who is she, Maalik?"

He raised his onyx eyes to hers. "After I fell, I did some research. She is a goddess of more ancient places than this. Countries have risen and fallen in her presence. She is Serqet to the Kemetians, Nemesis to the Akrosii. In Nerebus, she introduced herself as Dolor. It wasn't till later that I learned it was the Ancient Mirandelli word for pain. The goddess of pain. That's why she got so much stronger when she was torturing you."

The memory of the agony brought the feeling of bile rising in her throat. "Why is she here in Eilanmòr?"

"She won't just be in Eilanmòr. She'll be in Mirandelle, in Avalogne, in Visenya..." He sat forward. "She is a plague, Ailsa, hell bent on feeding on the souls of as many people as she can. That's who her slaves were, *Tentoria*. The Soulless."

"And she's the one who made you this way."

Maalik nodded. "I lost myself. Dolor exploited that. She convinced me that war could be stopped if I ended it. I had seen so many people die, so I thought, well, if I just killed one person, then I could save thousands."

"It wasn't your fault, Maalik. You wanted to do the right thing, the thing that would save the most."

"But she benefited from it. Do you know how painful it is to turn into a demon? I imagine it gave her more power than if the war had continued," he said bitterly.

"Oh my gods…" She had fed off him.

"That's just the thing. Gods. She's not the only one."

Ailsa frowned. "Not the only god?" *Of course not, we have many in Eilanmòr alone…*

"She's not the only one of her kind. She has siblings and they're just as bad, if not worse."

She shivered, the movement twinging the healing bones in her chest.

"Like I said, I did some research. There are four gods that call themselves the Soul-Eaters," Maalik continued. "Aside from Dolor, there is Chao, god of chaos. Then there is their sister, Timor, goddess of fear. No one who has ever seen the last of the Soul-Eaters has lived to describe him. Desper is his name."

"What does it mean?"

"Despair. He's the god of despair. When his sisters and brother have taken you and you are but a husk, it is Desper who finishes the job. The others merely take pieces of one's soul. He devours it."

"Let's hope he stays away."

Maalik's face twisted sadly. "That's unlikely. A war is coming, and no one believes me."

"I do."

The demon paused for a moment, before standing and coming to sit on the edge of Ailsa's bed. "Dolor has been trying to recruit me, ever since I became a demon," he sighed.

"But you've refused."

He nodded. "But I think I know why she tricked me into changing, aside from the power she gained. It seems they're looking for a way to reap all of the souls in Ossiana."

"How?" Ailsa breathed.

"There are legends of magical weapons. The Four Treasures. Four powerful objects. They are said to be the only thing that could kill a god. And if the Soul-Eaters can harness them all together, they could kill every god but themselves. They would have a monopoly over all of Ossiana. They could do anything they liked."

"Or," Ailsa said slowly, "someone could use the weapons to kill them."

"The only problem is, no one really knows what they are." His shoulders slumped. "Do you remember I mentioned something called the Cauldron of Life before? It's the only one I've found the name of. A drop of water from inside it can reverse any magic, including the removal of a soul."

Ailsa didn't care what the other treasures were. *That's the one we need to find.*

"That's the one I know most about," Maalik continued. "From my research, it seems that another treasure is a weapon that never misses. And one is some sort of magical stone that can transport you wherever you want—"

Now that sounded familiar. "The Stone of Destiny!" Ailsa grabbed his arm. "Maalik, I know where it is. I had it in my hands only a few weeks ago."

He gasped. "We have to get it, Ailsa. Before Dolor does. Where is it?"

"Right now? Around King Duncan's neck, I imagine. I don't suppose he'd let us borrow it?"

Maalik nodded. "If it's around the king's neck, it's safe for now. I need to find the other objects. I had hoped, with my soul back, I'd be able to go to the library in Edessa and find some clues."

"We'll get your soul back, Maalik. I promise." But there was something she didn't quite understand. "You said Dolor tricked you into changing for a different reason, aside from the power. What is it?"

"Each treasure is controlled by a different element, and they can only be wielded by beings who possess the correct magic. They're looking for someone with fire. And since I'm a demon," he flexed the skin on his arm, allowing fissures to grow, revealing his molten core underneath, "I fit the bill."

Ailsa sucked on a tooth. "Why doesn't she just find a different demon?"

"I think that's what she was alluding to while she was torturing you." Maalik shrugged. "She took a liking to me, but I think she's given up."

"So," Ailsa reasoned out. "They need fae with earth

magic, water magic and *air* magic too?"

He looked at her blankly, not understanding her train of thought. "I suppose."

"Like me," she huffed.

Immediately, his face shuttered. "You'll stay out of this, Ailsa. Dolor nearly killed you. Imagine what the other gods could do, whether you're fighting with them or against them. Anyway, you've got your own battles to win. Let's focus on getting you better so you can go to Ephraim."

She nodded and allowed him to wrap an arm around her shoulders. The thought of meeting the goddess again brought on another wave of nausea. And he was right, rescuing Harris was the most important thing right now.

Still, she couldn't help but wonder if today's worries would seem small in the face of a brewing war.

Chapter 53

"Ailsa? How are you feeling?" The voice was soft but insistent enough to wake her from the deep dark she was floating in.

"Okay. A bit sore." She stretched her muscles, wincing when her calves cramped. But that would mean... "Maalik, I can feel my legs," Ailsa breathed.

Maalik was by her side immediately, pushing her hair back to see her eyes, watching in wonder as she wriggled her toes. "He did it. Vasilii did it."

Ailsa's joy turned sour. "I still don't like him."

The demon let out a broken laugh. "I could kiss him right now!"

Kiss? Ailsa's mind was muddy as the demon wrapped his arms around her and buried his face into her shoulder, being careful not to snag her hair with his antlers.

"I'm so glad you're okay," Maalik whispered into her skin. She could feel his lips turn up in a smile.

She raised her hand and rubbed circles into his back as he held her, both needing the comfort. Ailsa felt Maalik's warm tears land on her neck, but didn't comment as she just let him hold her. She fought back the prickling in her own eyes, staring at the candlelight dancing on the ceiling of his cabin.

The next time Ailsa woke, the dawn light was creeping in the window. The bed was dipped to the side and when she looked over, she found Maalik, fast asleep with his arms and head on the mattress but his legs folded underneath him on the floor.

She watched him for a while, marvelling at how peaceful he looked in sleep. The tension in his face was completely gone. One strand of dark hair hung over his forehead. Ailsa's hands itched to push it back, but she knew it would wake him. Instead, she tried her best to get control of her newly healed limbs and rolled out of the bed without disturbing him.

Her stomach growled. How long was it since she'd eaten? She eyed the demon. How long since he'd eaten?

Ailsa slipped on her jacket and boots, all the while watching the demon for signs he would wake. *He must be exhausted. I'll go scrounge up some food for when he wakes.*

As quietly as possible, she opened the door and stepped out into the soft light. Before she could shut it again, something small and fuzzy flew out after her.

"Oh, you're up, are you?" Ailsa smiled at the brownie. "It's probably better that you come with me, otherwise you'll wake up Maalik."

Muck buzzed around her head in excitement and they set off into the woods together. Ailsa breathed in the fresh air, feeling like she hadn't had any for weeks. It felt so good to stretch the legs she thought she'd never move again, but her body still ached. "When I've rescued Harris, I'm going to sleep for a month," she told the brownie, zipping back and forward between the trees. "Though, I wonder if I'll get to. If Nicnevan is my mother, maybe they'll make me dress up in pretty dresses and hold court…" Ailsa groaned.

She missed having the peace and quiet of her beach. Ever since Harris and Iona had appeared, she'd been plunged head-first into adventure, and she wasn't sure she liked it. Yes, she'd finally found friends, finally been accepted. But if she was really being honest with herself, she preferred the calm of Maalik's cottage. "Maybe I'll come back here, after Ephraim…" Now that Maalik couldn't come with her, perhaps she could stay with him. *If he'll have me.*

Lost in her thoughts, Ailsa didn't realise she'd walked far until the sun was high in the sky and she reached the house they'd spied on when Wulver delivered his fish. There were no sounds of movement inside the cottage, but a gang of chickens pecked away happily at the ground. They must be out.

Then Ailsa spied a little table out beside the house's

short fence. On it were boxes and a sign.

"Eggs," Ailsa realised. It had been normal for people in her village to sell their extras on tables like this.

Stepping closer, she frowned down at the sign. How much were they asking for?

"You can have a box for free, if you like," said a little voice.

Ailsa jumped, looking around until she saw a little girl dressed in a pretty dress and an apron staring up at her curiously.

"I can't take it for free," Ailsa told her. "Your mother will get mad."

The girl smiled, revealing two missing teeth. "I saw you, in the bushes, when Wulver brought us the fish. My mama won't mind."

"No, there must be something I can do in exchange."

Just then, Muck flew forward, towards a hessian bag standing upright in the soil.

"They're seed potatoes," the girl explained. "My mama has to plant them but she's always so busy."

Muck hovered above the bag and then buzzed around it. To Ailsa's astonishment, the potatoes floated upwards and hung in mid-air for a moment. Then, the brownie made a clicking noise and they fired into the soil, burying themselves in the dirt.

The little girl clapped her hands. "Yes, well done!"

Muck bumbled over to the seedlings. Another few

clicks and more soil was pushed over them. Then she drifted back to Ailsa's side, looking quite pleased with herself.

"I might be able to help too," Ailsa said. She raised her hand, pulling slowly at a small cloud above them, until it glided gently down to the ground. It drifted over the vegetable patch and Ailsa twisted her hands together, as if wringing out a cloth. The cloud began to rain, just over the planted potatoes, until it dried up and dissipated into the air. For a moment, a rainbow hung the air above the vegetable patch.

"Wow," the girl squeaked. "You're both magic. Now you definitely deserve some eggs."

Ailsa smiled, before accepting the box that was shoved into her hands. The little girl sent them off with a wave and Ailsa couldn't help laughing at her exuberance.

They stopped on the way back to the cabin to forage some wild garlic. *It's not really breakfast time anymore*, Ailsa supposed. Maalik could still be asleep though.

She realised she was wrong about that when she found the demon on the path nearby.

"Ailsa," he called. "Where were you?"

"I wanted to surprise you. I brought breakfast. Don't worry, no animals were harmed."

To Ailsa's surprise, Maalik dropped the bag he was

holding and in three strides he was in front of her. Without a word, the demon gathered her in his arms and crushed her to him.

"Ailsa, you left the cabin."

"Yes, to get food," she laughed.

He leaned back, searching her face. "Without me."

That's when she realised. "Oh." She'd been able to leave without him. Without any resistance.

"The sacrifice has been fulfilled. It must have dissolved when you were injured. Ailsa, you can leave," he breathed.

Maalik drew back to stare at her face and Ailsa saw it. Underneath the awe, underneath the elation, there was a sliver of despair he was trying to hide.

Now she could rescue Harris, but she'd have to leave Maalik. Weeks of feeling bubbled to the surface. Ailsa reached out a hand, wrestling with her conscience. An image of mirthful eyes and copper curls.

I can't do this. Not until Harris had been saved.

So instead, she rested her head on his chest. Without hesitation, he tucked his chin on her head and gathered her closer again. And for a moment, listening to Maalik's heartbeat, Ailsa allowed herself to think about the desires of her heart.

Chapter 54

Ailsa rubbed at her eyes, unwilling to fall asleep yet. She had been sitting across from Maalik all night on the bed-couch, talking about anything except her plans for leaving.

Maalik passed her the bottle of whisky he'd found, and she took a sip, feeling it burn all the way down her throat.

"You don't have to drink it," he laughed when she made a face.

"I want to." Because it was something to do. Another distraction.

The demon lay back down, propping his head up with one hand. "What were we talking about before?"

"You were going to tell me about what they do to dead people in Kemet."

"So morbid," Maalik laughed. "Well, the Kemetians believe that you don't need your organs when you die, so they cut them out and place them in jars."

Ailsa hugged the pillow closer. "Gross!"

"Yeah, it is. They shove a rod up the nose and swirl the brains around so they can pull them out." He smiled sleepily, enjoying the faces of disgust she was making. "They leave the heart, though. So it can be weighed by Anubis, god of the afterlife."

"Is that true though?" Ailsa asked. "Do you have to pass some sort of test when you die?"

Maalik shrugged. "I have no idea. I was turned into an angel before I could find out."

"It doesn't really seem fair though," she grumbled. "What if your family couldn't afford to have all your organs pulled out?"

"I suspect all the mummification stuff is just a ritual to make the family feel better." Maalik accepted the whisky from her and took a swig. He didn't even wince. "From my experience, people are judged by their actions, not how light a bag of muscle is."

Ailsa leaned down to pet Wulver where he lay beside the bed. He gave a rumble as she scratched at his ears. "Tell me another one. Something a bit less macabre."

Maalik thought for a moment. "How about the story of Osiris and Isis? Osiris was the pharaoh—the King— of Kemet, thousands of years ago. He was murdered by his brother, chopped up, and the pieces of his body were scattered all over the land."

"I thought I asked for something less macabre?" Ailsa yawned. She didn't really mind what the story was, as long as Maalik kept talking, and she could keep putting off falling asleep.

He laughed. "I'll get there. This is a love story really. So, Osiris's wife, Isis, found out he had been killed and searched for years, all over Kemet, for the bits of his body. She never gave up. Finally, she found them all and put him back together. She asked the gods to resurrect him and, seeing what she had done for her love, they agreed to help. They turned him into the god of death and Isis into the goddess of life."

"Wow," Ailsa said, giving him a nudge with her foot. "You really got a raw deal there. Why didn't they turn you into a god?"

Maalik snorted. "All the spaces had been filled," he joked.

Ailsa smiled slyly. "I wonder what they could have made you the god of?" She tapped her chin. "Maalik, God of Old Ladies? Since you're so popular with them?" He pursed his lips, but she continued anyway. "Maalik, God of Books and Big Words?"

"How about you? You could be Ailsa, Goddess of Never Shutting Up?" She threw a pillow at him, but he caught it before it could smack into his face. "Goddess of Temper Tantrums?"

"You're one to talk," she muttered, sticking out her tongue. "I wouldn't want to be a goddess, anyway. People would want me to bless them all the time."

"You could smite people instead?" he laughed.

"I could do that now," she muttered, her eyes growing

heavy. She pulled the pillow out from behind her back and placed it under her head. There was no harm in getting comfortable.

"True," Maalik said softly. "What would I have to bring you so you wouldn't smite me?"

She yawned, rubbing her face. "Lavender bath soap. And a mountain of honey cakes." Her eyes closed, unable to stay open any longer. "My axe. And a plate of black pudding. From Dunrigh."

She wasn't sure if she mumbled anything else as her body sunk into unconsciousness. But she did think she heard Maalik whisper something, somewhere between wakefulness and sleep.

"I'd bring you all of that and more, if I could. Whether you're a goddess or not, you've got me. I'm devoted, body and soul—wherever it is—until we're both gone from this earth. And maybe even after that."

Chapter 55

Just after sunrise Ailsa jerked awake. She stood up, extracting herself from Maalik's arms, which had come around her in his sleep.

"It's too early, Ailsa," Maalik grumbled. "Come back to bed."

She hesitated, wringing her hands. "I think I heard something."

Maalik was immediately alert, sitting up from the bed with a start. Ailsa felt a warm breeze as he joined her at the window and she shivered. Gone were the sounds of chirping birds and insects. Instead, a heavy stillness cloaked the forest. There was something out there.

"What is it?" Ailsa asked Maalik.

The demon sniffed. "Three fae. Can you feel them?"

"No..."

"Focus on your magic. Can you feel theirs answering yours?"

Ailsa cast her power out like a web, letting it settle around the cottage. She couldn't feel much, just the life of the forest around her. She was about to voice her frustration, when Maalik placed a hot hand on her shoulder, steadying her. Ailsa fought to pull her attention from the demon behind her, but when she managed to gather her concentration, she felt something. There, moving closer, the three fae Maalik was talking about. And behind them another figure, human this time.

"Angus?" Ailsa whispered. Then she was pulling the door open and running out into the early morning mist. Ailsa could hear Maalik running behind her, but she was too fast. She crashed through the foliage, darting between trees, towards the lone human. But she had forgotten about the fae that surrounded him. Three fae. Her mind caught up with this realisation just as she almost barrelled into something large.

Ailsa gaped in horror as she took in first the chest, then the snout of the monstrous creature before her. It tossed its head, and she ducked, barely missing its sharp horn.

"What the hell is that?" Ailsa shouted as she looked up at the massive horse in front of her. "Why does it have a horn?"

She could hear Maalik behind her as the demon's snarl reverberated around the wood.

But it was the next voice, which had Ailsa sinking to the ground.

"Ailsa?"

Then, before she could let out a choking laugh, a bearded man lunged for her, wrapping her tightly in a fierce hug.

"Ailsa, we found you," Angus murmured into her hair.

"You did."

"I'm so sorry it took us so long. We followed a few wrong leads before Gris managed to pick up your trail."

"Are you alright?" said a female voice and then Ailsa was being hugged from behind by Iona.

"I'm fine, I'm fine," Ailsa assured them, unable to keep the smile from her lips. "Where *is* Gris?"

"Here," he growled. But the Fear-Laith had not joined their happy reunion. Ailsa raised her head from Angus's shoulder, to find Gris folded into a feral crouch, his teeth bared. "All of you, get behind me. Ailsa has been followed."

She frowned, before following his eyes to the demon, hovering behind them. "Oh, no. That's Maalik," she explained, shooting him a smile. "He's a friend." It had been a while since she had noticed how frightening Maalik could look. Now, in front of Angus, Iona, and Gris, she took him in with fresh eyes. Yes, he was eerie to look at, but there was nothing evil in the soft expression he wore.

"You made friends with a demon?" Angus laughed in disbelief.

"I'm friends with you," Ailsa snapped, letting him go. "I thought you'd be less shocked." She stood and crossed back over to where Maalik was standing. "These are the friends I was telling you about," she told him, taking his black hand in hers. He looked at the group with unreadable eyes. "Maalik has been looking after me," she told the others, her gaze drinking them in. "It seems like we've all got a lot to catch up on. Like how you have a unicorn now."

Iona bit the side of her cheek. "It seems she took a liking to Angus."

The prince puffed up his chest. "Ailsa, this is Laire." And to the horse, he murmured, *it's okay, she's the one we were looking for.* "Laire helped us find you," he explained.

"Well," Maalik said with no emotion. "You must all be tired. My cabin is just through these trees. You can rest and get some food before you all head off." Then he dropped Ailsa's hand and turned on his heel, back towards the house.

Ailsa's palm tingled as she watched him retreat.

"If you trust the demon, we trust you," Iona told her, looping her arm through hers. "Come on, lead the way."

It was worse than when Gris and Angus were sniping at each other.

The tension hung in the air of the cabin. Wulver and Muck had made themselves scarce somewhere and Ailsa didn't blame them. She tried desperately to cut through it but making people feel at ease wasn't exactly her strength.

"I'm sorry I disappeared, I just wanted to practise," she explained as they sat around stiffly, drinking their tea. "But Maalik helped me with that. He's a pretty good teacher."

The demon ducked his head and didn't reply.

"So did you learn to master your magic?" Gris asked. "You weren't doing very well before you went missing."

Ailsa fought the need to roll her eyes. "Yes, I think so. I had some chances to improve."

"How did your faerie powers manifest?" Gris demanded, leaning forward as if he was assessing a soldier.

"I grew some plants," Ailsa answered in a clipped tone. It wasn't exactly a lie. The seedlings she had watered with her powers yesterday would be growing, if a little slowly.

"Good," Gris grunted. "You're ready to head to Ephraim then."

Ailsa put her cup down and turned to Iona. "How far are we?"

The selkie was sitting primly on the edge of the couch, which had been hastily pushed away from the bed and tidied. "You were taken in the right direction. It'll take somewhere between a day and two days, depending on whether the faeries want us to find them. I'd really like to get going as soon as possible, if you're ready."

"Of course," Ailsa told her. Harris was waiting for them.

"Are you free to go?" Angus asked.

All eyes turned towards the demon hovering in the corner.

Maalik cleared his throat. "The sacrifice has been fulfilled, just in time for your arrival. Ailsa can leave whenever she wants."

The prince stood and stretched. "Good, because the sooner we can get to Ephraim, the sooner we can go home. I am done in with all this travelling. Oh, by the way," he reached into his pack, producing something metal and familiar. "I brought you something."

Ailsa was immediately up and across the room. "My axe," she breathed, taking the wooden handle from Angus. "Thank you." Ailsa tested its weight in each hand before tucking it into her belt where it belonged.

"Why don't you make a plan and get yourselves ready," Maalik suggested. "I'll go and get you some food to bring with you."

Angus and Iona nodded their thanks. Gris gave a grunt before launching into a list of preparations. "I'm going to repack my bag and I suggest you all do too. And the prince had better take this opportunity for a wash, you stink of sweat—"

No one noticed the demon slip out of the cabin. Except for Ailsa.

"Where do you think you're going?" Ailsa called to Maalik once she was outside.

He stopped, looking at her over his shoulder. "I've got some apples in my store, I thought they could be useful."

With a jog, she caught up with him. "I can give you a hand."

The demon shrugged and continued round the side of the house. At the back was a wooden hatch, covered over with pine needles and dried leaves. He bent down to lift it, revealing the pantry. But before he could reach inside, Ailsa grabbed his hand in hers.

"I wish you could come with me," she told him.

He raised his face to look up at her, the anguish he'd been hiding etched on his features. "You know I can't."

"Well then tell me to stay," Ailsa breathed.

He gritted his teeth . "You're free to go. The sacrifice is gone."

"Don't be so stupid." She reached out and tried to smooth his forehead with her other hand. "The bond has been broken since yesterday, and I'm still here. Don't you want me to stay?"

He squared his shoulders. "No."

That cut deep but she pushed the thought away. "Yes you do."

Maalik dropped her hand and stepping away. "Leave Ailsa. You have other people counting on you. Don't you want to save Harris?"

"Of course I do."

"Then *go*." It would have sounded sincere if his voice hadn't broken on the last word.

Oh no you don't. She could see right through this sorry attempt to push her away. Ailsa marched forward, until he backed up, cornering him against the side of the cabin. "Why are you doing this? I thought we were friends."

"I don't deserve to be your friend." Maalik hung his head. "I'm a demon."

"You are worth more than all the angels in heaven," Ailsa told him vehemently.

"Stop it. I want you to go." He closed his eyes and a single tear escaped down his cheek. "Please. Just go," Maalik whispered.

Ailsa watched him for a moment, waiting for him to cave in and take it all back. When he didn't, she growled at him. "Hear me now, I'm coming back for you, whether you want me to or not." Then she stalked away, giving him the space he needed.

Chapter 56

"You ready to go?" Iona asked when Ailsa returned to the cottage.

No, not even close. But she had a job to do. "Yes, I'm ready."

"Let's go then." The selkie gave Ailsa's hand a squeeze before heading out the door, followed by Angus and Gris. She could see the unicorn rise to meet them from where she had been lounging under a tree.

Gods, she's big. Ailsa had been secretly glad when Angus had explained Laire wouldn't let anyone but him ride her. Horse riding was not for her, even if they were magical ones.

She stood for a moment on the threshold, taking in the small space. How had it only been a few weeks since she'd arrived here, carried in Maalik's arms? It felt like a lifetime.

A growl had her jerking her head up. The door to Wulver's room creaked open, revealing his long nose. On his shoulder, Muck was dozing as if she had fallen asleep waiting till everyone else had gone. She made little crackling noises as she snoozed.

"Have you come to see me off?" Ailsa asked the wolf. He padded across the room so he could nuzzle into her side. "You really are a big softie," Ailsa chuckled. She placed a hand under Wulver's heavy head so she could look him in his ancient eyes. "Look after Maalik for me, until I can come back." She knew it didn't need to be said. After all, they'd been together without Ailsa all these years. Still, it made her feel better to say it. "And you—" she scratched the brownie's fuzzy belly, waking her from her sleep, "—give Maalik a hand, please."

Muck chirped something which could have been an affirmation.

Ailsa straightened. She was going to miss this place. *I'll be back soon, though.* Maybe if she kept telling herself that, it would one day be true.

Ailsa sighed as they headed off down the path, away from the cabin. After Maalik had dropped off some food, he'd made himself scarce. *He's not even going to say goodbye properly.* But then, before they could round the corner and lose sight of the house, she looked over her shoulder at it one last time.

Maalik was leaning out of the door, with one hand sunk into Wulver's fur and the other raised in a wave. Ailsa's heart leapt. His face was shadowed in from the clouds up above. With a flick of her fingers, she sent them scuttling across the sky, allowing the sun to shine down on the cottage.

Maalik looked up, letting the new light bathe his face with a smile, even as it caught the tear tracks glistening on his cheeks.

Don't do it, Ailsa told herself as she felt her own eyes reacting. *You promised yourself you'd never cry again.* There had been a lot of close calls lately. Ailsa waved one last time before the trees obscured the demon from view.

She felt a nudge at her side, and she blinked the sadness away.

"It seems that you've had an interesting few weeks," Angus murmured to her. "Who was that, Ailsa?"

She frowned up at the prince. "A demon."

Angus shivered. "I mean that is obvious. But who is he to you?"

"I'll figure that out once we've freed Harris," Ailsa sighed, leaving a little piece of her heart behind.

Chapter 57

"Why didn't we take the Stone of Destiny with us?" Angus groaned.

"It wouldn't have worked anyway," Iona told him. "Ephraim, has enchantments hiding it from unwelcome visitors."

Which was why they had been pacing back and forward over the same acre of trees all day. Eventually one of the fae would come out to meet them. At least, that's what Iona hoped.

"I feel like it's much easier in the stories," Angus continued. "Humans in the forest just stumble into faerie worlds all the time."

Ailsa sucked on a tooth. "I think I remember that most of those tales didn't work out well for the humans."

"Actually," Gris said, stopping in his tracks. "You might have a point. Maybe the Unseelie don't want a human in Ephraim at the moment."

"Are you saying I'm scaring them off?" Angus laughed.

"Maybe," Iona admitted. "We could always try to get in without you? If you wouldn't mind hiding?"

Angus gave a snort. "Absolutely fine by me. I'd rather

hide out in the woods with Laire and the bag of food than walk into an evil Faerie Queen's court." He turned to Ailsa, a frown touching his lips. "Will you be okay though?"

She pushed down the butterflies that were floating around in her stomach. "I'll be fine. Just keep your sword close, in case we have to fight our way out."

Angus nodded and ducked to give her a peck on the cheek, before leading the unicorn off into the trees.

Ailsa shook her hands out. "What we need is to get their attention." She widened her legs and clasped a fist towards the sky. Distantly, the rumble of thunder echoed through the glen.

"What are you doing?" Gris hissed at her.

She smiled. "Trust me, I've got this under control." She could feel the power building in her chest. *Let's show them what we've got.*

Yessss, her spirit guide agreed.

With a crackle that set all the hairs on her arms on end, Ailsa built up the electricity in the air. She rubbed the tendrils together, just like Maalik showed her; she intensified the charge, until it threatened to grow out of her control. Her ears popped at the change in pressure. Usually this would be when Ishbel took over, but all was quiet from the spirit guide. Whatever Maalik had said had worked.

"Stand back," Ailsa muttered to her companions.

Iona pushed Gris to the side, eyes wide with wonder.

"We have come to find Queen Nicnevan," Ailsa called to the seemingly empty forest. "Nineteen years ago, she had something stolen from her and we're here to return it." Then, louder still, she shouted, "I am the Queen's lost daughter and I demand to be let into Ephraim."

Then she brought her fist down on her other hand, pulling the lightning down from the air with it. It flashed, illuminating the trees in a bright light, before crashing to the ground in an explosion of leaves and dirt. Ailsa could feel the power reverberating underneath her feet as it was absorbed by the soil. She looked up, breathing heavily, at Gris and Iona, who were staring at something over her shoulder.

"Well," came a voice. "It seems we have found our lost princess."

Ailsa sucked in a gasp as she whipped round to find a tiny, thin man with green skin and large pointed ears watching her. He smiled widely, revealing needle-sharp teeth. "Welcome to Ephraim," he told her. "Welcome home."

Chapter 58

Walking into Ephraim was like entering a half-remembered dream: fantastical and unreliable. Even the air was different. It shimmered in the low light, like particles of stardust. Ailsa tasted it on her tongue, a combination of sweet, like vanilla and spice. But behind that, there was a bitter aftertaste.

Garlands of flowers between the trees swayed in the wind, their flowers tinkling like bells. From somewhere in the distance, Ailsa thought she heard a scream, but it was cut off before she could guess the direction and replaced with a voice singing a sweet melody.

Mushrooms and toadstools lined the path like tiny lanterns. Except, Ailsa realised, they weren't fungi. As they got closer, she could make out little faces peeking up from under the caps. The squat fae craned their heads as the group passed.

The woods were teeming with creatures, large and small. At first, Ailsa thought she was seeing faeries buzz around, but on closer inspection, they were insects the size of cats.

Dragonflies with wings like stained glass windows

hovered overhead. Bright beetles glinted on the ground. Giant snails slid over the trees, though instead of shells, they carried crystals on their backs. Ailsa was sure she even saw one with a human skull for a shell, but then it was gone, and they continued to move through the faerie camp.

As they walked, creatures appeared around them that didn't resemble anything Ailsa had ever known before. Snake-like eyes peered from the branches above and long, many-jointed fingers pushed aside the foliage below so their owners could get a better look.

Then, the trees thinned out and Ailsa caught a glimpse of two people in white moving through the gloom. They weaved along to the music, and as they got closer, she could make out more and more pairs.

"Are those faeries?" she asked Gris.

He didn't return her smile. "Look again and you'll see what Nicnevan really is."

Confused, she peered between the trees again. Now they were closer, she could make out the faces of the people. Ailsa felt a cold dread trickle down her back. The figures weren't gracefully dancing faerie couples, but a macabre impression of them. Spirits, pale as spilt milk, danced in the arms of ancient skeletons. The ghostly dancers twirled their skirts as they pranced between the trees. Several pixies and elves watched them from the branches with greedy eyes.

"Who are they?" asked Iona.

"Guests of Queen Nicnevan," replied the goblin leading them. "In life, these mortals believed they could make deals with faeries and deal with the consequences. Perhaps one wished that her sister's husband would fall in love with her instead. Or maybe, one wished she could live the life of a princess. All the wishes come true, but mortals never want to pay. So the Queen invites them here, after death, to provide entertainment for her court. It's a fair trade really. And most spirits seem to appreciate being reunited with their own bones."

A wave of nausea passed through Ailsa and she had to clamp her lips together to hold it in. Imagine spending your afterlife as nothing more than a puppet?

Finally, they came to a clearing, surrounded by a carpet of bluebells. Shadows flitted between the trees up above, letting them know they were being watched.

The goblin bowed low to someone out of sight. "I present to you the lost princess of Ephraim," he called.

All was silent for a moment. Ailsa touched the handle of her axe reflexively.

Then, from out of the gloom, a woman appeared. "Welcome, friends. We've been expecting you."

There was only one person in front of them, but at the same time thousands. If Ailsa fixed her eyes on her, she could see a tall, blue-haired woman, barely older than herself. She was dressed in a glinting silver dress that almost looked like it was made from tiny pieces of mirror. But then, if she looked away or allowed her gaze to become unfocussed, the woman's form shifted from young maiden to old crone—and every age in between— as if many people were sharing the same space.

"My Queen," Iona said, dropping into a curtsey.

"That's Nicnevan?" Ailsa murmured in shock.

"No, that is her half-sister, Beira, Queen of Winter."

The woman smiled sleepily at them, looking like she was trying to fight back a yawn. "Do excuse me," she said. "I'm not usually up this early, but my sister told me you were coming and wanted me to greet you."

"Will you take us to Queen Nicnevan?" asked Iona.

"Yes, in due time. But don't you want to rest first? You must have been travelling a while. When was the last time you had a change of clothes? Wouldn't you rather freshen up before meeting her?"

Ailsa managed a nod, watching as the woman's skin shimmered between smooth and wrinkled.

"Excellent." Beira waved forward a crowd of faeries that Ailsa was sure hadn't been there a moment ago.

They were all petite, with child-like bodies but adult faces. One of them grabbed her hand, making a clicking sound as she did. From between the flowers threaded into the girl's hair, two beetle-like antennae sprouted, moving independently of each other. Large eyes, shaped like a cat's, took up most of the faerie's face.

"Follow the wee-ones here and you'll find everything you need," Beira told them dreamily.

The girl who held Ailsa's hand tugged with more force than seemed possible, until she was being pulled out of the clearing and down a stone path, where many more faeries were skipping ahead. She tensed to fight but then turned to see Iona behind her and relaxed a little. Gris was growling at the two boys who had tried to grab his hands, but they just laughed as they circled him, leading him along in the rear.

"I'll see you at dinner," called the Queen of Winter.

Ailsa was really starting to wish she'd been able to stay behind with Angus.

Chapter 59

Ailsa had been told to stand in her underclothes as little goblins had woven silk threads around her body like spiders. Their tiny fingers poked and prodded until she felt like she had run through a nettle bush naked. They didn't let up until the faerie in the corner had given a nod, satisfied with their work. Ailsa was led in front of an ancient, cracked mirror so she could survey their handiwork. The dress barely covered her skin, but she had to admit that the placement of the embroidery was artfully done. Threads resembling branches snaked over her torso, as if trees were hugging her body. Delicate green leaves were woven between the stitches, becoming denser further down until they created a skirt of foliage. Underneath, her feet were bare, but they'd given her a silver anklet.

They'd been brought to a treehouse of sorts, though it wasn't so much a building *in* a tree as one made *by* the trees themselves. The trunks of towering oaks had intertwined to form a floor and walls, yet there was no ceiling. A charm of seven magpies sat in the branches overhead, looking down on them. Except, when Ailsa looked closely, they were just impressions of birds. Cogs and gears whirred inside their open chests as tiny pixies sprinkled their magic to keep them moving.

Nothing is as it seems here, Ishbel warned in her head.

Iona sat in the corner, having her copper hair worked into a plait that hung down her back. She too was wearing a beautiful dress, though the faeries had produced it, fully formed from somewhere. Ailsa suspected it had been made with a water-fae in mind. The teal satin reminded her of waves in a storm. Tiny pearls crested over her chest and shoulders looking very much like sea foam.

"Was it only a few weeks ago we were getting done up for the ceilidh in Dunrigh?" Iona asked, picking at a stray thread.

"I don't remember enjoying it then either," Ailsa grunted. The goblins around her tittered, seeming to enjoy her discomfort.

Iona sighed, looking her up and down. "You look as lovely as you did then, though. Maybe lovelier."

Ailsa felt her cheeks heat. "Is it time to go?" she asked the faerie with the cat eyes standing at the entryway.

The girl nodded, and gave a squeak before heading back out into the maze that was Ephraim. Before Ailsa could follow, Iona stopped her with an arm on her elbow.

"Eat whatever food you like, since you're not human, but do not drink the wine," she whispered. "Only full fae can handle it." Then, she too stepped out of the doorway.

At least it's not the other way around, Ailsa thought as her stomach gave a clench of hunger.

Outside the dressing room they'd been in, she was greeted again by the marvel that was the faerie court. From below, it looked like nothing more than a canopy of trees, but now that they were up in them, she could see how it was all engineered. Many oaks, alders and birch were woven together to make rooms like the one she had just been in. Rope bridges connected them, criss-crossing as far as the eye could see. Floating orbs were enough to light the way in the twilight. Ailsa reached out to one now, touching it with a finger. It burst, as if it had been a smoke-filled bubble, but reformed as soon as she dropped her hand.

They descended some spiral stairs cut into the nearest tree, though Ailsa couldn't tell if they were the same stairs they'd been led up an hour before. It was altogether too easy to get lost in the maze above the ground. That, Ailsa guessed, was the point.

Iona stepped off the stairs and gave a gasp. As soon as Ailsa tread on the ground, she knew why. The terrain was covered in a thick layer of moss, like a carpet. Her feet sank into the spongy turf and were almost enveloped by the cool green. This was why they hadn't provided them with shoes. To deny them this feeling would have been cruel.

The cat-girl led them on, until something white emerged out of the twilight.

It was as if the trees had been dressed for the occasion, too. Ivory silk strands, much longer and thicker than the ones on Ailsa's dress, had been spun together to create laced fabric. It had been strung up and sewn together, so that it draped from the large branches like a tent—though it was more spectacular than any tent Ailsa had ever seen. She could see at least five peaks in the structure, each taller than houses. More glowing faerie lights illuminated the inside, shining through the netting.

"Wow," Ailsa breathed.

Iona reached back and gave her hand a squeeze.

Their faerie guide motioned towards a gap in the pavilion. A blink later and she was gone.

"I suppose we're to go in then?" Iona asked ruefully.

Ailsa had expected there to be a large crowd, but thankfully there were only a few fae milling around, carrying plates of treats and sipping on drinks. Still, she could feel eyes on them as they wandered through the rooms.

Finally, they entered the largest space and found a low table, already laden with food. The table was empty, save for an uncomfortable looking Gris and the Queen of Winter. The latter was lounging on some pillows, almost completely horizontal. The former seemed like he was about to skewer someone with his fork. He looked like he had been brushed.

But where was Nicnevan? Ailsa shot Iona a questioning look.

Beira waved from the head of the table. "Come, niece. You can sit right next to me."

The woman hadn't changed clothes since they'd seen her earlier. *Though*, Ailsa thought, *when your form is constantly shifting, you're always changing*. She dropped onto the mint-green velvet cushion beside the Queen and tucked her dress in around her toes. Iona sank a lot more gracefully down beside Gris.

"You must be starved," Beira sighed. "Eat up, eat up, all of you. When faced with so much food, it would be a shame to waste it." Her body gave an almighty shiver. "It isn't winter yet, but it approaches."

Ailsa was glad to see food that was recognisable in front of her. After living on a vegetarian diet for so long, she immediately reached for the roasted pheasant sitting in the middle of the table. She piled her glass plate with as many treats as she thought polite. Iona went straight for the light and fluffy pastries while Gris grabbed a bowl of something. When he lifted the lid, Ailsa saw that inside was raw, minced meat. He dumped the whole thing onto his plate before tucking in.

"Now, tell me about what we've missed in the last nineteen years," Beira asked as Ailsa spooned out some mashed potato. "Was your childhood happy?"

Ailsa settled back down onto her pillow and tried to give the Queen a smile. "A woman named Heather MacAra raised me, in a little cottage near Arnish. I had an older brother growing up who I played with. When my —when Heather died—he was taken away and I was left alone. Eventually, I was chased out of my village. My neighbours were quite superstitious." A tiny faerie boy came around with a pitcher of wine. Ailsa shook her head when he reached her cup and watched on as Iona and Gris nodded, allowing him to fill theirs with the amber liquid.

Beira *tsked* and helped herself to a cherry. "So much pain. All of that could have been avoided if you had just been here. Now, how did you come to work for the crown of Eilanmòr? I heard that you went looking for the Stone of Destiny?"

Ailsa felt a shudder run up her spine. Of course they knew she'd been looking for the stone. "I met Iona and Harris. They needed someone to protect them, so I came along."

"We were so glad we met her," Iona piped in. "She saved my life more than once."

"Oh lovely. You must be very powerful then, just like your mother."

"I'm just good with an axe," Ailsa said with a shrug. She lifted a piece of pheasant to her lips, savouring the herbs on the skin. "I didn't know I had magic until recently."

"You'll have to show us what you can do." Beira smiled indulgently up at her. "Did you happen to meet the King when you were in Dunrigh?"

"Yes, before he died."

"Yes, I heard. I can't say I'm sad about that," she sniffed before shifting her sparkling gaze to Ailsa's. "He's the reason my sister is chained to the tree," the Queen said matter-of-factly.

Ailsa's stomach twisted and she set her fork down. "But the man who chained her to the tree is my father…"

"Yes. So you see, you are a princess in more ways than one."

But that means… If King Connall was her father, that would make Angus and Duncan… her brothers. She looked at Iona, silently asking if she'd known, but the selkie looked as shocked as she felt.

"Oh don't look so surprised," Beira continued with a laugh. "Did you really think she would have settled for anything less? They met when Connall was a young prince, during the war between Eilanmòr and Mirandelle. He was very gallant, I will say. When the war began, he was so ready to fight for his country, but his father said no. King Alasdair took Connall's older sister, Afric instead. So Connall came to the Forest of Frith, looking for adventure."

"Why doesn't everyone know this?" Ailsa asked, feeling a little numb. The King, the man she had met only a few weeks before, was her father.

"I'd only ever heard that the man had been a knight. Someone close to the King," Iona breathed.

"It had been a secret love affair," Beira explained. "But then, when his father and sister died, he had to go back to Dunrigh to become king. Nicnevan waited, expecting him to invite her. Then we heard rumours he was engaged to some lady he'd never met and I told her to stop waiting." She shrugged, plucking a pansy from the top of a cake and eating it. "Nicnevan went to Dunrigh for a few weeks, and when she came back, she was with child. We sent for Connall, expecting him to come straight away. But months passed, and she gave birth."

Something dark passed over Beira's face. "You were a few weeks old when Connall finally showed his face. He'd married that wench in the time he'd been away, and they were having their own baby. I hoped he was here to apologise but he took you and chained her to that tree." The Queen of Winter's body jerked again, changing rapidly between youth and old age. "I still remember her screams as you were ripped from her arms. But you're here now, and I'm so thankful."

Then Ailsa voiced the question she'd been wanting to ask since they'd arrived at the dinner. "Doesn't she want to see me right now?"

Beira's form settled again. "She'll come when she's ready. Can you even imagine the heartache of losing a child like that? To be betrayed by your lover?"

Ailsa nodded. *Don't press the issue. You're here and it seems safe.* "There's something else. A friend of mine went missing a few weeks ago."

"My brother was taken by some ceasg," Iona supplied.

"We had hoped I would find him here," said Ailsa, looking around as if Harris would suddenly appear.

Beira patted her on the hand. Her skin was like ice. "I'm sure you will. Ephraim is exceptionally large. But for tonight, you should all rest. Tomorrow you can look for him, after you've met your mother."

Ailsa felt a frisson of something run through her body. *Tomorrow...*

"Good," Gris grunted, standing from his place and draining his glass of wine. "If we're done, we should go to bed. Ailsa and Iona, I'd like to speak to you."

Chapter 60

"I don't like this."

Gris was pacing around one of the bedrooms they'd been given, surreptitiously looking out of the windows every time he passed. There was no glass, but somehow it felt warmer inside. "Why hasn't Nicnevan come to meet you?"

Iona frowned. "Beira said she just needed some time."

Ailsa chewed her lip and remained silent. If she was perfectly honest, she was feeling as anxious as Gris.

"And when you mentioned Harris she didn't react. What if he isn't even here?"

"We know he's here," Iona argued. "The ceasg took him. Harris told me they'd threatened to take him to Nicnevan when he was looking for the Stone of Destiny."

"But what if they didn't?" Gris growled.

"Or," Ailsa murmured, "what if he is here but Beira is trying to hide him? What if he's locked away somewhere?"

"My brother is here, I can feel it," Iona told them, sitting on the goose-down bed. "But I'm sure he's being looked after. Nicnevan might be surrounded by

Unseelie, but she knows the rules and can keep them in check. Harris is probably squirreled away somewhere in Ephraim, in a room much like this, with no idea we've arrived." She pulled out the combs in her hair. "Nicnevan must be trying to sound us out before she reveals herself. Then, once you're reunited, she'll bring us Harris."

It sounded so simple. Yet, Ailsa couldn't shake the feeling that Iona was wrong.

Things aren't as they seem, Ishbel whispered.

"Maybe we should go looking for him?" Ailsa said, sucking on a tooth.

Gris rounded on her before Iona could voice her disagreement. "You're not going anywhere. Nicnevan's court is too dangerous, especially at night. Most Unseelie are nocturnal and will not hesitate to hex you, no matter who you are."

"Just get some rest," Iona said, scooting up the bed so she could lie back against the pillows. "Everything will be fine once you've met your mother."

Ailsa nodded. "I'll walk you to your room, Gris," she told the Fear-Laith. Iona already seemed like she was falling asleep. So much for handling her wine.

Gris too, showed signs of growing sluggish as she walked him across the rope bridge to his quarters. His steps were heavier than usual, causing the structure to swing about. Ailsa had to grab onto the cables to keep an even footing. "In all those years watching over me, did you ever think you were wrong about who I was?" she asked his back.

The Fear-Laith stopped, turning to peer at her over his shoulder. "No, never. I knew you were royalty as soon as I saw you." He gave a half smile. "I didn't realise quite how royal you were though. Your mother is a queen and your father was a king. You do realise that makes you his first child?"

That's right, she realised numbly. Duncan was probably a few months younger than her, and Angus would have been born a year and a half later. "What do you think Angus will say when he finds out?"

Gris shook his head, continuing down the bridge and onto the platform that led to his door. "That would make him, what, fourth in line to the throne? I think he'd be pleased. Or, at least, I will. The question is: if you're the first of King Connall's children, should you be the Queen of Eilanmòr and Ephraim?"

"No," Ailsa told him definitively. "Duncan is king. And my parents weren't married." *I'm illegitimate.*

Gris shrugged. "People have ruled with less." He turned to go.

"Gris?" Ailsa called, gripping the bridge's ropes. "I feel like I've never really thanked you, for everything you did for me."

The Fear-Laith smiled. "Thank me by standing up for what is right. Thank me by being a good queen. Thank me by living." Then he closed his door softly, leaving Ailsa to go back to her room.

But Ailsa had had no intention of going back when she'd offered to walk him out, though the thought of curling up on the soft bed beside Iona was appealing after such a long day. Instead, she turned to the stairs, leading down from the platform high in the trees and went in search of Harris.

The woods of Ephraim were too quiet and too still as Ailsa searched for the selkie. Every movement was a creature ready to curse her. Every sound in the dark was a monster coming to eat her flesh. She jumped at every leaf crunch and twig snap until her nerves were frayed. The faerie torches had dimmed, creating shadows big enough to hide any number of assailants. Ailsa blew out a breath, willing the clouds to drift across the sky. The pale silver of the moon was revealed, allowing a little more light to shine on the forest floor.

Ailsa didn't know what she had expected of Ephraim, but it wasn't this. She'd always heard stories of raucous parties and midnight banquets in the faerie lands, but here they were, seemingly tucked up in their beds.

I don't trust it.

Movement attracted her attention and she ducked down behind a bush, gripping the hem of her dress in both hands. A figure stood further down the path, swaying slightly on the spot. Its head was twitching to the right, making strange jerking movements in time to the beating of Ailsa's heart. She ducked down lower, watching as the thing raised its arms out at its sides. Then, it raised another arm and another. Six arms snaked in the air, in a grotesque impression of a dance. Then there was a faint tinkling of bells and the creature threw back its head and made a noise somewhere between a laugh and a screech.

As she watched this freakish display with horror, a hand clamped over her mouth, muffling her scream.

"Ailsa, don't worry, it's me," whispered a familiar voice.

"Angus?" Her fingers clutched at her chest, trying to calm her thundering heart.

His body slotted in beside hers and they both watched as the six-armed creature shuffled away.

"What are you doing here?"

"Laire sensed something and we were able to cross into Ephraim," he explained impatiently. "Come on, you need to see this."

He dragged her back down the path she'd come from and then into the trees. She had to pull her skirts up and watch her bare feet to step over the knotted roots but somehow it felt safer to be away from the open trail. As they walked further, Ailsa was sure she could see a faint glow up ahead.

"Here, in this clearing," Angus told her.

The unicorn had been left to stand guard over the prince's discovery. She gave a whinny when she saw him and he raised a finger to his lips, bidding her quiet. Five standing stones rose from the moss-covered ground, covered in symbols that felt familiar somehow. The glow webbed between them like spider silk. But the massive boulders only caught her eye for a moment before they were snagged by two shapes on the floor in front of them.

Both appeared to be statues, though one was made from rock and the other from wood. The timber figure was lying on the ground with their hands up to cover their face. The stone figure had thrown an arm towards the other, as if reaching for them. They were covered in trailing plants.

"You're not going to like this," Angus muttered.

Her stomach plummeting, Ailsa stepped up to the stone statue. *Please no*, she thought at the figure. She removed the ivy with trembling hands and choked back a gasp.

They'd finally found Harris.

Chapter 61

Ailsa slammed the bedroom door open, unable to check her motions into something stealthy. She expected Iona to still be asleep; to her surprise, the selkie was sitting on the bed, wide awake and looking furious.

"Where did you go?" Iona hissed. "I thought we told you not to go wandering."

"I found him!" The words burst from Ailsa, too loud to be prudent. "I found Harris!"

Immediately, Iona's tone changed. "Where?"

Ailsa grabbed the other woman's hands. "He's been cursed. By Nicnevan or someone else, I don't know. And he isn't the only one. Come on, I'll show you." She pulled Iona towards the door, but just before they could go through the portal, the redhead stopped.

"Wait, I have something that might help." She turned back to her bag, rooting around inside until she found whatever it was she was looking for. Ailsa caught a glimpse of something small and grey before it was tucked into the pocket of the selkie's dress. "We should wake Gris too."

Ailsa bit her lip, bending to her own pack and

grabbing her axe. She had no idea how it could be useful, but she was sick of being in bad situations without it. Pulling her belt from her trousers and slinging it around her waist, she managed to make a decent hold for the weapon. "Okay, let's go."

The Fear-Laith had been asleep but, like any good warrior, he was up and awake the instant that Ailsa tapped on his door. She led him and Iona down the staircase and through the forest, trying her best not to run, until they reached the standing stones.

She found Angus and Laire where she'd left them, tucked up against the largest boulder.

"I thought we told you to hide?" Gris grunted at the prince. Was it Ailsa's imagination, or had the Fear-Laith spoken a little softer than usual to the other man?

"Laire sensed a strange pulse of magic coming from this clearing. I'm glad she did, otherwise you might not have found Harris for a long time."

Iona gave a choked sob as soon as she saw her brother, going closer to inspect what had become of him. "Oh Harris," she whispered. "What have you gotten yourself into now?"

"Is there any way we can save him?" asked Ailsa. "And the other one?" She gestured to the other man who, crouched on the ground, his arms covering his face.

"Something about him seems familiar..." Angus muttered.

Iona wiped her eyes. "Hold on, something told me to bring this." She pulled the object from earlier out of her pocket. Now Ailsa could see it resembled a rough cup or bowl, though it was no bigger than a thimble.

"The cauldron?" Angus asked with a frown. "Unless you're planning on making a whirlpool, I don't see how that's going to help."

"The Bean-Nighe told me I would find something in the village, and that it would save Harris." Iona held out the cauldron. "This is what I found."

"She could have been talking about Laire." Angus stroked the side of the unicorn's muzzle.

"I don't think so," Iona said. "You found Laire, not me. And under the water, it felt just like the Bean-Nighe said, that the cauldron was waiting for me."

Ailsa rubbed her thumb on the handle of her axe. Bean-Nighe? Cauldron? "What am I missing here?"

"The curse on the village was caused by this," Iona explained, holding it out in her palm. "I pulled it from the river so that they would tell us where they took you, but I seem to have some sort of connection to it. It told me it's called the Cauldron of Life."

Ailsa focussed on the object, feeling a shiver of recognition. *Do you remember?* Ishbel asked her. Her spirit guide sounded louder than ever inside her head. *Do you remember what the demon told you?*

"The Cauldron of Life?" Ailsa's heart jumped into her

throat. "I've heard of it! Maalik has been looking for it for years. It's one of The Four Treasures."

"What does it do?"

"I think he said it's supposed to heal people of magic. Something about a single drop of water from inside it…" Ailsa eyed the cauldron dubiously. *You'd only fit a single drop inside.*

Iona's eyes lit up and she nodded, placing the cauldron on the ground in front of her. "Stand back," she told them.

"Wait," Gris said. "If you're going to do this, Angus and I should go keep watch. You don't want to be crept up on when you're trying to save them."

Angus gave a jolt at his name. After a moment of open-mouthed staring at the Fear-Laith, he nodded and followed him through the gloom, with Laire trailing behind.

Well, there's a first time for everything, Ailsa thought, dumbfounded.

Iona waited until she couldn't see the two men anymore. Then she spoke to the object in front of her. "Will you grow, please?"

Ailsa gave a bark of shocked laughter as she watched the vessel expand, larger and larger. Now she could see the inside, so much more beautiful than the rough outer layer of rock. The polished white and blue stone shone faintly in the evening dim.

Once it had become so large that she could have easily fit inside it, Iona held up her hand. "That's enough," commanded the selkie. Then she smiled. "And now all we need is the water." With a wave of her fingers towards the nearby stream, the liquid was pulled upwards in an arc, landing in the cauldron with a splash.

"Do you think we need to leave it for a bit?" Ailsa asked.

But then she had her answer.

The cauldron's depths glowed brighter and brighter, turning the water inside into a sparkling swirl.

Iona held her hand out to it and it was as if she was feeling the change in the liquid. "I think it's ready now. Here goes nothing."

Then, with a flick of her hand, she sent the magical water towards her brother and the stranger.

Chapter 62

Where the water splashed over the selkie the stone glowed and then turned to skin, hair, and clothes. In a flash, the curse was removed, and he doubled over, taking deep breaths as his body was set free. Iona directed the liquid at the other man, until he too had turned fully back. Then with a final flick she deposited the water back inside the cauldron.

Harris recovered first, straightening up with a laugh. "Took you all long enough!"

Next, the stranger gasped, running a hand over the newly formed skin of his face. Harris reached over to thump him on the back a few times while the stranger coughed.

"It's ok, MacAra. You're safe now."

Ailsa blinked. *MacAra?* Why had Harris called the man by her name?

"Well, I think we're in the process of being saved, actually," Harris caught Ailsa's eye and grinned.

The man beside him shook himself and looked up at his rescuers.

Ailsa's heart stopped in her chest. It had been years.

He'd changed his hair and he was a lot taller now, but he was unmistakable, even after all this time. "Cameron?" she breathed.

Her brother's eyes widened in recognition. "Ailsa?"

"Surprise!" Harris said, looking smug. Ailsa had an urge to hit him.

Cameron stumbled up, grabbing Ailsa by the shoulders when he reached her. His hands shook, though his grip was strong. "I've been looking for you all this time."

She drank him in, staring at his eyes. They were the same shade of blue as hers, but the delicate skin under them was bruised, as if he hadn't slept in days. His hair must have been bright purple once, but now it had faded to a dull lavender, with brown roots growing out. His cheeks were thinner than she remembered, and he'd grown into his ears. There was a light dusting of stubble on his jaw which looked straggly and unkempt. But his mouth twisted into a smile, revealing one of his front teeth was slightly crooked and she knew without a doubt that it was him.

"Cameron, I..." Ailsa fought to keep the tears at bay, "I don't even know where to begin."

"Let me fill you both in," Harris smirked, placing a hand on his hip. "Cameron, here, has been a prisoner of Nicnevan for a few months now, but before that he was a soldier, exploring the world, presumably looking for his long, lost sister. Ailsa on the other hand has been terribly busy lately, saving the world, finding out she's a mythical creature, and dancing with handsome selkies."

Iona strode up to Harris, searching his face and body for any wounds.

"And here I thought you would be waiting at home worrying about me," he said with a roll of his eyes.

"I couldn't let you have all the fun this time," Iona said. "And what about you, Harris? Fill me in."

His smile dropped into a pout. "I've been, you know, hanging around. Actually, you could say I hit rock bottom."

Iona pinched him. "Stop showing off."

"Just making light of a bad situation," he winced. "I was brought here by a few of Nicnevan's cronies. Then, when I tried to escape, I was punished. That's basically it."

"Well, I'm glad we found you both," Ailsa said, grabbing Cameron's hand. "We're getting you out of here." Because now there was no way she could meet Nicnevan. Not when she'd done *this* to her prisoners.

"How exactly are you going to do that?" asked Harris.

Then, Ailsa heard something that made her blood run cold.

"Go!" Gris shouted through the trees. "They're coming."

Oh gods. Ailsa looked Cameron up and down. He was swaying on the spot, as if he was about to faint at any moment. How were they going to get away with him in this state? "We have to go. Now."

The Fear-Laith crashed through the darkness, raising his sword and baring his white teeth.

Harris yelped, his eyes bulging. "Who is that?"

"My monster," Ailsa said.

"The alarm has been sounded. Nicnevan knows you've rescued her prisoners." Gris reached out as if to grab her, but Ailsa shook her head.

"Take my brother and run. We'll spread out and try to lead them away."

"It's too late," Iona told them. "We're going to have to fight."

Another figure materialised from the trees, looking around wildly. When Angus's eyes found Harris, he let out a breathless laugh. "Good to see you've shown up to be useful."

Cameron's mouth popped open and the blood drained from his face.

Ailsa watched in shock as Angus saw her brother and stopped in his tracks. "Cam?"

"Angus?" Cameron croaked.

Then the prince did something very stupid, considering they were about to fight the whole Unseelie Court. He dropped his sword.

"But how do you two know each other?" asked Harris.

Angus's ears pinked and he bit his lip. "Do you remember I told you once I met someone when I was training in the army?"

Ailsa thought back to a conversation around a campfire a few weeks ago. They'd been talking about family, childhoods and first loves. "Oh my gods, Angus— it was my brother?"

The prince's mouth dropped open. "Your *brother*?"

Then, a honeyed voice drifted out of the dark.

"Well, isn't this cosy?"

Chapter 63

When Ailsa had imagined meeting the Queen of the Faeries, she had expected the reunion to be heartfelt and bittersweet. Instead, all she felt was fear.

A thousand faerie lights illuminated around them, casting the forest in almost daylight. Ailsa had thought the magical threads between the standing stones reminded her of spiders' webs. Now she realised the trap they'd walked into.

Beyond the stones, a huge willow tree eclipsed the space; massive and gnarled. Its moss-covered trunk was too large for even two people to wrap their arms around. The leaves spread out in a thick canopy, creating a natural, living roof of green. Lower down, its roots tangled together, spreading out as far as the eye could see. Directly below the trunk, those roots created a monumental throne and in it sat the mesmerising, haunting, Faerie Queen. Nicnevan. This was the woman who had haunted her nightmares and her dreams. This was the woman who could be her mother.

She was not what Ailsa had expected.

Her golden hair was cropped—to show off her

pointed ears—and decorated with a crown of blossoms which flowed over her shoulders and down into her pale pink gown. Her skin was flawless, yet it had a green glow around, it as if she was lit from the inside. A thin silver chain encircled her bare ankle and twisted away into the undergrowth. Only her eyes, cat-like and calculating, betrayed the image of innocence.

Delicate. Feminine. *Deadly.*

Nicnevan tapped her long nails on the bark of her throne and the piles of leaves and flowers that lay on the floor around her feet began to shuffle. Transfixed, Ailsa watched as faces emerged and then they yawned and stretched their bodies, unfolding like flowers. The tiny pixie children shuffled about so they could drape themselves at the queen's side. She stroked the rosy cheek of a boy beside her and regarded the group.

"Well, it seems that you found my prisoners, finally. I had wondered how long it would take you."

There was tittering up in the trees overhead and Ailsa realised, with dread, that the boughs were completely full of fae. But these couldn't be mistaken for the cheeky faeries they'd met earlier. These were the Unseelie.

Hundreds of creatures with sharp pointed teeth looked down upon their small group. There was something wilder, more primitive, about these monsters, as if they hadn't changed since the dawn of time. Their cackles sent a shiver straight up Ailsa's spine.

Nicnevan waved an elegant hand towards her. "And this is my lost daughter I've been hearing about?"

"I found her when she was a baby," Gris grunted. "Beside the body of a felled faerie."

The Queen tilted her head towards him. "I suppose I should thank you for saving her?"

"If it weren't for him, I'd be dead," Ailsa told her truthfully.

Nicnevan nodded. "So if it weren't for him, you wouldn't be here?" Then she waved a hand and out of the ground grew the stem of a single plant. It curled upwards in a spiral, in front of the Fear-Laith, covered in wicked looking thorns. When it reached shoulder height, the bud opened, revealing a crimson rose.

Gris smiled at Ailsa. *This is it*, the smile said. *I did it*.

"It's a shame," Nicnevan drawled. "That you didn't leave well enough alone."

Then the plant's stem snapped out and shot straight through Gris's chest.

"No!" Ailsa screamed.

The Fear-Laith made a choking noise, before crumbling to the floor. Ailsa ran for him, paying no mind to the laughter from above. She slid on her knees, and turned Gris's shoulders so she could look at his face. Blood was already starting to dribble from his mouth.

"I'm sorry," he croaked.

"Just hold on, I'm going to get you out of here," Ailsa

told him. Behind her, she could hear someone crying, though she wasn't sure who.

Then, before her eyes, the fur on his body disappeared, revealing the dark brown skin she remembered him having when he had trained her. His eyes went from red to chestnut, even as they glazed over.

"Gris, I need you to stay with me," Ailsa shouted at him. But it was too late. Mere seconds had passed, but Ailsa felt her whole world shift again as the Fear-Laith, her monster, her friend, closed his eyes and let out his last breath.

"Why?" The word came out gritted through teeth. When she had no answer, Ailsa looked up at the queen and screamed it again. "Why?!"

Nicnevan looked impassive as she drummed her fingers on her throne. "I punished the one who brought you to me. Did you know that when changelings meet their mothers they change back to their true form? And yet, not a single hair on your head, nor freckle on your face has changed. You still have that ugly mark on your cheek. Dear little girl, you are a changeling, but I'm afraid you aren't mine." She grinned. "But you knew that already, didn't you?"

Then, louder still, she called to her court, the Unseelie watching in the trees. "This fae thought to trick your Queen! She came to Ephraim to fool a grieving mother and rescue her selkie lover."

They hollered and screamed, shaking the branches until leaves were raining down on them.

Nicnevan raised her chin. "Did you know, you're not even a faerie? Would you like to find out where you truly belong?"

Ailsa, still kneeling on the floor in front of Gris's body, only had the energy to spit in the Queen's direction.

"Tell you what, let's play a game," Nicnevan said with a sneer. "If you can defeat me in a test of magic, I'll tell you what you want to know." She looked to all of Ailsa's companions. "And I'll let the rest of your friends go."

Ailsa turned to them. Iona had collapsed on the moss, with Harris's arms around her as she sobbed. Angus was clutching Laire's shoulder, as if to hold her back. Cameron had propped himself against a standing stone, gripping the rock with white knuckles.

She swallowed, forcing down her rage. "And if you win?"

Nicnevan shrugged her slim shoulders. "You'll be dead."

Chapter 64

*A*ilsa had a moment of mourning, before she tore at the wispy dress until the fabric hung ragged above her knees, wishing she had her trousers on.

The forest around her writhed. At first, Ailsa thought she had been surrounded by snakes, but then the shapes twisted off the earth, revealing themselves to be thick vines. Behind her, she heard Iona give a cry as they rose, threading together to make a barrier, cutting Ailsa off from her companions.

Ailsa rubbed the sweat from her palms and flexed her hands, trying to build up static.

"Now would be a good time to take over, Ishbel," she muttered as Nicnevan grinned.

"Too hot? Let us help you," the Queen said, waving a hand. Beira stepped out of the shadows, her face impassive as she surveyed the scene.

The ground rumbled, and Ailsa pitched forward. She landed hard on her back, eyes closed in a groan. But then, when she opened them again, the scene had changed. The whole forest was blanketed in a layer of snow and ice. Ailsa felt the cold sink into her bones, biting at the bare skin on her legs and feet. She blinked away the frost that had already formed on her eyelashes. Then the Queen of Winter collapsed against a tree, her powers spent.

"Is that better?" asked Nicnevan.

Ailsa gritted her teeth and stretched out an arm to the heavens. *Come on, come on*, she thought to the sky. Thunder answered somewhere, too far away.

"Oh no," Nicnevan drawled. "It's not that easy." The Queen brought a hand up, sending something dark and sharp whipping at Ailsa's face. It stung, bringing tears to her eyes. She spat the blood from her mouth, leaving a trail of crimson on the white snow. She was thrown to the side before she could build up a charge. Something snaked forward in the sides of her vision and she rolled, just in time to watch the vine snapping where her head had been.

Nicnevan laughed. "They told me you were powerful, but this is pathetic."

Anytime now, she thought to herself. But every time she tried to raise a hand to the sky, she was forced to dodge another snapping branch.

The Faerie Queen stood, shaking off the little pixies that were clinging to her. Her fingers made a clawing motion in front of her, then many more vines and stems burst from the earth towards Ailsa. There was nothing she could do to avoid them as they wound around her body, freezing her in place.

"How could you have thought you could possibly be my offspring?"

The vines wound themselves tighter and tighter around her body, squeezing the breath from her lungs. But then, one of them must have rubbed against the blade of her axe as it suddenly snapped. It was just enough for Ailsa to get her hand around her weapon so she could pull it through the plant-matter, cutting it from her body. Then, almost on instinct, Ailsa's arm flew forward, throwing the axe at the Queen.

At first, Ailsa thought it was a missed shot, but then a trickle of blood bubbled on Nicnevan's arm.

The Queen snarled, sending more branches at her, but Ailsa took advantage of her momentary slip of control to roll to the side and out of the way.

You don't need to use your hands, Ishbel told her. *Just will the air to do your bidding.*

"Do you want to take over on this one?" Ailsa huffed but her spirit guide was silent.

The wind was beginning to whip up, growing stronger and answering her call, but it still wasn't enough to do any damage. Dirt and snow clung to her bare arms as she pushed herself up to face the faerie. Nicnevan had stepped forward, away from her throne. Up above, the Unseelie had stopped laughing.

"Do you know how many changelings have come

here, pretending to be her?" the Queen asked, curling her lip. "Whether they meant to deceive or not, it doesn't matter. Every time it happens a piece of my heart chips away." She made a fist in the air and Ailsa's feet began to shake. "The only thing that stops it from breaking is killing the imposters." Nicnevan slammed her fist down on the ground and the earth exploded.

Ailsa pitched to the side as rock and soil cut through the snow. The earth she was on was pushed up, up, up into the air, higher than the trees. On her hands and knees, she looked over the sides of the pillar of stone at her companions, a dizzying distance away.

"When I am finally freed from this tree, I am going to hunt down every single person responsible in Eilanmòr," Nicnevan shrieked up at her. "Then, I'm going to go to Dunrigh and take the throne that should be mine— and not even the Stone of Destiny will stop me."

But as the Queen screamed below, Ailsa filled her lungs with the fresh air. Closing her eyes, she imagined the clouds rolling in, the vapour sparking together, funnelling their power into her. "That'll be hard to do, when you're burnt to a crisp." Then, raising her hands to the sky, Ailsa jumped from the stone column.

The lightning caught her in mid-air, and immediately her body was alive with electricity. It was more, much more, than she'd ever felt or imagined. Every nerve, every hair, sparked with energy, until she was sure she'd been disintegrated by the force. *If this kills me, at least I'm taking her with me*, she thought as she unleashed it all on the Faerie Queen.

Nicnevan threw her arms out at the last minute, sending plant tendrils up to shield herself. The electricity burned through the vines, knocking her to the foot of the throne. The pixie children scattered, hiding in the bushes as the Queen groaned.

Ailsa landed on the ground, now devoid of snow. The power she had felt a moment before was diminished, but she did her best to stand tall so as not to let her adversary know that. Her body ached, as if she'd been scorched from the inside and she couldn't stop her muscles from twitching.

"I suppose you have proven yourself," Nicnevan sneered, her body steaming slightly from the hit of power. She waved her hand in the air and the barrier between Ailsa and her companions shrivelled away.

"Ailsa!" Harris shouted, running for her. Behind him, Iona also tried to race forward but she was held back by a shaking Angus.

Harris skidded to a stop in front of her, one hand coming up to cup her face, the other grabbing what was left of her dress. "We have to go, now."

And for one fleeting moment, Ailsa thought she had won.

Then, Nicnevan looked at Ailsa with the same smirk

on her face as before. Harris's grip tightened at her waist. Ailsa glanced up at him, but he wasn't looking at the Queen. Instead, he was looking at the forest behind her.

"You can go," Nicnevan conceded, shrugging her shoulders. "But I can't promise that you can leave." Ailsa turned to face the next horror. The glow of the faerie lights was only bright enough to pick out four sets of yellow eyes in the shadows of the forest.

"Ailsa, now!" Harris tugged at her, but she couldn't move. A thrill of fear shot through her body as four great hulking masses stalked into the clearing. Their lips were pulled back in snarls over gleaming white teeth. Growls ripped from their mouths and her hair stood on end. The wolves' breath turned to steam in the cold night air.

"Run!" Nicnevan breathed.

Chapter 65

Harris grabbed Ailsa's arm and her trance was broken. They turned on their heels and bolted for the cover of the trees. Ailsa panicked as she glanced at Iona, Angus, and Cameron, still beside the standing stones, but then the wolves were rushing after her and Harris. The beasts howled behind them, as if to signal the start of the hunt. Ailsa could hear the heartbeat in her ears as they sprinted through the crushing darkness of the forest. As they flew over the detritus her bare feet ripped on the jagged stones. Ailsa's lungs burned with the effort of running but the sound of snapping jaws pushed her forward. The branches tugged at her dress as they ran a breath away from their pursuers.

Then, suddenly, they were out of the forest again, and back in the same clearing with Nicnevan and the standing stones.

"You'll have to try harder," she cackled.

Had they run in a circle? Or was this another magic trick?

One of the wolves' teeth barely missed Ailsa's ankle but as she turned to see where the creature was, she slipped. Beira's snow had been replaced by clinging mud. The clay was thick and it pulled at her body. Ailsa could see Harris ahead, as he realised what had happened. He looked on in horror from her spot on the ground to the wolves tearing through the trees behind her.

"No!" Ailsa screamed at him as he made to come back for her. As she held out a hand to stop him, he skidded to a halt. An opaque wall of mist drifted up from where he stood, cutting him off from her. His fist came up to swipe it away but instead of touching cloud, his hand was met with an impenetrable barrier. He looked in shock at Ailsa as she concentrated on keeping the partition in place.

"Get them out of here," Ailsa shouted as she turned to meet her fate. She didn't miss the look of anguish that crossed his face. If he managed to save their friends, it would all be worth it.

The pack was slowing now, coming to surround their prey. Ailsa's eyes met with cold yellow ones and she sent a prayer to the gods. *Make it quick.*

Ailsa felt a single tear escape her left eye and she quickly swiped at it. She would face death with dignity. She couldn't bear to let her companions see her sob as she was taken. If this was to be the last they saw of her, then let them remember she stood with courage against her end. She heaved herself out of the mud until she was upright. Her dress clung damply to her body and she shivered. Finally, Ailsa curled her lips and looked at the wolf in the centre of the pack dead in the eye. She growled low in her throat and braced herself to be torn apart.

The animals stopped moving towards her and lowered their ears. Ailsa's heart beat once; twice. One by one the wolves approached her until she could feel their hot breath on her face.

Please, let it be quick.

Then, something large came barrelling from behind, shooting out of the darkness, landing right in front of her, growling louder than any of Nicnevan's wolves.

"Wulver?" she gasped in astonishment as she recognised the creature.

The huge forest guardian growled deep in his chest, daring the smaller wolves to fight. His snarl sent a shiver up Ailsa's spine. *I'm glad you're on my side*, she thought in wonder. The wolf pack hesitated, tucking their tails under them.

"Attack!" Nicnevan screamed, stalking towards Ailsa, her hands curling into claws. "If they won't kill you, I'll do it myself." Her steps took her near the standing stones, dangerously close to Iona, Angus, Cameron, and Laire. But she didn't even look in their direction. She only had eyes for revenge.

Listen to me, said a voice in Ailsa's head. *Use the cauldron.*

Ailsa raised her hand in the air, building up a charge again. Then, just as she brought down a thread of lightning at the Queen, she screamed her instruction to her friends. "Push the cauldron!"

What came next happened almost in slow motion. The lightning cracked down an inch away from Nicnevan's feet, just as she sent another thorned vine at Ailsa. It slashed at her cheek, right under her changeling mark. As Nicnevan dodged back to avoid the bolt of electricity, Iona darted forward, pushing the cauldron over.

The liquid inside rushed out of the pot, straight towards the Faerie Queen. Her mouth opened in shock but she didn't have time before it hit her. It engulfed her body in a tidal wave, far larger than should have been possible. Behind the curtain of water, Nicnevan gave a shout of surprise, which quickly turned into a terrible wail. The water swirled around, defying gravity as it fell up and down all at once. The Queen's screams pierced the air—so loud that Ailsa had to cover her ears. Finally, as all the liquid fell to the earth, the shrieks choked off, leaving a deadly silence.

The sparks of lightning and drops of water cleared and Nicnevan's body was revealed. It had completely turned to wood and stone.

Ailsa let out the breath she'd been holding and turned to Harris in astonishment. The mist wall dropped away but he stood fixed as if still trapped. He looked at Ailsa for an eternal moment and then dropped to his knees. His hands sank into the soil and he bowed his head.

"What did you just do?" he rasped.

Above, in the boughs of the trees, the forest came to life with howls and screeches. The Unseelie became frantic as they realised what had happened to their leader. Then, quickly, they disappeared, darting off into the woods so that the same wouldn't happen to them. The pack of wolves backed away from Wulver's growls, until they too slinked off.

"I think," Ailsa said with awe, "we've just defeated the Faerie Queen."

Chapter 66

"Yes," Harris said. "But how?"

"The Cauldron of Life," Iona breathed from behind him. "It doesn't just remove magic like I thought, it also stores it so it can be used again. Yours and Cameron's curse was in the cauldron, and two curses were strong enough to incapacitate Nicnevan, it seems." She gazed down at the queen's body, still with a silver chain attached to her ankle. It led back to the willow tree, where all the pixie children were watching them. One at a time, they burrowed into the leaves and flowers again, becoming as dormant as Nicnevan.

"How did you know the cauldron could do that?" asked Angus.

"A little voice told me." Ailsa reached a hand to pet the fur on Wulver's back. The great wolf tensed, before leaning into her side, sharing his warmth with her as she trembled.

They burned Gris's body where he lay. It was the least Ailsa could do for him, after everything.

"You did well, Ailsa," Iona told her as they watched the flames engulf him. "He would have been proud."

"I couldn't be what he wanted me to be," she whispered back. "He was so sure I was Nicnevan's daughter. He paid for that mistake with his life."

"You defeated her and saved us all. That's all he wanted."

Maybe, she thought. But she was still too raw to accept it. Instead, her eyes drifted to where her brother was propped up against a standing stone. "We need to get Harris and Cameron back to Dunrigh to recover."

Iona nodded. "Now I wish we had the Stone of Destiny." She muttered something to the cauldron beside her and it shrunk again until it was small enough to fit in her pocket. "I don't think I'll be letting anyone have this."

Ailsa's stomach twisted. Hopefully, Iona didn't mean that.

The two women managed to make it back to their room without seeing a single other fae. It was as if they'd all vanished. Ailsa discarded her ruined dress, finding her old travelling clothes and slipping them on as the sun rose through the trees.

They found the others near the huge white tent, stocking up on food and water. Suddenly, Ailsa realised how hungry she was as she spotted a plate of biscuits. As she munched on them, she eyed the wine regretfully. *I could do with a drink right now.*

Someone stepped up beside her, grabbing a treat for himself. "Hello," Cameron muttered, ducking his head.

Ailsa gulped her mouthful down. "Erm, hey."

"It's been a long time."

"Five years," she agreed.

Cameron's eyes—the same icy blue as hers—were filled with regret. "Do you think you'll ever be able to forgive me for not finding you?"

"It's fine," she said. "I found *you*."

"Ailsa, I'm sorry. I'm your big brother and I let you down."

She squirmed, unwilling to have this conversation now. "Just... let's forget about it, eh? Don't you have someone else you should be speaking to just now?"

"Angus? I think he can wait for a bit." He turned to look at the prince outside the tent. "How exactly do you know him?"

"Well, there was this whole thing about saving the kingdom..." She considered him for a moment. "Cameron, I feel a bit strange about saying this to you, but Angus is like a brother to me. But, I suppose, I'm not related to either of you."

Cameron's mouth twisted. "Ailsa—"

"Did you know?" she asked, chewing her lip.

"Yes."

"Did our mother?" Her voice came out in a whimper.

Cameron nodded. "We both did. And we loved you. I loved you just as much as the sister I lost. I still do."

Ailsa swallowed thickly. "Thank you. The last few years... they've been tough. Just... give me time."

He placed a hand on her shoulder and gave it a squeeze. "You can have all the time you need."

"And do us both a favour and go speak to Angus, please." She tried to laugh but it came off as more of a sob.

"Yes, m'lady." Cameron kissed her on the cheek and then he limped off, to where Angus was tending to Laire.

"Brothers," Iona said from behind Ailsa. "Seems that both of ours have to be watched more closely in future."

Ailsa nodded her head in agreement before stalking off in the opposite direction. There was someone else she desperately needed to speak to, now that it was all over.

The selkie was rooting around in a pile of apples, looking for the best one. She cleared her throat to let him know she was there. "Harris, can I speak to you?"

He dropped the fruit and turned with a huge grin. "Ah, there she is, my fierce rescuer." The breath whooshed out of her as he picked her up and spun her around. Ailsa grasped at his shoulders until he set her down on the ground. "When we get back to Dunrigh, I'll make it up to you."

Harris bent his face to hers, as if to kiss her. Before

she realised what she was doing, Ailsa tucked her face into the crook of his neck and wrapped her arms around him in a hug. He hesitated for a beat, before returning it.

After a moment, Ailsa pulled away, unable to look Harris in the eye.

"What is it, Ailsa?" he asked, his smile gone. "What did you want to speak to me about?"

"I'm just... glad you're safe," she told him, letting out a breath.

"Thanks to you," Harris said, tilting his head at her.

She could see he knew something was wrong, but now wasn't the time. "Looks like we're about to head off again."

"I was just about to pack some supplies," he said, nodding to the apples.

"I'm just going to say goodbye." She motioned to the great hulking body of the wolf, who had lain down among the bushes.

"Okay, don't be too long."

Ailsa shoved her hands in her pockets as she walked away from the selkie. She'd have to work up the courage to tell him. *When we're back in Dunrigh*, she thought to herself.

If it hadn't been obvious before, the hug had confirmed it. Where there had been a spark only weeks ago, now there was just the comfort of friendship.

When she reached the wolf, she knelt to whisper in

his ear. "I know that he won't believe it, but I'll be back for him. And when I do return, I won't stop until he has his soul back."

Wulver whined.

"Look after him for me."

Then the forest guardian stood, nuzzled her side one last time, and ran off into the gloom, back to her demon.

Ailsa watched her brother sleep as she walked beside the unicorn. Everyone but Angus had been surprised when she'd allowed Cameron to ride her, but Ailsa was thankful. There was no way he would have been able to keep up, not with his human body. As soon as she moved, he'd fallen asleep, absolutely exhausted. Dozing against her neck, he looked half like a prince from a faerie tale and half like a vagabond. Just like in the games they used to play as children. So much had changed through the years and yet so much hadn't. Back then, she had followed him everywhere and he had protected her. It felt good to have it the other way round for once.

She was no closer to finding her real place—her real identity. Still, seeing her friends together, it finally hit her. Finding Harris wasn't the only reason she'd come to Ephraim.

She'd been desperately looking for somewhere to belong, for a family. And here they were. If she could choose, she couldn't think of a better group of jokers and scoundrels to call her own.

And so, she trekked out of Ephraim with her adopted family, a little worse for wear, but still standing.

Chapter 67

*F*ifty miles away, the young woman felt the cloud of her mother's influence extinguish suddenly. She dropped to her knees, in front of her daughter's cot.

"Mama," the infant babbled, not yet aware enough to be concerned.

"We're safe," the woman told her anyway, gathering the little girl in her arms. "We don't have to hide anymore, *mo ghaol.*" Then, blinking back tears, she said a thanks to the gods for whoever had vanquished Nicnevan.

Little did she know that, as she basked in relief, one of the gods was watching her and making plans.

The End

About the Author

Caroline Logan is a writer of Young Adult Fantasy. *The Stone of Destiny* is her debut novel, and is the first in *The Four Treasures* series.

Caroline is a high school biology teacher who lives in the Cairngorms National Park in Scotland, with her fiancé. Before moving there, she lived and worked in Spain, Tenerife, Sri Lanka and other places in Scotland.

She graduated from The University of Glasgow with a bachelor's degree in Marine and Freshwater Biology. In her spare time she tries to ski and paddle board, though she is happiest with a good book and a cup of tea.

Follow Caroline online:
Instagram: @bearpuffbooks
Twitter: @bearpuffbooks

Acknowledgements

How have I managed to write two whole books? The only explanation I can think of is ghosts.

Anyway, throughout my most recent haunting, a bunch of people were super cool and made my cold heart grow at least three sizes. Unfortunately, this book has ended up bigger than *The Stone of Destiny*, so I'm short on space for all of my gratitude. I'm sorry I won't get to mention everyone by name, but you know who you are.

The biggest of thanks to Anne Glennie at Cranachan Publishing for sticking with me and allowing me to put another book baby into the world. I've never met someone who works as hard as you do. You're my hero.

Thank you to my Dad and Linda, and my Mum and Stepdad, and my sister Rachel, for supporting me during book launches and general life. I bet all your friends are sick of hearing you push my book at them, but I am so thankful for it. Also thanks to Diane and Neil, Blair and Martin for supporting my books as much as my parents do!

Thank you to all of my fellow #clancranachan authors. I feel so lucky to be part of this awesome team. Also

big thanks to Antonia Wilkinson for her marketing
wizardry.

To all my wonderful friends, family and coworkers
who have supported me at the beginning of my writing
journey. Special thanks to Martin Kinnear and Cara
Donald for being my sometimes housemates and for
coming to two book launches, 170 miles apart.

Thank you to my online friends and the reviewers
who've read and helped promote both books.

And finally, to my wee family—Vince, Ranger-Danger
and Scoot-Patoot—I love you.

A Four
Treasures Novel

the
Sword
of
Light

Book 3

Coming Soon